THE UPROOTED

by

William B. Makowski

Published in Canada
by
SMART DESIGN
Promotion Agency
6-2550 Goldenridge Rd. Unit 6
Mississauga, Ontario L4X 2S3, Canada

Mississauga, Ontario, Canada
2002

ISBN-0-9694698-1-0

Printing by Nova Printing
Tel. (905) 281-3231, Mississauga
Ontario L4X 2S3 Canada

PRINTED IN CANADA

The uthor has applied funds from
The Barbara Piasecka Johnson Foundation,
c/o BPJ Holding Corporation
4519 Province Line Road
Princeton, New Jersey 08540 USA,
towards the printing of this book.

Special thanks to:

The Barbara Piasecka Johnson Foundation
for a $16.000 (Can. F.) grant
towards the printing of this book.

Museum of Independence in Warsaw, Poland
for allowing publication of the historically unique
photographs.

Ms. Mariquita Weslawska of Warsaw for her
help in acquiring the photographs.

Barbara and Matthew Nassius for their generous
help and advice during the process of preparation
of this book.

Margaret Pogorzelska-Bonikowska for her generous
help in preparimg this manuscript for publication.

This book is dedicated to
my four-year-old brother Ryszard
who did not survive the Soviet Union's inhuman conditions
and who is buried somewhere in the sands of Uzbekistan

Chapter One

Jan Tabor was jolted awake by the sound of a woman's voice, an ear-piercing, urgent wail. Listening more attentively, he realized that she was yelling, "The horse is drowning! The horse is drowning!"

He jumped out of bed with all the swiftness and agility of his fifteen years. Throwing on some clothes, he dashed through the adjoining woodshed to the street, which was swarming with people of all ages, all running in the same direction. He followed the crowd, soon overtaking the slow runners. He passed a group of old women who, with uplifted skirts and wild eyes, were bounding ahead with surprising speed. "Horse is drowning, horse!" he heard them yelling. "Whose horse?" someone asked.

"The priest's horse, the priest's chestnut."

The men were carrying axes, spades, sticks, and ropes. One man was carrying a fishing net.

Ahead of the crowd, like the commander of an infantry battalion, ran Jan's Aunt Fela, known in the village as Fat Fela. Despite her bulk, Fela was running like a forest roe-deer, with disheveled hair, clenched fists and red sweaty face. Spotting Jan beside her, she inclined her head toward him. "The horse is drowning! The horse is drowning!" she roared, nearly deafening him.

"Where?" Jan yelled back.

"In the marshes behind the blacksmith's shop," Fela yelled, pointing toward the nearby marshes. Amid the cries of people and the barking of dogs, they reached the marshes. The horse's head and neck were visible about 50 metres from the bank of the marshes. Jan presumed it had been chased by wild animals, probably wolves, and had sought sanctuary in the marshes, where it had been swallowed to the neck. Frantic attempts to free itself had caused it to sink deeper into the quagmire, its legs entangled in the rotting vegetation. The prolonged struggle and fear had weakened the animal. Exhausted, it stopped jerking, its laboured breathing broken by an occasional frightened whinney.

The crowd grew silent, almost as though someone had given a command. Even the dogs stopped barking. The men put their axes and sticks down, and all the people stood still, mesmerized by the spectacle before them.

"Fetch me a rope, or maybe two," Fela called out suddenly. When the villagers did not move, she thundered, "Quickly!", startling them into motion. Two ropes were found and Fela coiled them. Then, hiking up her skirts, she stepped into the marsh and began wading through the reeds. She had not gone very far when the mud and vegetation began pulling at her. She was sinking deeper with every step, but the sight of the drowning horse drove her forward until she realized that she was in danger of meeting the same fate and could go no further.

"Help! Holy Mother, help!" she cried. Four strong men dragged poor Fela out of the bog with the help of a long pole and assisted her to a nearby log where she sat, visibly shaken.

The village reeve then took command. "Someone small and light is needed," he yelled.

The people exchanged glances, but no one responded. Then everyone's gaze seemed to shift at once. Jan realized they were looking at him.

"Oh no, not me," he called out. "No way, go to hell!"

He probably would have been left in peace, were it not for his sisters, who suddenly emerged from the crowd and stood by his side. Maria and Helena were Jan's joy and aggravation. They made his life a complexity of unwanted challenges, confrontations and surprises. The two girls made a point of ganging up on their brother, leading him into all sorts of trouble, then laughing when he was punished for his misdeeds.

As soon as Jan saw his sisters beside him, he knew that he was trapped.

"He won't go, of course," said Maria in her seemingly innocent voice. "Jan won't go, Helena, will he?"

"No, he won't," Helena responded.

"Oh, yes, he is brave with us, but..."

"So, I guess one of us should go, Maria."

"Yes, Helena, since I am older than you, I will go."

Jan, knowing his sisters, wouldn't have been surprised at all if one of them did actually go. He couldn't possibly allow that to happen.

Grabbing the coiled rope lying close to his aunt's feet, he waded into the marsh, remembering his grandfather saying, "If you ever find yourself on quicksand or marsh quagmire, spread yourself as if you were swimming - don't forget!" He stretched out as far as possible, almost swimming in the bog, using all his strength to move toward the horse. The horse gazed at him and nickered softly. The animal started to struggle again as he reached it and Jan knew he had to calm the beast before it entangled itself even more.

"Steady, boy, steady," Jan said, stroking the horse's neck with one hand while winding one end of the rope around it with the other. Then, securing the rope around the animal's neck, he began to make his way back slowly, uncoiling the rope.

"Atta boy, come on..." the crowd was roaring, encouraging him. Jan's strength was waning and he felt himself sinking deeper into the quagmire. He started to swallow mud; the acrid taste and the stench of rotten vegetation became unbearable. His legs were trapped in the mud and vegetation and he felt a surge of panic; drowning seemed certain. His hands groped frantically for the support of the rope. He saw his mother's smiling face as she lovingly stroked his hair, then remembered her on her deathbed. He had only been seven then, yet the memory was vivid. He saw himself kneeling at her bedside, praying to Holy Mary to spare his mother's life. Then the memories, the crowd and the bog disappeared into blackness.

Jan slowly opened his eyes to see his sisters staring at him with tear-filled eyes. He tried to get up and realized that he was surrounded by the villagers. All eyes were on Jan, expectant and worried.

"He's alive!" someone in the crowd shouted, and others took up the cry.

"He just swallowed a bellyful of mud, but he's still breathing."

"He is one of the Tabors, isn't he? They are a tough lot."

"What happened to the horse?" Jan managed to whisper.

"The horse is all right; the men pulled it out," said Maria, who was sitting close to him.

"Thanks to you, Jan," Aunt Fela added.

"You're a hero now," said Helena.

"What happened to me?" Jan asked, shakily rising to his feet.

"You were pulled from the mud by the villagers," Aunt Fela said, gesturing to the surrounding people. "We made a human chain," she explained.

"It wasn't far to pull, since you were only two or three metres away from solid ground," said Helena, laughing. Jan and Maria joined her, Jan laughing the loudest, until the tears started to roll down his mud-covered cheeks.

"He's a brave lad, that Tabor," someone remarked.

"And strong for his age," added another.

Jan, blushing, pretended not to hear their compliments, although he felt a surge of pride and satisfaction.

It was only when Jan and his sisters were walking home that he noticed how filthy he was. His clothes were soaked through and caked with acrid mud. Shivering uncontrollably because of the cool April wind and the recent excitement, he started to run toward their cottage. His sisters were soon left behind.

Entering the cottage, he tried to sneak into the bedroom to change his clothes. He almost succeeded, since his grandmother, busy baking bread, didn't notice him at first. However, before he had taken three steps toward the bedroom, he heard a shriek which stopped him cold. Almost before he knew what was happening, his grandmother, shouting incoherently, pushed him into the adjoining woodshed, where she ordered him to remove his clothes. Within a few minutes, he was sitting in a long, wooden bathtub filled with cold water.

In the meantime, the cottage had filled with people chattering excitedly about the recent drama at the marsh. Aunt Fela's voice rose above those of the others. "Michal," she boomed, turning to Jan's father, "that boy of yours is a marvel!"

"A marvel indeed, Fela, he almost got himself killed," Jan's grandmother said in a trembling voice.

"Well, come on, Matylda. The boy did the right thing," observed Jan's grandfather.

"He is brave, I tell you!" cried Aunt Fela. "Some day, as we often say, he will be 'somebody'," she added.

"He will grow into a tough man...and..." Grandfather was looking for a word.

"And a compassionate one," supplied Jan's father.

"Compassionate, maybe - but a reckless one for sure," lamented Grandmother.

Splashing water lazily over his body, Jan listened to every word. He was pleased to hear all the compliments, and yet he felt that he did not deserve them. Remembering how scared he had been in the marsh, he wondered how he could be considered to be brave. He didn't understand exactly what they meant by compassionate, but by their tone of voice, he knew that it was something good.

"People who like animals are usually good people," he heard his grandfather say.

"And animals, in turn, are good to such people," said his father.

In the woodshed, Jan reflected that he liked animals, but he was still unsure about the other comments he had heard. Well, anyway, it was nice to feel important.

"Remember that old Antoni, who broke both his legs while hunting?" asked Aunt Fela. "The one whose horse saved him from the wolves?"

"Oh, yes, I remember," Jan's father said. "Is it true that the horse guarded him all night, lashing out at the wolves like crazy until help arrived?"

"Yeah."

"Oh, talking about the horse, I completely forgot that I'm supposed to drive to Pinsk today," Michal Tabor exclaimed.

"With Jan? If he is ready," added Grandmother.

Hearing "Pinsk", Jan jumped out of the bathtub and dressed quickly. He enjoyed these occasional excursions to Pinsk, the largest town in the area; there was always something fascinating to see there. He particularly liked their visits to the marketplace, where he couldn't take his eyes off all the things for sale. It seemed to him that everything was there, from kitchenware to farm wagons. The best part of all was eating sugar cakes and drinking lemonade in one of Pinsk's restaurants.

He stood before the mirror to comb his hair and regarded his reflection critically. He saw a prominent nose, bright blue eyes and slightly curly blonde hair. He had the lightest hair in school, almost as white as linen, and envied his classmates with darker hair. Short for his age and skinny, he was always trying, without much success, to gain some weight.

Sighing, he left the house and noticed that his father was still in the barn, probably hitching their grey mare to the farm-buggy. Waiting for his father, he scanned his surroundings. Their house, built of logs like the others in the village, was located on a small hill. His eyes passed over the scattered cottages below, the marshes surrounding the village on three sides, and the one road which led out of Zamosze, connecting the village with the nearest town of Bostyn and, beyond that, Pinsk. His eyes rested on the more elevated areas of the marshland covered by thick, coarse grasses, reeds, and osiers. He watched a flock of wild geese as they ascended and then dived back into the water in search of food.

To his left, beyond the marshes, was the dark blue line of a coniferous forest growing on sandy plains. Feeling weak in the legs, he sat on the low shelf of earth which ran in front of the house and offered some protection from the cold winters. Like the other houses in the village, it was small and low, sunk into the ground by time. Jan often wondered how old their house really was. He had asked his grandfather, whose only response had been "old, very old," followed by an impatient hand gesture, as though the boy was an irksome gnat.

His thoughts were interrupted by the wagon's rattle. His father slowed just enough for Jan to jump on the wagon and settle himself as comfortably as possible. He looked back at the barn, which was really no more than a small wooden shack. Like most of the barns in the village, it had a large stork's nest on the thatched roof. Jan waved at the big bird, which, standing on one leg, responded with a chatter.

"Goodbye, I'll see you later," Jan waved at the bird once more. As they drove through the muddy streets in the direction of Bostyn, they passed the village's wooden cottages with thatched roofs. Each cottage had a small fenced-in garden in front, and behind the cottages stood barns and stables. Outside the village to their right, stretching as far as the marshes, were small fields. Some of them were already showing short sprouts of rye, but others, potato fields, Jan thought, were still dark grey.

The day was sunny and warm for the end of April, with pleasant breezes blowing from the east. The birch trees along the road were at their fullest, green splendor.

When they had left the village far behind, Michal Tabor put his whip aside and, clearing his throat, said, "I am proud of you, son."

Startled, Jan was silent.

"Sometimes a man must make a decision. Sometimes a bad one, sometimes good, but a decision nevertheless," he continued. "You made a good one, Jan. You saved the life of an animal."

He picked up the whip and urged the mare to a trot, overtook three other farm wagons, then slowed down again. Two of the drivers, recognizing Michal Tabor, left their wagons and joined them, nestling comfortably in the hay on Tabor's wagon. Their plodding horses continued to pull the wagons.

The men spoke Byelorussian. Jan didn't know the men, but he was certain they were not from Zamosze. All Zamoszans were Poles, so they had to be from one of the neighbouring Byelorussian villages. He knew that there were many villages which were either Byelorussian or Polish. According to his maternal grandfather, Antoni, there were by far more Byelorussians than Poles. He had also told Jan that Zamosze was mainly inhabited by either Tabors or Dabrowskis, who were related to one another. Jan's father and grandfather had told him that Poles were different from Byelorussians. Poles, like the Tabors, were descended from the lesser nobility; Byelorussians were peasants.

Now, sitting at the rear of the wagon, his legs dangling, he heard his father talking fluently in Byelorussian. He was dressed in linen trousers, linen shirt and wool blazer, the same as his Byelorussian companions. Jan wondered what made Poles different. 'Well, sure,' he thought, 'we Poles are all Roman Catholics and the Byelorussians seem to be all Greek-Orthodox. But that's good,' he concluded. 'We celebrate two Christmases and two Easters. No school for a long time,' he smiled happily. He started whistling, but meeting a disapproving glance from his father, continued with his thoughts.

'Sure, there is some name-calling between Byelorussians and Poles - even fights. They call us Polacks! Smart-pants lords! We, in turn, call them peasants! Manure-movers!' And yet, he had met many Byelorussians attending Polish weddings, dances and birthday parties in Zamosze, having a good time with the villagers. His family had attended a wedding in a neighbouring Byelorussian town called Motol and had talked about it for a week after.

The wagons, after hours of rolling over the bumpy track, reached a road covered with fine gravel. Jan heard the whistle of his father's whip and the wagon started to move faster. On both sides of the road, as far as he could see, spread the marshes. Even though it was late spring, they were still covered with water and resembled a huge lake.

They reached Pinsk in the early afternoon and followed the cobble-stone street which led them straight to the town's market. Jan loved the market. The numerous booths with farm implements, news-stalls with newspapers and magazines, tables full of meats, bread, herrings, and pastries fascinated him. Running from one display to another, he wanted to see, touch and smell everything. One other place that intrigued him was the horse market. The great assortment of horses, hundreds of them, was located on the outskirts of town. Michal Tabor, like his son, enjoyed the horse market.

"It's nice to at least see the horses, even though I can't afford to buy one now," he told his son.

Most of the horse merchants, Jan noticed, were Jews, but most of the buyers were either Byelorussian or Polish farmers. Jan pulled his father toward an old Jew who, holding his horse's bridle in one hand and gesturing with the other, was praising its qualities in broken Polish.

"Noo! Look at that horse, friends. Did you see a better one? Noo! Look at her teeth. It is a young horse, almost a foal, noo?!"

"If she is so young, then why are her teeth yellow? Hmm, why?" asked a stooped Byelorussian peasant, looking around, obviously expecting praise for his wisdom.

"Oy! Yellow teeth? He is saying yellow!" screamed the merchant. "You crazy? Look! Look at these teeth; they are like pearls. It is you that has yellow teeth, not this mare."

"Will it bear a foal, Yankiel?" somebody asked from the crowd.

"Foal? You crazy? Of course she will," cried the merchant, raising the horse's tail.

"Tfoo!" spat the peasant.

"Tfoo yourself!"

Jan and his father left the merchant and his mare, laughing loudly.

"I am not sure, Father," said Jan, "but I think that mare is old."

"Old!" scoffed his father. "She is dying of old age!" he exclaimed. Jan, after witnessing such a blatant display of human greed, shrugged his shoulders, found the humour in the situation and chuckled to himself.

By nine o'clock, after buying necessary supplies, they left Pinsk and headed home. The wagon moved slowly in the darkness, jolting crazily on the bumpy country road, its big wheels brushed by wayside marigolds and coarse grasses.

Their horse, an old veteran, skillfully avoided large puddles, deep holes, stumps and logs, confident and sure-footed as ever. There was silence between them, broken only by Michal's occasional sighs. Jan knew that this was a sign that something really important was bothering his father.

"What's the trouble, Father?" he finally asked.

"War."

"War?"

"Yes, war, son! War with Germany."

Jan had read something about it in the newspapers and heard rumours, but hadn't paid much attention.

"Why, Father?"

"You see, Hitler, Germany's leader, threatens to attack Poland."

"Buy why?"

"Good question, son! Good question," sighed Michal Tabor. "It looks to me like the war is unavoidable," he added.

"We will beat Hitler, won't we?"

"I don't think so, son," his father replied. "You see, son, we started to build our army only three years ago. We need another five years at least."

They drove in silence, interrupted occasionally by flocks of shrieking ducks and geese, which Jan thought were heading toward an island in the midst of the marshes. Michal Tabor, his eyes half closed, appeared to be absorbed in thought. Jan, noticing his father's preoccupation, didn't want to disturb him. Making himself more comfortable on the hay, he thought about the war his father had spoken about. He had read a lot of books about wars:

wars with Tatars, Turks, Germans, Russians. Sure, people died in all of these wars, but there was a lot of excitement, too. He recalled the descriptions of horsemen dashing toward their enemies, swinging their sabres, bands playing marches, girls with garlands, greeting their heroes... And yet, any time his father or grandfather mentioned war, they became withdrawn, even sad, like his father right now. He looked at his father again and hesitantly asked him, "Father, you were in the last war, in 1914, wasn't it?"

"Well, yes, I was. Why do you ask?" Michal asked.

"What was it like?"

"Terrible."

"Terrible? Why?"

"People died. That's why it was terrible."

"Why are there so many wars, Father?"

"Because some people are greedy. They want something that doesn't belong to them."

"What do the Germans want from us?"

"They want to have a piece of our land. They call it the Polish Corridor."

"Well, why don't we give it to them if it would avoid war?"

"Well," said Michal Tabor thoughtfully, "today they will take the Corridor and tomorrow the whole of Poland... and... perhaps the whole of Europe."

"We can't allow them to do that, can we?"

"No, we can't!"

"Will you go to war, Father?"

"Yes, I will." Then, after a long silence, he added, "So will you if it's a long war." He whipped the horse several times, angrily.

The wagon moved faster, jolting on the bumpy roadway. Burying himself deeper in the hay, Jan let his imagination float over the battlefields of the wars he had read so much about.

A few days later, instead of doing his homework, Jan went to see his friend Moyshe.

Besides Tabors and Dabrowskis, Zamosze had two Jewish families, the Norkins and the Goldbergs. Moyshe, the head of the Norkins family, was the village blacksmith, and Shloma Goldberg owned the inn.

Both families, Jan had learned from Moyshe, were as old as Zamosze itself. Moyshe had once told Jan, "I think we can trace our ancestors for at least three hundred years."

"More like three hundred and fifty," added his wife, Rifka.

Moyshe, a tall, muscular man of about fifty years of age, liked Jan and was amused by the young boy's curiosity. One afternoon after his return from Pinsk, Jan arrived at Moyshe's shop to find him swinging his hammer vigorously as he made an iron rim for a wagon wheel.

"Moyshe!"

"Yeah, Jan."

"Moyshe, there will be a war, I think."

"Sure, there always is war, Jan."

"Yes, but we may lose it."

"Who knows? Maybe yes, or maybe no!"

"But, Moyshe, what will happen to us, if we lose the war?" Moyshe continued with his work, so Jan went on. "I read that the Germans are vicious, especially to Jews, Moyshe."

Moyshe hammered faster, as though he wished to smash the iron to pieces.

"I read about them beating the Jews, burning their books..."

Moyshe suddenly stopped swinging his hammer and, wiping his face with his hand, sat beside Jan.

"Jan," he said, "if Hitler wins, we will be killed, or we will be scattered all over the world."

"Then we have to beat him!"

"It won't be easy, my boy! It won't be easy," said Moyshe, sighing.

"Maybe England and France will help us?"

"Maybe," said Moyshe, resuming his work. However, as soon as Jan left, he stopped working and sat down heavily on a wooden stool. Jan's simple questions had stirred Moyshe's fears more than the boy could possibly imagine. Moyshe, like his late father Abram, his grandfather and past generations of Norkins, had always lived in fear. He was a Jew, wasn't he? Some of these fears were the product of excessive imagination or oversensitivity, but most were real - too real, unfortunately. How well he remembered what his father had told him about the Cossack pogroms before World War I and the horror stories about the beatings, indignities and ridicule experienced by the Norkins, Goldbergs and other Jews. Was it really important who inflicted such suffering upon his people? 'It seems, though, that things are worse for us during a war and now there is going to be another war and it will reach us soon.'

He went outside and gazed at the nearby marshes and his beloved Zamosze. "I hope we survive," he sighed.

****

Walking home from Moyshe's blacksmith shop, Jan noticed with dismay that one of their cows had broken through the fence and wandered into their neighbour's garden. "Marta's garden of all places," he moaned, running toward the cow.

The widow, known as "sharp-tongued Marta", was the village's worst curse. Gossip had it that she had killed her husband with her tongue.

Before Jan could retrieve the cow, Marta was there, waiting. She was like a watch dog, guarding her property day and night. "So, Jan, it is your cow, eh?" she hissed.

"Yes, ma'am, sorry, but..."

"Sorry, eh, you little bastard! You are sorry!" The hiss became a roar. "You will be sorry when your stupid old cow dies tomorrow. Tonight she will breathe her last. Her calf will die, too! I will cast a spell on you, your father, your..."

Jan chased his cow toward their barn, running as fast as he could to escape Marta's ranting.

He raced into his house, almost colliding with his grandfather, who, while puffing on his pipe, had observed the incident. "Marta again, eh?" Grandfather chuckled.

Antoni, Jan's grandfather, had two passions in life: beekeeping and story-telling. His apiary had sixty hives; next to the reeve's, it was the largest in the village. The Dabrowskis' honey was even known in Pinsk. Jan and his sisters were very proud when they overheard, in Bostyn, someone saying, "That son-of-a-gun, Dabrowski! He has the best honey in the county."

His grandfather's other passion, however, was more interesting to Jan. Grandfather was the greatest storyteller in the world. The winters in Zamosze were boring, especially the long, dreary evenings. Jan's grand-mother was the unofficial leader of the village women, and most of the danc-ing, knitting, sewing, wedding, and christening parties were held in her house. Usually, half of the village was present. On these occasions, Jan's grandfather would tell his stories about the devil or ghosts. To Jan, they were as terrifying as hell itself.

May and June of 1939 were rainless, turning the meadows brown and dry-ing the marshes to such a degree that Jan and his sister could walk for kilo-metres without wetting their feet.

"We haven't had such dry weather since as far back as we can remember," Jan heard the villagers say. After school, he helped his father with the hay, or worked in the field picking potatoes and other vegetables. The harvest was poor and he heard his father sighing more often than usual.

Maria, eighteen, and Helena, eleven, helped their grandmother with the domestic chores. "My two helpers," Jan often heard her say to her neigh-bours, "what would I do without them?"

Jan and Maria attended the Bostyn high school; Jan in his first year, Maria in her fourth and last. Helena was in the fourth grade at Zamosze elementary school.

On Sundays, the whole family attended the little wooden church, where each of them had to go to confession. Although most of the villagers liked Father Kowalski, he was known for giving a stiff penance. In Jan's case, it was usually five "Our Fathers" and five "Hail Mary's". However, since Jan's participation in the rescue of the priest's horse, the penance miraculously had been reduced to only one of each.

The end of June was approaching and he was happy that school would soon be over. His only problem was the trouble in school which had recently clouded his life.

The majority of pupils in the Bostyn High were Byelorussians, followed by Jews, with a sprinkling of Poles.

Jan had been beaten up more than once by Byelorussian bullies. It eventually became so bad that Jan's only recourse was to run straight home as soon as school was let out. Maria, a strong girl, did her best to defend him in these daily scuffles, but this was not enough. Both of them were constantly coming home with bloody noses. They had several discussions with their father about this problem.

"Try to avoid them... those savages," was their father's response.

"But, Father," Jan objected, "what can I do when they are waiting for me day after day? Run all the time?"

Father's silence was enough for Jan to realize that his father had no solution to his problem. He would have to solve it alone.

He knew that there were not enough Polish boys and girls to ward off the Byelorussian attacks. Some other help was badly needed. The second largest group of boys and girls were the Jews, but rumour had it that they would not fight.

"Jews are like skunks and rabbits," the peasants said. "Show them a stick and they run like hell into the forest!"

"One Byelorussian, or a Pole, for that matter, can beat up fifty Jews! They are weaklings, you know," spat a Byelorussian peasant, describing the Jewish character to Jan. "They just count money, sell rags and eat lots of herring and onions!"

Jan was puzzled by what they said, because he had seen old Moyshe swing his sledge hammer as though it was a feather.

The only Jew who attended the high school from Zamosze was Roova. He was two years older than Jan, and the only son of Shloma, the inn-keeper. The two boys had little contact because Jan was not permitted to go into the inn. However, though he never told anyone, he had been there several times.

His first visit had made a great impression on him. It was early afternoon. In the semi-dark room, he spotted several peasants, Polish and Byelorussian, sitting at long tables, drinking vodka and eating herring. Behind the bar stood Roova's father, a skinny man with a long grey beard, who served the vodka and herring while observing every movement in the room with his dark, piercing eyes.

"Ivan!" he addressed a mustachioed peasant seated at the far end of the room. "Ivan, your plate is empty; more herring, eh? Stefan, your cow died, I hear. Oy, oy, too bad! Another vodka, Stefan? How is your wife, Antoni? I heard she's pregnant again. You need another vodka, Antoni? Vat's the matter, Nikolay, are you sick today? Have another vodka. Vat? No? No more credit for you, Vasili, you already owe me five zlotys."

"I am selling my horse - that black one - Shloma. I will pay you back. Give me another."

"Look! Look at him, people!" Shloma cried. "Vat does he think I am, a Lord of the manor or vat? Vy should I give you anything?"

Jan was fascinated by Shloma's accent and his wit.

On Thursday, the market day in Bostyn, Jan and Roova made a pact, when the boys were wandering around the marketplace after school, looking at the handicrafts, meats, live fish, cookies, bread, and pastries being sold by the peasants.

He spotted Roova standing at the cookie kiosk, contemplating whether or not to buy. Each cookie cost ten groshen, or twelve for one zloty. Looking at Roova, Jan had an idea. Roova was a little quiet for Jan's taste, but he respected him because he was strong as well as smart. Roova was a good student, getting A's in all his subjects, as well as being the undisputed leader of the Jewish schoolboys.

After long bargaining, Jan persuaded Roova and his gang to protect him from the Byelorussian boys, for one zloty a week. Roova agreed to help Jan, providing Jan paid in advance. The plan was that Jan, instead of running home immediately after school was dismissed, should linger around the schoolyard, provoking the Byelorussian boys. The rest would be up to Roova.

Jan would remember the next day for a long time. He deliberately remained in the schoolyard. Hands in his pockets, he insolently confronted a group of belligerent Byelorussian boys. The reaction was immediate.

"Hey, Polack!" one of the gang members yelled at Jan. "Are you still here? Go home, you shitty Polish lord." He was joined by other cursing boys, who moved threateningly toward Jan. Jan's legs became weak and he began to tremble all over, but he didn't run away. They were advancing, sticks in hand, removing belts from their pants.

There was no sign of Roova and his gang. "Where is Roova?" Jan thought, petrified with fear. "The Jewish bastard chickened out," Jan almost screamed. "He's betrayed me, the bloody skunk."

They circled him. He felt a stick hitting his back, then another and yet another. Paralyzed by pain and fear, he just stood there. He felt a blow to his left knee which had been delivered by a stout Byelorussian, who, holding a long stick in his hands, was particularly aggressive. The excruciating pain made Jan abandon all caution. He lunged forward, knocking down his adversary, who, not expecting such fury, yelled for help. In the heat of combat, Jan punched and punched his fat adversary's face, blindly and mercilessly.

Finally, Roova and his gang appeared and surrounded the Byelorussians. There were as many Jewish boys as Byelorussians, but they made an incredible racket, yelling to each other: "Moyshe! David! Shmuel! Sruel! Yankiel!"

Jan, realizing that his rescuers had finally arrived, stood up and helped his bleeding adversary to do the same. The fury of battle between them had abated by then, and they stood side by side, watching the fight. Jan saw that the club-swinging, stone-throwing Jews had the upper hand over the dumbfounded and slower moving Byelorussians. Not for long, though, because the Byelorussians regrouped and began to fight back with surprising energy.

The fight would probably have continued for some time if it hadn't been for the appearance of four blue-clad policemen who parked their bicycles by the fence and went into immediate action, swinging their rubber batons freely and indiscriminately. Jan was hit on the back by a burly policeman. He decided to take his injured adversary with him and, limping, retreated to the safety of the street.

"The battle of nations", as the fight was later called, was the subject of widespread gossip and rumours. The Byelorussian parents said that the fight had been instigated by the Polish authorities, who just wanted to prove who was the boss in Bostyn. Jewish parents, on the other hand, claiming that another pogrom was in the making, said that today their children were the victims and tomorrow it would be all of them.

The school authorities sent an inspector from Pinsk to the school on the day after the fight. He accused the director of the school of negligence and threatened dismissal if there were any further disturbances.

The police, accused of brutality, by both the Byelorussians and the Jews, were told by the Police Commissioner in Pinsk to straighten out the situation or be fired *en masse*.

The mayor of Bostyn, a Byelorussian, in order to relieve the tension, called a meeting of parents and school authorities. The meeting took place on Monday evening in the school hall. It was only 10 p.m. when Michal Tabor returned and, to Jan's surprise, went straight to bed without his usual conversation with his family. Jan had enough time, though, to notice that his father had several bruises on his face, especially on the bridge of his nose.

Arriving at school the next day, Jan saw two old janitors clearing debris from the school hall. Chairs, desks, lamps - even the portrait of the President of Poland - were all in pieces.

Jan was never told exactly what had happened, but the rumour was that the fight had been started by none other than their neighbour, Marta, who, even though she had no children in school, had attended the meeting. The same rumours said that the mayor had denied Marta the right to speak at the meeting. She had then delivered a series of curses to the mayor and, indeed, Byelorussians in general. He, in turn, had called her a fat trollop and a strumpet and ordered her to leave the hall. Instead, she attacked him, scratching his face badly. One of the mayor's supporters, springing to his defence, had kicked Marta's fleshy behind. Then everyone had joined the melee. Even Father Kowalski, while pleading for peace, had been punched several times.

A few days after the meeting, a stained glass window in the Jewish temple was found broken, two Byelorussian lumberjacks were badly beaten, Sophie's dilapidated barn was burnt to the ground and Jan was beaten up by three Byelorussian bullies. "It looks like my friends need more money to protect you," Roova shrugged.

Thankfully, not all the Byelorussian boys were unfriendly to Jan and the other Polish boys. Wasil and Jossif, for example, were Jan's best friends. Together, they explored the nearby forests and marshes, looking for birds' nests, swam in the marshy pools, or skated over the ice-covered rivers and creeks in winter. They strolled barefoot over the marshes in late spring or summer, played Indians in the forest or just simply daydreamed in the forest clearings.

Sometimes, on summer evenings, they sat on the bench in front of Jan's cottage, listening to the chirping of birds, or the croaking of frogs, and just talked.

However, some evenings, especially when he was alone, sitting at the edge of the marshes, looking at the endless expanses, he felt sad. At those times, he missed his mother most. He missed her warm smile and her gentle caresses when he rested his head on her lap. 'Where are you now, Mama?' he wondered, gazing up at the stars. 'Can you see me now, Mother? It has been eight years since you left us. I miss you so much.'

There was silence from the stars above. In front of him, the fog was slowly blanketing the marshes and the distant forest was merging with the horizon, forming a dark blue line.

"Where were you so long, Jan?" Grandmother would ask. She was a small, hunched woman, who always seemed to know Jan's feelings and tried hard to make him happy. Grandmother loved all three of the children, but it was common knowledge that Jan was her favourite and he usually got something extra from her: an apple, candy, or sometimes an egg. Although his sisters never mentioned Jan's privileged place with their grandmother, occasionally their resentment was expressed by a pull of Jan's hair, or a kick, for no apparent reason.

****

Although the world's current news seldom reached them, they learned from the newspapers occasionally brought from Bostyn that Germany had occupied Czechoslovakia and that Hitler had threatened to invade Poland.

Jan, like most of the villagers, was concerned. However, lately, he had heard in school about the great military strength of Poland, its mighty infantry, navy and cavalry. In fact, he firmly believed that if the stupid Germans dared to attack Poland, they would not only be beaten, but would lose Berlin as well. His father was of a different opinion. A veteran of World War I, during gatherings at his home, he had often voiced the opinion that Poland was not prepared for war with Germany.

News of Hitler's demands and threats became more frequent. On the third Sunday of August, the village priest told his congregation that he believed that war between Germany and Poland was inevitable and that they, as good citizens, should do everything to help their fatherland.

Three days later, Jan's father and a score of other men volunteered for the army and left for Pinsk, the mobilization centre. Jan was very sad, but he did not believe that his father would be gone for very long. Michal's departure was so sudden that there was no time for a proper farewell. There was only time for him to tell Jan to look after his family and the farm. After a hurried embrace, Michal leapt onto the wagon with the other men and Jan ran after them for a kilometre, waving and calling goodbye.

Walking back toward the farm, he noticed that the skies were filled with low, dark clouds. He kicked a stone along the dirt road as he walked. It would be years before he saw his father again.

On September 1, 1939 - six days after Jan's father's departure - Poland was invaded by the Germans. The village radio, located in the reeve's cottage, told the people about the brutal attack and the rapid advance of the German armies. Jan found it difficult to understand what was going on. He felt frustrated that he couldn't actively participate in the defence of his country. Radio reports were often interrupted by the announcer saying "Uwaga Nadchodzi, Uwaga Nadchodzi!" (Watch out, planes are approaching!) Gathered around the only radio, the villagers heard the drone of powerful aircraft motors, followed by the thuds of exploding bombs. Warsaw was being bombed. The villagers hated to admit to themselves that Poland had too few planes, tanks and men to cope with the German onslaught.

"How do you know that they are German planes?" Adam Dabrowski, Jan's uncle, known for his belligerence, asked. "We are probably bombarding goddamned Berlin right now!"

"Don't kid yourself," argued a peasant. "The German bastards are strong; it's difficult to kill the sons-of-bitches. They are like cockroaches."

"But what about France, England, perhaps even America," insisted Adam stubbornly. "Aren't they our allies?"

"France?" Edward Koziol, the local school teacher, scoffed.

"What's wrong with France?" hot-tempered Adam demanded.

"It's rotten! That's what is wrong with France," retorted Koziol. "I was there last summer. I was only there for two months, but from what I could gather, pacifism is like a disease there. No one will fight. You can't count on France, or England for that matter. England's totally unprepared."

"The Russians will help us," a young farmer said. He was suspected, although there was no proof of it, of being a socialist.

"Shit on the Russians," exclaimed Adam Dabrowski, spitting on the floor with indignation and disgust.

"Why shit on them?" persisted the young farmer. "Aren't they Slavs like us? They're almost like brothers. Besides, it is in their interest to help us. Aren't the Germans their enemies too?"

"Brothers? Oh my God!" exploded Adam, red in the face. "Cain was Abel's brother, too, wasn't he? If the Russians are our brothers, then why have they kept us under their bloody Siberian boots for over a hundred years?"

"I'm afraid we can't expect any help from the Soviets," stated the teacher calmly. "If they do march into our territory, it will be impossible to get rid of them."

"So if my poor peasant's head is thinking clearly, then what you are saying is that the Germans are our enemies, the Russians are not our friends, and the allies are somewhere, but nobody has heard from them," said Adam, shaking his head.

Jan listened to every word, and although he had questions, he decided to be quiet. He was afraid of being ridiculed by his elders. He wanted to know what happened to the people in a country occupied by a foreign army. What would happen to those who fought against their enemies and survived? Would they be punished? He worried about possible defeat and the fate of his father.

After this discussion, the group dispersed to do the chores, which, war or no war, still had to be done. They heard about the heroism of their own soldiers and civilians fighting against overwhelming forces and about the bombardment of cities, towns and even villages. They also heard, over the village radio, appeals for calm and maintenance of order, and pleas for solidarity. It soon became apparent to them that the Polish armies were falling back and that they could not stop the Germans' invasion of their country. Jan waded over his beloved marshes for hours, worried and unhappy.

Every word, gesture or look from the people he knew suggested fear, uncertainty, and resignation. Resignation was the worst, he thought. He wanted to act, to do something. Instead, like the others, he could only wait.

On September 12, the Zamoszans saw six German planes flying low over their village, and shortly after, they heard a series of explosions.

"It sounds as though Pinsk is hit!" someone shouted. Next day the road from Pinsk to Zamosze was flooded with refugees - on foot, on bicycles, in horse-drawn wagons, and occasionally in automobiles and trucks. The people were fleeing to the east, toward the Soviet border, hoping for help, food, and shelter in Russia. Villagers who knew the Russians expressed doubt. Zamosze was, after all, only 100 kilometres from the Soviet border, close enough to learn what was going on in that country from the smugglers and political refugees who occasionally stopped in Zamosze.

Jan and his sisters helped their grandparents to hide their livestock in the pine grove, as far from the road as possible. In the darkness, it was difficult to get the pigs into the makeshift pens. Jan hoped that all the animals would be safe. Desperate and hungry, the refugees would not respect property. The barn, left open, soon became a place where people stopped to sleep before pushing on. Old and young, all were possessed by one idea - to move eastward as far as possible, away from the invading Germans.

"Warsaw is burning!" they cried in answer to questions from the people of Zamosze. "The roads are bombarded." "Our armies are defeated." "Defeated..." "Cities in ruins..." "The Germans are executing people!" "God help us!"

Soon the village was swarming with refugees, asking for food and lodging. Jan's home sheltered eight families - thirty-seven people - for six days. Four little children slept in Jan's bed, more on Maria's and Helena's, while they slept on the floor. Some of the refugees were from Warsaw, others from as far away as Poznan. All were hungry. Luckily, Jan's potatoes had been harvested. Maria and Helena had enough of them to feed the hungry people. Grandmother spent almost all day cooking for the refugees. "The German planes attacked the highway we were on," said an old bearded Jew in a soiled black coat. "Hundreds were killed by the machine guns. Murders! In broad daylight."

"Our planes must all be destroyed," said another man, sadly.

"The Germans are everywhere, attacking everything that moves."

This was terrible news for the Zamoszans. Poland was on its way to defeat.

"Where are the goddamned French and English?" someone asked in desperation. "Aren't they our allies? What are they waiting for?"

Jan wondered where his father was. Was he alive? Father was always strong and clever, but... Jan prayed more earnestly than he had ever prayed in his life.

A few days later, Polish soldiers appeared among the refugees. The men were tired, hungry and grim; many wore blood-stained bandages. Some were mounted; most walked or limped. Usually, they moved in military order, formation after formation, day and night.

On September 17, Walter Plater, who was suspected of being a Communist, ran through the village street, yelling excitedly, "The Russians are coming! The Red Army is coming to help us!"

People rushed into the street. "When? Where? How many?"

Walter Plater ignored their questions and continued to yell. "We are not alone! Now we will beat the Germans!"

Indeed, news came that a huge Soviet army had crossed the Russian-Polish border and had engaged the Germans. For historical reasons, Polish sentiments were not pro-Russian, especially not pro-Soviet. Nevertheless, the villagers were happy to hear that help was coming, and their hearts warmed to the Russians.

"We can still be friends with them, you know," Jan heard the villagers saying. He was happy because he thought that the Russian involvement would help to end the war and hasten his father's return.

One day a small airplane with a red star on its side appeared in the sky over Zamosze. A rain of leaflets was dropped. Most landed on the street, some in the gardens, or on the roofs of the buildings, some even reached the marshland. People grabbed them curiously. Jan found one, and brought it home to read. Grandfather, Grandmother and his sisters clustered around Jan to hear what it was about. Though the Polish grammar was poor, the message itself was very clear.

"Soldiers! During the last few days the Polish army was finally smashed. Soldiers of the cities of Tarnopol, Galicz, Rowno, Dubno, over 60,000 of them, voluntarily came to our side.

Soldiers! What's left for you? What are you fighting for and with whom? Why are you endangering your lives? Your resistance is useless. Your officers drive you towards senseless slaughter. They hate you and your families. It was they who executed your delegates whom you have sent with a proposition to surrender. Do not trust your enemies. They want your death.

Soldiers! Kill your officers and generals. Don't obey the orders given by your officers. Kill them out from your land. Come to us with no fear, come to your brothers, to the Red Army. It is here that you will be able to find attention and consideration.

Remember that only the Red Army will free the Polish nation from this ill-fated war and will give you an opportunity to begin a peaceful life.

Trust us! Red Army of the Soviet Union is the only friend you have.

S. Timoshenko
Camandarm, First Degree
Ukrainian Front"

Jan finished reading. For a while, no one spoke.

It took a while before people realized the terrible truth. Those who had hoped that the Soviet Army would help Poland were disappointed.

"We thought the Soviet Union would help us!" someone shouted. "Instead Russia and Germany are now allies!"

"I told you not to trust Russkies," someone else said. "They've stuck a knife in our backs!"

"How can we defend ourselves against the Germans and Russians at the same time?" others asked. "There are millions of them. What will happen to us?"

Soon it became clear to everyone that Poland had not the slightest chance of defending itself and that a time of great suffering was beginning.

Then the Red Army arrived. The soldiers were dressed in mud-coloured uniforms and round caps which tapered to a ridiculous point at the top. The caps were adorned with a large red star, the only shiny item, Jan remarked. It seemed to him that the Red Army cavalrymen rode wherever they chose. By the thousands, they galloped over the fields and meadows, with no regard for property.

On the road, tanks, trucks and cars moved day and night. Fortunately for them, Jan thought, the summer had been dry, in fact, completely rainless. Behind the motorized units, thousands of infantrymen marched. The fields and drier meadows swarmed with cavalry. Jan heard some of the soldiers speaking Russian, Ukrainian, and other unknown languages. He heard their droning singing. The most popular song, sung virtually by all of them, was "Katiousha".

> " When the apple and pear trees were blossoming,
> When the mist was rolling over the river,
> Katiousha would come to the water's edge to
> sing about the prairie eagle and her beloved one..."

To Jan, these songs revealed a new world, full of melancholy. The soldiers sang on every possible occasion: while marching, riding an open truck, even while roasting a requisitioned cow or pig.

"Nobody pays any attention to the birch tree," they sang while roasting Jan's third cow. "I'll go to it, break off a twig, make a whistle and play to myself."

Jan understood enough Russian to realize that these soldiers were homesick. He increasingly experienced a feeling of sadness, sensing the terrible times ahead.

By the middle of October, the villagers learned that Poland had been partitioned again by Germany in the west and Russia in the east. Ahead of the Soviet Army, with it and behind it, came the Soviet Police, the notorious K.G.B. They were known for their brutality, their ability to break and bend, to use or abuse the unfortunates who fell into their hands. Soon, the K.G.B. took over power from the Red Army and became the real rulers of the eastern part of Poland.

The people in Zamosze soon knew the terror of the K.G.B. Eighteen men and six women of the village were arrested and disappeared within four weeks of the occupation. There was no apparent pattern to these arrests. One night it was the reeve, another night an illiterate peasant, then a forest ranger, and a housewife. Jan's uncle and aunt were among those who had been arrested.

The autumn of that year was particularly sunny and warm, as though nature wanted to ease the misery imposed by the invaders.

The marshlands around the village retained their green colour as though it were the beginning, not the end, of the warm season. The old timers predicted a cold winter; as Jan's grandfather stated, "a warm autumn foretells a cold winter." The farmers ploughed their fields, not knowing whether they would be allowed to harvest them. Jan, with the help of his sisters and occasional help from his neighbours, managed to plough and seed their three acres of land.

The mild weather ended abruptly at the beginning of December, 1939, when there was a severe snow storm, followed by very cold temperatures. The family, having lost all their pigs and cows to the Russians, was facing starvation. Christmas, usually such a happy time, was sad, lonely and meager. There had been no news of their father since the day he left. The people of Zamosze were now so fearful of the K.G.B. that they did not even dare to visit one another.

A rumour spread that Walter Plater, in order to establish a good relationship with the new rulers, was an informer, denouncing his own neighbours, particularly those with whom he had a disagreement. His first victim, so the rumours said, had been the village priest who was arrested and, like the others, disappeared. Plater was seen parading in cavalry boots which, Jan was told, he had pilfered from the Polish soldiers. To enhance his importance, he had asked for and been given a long mud-coloured Soviet army coat and Siberian fur hat. Thus attired, he was often seen marching arrogantly down the street.

Jan's grandfather suspected that there were others, who, driven by their own terror, or in the hope of ingratiating themselves with the new rulers, went to the police with ridiculous stories about their neighbours.

Winter brought more hardships. Cold, dry winds from the east swept over the countryside, piling up enormous snow drifts and snapping trees in the bitter cold. Deeply covered in snow, and held for weeks in the grip of sub-zero temperatures, the countryside was like a huge corpse, cold and still.

On the night of February 9, 1940, Jan, his grandparents, and his sisters sat in the kitchen. His grandfather brought out a jar of honey so that his grandmother could sweeten their tea, since there was no more sugar in the stores. It was hard to believe that the stores in Bostyn, always loaded with meat, sugar, herring, candies and bread, had been emptied by the Red Army soldiers, who were requisitioning everything in sight.

Grandfather smoked his pipe and complained that only one package of tobacco was left, hidden in the basement. Grandmother worked on a scarf she was knitting for her husband. Helena and Maria sat on the floor, sipping their tea. Jan, with a cup in his hand, studied the Russian newspaper, trying hard to translate it.

Around the village, frozen trees cracked in the fierce wind. From the forest, a pack of hungry wolves moved toward barns and chicken coops as if to finish the job started by the Russians.

In the town of Bostyn, Soviet soldiers confiscated hundreds of horses and sleighs. Early next morning, horses and sleighs were being driven from Bostyn, some east, some west, some south. Soldiers armed with rifles rode on the sleighs.

A large sleigh, bearing three soldiers, traveled toward Jan's house. The horses jogged steadily through the snow, their breath freezing about their bridles. One of the soldiers, back to the wind, started to sing and the others joined him. "Make my couch beneath the green pine tree. Do not whisper about me, pine tree. Let me dream of my beloved."

The melody floated gently in the early dawn, echoing softly through the woods, across the silent fields of snow. When the song ended, one of the soldiers drew a bottle of vodka from his pocket. "Kholodno (cold)," he said. Let's soothe our dry throats, comrades."

"Da, kholodno," the others agreed.

"Watch, don't drink too much, Ivan, it's the last one we have," the driver said, but he himself promptly took a sip when his companions passed him the bottle.

"Rotten business," Ivan observed.

"What?"

"All these arrests. What's the point?"

"They deserve it. These Polish farmers are rich."

"Come on! They look poor to me," argued the soldier, gazing at the thatched roofs of Zamosze.

"Like hell they are. They're capitalistic parasites. They've got cows and horses, pigs and chickens."

"You mean they had them, before we ate them!"

They drank once more and fell silent. It was daybreak when they entered the streets of Zamosze amid barking dogs.

Chapter Two

Jan's sleep was interrupted by impatient thumps on the door and harsh Russian voices.

He pulled on his clothes frantically, praying, "Holy Mary, Mother of God..." He was scared and sweating, even though the room was cold. Rushing out, he noticed his grandfather's clock. It was 6 a.m. "What do these Russians want so early in the morning?" he mumbled. He noticed that his grandparents and his sisters were also awake and gathered in the kitchen. Unbolting the door, he was confronted by three Russian soldiers. Their leader, a short man with a cadaverous face, entered first and immediately pinned Jan to the wall of the corridor.

"Do not move! Spread your legs, put your hands up... Da! Da! That way, at the wall!" Terrified, Jan did as he was told.

Grandmother stood near the fireplace, terror-stricken. The soldier who had been close to Maria, suddenly grasped her shoulder roughly and clamped his hand over her mouth. Jan moved toward Maria to help her. The soldier in charge caught Jan by the collar and pushed him to his knees on the floor. "Now get up and stand quietly over there." Jan slowly got to his feet, trembling with fear and anger. The soldier released Maria, then began to search the house for arms, but found none.

The soldier in charge pulled out his pocket watch and looked at it for a moment. "I am giving you half an hour - no more - to collect your belongings," he announced. "Then we will leave. Now move! Bring food unless you want to starve." His Russian was harsh and accented; Jan thought that the man must be Mongolian.

"Where are you taking us?" Grandfather asked.

"You will find out soon enough, old man," the soldier replied. "Don't ask questions, just do as you're told," he added impatiently.

The family gathered together in the hallway. They were strangely dressed, layered in the warmest clothes they owned. The girls carried bread, cheese, meat and a few garments tightly rolled in blankets. Jan assisted Grandfather, who had difficulty in walking, while Maria and Helena kept Grandmother between them. The strange procession moved outside.

They were ordered onto the waiting sleigh. One soldier picked up the reins, the other two sat behind the captive family, and the sleigh started to move. Behind them and ahead of them, Jan saw a string of sleighs carrying their neighbours into the unknown. "Where are they taking us?" asked Grandmother in a shaky voice. "Siberia, I think," Grandfather answered. They did not speak, but gripped each other's hands tightly as the sleigh moved along the snow-covered road.

The prisoners, pulled suddenly from their beds, were too frightened to talk. Their captors were also silent. Their eyes, it seemed, were avoiding their passengers, wandering instead over the snow-covered fields, marshes and distant forest. The silence was interrupted by the occasional whistle of a whip. Jan could not control his trembling and was ashamed of himself.

They approached the familiar pine grove. Jan's eyes scanned the branches, which, because of yesterday's storm, were weighted down under a downy powder of snow. Some of the trees, he noticed, had not withstood the vicious storm and had been hurled to the ground. Their roots, removed from the life-giving soil, were now exposed to the merciless elements. Jan had seen many trees uprooted, some by storms, some by age and others by man. That morning, however, staring at the vulnerable roots, he felt sadness for the fate of those trees. Only a few days ago they had been standing proudly, their green crowns facing the skies, their roots anchored securely in the ground. He consoled himself with the knowledge that in the spring their place would be taken by young saplings and life would go on in the grove.

Jan looked back at their cottage, then the village, until they were hidden by the trees. He wondered if he would ever see them again.

By eight o'clock they reached Bostyn. A few minutes later, they realized that they were going to the railway station. The platform was crowded with families from Zamosze, nearby villages and the town of Bostyn itself. Fear was so great that neighbours who had lived together for generations failed to greet each other. Jan recognized Mr. Wojek, the postman, with his seven little daughters. Beside him stood a teacher from Jan's school, looking frail and shaken.

There were peasants, lumberjacks, small businessmen, railway workers, children, old men, and women. Most stood silent, too anxious to risk speech.

Others talked nervously, eyeing the Soviet soldiers who formed a loose ring around the crowd. Most of the people spoke Polish, but Jan heard some Byelorussian and Yiddish as well. "Where are we going?" "Where are they taking us?" "Mama, I'm cold..."

In the early afternoon, light snow began to fall. People huddled together for warmth. Jan stamped his feet, trying to stay warm. He noticed that his grandparents looked pale. Grandfather leaned heavily on his cane and Grandmother sat unmoving on a bundle of clothes. Just as the light was fading from the sky, they heard a train whistle. Jan stood on the bench to see what was happening as the station clock struck five.

He saw the silhouette of the approaching train. It was a freight train, unusually long. When it stopped, the Red Army soldiers sprang into action. Rifles in hand, they started herding the crowd toward the freight cars.

"All aboard!" The command rang out in the cold air, echoed by soldiers all along the platform, "All aboard!" The first families clambered into the cars, soldiers urging them on from behind.

Jan, helping his grandfather, moved ahead, knowing that the rest of his family would follow. They hurried to the train and made their way on board. When the car was full, the door was barred and locked. They stood side by side, breathing heavily in the darkness.

"Who has a lighter?" someone asked. "Matches, for Christ's sake, matches!"

A burning match did not illuminate the interior of the car very much, showing only a few frightened faces. Then somebody spotted four kerosene lanterns hanging on the wall of the car and rushed to light them.

The large car, normally used to deliver grain, machinery, livestock and other goods, had been converted for other purposes. Jan spotted rough bunks, in four tiers, lining the sides of the car. The space between the tiers was so small that each person had to crawl to his or her space. A grown man or woman could not sit or kneel.

"Ten to a bunk!" a voice called out. The owner of the voice, Jan realized, must have already figured out how many of them there were and calculated the distribution of people.

Reluctantly, the families settled themselves in the crude bunks. Jan and his family shared a bunk with another family of five, consisting of a tall bony peasant, his plump wife and three teenaged daughters. The man took charge of both families. "You sleep at the end there," he told Jan. "Roll over on your side so there is more room. Now you, child..." After some manoeuvering, they were settled.

"I'll never be able to sleep like this," Helena complained.

"Hush child, hush," Grandmother tried to calm her. Maria was weeping. Jan felt as though he was trapped in some devilish cage. His eyes fell upon two small openings, meant for ventilation, but now barred. Unable to sleep, he lay still on the hard boards of the bunk.

Many people were sleepless in the stuffy car. Jan could not shut out the sounds: sighs, whispers of mothers trying to soothe children, muttered curses. The woman next to Jan lay uncomfortably on her rolled-up coat. Her lips moved slightly as she prayed. Maria and Helena talked in whispers. Their grandparents were quiet and Jan was afraid, weak and exhausted. The train lurched suddenly and began to roll steadily forward. They were on their way - on their way to where? The rhythm of the wheels and the swaying of the freight car finally lulled Jan to sleep.

When he woke up, he was bewildered. Where was he? Why did all his bones and muscles ache? Then the sounds of the train reminded him. His eyes met his grandfather's and Jan saw the pain in them. Grandmother reached for his hand, squeezed it weakly, but said nothing. His sisters were still asleep. He had to find a washroom; where was it? Careful not to disturb his sisters, he slipped from the lower deck to the floor and looked about him. In the central area of the car, there was a heater and a stove pipe which carried the smoke through the car's floor. Close to the door was the toilet, a hole in the floor with a half-circle of jute sacking hung around it.

A man sat on the floor beside the heater, feeding wood through the open door to keep the flames alive. He was about twenty, Jan guessed, thin, with sharp features. It dawned on him that there, in front of him, was Walter Plater, the village communist. The same Plater who had brought the joyous news to Zamosze about the Soviet Army crossing the Polish border.

Jan had heard a lot about Plater, but had never had a chance to talk to him, even though they were from the same village. Gossip said that when Plater was ten years old, his father had emigrated to Canada and his mother had died soon afterward. He had been adopted by an aunt in Pinsk, where he had finished high school and Lycee. While in his last year in the Lycee, he had become involved with the communist movement. He had been found out and had spent a year in jail.

Jan carefully scrutinized the man in front of him. When their eyes met,

Jan noticed that Plater's eyes were steady and forceful, but not without warmth and humour.

The silence was broken by Plater. "Bastards! Fat bastards!" he hissed.

"Who?" Jan asked, surprised.

"What do you mean, who, stupid? The bloody Bolsheviks."

"Is that so?" Jan retorted. "Wasn't it you who ran through the streets of Zamosze like a cat with its tail cut off, yelling 'the Red Army is coming to help us'?"

"Oh, so you saw that," Plater smiled, unperturbed. "Ya," he added, "it was I who brought the news."

"So?" Jan persisted.

"So, shit! So, nothing! After I learned that they came not to liberate us, but to partition us - with their good friends the Germans - I told them what was on my mind. I told them that I was a Marxist, and they told me 'you are not a Marxist.' I showed them my I.D. from the Polish Communist Party. I had one hidden in the lining of my coat," he grinned wryly. "The Commissar hardly looked at it. He told me that true communists are only in the Soviet Union and that Polish so-called communists needed to be re-educated in Siberia. I couldn't believe my ears. So I told him that a communist is a communist, regardless of whether he is Polish or Russian. Then I asked him why they were sending agents to organize us, and what about the International Communist solidarity and the united workers of the world? Do you know what that bastard was doing while I was talking to him? He was picking his rotten teeth, preoccupied with what he found between them! Tfoo!" Plater spat on the floor with disgust. "I became desperate," he continued. "I told him that for my beliefs in communism, I had sat for almost a year in jail. I told him that we had been used when we were needed and now... The Commissar just leaned back in his chair and laughed - laughed, can you imagine?"

"And what happened then?" Jan asked, his curiosity mounting.

"I lost my temper and told the red bastard what I really thought of them, their treachery, their stupid, ragged Red Army, and their Stalin-Ribbentrop pact, which partitioned Poland between Germany and the Soviet Union. As a result, he called two of his K.G.B. thugs to beat me up and take me to jail. On the way to prison, I escaped into the forest. It was too bloody cold there, so after a few hours of wandering, I met Ignacy Dabrowski - there, that man lying on the third deck - and asked for shelter. That was last night. This morning, I was riding in the sleigh. The rest you know."

Jan was very impressed by his new-found friend, Plater. 'He is brave,' he thought. 'He stood up to the Bolsheviks.'

Plater returned to his bunk. When there was a little space, Jan crouched in front of the stove for warmth. When he could, he looked out through the cracks of the wagon. Peering through a crack that appeared to be slightly wider than the others, Jan desperately tried to see the area that they were passing through. All he could see were fragments: an occasional railway station, snow covered fields, a grove of trees, or a hamlet.

Jan didn't know much about the Soviet Union. What little he knew he had learned from his grandparents, his father, or the few schoolbooks and newspapers that he had seen.

As a young girl, Grandmother had lived for ten years in Moscow, before the Revolution. She never tired of talking about the Russian capital. "Oh Jan, you cannot imagine how beautiful the churches are, and the Kremlin. Oh, and the markets, so many things to choose from and buy. And the people Jan, so nice, such well-dressed ladies and gentlemen."

"How about the peasants?" asked Grandfather, who didn't like anything about the Russians. He always remembered the time he had been whipped by a Cossack cavalryman during a students' rally.

"Peasants? Well, peasants everywhere are poor, of course," Grandmother explained.

"Poor? She is telling me poor! You mean the poorest on earth."

"Well, maybe." Grandmother did not want to argue. "And wheat! Jan!" she continued. "Endless fields of wheat in the Ukraine, close to Kiev. I was there twice with my grandfather."

"Why did they revolt if life was so good under the Czar?" Jan asked.

"Aha!" interjected his grandfather, glad to have an ally. "That's the point, my boy! A few rich and the rest poor! That's Russia for you."

"Still, it was a nice place," Grandmother said, not giving up.

Jan was thinking about the story he had heard from his father on the subject of Russia. His father had taken part in the war between Poland and the

Bolsheviks in 1920. He had been captured by the Red Army and had spent a year in prison. He had a different story to tell his son. "Jan, I saw the Soviet police executing old men and women, children, anyone they captured, for no reason at all. I myself was supposed to be shot, but I managed to escape."

"Why did they want to shoot you, Father?" Jan asked.

"Good question, son! They had wagons loaded with garbage and I was told to pull one - like a horse. Being weak from hunger, I collapsed. So they decided to shoot me."

"They didn't feed you enough?" Jan had asked, puzzled.

"Feed? Oh, my God! I would have died in the first few weeks if it weren't for the camp cook."

"How was that?"

"Well, I addressed him once in Yiddish, and he thought that I was a Jew, so he usually arranged to give me a bit more soup and black bread."

Only last year, Jan had met a boy of about his age, whose family had managed to escape from the Soviet Union. The boy's name was Kola, but the boys in Jan's class nicknamed him "Sibirak", a person from Siberia. Sibirak didn't want to talk about his life in the Soviet Union, but once, when pressured, he had exploded, "Hell! Hell on earth, friends."

Hell or Heaven, Jan wanted to see more of the land he had heard so many conflicting stories about. He borrowed a sharp knife from the peasant on his bunk and started to cut the board, slowly enlarging the crack in the weathered wall of the freight car. Soon his efforts paid off, because he was able, without moving from his bunk, to see more of the passing Soviet countryside. The land was flat, endless. Covered in snow, it looked monotonous and somehow sad. It didn't seem as peaceful or welcoming as the marshes and forests of Zamosze in winter.

Jan was astonished to find that many fields had heaps of grain stacked and abandoned. He shared this information with his neighbour, the peasant.

"Come on, you are lying!" the peasant exclaimed.

"Look for yourself," Jan said, moving away from the wall.

"Of all the goddamned..." cursed the peasant. "Hey, Wladek, Janek,

Grzegorz, come here! All of you, come here! Look! Look through this shit-ty hole! Look!"

Jan was surprised and a bit proud of the commotion caused by his dis-covery.

"Sons-of-bitches!" cursed the peasant called Wladek. "They harvested it, but they didn't store it."

"Looks like it."

"But that is a crime!"

"At home I would carry the grain on my back, never mind a horse."

"I would thrash it right on the field."

"I would sooner give it away than leave it like that!"

"Maybe they went on strike," someone suggested.

"Strike in the Soviet Union?" Wladek scoffed. "They shoot strikers!"

From that time on, Jan was known as the observer. He would look through his little hole and pass on what he saw to the other passengers. "Hey observer, what's new now? What do you see?"

But there wasn't much to see. All they passed were poor-looking hamlets, villages and towns. The towns, Jan realized, were few and the train would pass them at considerable speed. Usually, he had noticed, the train stopped only before or after a town.

"They don't want to show us their miserable towns," somebody said sar-castically.

"Or to show us to the towns," somebody added.

A few times Jan observed people standing around or working at the small railway stations. They were dressed in heavy cotton coats, men and women alike, and they wore long boots. What was particularly strange to Jan was that the few people he did see always stood with their backs to the train. As much as he tried, he never managed to see their faces.

"Why are they turning their backs?" he asked Plater once, when they were both sitting close to the stove.

"Maybe they have ugly faces! Most likely they have been told not to look at us."

The hours passed. "Where are they taking us?" That question was asked again and again. Siberia was the most frequent guess. They wouldn't be the first Poles sent to Siberia, someone remarked. The Czars had been doing that for more than a hundred years.

The train sometimes stopped for hours, sometimes it crawled at a snail's pace. The men surmised that the Russians wanted to keep secret what they were doing to the Polish people.

The second night was much more difficult. People were thirsty. They had some food that they had brought with them, but there was no water and the children began to cry. The stuffy air, first too hot, then too cold, together with the incredible congestion and odour from the "toilet", was unbearable, especially for the children and the very old.

On the morning of the third day, the train stopped, to their surprise, in a large town. The door was unbolted and slid open. After so many days in darkness, the sunlight was painful to their eyes and the prisoners tried to shield them. A Soviet soldier appeared and announced that six men were needed to carry boiled water. Jan and Plater volunteered at once. They were given a large pail each and lined up in pairs, squinting in the sunlight. Six soldiers with rifles surrounded them as they made their way into downtown Smolensk. Even though it was bitterly cold, they were glad they had volunteered for the job.

At first, their legs were stiff and aching, but after a while they were walking almost joyfully. They were amazed at what they saw of the Soviet Union and its people. They felt as though they had found themselves in a lifeless city. They passed desolate, shabby buildings without a single store, window display or advertisement. The strangest thing to Jan was the seeming indifference of the Soviet people. Shabbily dressed men and women, huddled in their winter coats, with felt boots on their feet, passed like shadows, without a single glance at Jan's group.

"Plater!" Jan turned to his companion. "Why do these men and women pay no attention to us? They act as though they don't see us at all. After all, we are dressed differently, with these soldiers around us, and they just don't seem to notice us at all! Why is that?"

Plater was puzzled too. "Maybe they are used to this kind of sight, Jan." After a while he added, "Or maybe they are afraid to look at us! Maybe they pretend not to see us for fear of becoming prisoners like us. But we will learn the reason soon enough," said Plater pensively.

Sleighs pulled by one horse, or occasionally by two, and driven by heavily dressed men and women, passed to and fro. Here and there, they noticed an army truck which, honking loudly, tried to make its way through a narrow street.

Turning right onto another street, they passed a stocky old woman carrying a bundle of wood on her back. Her slow progress suggested that it was much too heavy for her to carry. Jan, manoeuvering himself closer to the woman, looked at her face intently. She seemed grim and tired.

They reached their destination which was an old building with steaming water taps placed in a row along one of the inside walls.

A sturdy old woman supervised this water service. Her simple duty was to make sure that the water taps were closed properly. Jan moved close to her and greeted her in Russian. She murmured something incomprehensible under her breath, turned her back on Jan and continued with her work.

"Babushka! (old woman)," Jan said. "Do you know where they are taking us?" He waited for an answer, but the woman lowered her head as though looking for something on the floor. "Babushka, please!" he persisted.

"We are Poles... prisoners..." he realized then that he didn't really know what to say. "How is life here, Babushka?" he asked haltingly.

The woman raised her head and met his eyes angrily. "Kharasho! Kharasho, malcheek! (Good! Good, young man!)," she said harshly. Jan spotted a guard pushing his way toward him. Swiftly, he moved to the other side of the hall.

On the way back to the train, he told Plater about his conversation with the Soviet woman. "What do you think of that?" Jan asked him.

"They live in fear here! That is the obvious conclusion."

"Fear? Why would that old woman be afraid to talk to me, Plater?"

"Maybe it's fear of speaking to any stranger."

They walked in silence for a while, then Plater said, "I didn't tell you this, but I tried - before my arrest, that is - to strike up a conversation with the Soviet soldiers in Zamosze and, like your Baba, got nowhere with them. 'Kharasho! Kharasho!' That's all I could get from them. They told me life was good, food was plentiful and the houses were krasivye (beautiful)."

What Jan had managed to see during their brief stops made him think that it wasn't good at all, and certainly not beautiful.

Even though it was March, thick snow still covered the streets and the buildings. The heavily bundled people they saw on the streets, with clouds of steam coming from their mouths, were plodding over the snow covered sidewalks.

Jan was eager to leave the train at every opportunity - cold or not. He wanted to see the life of the people here and then talk with Plater, who had become a close friend. One of the things that puzzled Jan was the obvious shortage of bread and the long lines for everything.

"Not vodka," said Plater. Indeed, Jan saw many people carrying bottles of alcohol on the streets. "I suppose that's the way these poor wretches try to keep themselves warm," Plater continued.

The train sometimes stopped at railway stations, where Jan, Plater and the other volunteers could fill their pails with hot water.

"Look, Plater! I can't believe it!" Jan yelled to his friend, pointing at the people on the station platform. There were people of all ages everywhere, on the benches and floors and in the passageways. Some were sleeping, most were lying or squatting, their bundles of belongings in close sight. They were staring ahead passively. Jan noticed that the crowds were usually quiet, even though there were many children.

"Subdued or tired," he observed to Plater.

"Probably both, Jan. Look carefully at their faces! They don't smile... and see how thin they are."

"Let's go and talk to them," suggested Jan.

"I don't think it would be wise," said Plater. "Look behind you," he added quickly. Jan turned his head and found himself eye-to-eye with a Soviet guard, who, motioning with his rifle, told them to hurry up with the water and get ready to return to the train.

"This is a problem, Jan," Plater remarked while they were walking back. "We won't see much of life this way, will we?"
"Hardly. Not with a bayonet so close to your ass," answered Jan.

"Maybe it is not so smart to see it anyway."

"I don't understand, Plater," Jan said with annoyance. "Tell me why everything seems to be so lifeless here. No laughing, no talking... no flirting, damn it! There seems to be no joy in life here... No... No..."

"No soul," Plater finished for him.

Conditions in their freight car deteriorated further. Most of the food they had brought with them was gone. Unsanitary conditions and the lack of cooking facilities resulted in an epidemic of diarrhea, mostly in the children. Overcrowding, hunger, thirst, the crying of the children, and the horrible stench made life unbearable. Four children and three elderly people died in the third week of the journey. Sometimes, after long maneuvering, their train would stop outside a town, where it would stand for days.

Jan began to observe the other passengers more carefully. He noticed that people had begun to form cliques, "a natural selection", Plater observed philosophically.

The lower right bunk was occupied by eight adults and two boys in their teens. This group was dominated by a husky, forty-year-old woman, nick-named Aunt Grizelda by Plater. This muscular lady, with straw-like hair and a face like a boxer dog, had assumed indisputable leadership over her bunk and tried hard to extend her domination over the whole car.

"Would somebody tell that filthy peasant to cover his ass," she yelled, pointing at an old man. "Hey, you there! Yes! Yes! You, the fat one. If you must shit, do your shitting in the night so we don't have to look at your fat ass!" she roared at a stout woman who, with four small children, was having a particularly difficult time. "Do you have to scratch your nuts so openly?" she berated Plater, who was infested with lice. "What's going on here? No culture! None of you have culture."

Plater was offended, and at the same time, amused. "I must try to observe what makes the way she shits so different," whispered Plater into Jan's ear.

The upper left bunk was under the command of a tall black-bearded man called Rene. Rene, born in France of Polish parents, was a coal miner who had decided to immigrate to Poland a year before the outbreak of war. "I wanted to live in the country where my parents originated," he told Jan, "because, you see, even though I was born in France, I spoke Polish, followed Polish traditions, read Polish and always wanted to live in Poland."

"Do you regret moving to Poland?" asked Jan.

"Well, we spent a wonderful year in Poland. We bought a house and 20 hectares of land, and everything was good," he pointed his finger around him, "until this!"

They passed Moscow at night and, in spite of his efforts, Jan saw nothing more than a string of log cottages. "We probably only touched the outskirts," Plater explained.

In the morning, they began to speculate about their destination again. "Well, Plater, since you are so smart, tell us where we are heading," one of the men demanded. He disliked Plater and constantly tried to show him up.

"Since we passed Moscow last night," Plater started in a lecture-like tone, "it is important to establish our direction. Once we know the direction, it will be easy to establish our destination."

"Smart, eh?" the man jeered. "How do we establish it?"

"Well, Jan here is going to give us the name of the next town and then leave the rest to me." Jan went to his observation post, while the men surrounding the stove waited. "You see," Plater continued lecturing the cluster of men around the stove, "if, after Moscow, we turn north, then we are heading into the sub-Arctic Soviet Union, the Taiga. If so, we will work in the forests."

"What if we head straight east?" another man asked.

"Then we will either work in the Kolyma salt mines in the far east of the U.S.S.R., or help the Soviets in their construction of the Trans-Siberian Railway."

"Beautiful, very exciting," someone commented dryly.

"If, on the other hand," Plater continued, unperturbed, "the train turns southeast, then brothers, we will work on a collective farm in Kazakhstan or dig irrigation ditches in Uzbekistan."

"Where in hell is Uzbekistan?" somebody asked.

"In the Caspian Sea area." Plater was in his element.

"Maybe you are full of shit," somebody who didn't like the prospects exclaimed angrily. "Maybe we will work in factories, producing ammunition, food..."

"No, my dear friend! They need miners, lumberjacks and farmers; all free labour, of course."

"Free?" piped in Aunt Grizelda, who had been unusually quiet. "Free? Over my dead body! Why should I work free for the lousy Russians? I had to pay my servants, so they should pay me!"

"It could very well be over your dead body," an old man, sitting close to the latrine, observed. "And, as far as paying your servants, you paid them bloody peanuts. One zloty a day, I believe."

"Those lazy no-goods weren't worth any more!"

"Vologda!" Jan called out. "We're just passing the town of Vologda!"

"Aha!" said Plater. All heads turned to him. Feeling his importance, Plater wasn't in a hurry. "It seems we are turning straight north."

"The Taiga, then."

"Yes, it would appear to be the Taiga," Plater agreed.

The stops were becoming more frequent. Jan could see that the forests were increasingly dense. The railway stations where they stopped were piled with logs, boards or two-by-fours.

Plenty of water was supplied, but food was getting really scarce. The soldiers distributed food only occasionally. Two more people died and their bodies were taken quickly from the car. The train rolled on. The health of Jan's grandparents was getting worse; they could hardly move off the bunk, even with the help of their grandchildren.

On the 27th day of their journey, the train stopped. Besides the usual activity of the trainmen, banging the wheels with hammers, they heard many voices and the neighing of horses. Soon after, the door was unbolted by a soldier and they could see a shack, with the name "Plyesetsk" written in Russian. Looking around, they saw a few huts and a sawmill. There was wood everywhere, piled in long rows, mostly short logs and boards. The station was crowded with horses and sleighs.

"Look!" Jan yelled to Plater. "Look at those horses! I've never seen anything like them!" Plater was puzzled, too, but after a while, Jan heard him say, "Siberian horses."

The horses were short, with abnormally large heads, thick hair covering their bodies and long, bushy tails that swept the ground. The sleighs were constructed of two high-fronted runners, held together by two cross-beams. They held a centrally placed platform, low and uncomfortable looking. The drivers were so huddled in their coats, fur hats and rags, that it was difficult to tell that they were men at all.

The prisoners were ordered to leave the cars and board the sleighs, four persons to a sleigh. Jan made sure that his family rode together on one sleigh, while he went in another one with only three passengers.

They started their journey along a slippery, sleigh-flattened road, which led straight into the great forest ahead of them. The cold was so bitter that in spite of his old fur hat, his ears were freezing and his feet began to go numb.

"Where are we going?" he asked his driver. There was no reply. Jan thought maybe his Russian was poor, so he repeated his question. The man turned his head toward Jan, pulled the rag from his face and said, "Nieponimayou (Don't understand)."

The man's face was of a yellow tone with prominent Mongolian features. 'He probably doesn't speak Russian,' thought Jan.

"Davay! Davay! (Get going)" the driver shouted, whipping his horse mercilessly. The wind was so cold that Jan gasped with every breath. After six hours, the road twisted to the right, rounded a curve, and they arrived in a clearing. At its centre was a cluster of barracks. The late afternoon sun glinted on snow-covered roofs, and tall columns of smoke rose from the chimneys, white against the grey sky. As they came nearer, the captives saw that the wooden buildings were very simple, box-like structures. The camp seemed to be enclosed by a high wooden fence. The gate stood open, ready to admit the column of weary prisoners, and above it, crudely painted, were these words: "STRANA ZYLAYET DYEREVA (the state needs lumber). Welcome to Nukhto-Ozyero Lumber Camp."

The sleighs proceeded slowly until they reached what appeared to Jan to be a square. Looking curiously around, he saw many wooden barracks clustered around the square. Most of them were square, but some were long and narrow. Other than the prisoners and drivers, there was no one in sight. The drivers led them, family after family, into their respective barracks. One such driver, a list in his hand, called the names Dabrowski and Tabor. After scrutinizing them one by one, he ordered them to follow him. Jan's legs were so numb from the cold that walking was an effort. The deep snow made their progress even more difficult. Even though Jan's pocket watch, which he had managed to take with him from Poland, showed four o'clock, it was already completely dark. They were allotted one room in barrack Number 18. The room was dark, except for a dimly lit lantern, which was placed close to the wood stove in the centre of the room. The stove was burning, emanating a welcome warmth. The room reminded Jan of the railway freight car, except that it was smaller. It had wooden bunks, four in all, and even the wood stove was the same. The beds, he noticed, were covered with half-rotten grass, coarse and sharp.

They all gathered around the stove, trying to warm their frozen hands and feet. Jan noticed a pile of wood close to the stove and laid out the logs so that they could sit down. No one spoke. Jan could see the exhaustion of his grandparents and sisters. He was tired, cold and hungry himself. Sitting close to the stove, he felt numb in spirit and body. The experiences of the past few weeks made him want to cry and yell in desperation, but he some-how felt that the survival of his family would depend a lot on the way he acted. 'Jan will be somebody' the words of his family and villagers rang through his mind. 'Well,' he reflected, 'maybe I'll have to be somebody to survive here...' His pale blue eyes rested on the wood stove as though he expected some sort of inspiration from it.

"Do we have any food left?" he asked, breaking the silence.

"No, child," Grandmother answered.

He closed his eyes and imagined that this was just a nightmare and that when he woke up, he would find himself back at home. 'I must do some-thing,' he thought. 'Any action is better than just sitting in despair.' He raised himself to his feet heavily. Grabbing his grandmother's arms gently but firmly, he urged her to lie down on one of the lower bunks. Reaching for one of the bundles on the floor, he found an old blanket that he thought could serve as a sheet for her bed. He did the same thing with his grandfather who had been lying down on his old, crumpled shirt. Having done this, he turned to his sisters only to find them asleep.

To Jan, they looked like two oversized dolls. He sat by the stove for a long time, tears rolling down his cheeks. The barrack was quiet, except for the winds howling outside. Their force was very strong; the barrack shook under their lashing. He shuddered and, feeling cold, limped slowly to his own bunk. It was only then that he realized that there was no place left for him. Spreading his coat on the floor, he lay down next to the stove and went to sleep almost at once.

He had only slept for a little while when he was awakened by a strange itching all over his body. Jumping up, he grabbed the nearby lantern to find the cause. His coat was swarming with bed bugs. Raising the lantern, he saw that the walls and floor were also covered by the slowly moving red bugs.

He was filled with revulsion. He had heard about these bugs, he had even seen them, although none as large, or as many at once. He went back to the stove, reluctant to close his eyes. However, tiredness won out and he fell into a fitful sleep.

Although the Polish prisoners upon their arrival had seen only the drivers, there were other people in the camp. The prisoners had no way of knowing that they were being observed. From the dark barracks, through the windows, hundreds of eyes were peering at them, curious and excited. They were the eyes of the Soviet prisoners, mostly families like themselves, with a sprinkling of single men and women. There were about three hundred of them. Some were recent arrivals, but some had been there for many years. There were even some who had been born in this camp.

****

Comrade Ivan Vasilyevich Kovalenko, the Political Commissar of the Nukhto-Ozyero Labour Camp also watched the prisoners. Had the Polish prisoners seen his eyes, they would have noticed a difference. His, unlike the others, were hostile, cold and calculating. They were small, almost completely hidden in folds of skin. Nevertheless, they were piercing eyes, seeming capable of penetrating a man's soul, especially if that man was an enemy. Standing at the window, his eyes bored into the crowd of Polish prisoners walking beside his barrack. In order not to miss anything, he flattened his snub nose to the window pane, disregarding the discomfort caused by the cold glass.

"Look at those rotten capitalists," he whispered to himself. "Look at the way they are dressed: elegant coats, fashionable shoes, colourful hats... Tfoo!" he spat, straightening his shabby, mud-coloured coat. The coat was too long for his chubby, short body, almost reaching the ground. This particularly annoyed him because when he walked outside, the coat's hem inevitably became wet.

"We will see how these Polish lords cope with the snow here!" he growled loudly. "Especially in their short coats." He laughed without humour. He hated snow and cold weather. Indeed, he hated all of goddamned Siberia. He had only been in Nukhto-Ozyero for two weeks, and already he hated it. "This sure isn't Odessa, this Nukhto." The rest of the Polish prisoners, he noticed, had disappeared from view and the drivers had headed toward the gate and Plyesyetsk. He left the window and went into his small kitchen, where he poured a large glass of vodka. His thoughts wandered to his native Odessa, where, until recently, he had been a police officer. 'A lowly functionary,' he thought sadly. This had worried him a great deal because, being an ambitious man, he wanted to have more power and respect. As it was, he wasn't getting either. Other, lesser men, were promoted and respected, but a big fig for you, Ivan Vasilyevich. His superiors had called him an uneducated peasant behind his back and assigned the dirtiest jobs to him. His co-workers in the police force, especially fat Natasha, often called him a "sveenya" (pig). 'Blyad (whore),' he thought, spitting into the corner of the kitchen. 'And the citizens?' he sipped vodka until he had reached the bottom of the glass. 'They despised me and feared me.' That they had feared him was understandable. According to his philosophy, citizens should fear policemen, otherwise how, for the love of hell, would they obey the law?

But it hurt him deeply that they despised him. Why? Was it their ignorance? Hostility to the system he guarded? "Somebody has to crack the whip," he murmured, pouring another glass of vodka. "That's why I was sent here, to whip these capitalistic Poles. They promoted me before sending me here!" He laughed bitterly. "Some goddamned promotion. It smells more like an exile to me. Tfoo!" he spat again. "Justice, eh?"

Noticing that the bottle of vodka was empty, he sighed and went to bed. The bed bugs, as though they had been waiting for him, attacked him instantly. Tossing and turning, he cursed the authorities for promoting him to Political Commissar and the Poles he would have to supervise.

While Ivan Vasilyevich was busy observing the Polish prisoners from Barrack Number 2, his superior officer, Aram Visaryanovich Zhukhvili, was watching them from Barrack Number 1. He was a tall, lean man with shaggy black hair. His narrow, elongated head, hollow cheeks, and aquiline nose reminded one of a vulture. His appearance was softened somewhat by his large, dark blue eyes. Like Ivan Vasilyevich, he had arrived at the camp only recently. Unlike Ivan Vasilyevich, who had been promoted, he, Aram Visaryanovich had not only been demoted, but exiled as well. In Tbilisi, the capital of Georgia, he had occupied a high position in the police hierarchy, but one day he had been told bluntly, by his superiors, that he would go to Siberia, either as a commandant or as a prisoner.

"In Siberia, comrade, you will either learn how to be a good communist or you will die," his superior had said.

"But why? What did I do wrong, comrades?" he had asked.

"You are too soft. You must learn how to be tougher, stronger, thus a better communist, comrade."

So here he was, receiving Polish prisoners instead of being a shoemaker, as his mother had often suggested. He had argued that was a job for peasants, to which she had retorted, "It is safer, son, to be a shoemaker than a

Police Commissar."

"Maybe I should have listened to her. Maybe she was right, after all." He looked at the prisoners passing by his window, his eyes lingering on the men's boots. 'Good leather,' he thought. 'Must be soft, too.' He had never met Poles before but had heard a lot about them. In the school he had attended, the teachers had said only negative things about Poles. They had called them "parasites", "lords", "exploiters of the poor" and "enemies of the working class." At home, however, when the subject of Poles was raised, he had heard a different viewpoint. "Brave people", "freedom loving like the Georgians" and "friendly."

"Well, I will see soon enough what they are really like," he murmured. "I wonder what that son-of-a-bitch Ivan Vasilyevich thinks of them." The thought of his second-in-command made him angry. 'I'm sure that he is already sniffing with his Asiatic nose, hoping to find a spy among the newcomers. Whatever he thinks, nothing good will come of it, only trouble. Trouble for me. Two weeks with that man has been enough to see that he is a complete bastard. His constant insinuations, questions about my past, my opinions of Stalin - all asked in a seemingly friendly but shamelessly fawning way - make me sick. I must get rid of him somehow,' he thought, 'or else he will get rid of me.' The prospect of conflict with his deputy made him tired. Yawning widely, he decided to go to bed.

Three hundred metres away, flanked by two armoury buildings, stood Barrack Number 4. It sheltered the camp offices, a small store and a bakery. Two men stood by the bakery window, eating steaming black bread.

"Here are your workers, Nikolay Davidovich," said one of them, waving his hand toward the Polish prisoners. His grey hair, stooped posture and trembling voice indicated his age.

"Workers, indeed," answered Nikolay Davidovich. "Children and old women, mostly. How in hell will I fulfill my quota with those... those children?" he spluttered.

"You are the Work Manager. It is your problem; I am just a baker, you know."

Nikolay Davidovich, until a week ago, had been the Work Manager of the Plyesetsk Lumber Depot, where he had been born and raised. With little notice, he had been told to pack and move to Nukhto-Ozyero, where he was to teach the Polish prisoners "what real work is all about."

Nikolay Davidovich had spent more than half of his 42 years in the Taiga forests, first as a worker, then Supervisor and eventually Manager. He knew his work well, so on learning about his new assignment, he had asked pertinent questions.

"How many prisoners will I manage?" he had asked his superior.

"Fourteen hundred. Add to that our people, an extra three hundred or so."

"I see. Out of these fourteen hundred prisoners, how many are of working age?"

"Hmmm... let me see," the official was busy with calculations for a while. Then, raising his head, he said, "Considering that everyone from the ages of 16 to 70 must work, I estimate that you should have 800 workers."

"What about food supply?" Nikolay Davidovich had asked. He was a practical man.

"400 grams of bread per working person, 200 grams for non-workers, cabbage soup once a day, and hot water. Anyway, you will be given a chart which you must follow."

"They won't survive long on that diet," Nikolay Davidovich observed with concern.

"Then they will die."

"And then?"

"Then others will be sent by Moscow to replace them."

"What about warm clothes?" persisted Nikolay Davidovich.

"What about this, what about that!" the official exploded. "They will get what we give them! One more thing, comrade. Work them six days a week, or seven if necessary. We must reach the Tundra by next winter, or we will all end up in the Vorkuta coal mines. Our comrades in Moscow are going to make sure we will be sent there."

Scrutinizing the prisoners passing outside the bakery window, Nikolay Davidovich became so perturbed that, for a moment, he stopped eating his bread. "Where are all the goddamned men, Alosha?" he exploded.

"In German prisons, I think."
"Or ours."

"Whichever," the baker shrugged. "Either way, it is your problem."

"Your problem! Your problem! You sound like a parrot today, Alosha. How about you? It is also your problem. Where in hell do you think you will get enough flour for bread, eh, Alosha?"

"No problem! Less flour, less bread; that has happened before, you know."

"And no flour, no bread!" Nikolay Davidovich snapped. He turned abruptly on his heel and left the bakery.

"And no bread, no work," Alosha said quietly. "Then you and I will rot in jail, my friend."

Chapter Three

In spite of the bed bugs and the unfamiliar place, Jan and his family managed to get some sleep that first night. In the morning, they were awakened by loud banging at their door and a harsh Russian voice. "Davay podnimaysa (get up). Davay! Davay!"

They dressed quickly, the children helping their grandparents, then they went out into the still Arctic darkness. The huge yard was crowded with people. In the middle there was a fire. A group of Soviet officials were standing around it, warming their hands. Still half asleep, Jan looked around. The crowd was unusually quiet, expectant. The silence was interrupted only by an occasional cough, someone blowing on his hands or jumping up and down to keep warm.

The Soviets left the fire and approached the crowd. "My name is Nikolay Davidovich Tikhanov," said the tallest of them. "I am the Manager here. Our task today is to assign a job to everyone between the ages of 16 and 70. If you are in this age group, you must work! I repeat, you must work!"

'Thank God,' Jan thought. 'That excludes our grandparents and Helena.' Both of his grandparents were over seventy, and Helena was only eleven. "That leaves two of us," he said, turning to Maria. She smiled sadly, but said nothing.

"Those of you who work," the Manager continued, "will receive 400 grams of bread a day. Those under 16 and over 70 will get 200 grams a day. However, those of you of working age who refuse to work will get nothing! Nothing!" He paused to allow his words to register. "You must learn today, right now, that in the Soviet state, those who do not work, do not eat. You must remember that you will be here until you die. This is your home now!"

He was flanked by the other camp officials, all dressed in heavy koofaykas (cotton-padded coats), large fur hats, cotton-padded pants and valonki (high woolen boots). They were introduced as Supervisors or

Brigadeers of various work sections such as lumberjacks, teamsters, carpenters, and food suppliers.

"And now," the Manager ordered, "line up at the office for your job assignments."

The line was long and moved slowly. In an effort to get warm, people jumped up and down and beat their hands together. "We shouldn't work for the bastards," Jan heard someone say.

"No? You want to starve?" someone responded.

Jan's turn came about noon. He entered the camp office, where he saw four men sitting behind a long desk, each holding a pencil and pad. He disliked one of them instantly. The man was fat, with a small, flat nose and a bald head. What disturbed Jan most was the man's eyes. They were small, unblinking, and seemed to bore into him. Jan felt a tightness in his gut. The man, sensing Jan's apprehension, smiled crookedly, which further deepened Jan's disgust and fear.

After checking Jan's muscles with disappointed grimaces, and noting his name and age on the lists in front of them, they assigned him to the teamster brigade. Jan couldn't understand their smirks or the glances they exchanged.

Later, he learned that when assigning jobs, the officials followed certain well-established criteria. Plater, who had tried to analyze the job allotment, told him that the prisoners the Russians hated most were those with a certain amount of education. They were thought to be parasites, blood suckers, the product of the capitalistic system and they needed to be re-educated by hard physical work. Plater, who could speak and write Russian and was generally well-educated, was assigned to the lumberjack brigade, whereas a Byelorussian who had been a forest ranger in Poland with only four years of education, was given an office job. Aunt Grizelda not only claimed to have had a higher education but had also had servants before the war; she was the epitome of everything the Russians held in contempt. She was assigned to the nearby quarry - one of the hardest jobs in the camp.

Twenty-eight women were assigned to work at the quarry. All but one were Polish. Some of them were the wives of Polish landowners, others were teachers or office workers, and two of them were medical doctors. The camp officials called them 'the Bloodsuckers'.

"Now they will pay for their exploitation of the working class," the officials said. "They must be re-educated...or die."

'The Bloodsuckers', unlike their peasant counterparts, were unused to hard physical work and harsh weather. Their expensive winter coats were well-tailored, but much too light for sub-zero temperatures and cold Arctic winds. Their elegant, well-fitted shoes were suited for a dance floor, but useless in the Siberian winter.

It didn't take long for their Russian supervisor to realize that only about one third of them could even lift a pick or a shovel, never mind splitting or shoveling rocks. "It doesn't matter," he was told by the camp official to whom he complained. "They have been assigned there to die... We don't even need the rocks."

At first, the women refused to work, started a fire and sat around it in a tight circle, singing Polish songs.

"What's the use? We will all die here anyway," they said.

They answered the continuous orders and curses of their supervisor with more and more songs.

"You will die of starvation, you Polish whores!" he screamed. "You won't get one gram of bread tonight!"

"Shut your filthy mouth, barbarian!" one of them yelled back. "Take us back to Poland, you louse-infested bolshevik!" The others chorused their encouragement.

That night, their bread rations stopped. They became weaker daily, and some had to be dragged out of the barrack by the K.G.B. men.

On the third day, 'Aunt Grizelda' addressed the squad. "Sisters, the Soviet barbarians will starve us to death. We must fight for survival as long as we can. We must begin to work. We will endure!" So saying, she lifted a pick and started to strike an enormous rock. They followed her example, some with reluctance, others with surprising determination. Soon, Grizelda's hands were bleeding and her legs and back were numb, but she worked until the end of the day.

Thus, the people in the camp saw a procession of haggard women, dragging their feet as they carried their picks and shovels back and forth between the camp and the quarry, day after day, day after day.

Those who cared to count noted that only twenty of the twenty-eight women assigned to the quarry returned to the barracks alive. A few weeks later, only seventeen...then thirteen...then eight...

Then one morning only one woman was left - Grizelda. The poor creature's feet were wrapped in rags tied with string. Her coat lost a sleeve and the rest was in tatters. Her bony knees showed through the holes in her cotton trousers. She crawled toward the quarry, dragging her pick behind her. Hours later, she was brought back, frozen to death.

****

By the end of the first day in the camp, all the prisoners had their jobs which, while not as murderous as quarry duty, were far too difficult for most of them.

That evening, Jan was sitting by the stove when his grandfather beckoned him to the bunk where he lay. Jan jumped up from the log he occupied and stood next to his grandfather.

"Jan, I want to talk to you about something that worries me," Grandfather said quietly. "Your grandmother and I are old, and God knows we won't live to see Poland again."

"No, Grandfather!" Jan exclaimed, but Grandfather gestured for silence.

"You children must survive," Grandfather continued. "I have a feeling that only the fittest will survive here. The fittest and the smartest; remember, the smartest. I have always thought you were smarter than other boys your age, and I think you will be able to take care of your sisters. You are a man now, you understand?"

"What do you want me to do, Grandfather?"

"Learn how the Russians have survived here...get friendly with them...and learn as much as you can."

"Yes, Grandfather," Jan promised.

****

There was a man in the camp called Mikola. Jan had met him briefly in the camp office and exchanged a few polite words with him in Russian. He was a seventy-year-old Ukrainian prisoner who had impressed Jan in several ways. Despite his age, Mikola's back was as straight as a sugar cane. With powerful leg and arm muscles, he emanated physical strength and confidence. Jan already knew that Mikola was a carpenter, assigned to a huge barn-like structure where he fixed broken sleighs. Jan could not work until his sleigh was repaired, so he decided to pay a visit to Mikola. Mikola greeted him warmly as though they were old friends.

"Sit down, young man, sit down."

"Thank you, sir. My name is Jan."

"What can I do for you?"

"Will my sleigh be ready soon?"

"Yes, it's ready now. I understand you are to be new zhvozcheek (teamster)," Mikola said. "Well, I hope that you will take good care of your horse,
not like those oorkies."

"Oorkies?"

"Oh, pardon me. I forgot that you are new here. Oorkies are criminals,
my boy, really bad criminals."

"Do they get worse treatment from the authorities than we do?"

"No!" said Mikola, angrily. "They are treated better."

"But why? You said they're criminals!"

"Sure, but they are considered less dangerous for the Soviet authorities
than you are."

"I'm not dangerous to anyone!" Jan exclaimed.

"Maybe not now, but in the future you might be. You, and others like you,
may question the validity of the Soviet system. The oorkies don't.
Politically speaking, they are loyal citizens of the Soviet Union."

"Are there any oorkies in this camp now, Mikola?"

"Yes, three of them, and you had better stay away from them, malcheek."

"Are there many prisoners in the Soviet Union, Mikola?" Jan asked.

Mikola laughed bitterly. Lowering his voice almost to a whisper, he
asked, "Ever heard of the Gulag?" Jan shook his head. "They say that the
Gulag area stretches from the Kola Peninsula in the west to Kamchatka in the
east - some 10,000 kilometres. It is full of camps like this and many far
worse. Some call it simply 'Siberia'."

"Who says?"

"The prisoners, who else? In my fourteen years here, I've met a lot of them. Some were transferred from the Kolyma, some others from Novaya-Zyemlya, Vorkuta, Taymyr Peninsula, Pechora Valley, or other parts of the Gulag."

"How many did they send to these camps?"

"Nobody here knows exactly how many were deported to Siberia, but I hear there were six million Ukrainians alone." They sat in silence. After a while, Mikola resumed his story. "Some of the prisoners were sent from here too," he whispered. "They were never heard from again."

The day after his conversation with Mikola, Jan was told to report to the stable where the Stable Supervisor would assign him a horse. The supervisor of the stable was Olga Stepanovna Kolov, whose reputation had already reached Jan's ears.

He met her at a most inappropriate time, it seemed. She was in the process of spanking a "zhvozcheek" (teamster) who had been stealing oats.

Jan had never seen a woman spanking a man, a fully grown man at that. Nor had he seen such a tall and muscular woman. The heavy clothes she wore further accentuated her size. Her face, red with anger, was like a full moon. She was spanking the man, holding him by his feet so that his moustache hung absurdly upside down.

"Yey Bohu, ne budu whze kral (So help me God, I won't steal anymore)!" her victim yelled.

"You mouse's ass! You ox's tail! You, you...mammoth's fart!" Jan couldn't believe his ears. Marta, the neighbour from Jan's village with a mouth as foul as any man, was an angel in comparison to this forbidding woman.

Olga Stepanovna, using her right hand, continued spanking the man's rear. The victim, seeing Jan, started to yell, "Help! Help! For the love of God, help!"

Realizing they were not alone, Olga Stepanovna decided to let the man down. He immediately scurried out of the stable, moaning like a wounded dog. Jan just stood there, his mouth open.

"Well?" she thundered at him.

"I, I..." he stammered.

"You what?"

"I came to get a horse."

Olga Stepanovna looked him up and down contemptuously. "A horse? Why do you need a horse, Polack? Eh, what for?"

"For work," said Jan meekly.

"Work, eh?" she repeated, glancing at him again. "Where are your papers?" Jan handed her a piece of paper from the camp office with the name of a horse. "Choodak?" she roared, after reading it. "Choodak? Don't they know in that shitty office that Choodak refuses to work?"

"Refuses?" Jan repeated, confused. "How can a horse refuse?"

"Come with me, you shitty Polack, and see for yourself! I would refuse to work myself if somebody did to me what they did to that poor animal."

Puzzled, Jan followed her to a nearby stall. In the dim light of a lantern, he saw a horse that was small, even by Siberian standards. With protruding bones, disproportionately big head and somewhat crooked legs, it was the ugliest horse he had ever seen. There was no comparison between this piteous creature and the tall, graceful horse he had saved from the marshy quagmire in Zamosze. Choodak, however, had a beautiful mane and a long, bushy tail. Olga Stepanovna lifted its tail, revealing an enormous scar. Seeing Jan's horror and surprise, Olga Stepanovna exploded that "an oork son-of-a-bitch burned this poor horse's ass! Loaded too much on it and then thought that a firebrand would help to move him."

The horse, as though sensing that they were talking about him, raised his head from the manger, and turned his gaze on them. Jan could see the wariness and mistrust in the animal's eyes. Touched by Choodak's (Funny One) mutilation, he stroked his neck, head and back.

Seeing Jan's gentleness with the horse, Olga Stepanovna became more amiable. "After those bastards were finished with him, he refused to work. They wanted to kill him for meat, but I put my foot down and they've let him be. For how long, I don't know. And now, those pigs in the office want you to get him to work, bloody jokers." She was pensive for a moment. "Well, try him, malcheek," she said softly.

****

Hitching Russian sleighs was new to Jan. Olga Stepanovna made an exception and helped him. Not, however, without delivering a litany of filthy curses. "Treat him carefully, you mother-fucker!" she warned as he left.

The sleigh, he noticed, had been cleverly designed to carry logs. It was simply two long runners, curved up at the front and held together by three crossbars. Logs were piled on two of the crossbars and the third held the runners together at the top of the curve in front. The driver had to balance himself on the curves of the runners and bend forward to hold the reins, which passed over the front bar.

On his way to join the work team, he began to worry. If Choodak wouldn't pull the load, as Olga Stepanovna had predicted, he and his family would be even hungrier than they were already. If Maria was the only person working, there would be less bread for the family.

Arriving at the cutting area, Jan was greeted by the ribald remarks of the predominantly Russian lumberjacks who all knew the story of Choodak's stubborn revenge.

"Oh, great! They send a horse that won't work!"

"And look at the driver - he probably hasn't worked a day in his life!"

"Maybe he needs a fire under his ass, too!"

"Leave him alone - he's just a boy."

Jan, hurt by the lumberjacks' jibes, sat motionless. The horse lowered his head and sniffed at the snow, searching in vain for a blade of grass. All around, the trees creaked and groaned in the breeze. The snow reflected a pale, cold light from the grey sky.

Despite their barbed remarks, the lumberjacks were, in fact, worried. They were angry with the Administration for sending an inexperienced, skinny youth to act as a regular, strong-bodied teamster. The presence of Choodak further concerned them since they knew about his temperament. They all had a daily quota to fill, and failure to do so would decrease their rations of bread. Thinking that if Choodak wouldn't pull the load, they would get rid of both the horse and the boy, they overloaded Jan's sleigh.

Jan stroked Choodak's neck and combed the horse's mane with his fingers. He stepped on the runners of the sleigh and drew the reins taut, then slackened them a little. "Davay, Choodak! Davay! (get going)" he cried.

The lumberjacks put their tools aside to witness the spectacle. Choodak felt the gentle tug and heard Jan's voice, but made no attempt to move.

"Davay!" Jan cried in frustration. Choodak responded by burying his head in the snow, which brought a chorus of laughter from the lumberjacks. "Davay, Choodak!" Jan repeated pleadingly. Choodak turned his head and Jan could have sworn that the horse winked at him. Suddenly, Choodak raised his head high, stretched his muscles and began to move the load. Jan heard the excited voices of the lumber-jacks behind him, but paid little attention; his eyes were on Choodak. At that moment, Jan became a zhvozhcheek, a teamster.

After that, Jan always made sure that the sleigh wasn't overloaded and that the harness was comfortable and in good repair. Unlike the other teamsters, he never used a whip or yelled at his horse. Choodak reciprocated by doing his job, and by taking care of Jan in the only way he could. During the biting Arctic blizzards, when visibility was zero, Jan would let the reins go, relying completely on the horse's instincts to take him to work or back to the barracks.

Jan and the horse became celebrities among the Russian workers. "They work well together, those two," they would say, watching the odd pair.

As time went on, however, the extreme cold and poor food began to take their toll on both Jan and Choodak. Jan's clothes, warm enough for the Polish winter, were totally inadequate for the Arctic. His light boots were in pieces within a few weeks. He was warned by the Russian prisoners that he would lose his feet to frostbite unless he wrapped them in heavy rags. He followed their advice and, although it felt awkward, he was warmer. Maria's coat was far too light, so she had to wear two coats, her own and her grandmother's. The warmest piece of clothing Helena had was a woolen nightdress which almost reached her ankles. It wrenched Jan's heart to see his sister standing in the soup line in the bitter cold, wearing a tattered winter coat over her night-dress and bed-socks wrapped in rags. He had offered to take her place once.

"Please don't try to stop me," was her immediate answer. "It's the only way I can help and, besides, you have to work in the forest." Jan had consented, but he was still concerned.

Cabbage soup and black bread was their whole diet. The soup was issued in the morning before work and in the evening. It was considered good luck to find any cabbage. The prisoners were given tallons (wooden coupons) for their work and used them to buy soup and bread rations. It was necessary to take a place in line two or more hours before the kitchen opened. Hundreds of people stood in the cold at four or five in the morning, pushing, cursing and complaining. Everyone wanted those meager portions of soup, knowing that only the first few hundred would actually get any, and that the tallons issued for that day would be obsolete the next.

Jan's lunch consisted of a piece of bread. No matter how he tried to protect it from the cold, it was always frozen by lunch time. Every day the workers made a fire, pierced their bread with sticks and held it over the flames. The result was that the bread's outer layer was burnt, while the inside remained frozen. A severe stomach ache would usually follow.

Bread! It seemed that all everyone talked about was bread.

"Remember, Antoni," Grandmother would ask, "when I baked bread from the wheat you brought from Bostyn?"

"Sure, I remember, but don't torture me, you know how hungry I am," grumbled Grandfather.

"Remember when we would walk to the marshes eating whole wheat bread and jam?" Maria asked Jan. "Oh, it was such good bread," she said with a sigh.

"Please, stop it!" Jan cried, salivating. He heard similar talk every day from his co-workers, in the stable from Olga Stepanovna, from the children in the corridor of their barrack.

In the camp office, there was a daily list showing which working brigades had completed their quotas and which had not. The prisoners were constantly urged to work harder. "Those who do not work, do not eat," was the slogan written on a large blackboard in the camp office.

****

The close bond that Jan had established with Choodak gave him more confidence in himself. Responding to the horse's good nature, intelligence and devotion, he treated him gently and took good care of him. When she saw that Jan was the only teamster who brushed his horse every evening, Olga Stepanovna was so impressed that she secretly increased Choodak's ration of oats.

The exercise and extra food revitalized the horse, making him stronger and livelier. He welcomed Jan every morning with joyous neighing and stamping. Olga Stepanovna, who seemed to love horses above everything, showed her pleasure by alternately patting Jan's heavy fur hat and stroking Choodak's mane. All this was accompanied by her customary stream of profanities.

March 17th was a memorable day for Jan. Except that the morning was even colder than usual, the day began like any other. However, by noon there was a sudden increase in the wind velocity and snow started to fall. By the end of the day, the light snowfall had become a "buran" (blizzard). Olga Stepanovna had told Jan that buran - that most dreaded element in Siberia - had been responsible for many deaths in the camp. "It killed nine people in 1938," she had said, "and as many horses."

That day, the teamsters had been allowed to go home an hour earlier. But, as Jan soon learned, it was too late. Only when he had left the shelter of the forest did he understand the real meaning of Olga Stepanovna's description of the buran. The sharp, icy flakes carried by the cold, howling winds lashed them with a force that frightened and astonished Jan. The fury of the storm reduced visibility to zero. It was as though a huge wall of snow, driven by the devil himself, was falling upon the boy and the beast. The wind forced Choodak to halt. To protect himself, the horse lowered his head and buried it in the snow.

Powerless against the howling winds and piercing cold, Jan sat on the sleigh without moving. The pain caused by the cold was gradually replaced by a blissful numbness. He felt very sleepy. He saw himself walking across the meadow on the outskirts of Zamosze. It was a warm, sunny day. He was on his way to fetch their horse. The horse, seeing Jan, neighed happily. He always neighed when he saw Jan, but today it seemed to be much louder than usual. Jan opened his eyes as the neighing continued.

"Oh, God!" he cried. "It's Choodak!" He pushed back his fur hat, exposing his face and eyes to the winds. The ice-flakes stung like needles. He stepped off the sleigh and found himself up to his waist in a snow drift. He inched forward, hoping to reach the horse. Choodak was almost buried, and his heavy groans indicated that he was near the end of his endurance. Jan knew that unless he acted quickly, the horse would die. Sobbing with rage and desperation, he managed to unhitch the sleigh. Taking hold of Choodak's tail with both hands, he cried "Davay, Choodak!" as loud as he could.

Choodak freed himself from the drift and struggled through the deep snow. Jan, clinging blindly to the horse's tail, trusted Choodak's sense of direction to lead them to safety. The wind whipped against Jan's face and he tried to pull his hat down for protection. He lost his footing and his other hand slipped from Choodak's tail. He swung his arms frantically ahead of him to find the horse, lost his balance completely and fell headlong into the snow.

He could see nothing but whirling white and had no idea where the barracks were. He made an effort to get to his feet, but his legs were too numb. After a few more desperate tries, he fell into a deep, powdery snow drift. He was wondering how long he had been lying there when he felt a gentle nudge and heard familiar snorting. He struggled to his knees and stretched his arms toward the sound. He found the horse's neck and, holding on to Choodak's mane, slowly stood up. He was too weak to mount the horse, so he tightened his hold on the mane and urged Choodak to move ahead. His hands were slipping off the mane and he knew that he wouldn't be able to hold on much longer. But he also knew that his life depended on it. Using all the strength he could muster, he held on. Then everything became blurred, and he was falling into a soft, down-like comforter. Choodak nudged him with his nose again, but this time the boy did not respond. Fortunately, they were only about twenty metres from the stable and Choodak's neighing was heard by Olga Stepanovna, who carried Jan the rest of the way.

When Jan woke up, he saw that he was lying on a pile of hay. In the dim lantern light, he saw Olga Stepanovna's smiling face. "Thank you," he murmured.

"Thank Choodak, not me," she replied, massaging his legs with her huge hands.

****

The days passed slowly. Winter still held the camp in its grip. Although it was now April, it was still as cold as March had been. The Russians, when asked how long their winters lasted, were delighted to say that they were "twelve months and the rest is all summer." This prompted Plater to observe that the Russians had a peculiar sense of humour.

"Listen," he said to Jan, with annoyance. "The other day I asked one of the Russians how is life elsewhere in the Soviet Union. And do you know what he said? 'In the Soviet Union, here or elsewhere, life is good... You will live, but you won't be able to fuck women.'" He spat with disgust.

"What the hell did he mean by that, Plater?" asked Jan innocently.

"I don't know, but I think he was trying to tell me that life in his country is not as good as some people think," Plater answered, turning his head to hide a grin.

Most of the Russians they met were friendly and usually they would answer questions about life in the Soviet Union. However, any time they were asked why they had ended up in the Nukhto-Ozyero camp, they, except

Olga, became mute. Nothing could make them answer that question.

"Strange," Maria observed one evening after Jan had told his family about his encounters with the Russians. "The Russian women almost tore my coat apart, examining its quality," she added.

"Little did they know that it is Grandmother's old coat," Jan laughed.

"Poor souls," sighed Grandmother. "Some of them have never seen anything except felt coats, pants, and boots."

"Did they tell you why they were brought here?" asked Jan.

"No! Even though I asked them many times," Grandmother answered. "Funny, isn't it?"

"Poor people," said Grandfather with pity in his voice.

"I gave one woman an old kerchief," Helena said, "and she kissed my hand."

"Poor wretches," sighed Maria.

Plater, in spite of his heavy work load, paid frequent visits to Jan's barrack. He would share philosophical thoughts as he placed himself as comfortably as possible near the stove. One evening at the end of March, while visiting Jan's family, he astonished them all by announcing "I am going to escape soon."

"What?" they cried. "Escape?"

"Yes, you heard me. Escape!"

"Where to?" Jan asked.

"To Poland, where else?"

Jan's grandfather, who was usually too weak to talk, spoke up. "But Poland is under the bloody Germans!"

"Well, Germans, or no Germans, it is still our country. I would like to fight, even if I get myself killed doing it. It will be better to die in my own country than to rot here."

Jan looked closely at his friend. Plater's short coat didn't quite protect his scrawny body. His beard was scraggly and his face pale and drawn. Despite his poor health, his eyes burned with determination.

"I can't stand it anymore!" Plater exclaimed, so loudly that Jan was afraid he would be heard in the corridor. "I tell you, I can't!"

Jan wasn't sure, but he thought he saw tears in his friend's eyes. He had heard through the grapevine that Plater had been beaten several times by the K.G.B. for criticizing communism - the very philosophy he had believed in so fervently before he had been torn away from the life he had known.

The Polish prisoners still despised Plater for what they saw as his betrayal in Zamosze. "That stinking commie," they would whisper. "Now he is learning about the Bolsheviks, isn't he?"

Jan was the only one who didn't take Plater at face value.

One day, close to the end of April, Plater didn't show up for work. At first no one really noticed, so there was some surprise when the K.G.B. started to search the barracks, asking for Plater. After ten days without any sign of Plater, Jan believed that his friend had managed to escape. However, the next week, Olga Stepanovna told Jan that Plater had been caught, beaten badly, and locked up in one of the Gorki prisons.

Shortly after Plater's attempted escape, Jan developed "hen's blindness" and could see only with the aid of bright light. In the long Arctic night, he was blind most of the time. The Soviet doctor told him that his blindness was caused by "avitaminosa", a vitamin deficiency, and that nothing could be done about it because there was no cod liver oil available.

"Oh my God," he moaned in desperation, "I'm going blind! I'm going blind!" The thought of losing his sight terrified him. "What will happen to me and worse... to the rest of my family?" he thought, sweating in spite of the cold northerly winds. "If I go blind..." he whispered to himself, "I won't be able to work. That means half of one bread ration... Oh, God, please don't take my sight away," he prayed.

He went through the agony of going blindly to the stables, following a path in the snow. The lanterns there, dim though they were, gave enough light to enable him to find Choodak and lead him out of the stable. By then, he was experienced enough to hitch the horse without his sight. It was up to Choodak to lead Jan into the forest, where there were huge fires set up, not only for Jan, but for others with the same affliction. Once their sleighs were loaded, their horses were experienced enough to take them to the unloading depot.

In Jan's barrack, there were several deaths from avitaminosa. One evening, when he was already half asleep, he was summoned to a neighbour's room, five doors away. A woman knocked frantically at Jan's door, wailing that her husband was dying and begging Jan, who spoke Russian, to fetch the doctor.

Jan went to see what was wrong with her husband. The woman held a lantern and by its light, Jan could see that the man was lying on one of the bunks with four children between the ages of five and twelve around him. He lay still, his large, feverish eyes focused on Jan. The woman lifted up a tattered blanket, stained with blood and dirt. To his horror, Jan saw that the man was a mass of sores oozing vile green pus. Jan was nauseated by the smell of rotting flesh. Some of the wounds were so deep that Jan could see bare bones. The few unaffected patches of skin were blue.

Jan's stomach turned in revulsion; he thought he would vomit. He ran outside as fast as his weakened legs would carry him. The air was cold but mercifully fresh, and after a few moments, his nausea subsided, and he started to run to the doctor's office. He knocked frantically on the door. After what seemed a long time, the door opened and a young woman doctor invited him in. Listening to Jan's outburst patiently, she spread her hands, palms upward, helplessly.

"Can't you do something for him?" Jan pleaded.

"There are over two hundred cases like this, young man," she said quietly.

"They will all die?"

"They will."

"And you will do nothing to help them?!"

"Don't yell at me," she said defensively. "Go talk to the Administration! The K.G.B.! To Stalin himself! They make sure that I can do nothing." She turned her back on Jan abruptly, and he noticed that she surreptitiously dried her eyes with the corner of her white smock. "Forty-three others are dying of severe frost bite. Normally an amputation would help, but..." her gesture encompassed the room. Jan followed her hand and realized that there were no bottles of medicine, no instruments and no first aid kits. Apart from a single bed, there was no evidence that the room was an infirmary.

"Doctor, can't you at least go to that man and just... be there for a while, please?"

The doctor didn't answer. She just stood there in the middle of the infirmary, looking at Jan. He felt terribly uncomfortable under her stare, so, shuffling his feet nervously, he mumbled that he had to go. As he grabbed the door knob, she said, "I will be there in a minute, malcheek... What's the number again, 18, room 5... I will be there... And, oh, how is your 'hen's blindness'?"

"Bad, Doctor, getting worse. Will I lose my sight, doctor?"

"Not in the daytime," she answered. She looked pensively at Jan for a long moment. "Come back tomorrow and I'll find some cod liver oil for you," she said quietly. "About twelve tablespoonfuls should cure you."

"So you have cod liver oil, after all," said Jan.

"Yes, I have, but it's not meant for prisoners."

"For Commissars?" Jan asked.

"Please, go now. Come back tomorrow, and I'll help you - I promise."

His visit to the dying man's room and the sight of his suffering generated terror in Jan. He knew the nature of his sickness by now and he also knew that 'hen's blindness' was just the first stage. Leaving the doctor's barrack, he stood outside oblivious to the stinging Arctic wind. He pictured himself lying on his bunk and saw his flesh slowly disintegrating: first on his legs, then his nose and ears, and finally his whole body. His strong young heart would continue to pump blood, keeping him alive to suffer. Foul-smelling fluid would ooze from his sores and spill all over his bunk, but of course by then, he would be totally blind. He wouldn't be able to see, but he would hear the whispers and sobs of his sisters and his grandparents. Then, when he was dead, they would soon follow; they would all die of starvation.

He raised his tear-filled eyes to the dark, indifferent sky. "Oh, God," he prayed, "spare me... so I can help them. Give me courage and strength."

A strong gust of wind whipped his back with such force that he was pushed forward. Not wanting to return to his barrack just then, he walked blindly around the camp until he found himself in front of the carpentry shop and went inside to see who was still hammering. Only one carpenter, the night duty man, was working, a Russian whom Jan had met before.

"What can I do for you, young man?" the carpenter asked.

"Oh, nothing. I was just walking and it's cold outside, and... and I saw the lantern light shining from your shop."

"Well, look around, if you wish," the good-natured Russian said, with a wave of his hand.

Jan noticed that there were only two things in the carpentry shop: broken sleighs and crudely built coffins. He stared at the rows of coffins. They were of all sizes, but most were small - no more than four feet long. There were so many of them!

Jan's thoughts turned to the nearby cemetery, where he had seen so many of these coffins sticking out of the permanently frozen ground. His spirits sank even more.

****

The days were spent performing heavy work in brutal cold, and the nights were not much better. Enormous piles of snow, bitterly cold winds and ice-bound Lake Nukhto, were hardly signs of spring. The family's clothes had become pitiful rags, and it was doubtful whether they would last until summer.

To Jan, the most dreadful moments of the day were in the mornings, when the loud and persistent sound of a gong awakened everyone. He lay on his bunk unwilling to get up, even though he knew that he had to. Their lives depended on it. The darkness and the whistling sounds of the wind that he knew would be cold and piercing made him shiver.

The stench in the room caused by unwashed clothes, their own bodies and the bed bugs seemed a blessing to him at such moments. What a pleasure it would be if he could lie in bed for another minute or two! In his imagination, he saw himself struggling through the huge snow drifts toward the barn, shivering and hungry, always shivering and always hungry. The barn, Choodak, Olga, then the forest - heavy work, loading and unloading, then riding back to the camp in the darkness again. Today, tomorrow, day after day. He remembered the Camp Manager telling them, "Work or die. There is no return to Poland for you. You will all die here. This is your home."

'But then,' he thought, finally getting out of his bunk, 'there is a spark of hope. At least, I think there is.' Some prisoners, Jan knew, had been receiving letters from their friends who had not been deported and were still living in the area which used to be Poland. "Have hope," these letters urged. "Aunt Frances and Aunt Agnes will visit us soon." These were coded messages which were supposed to fool the Russian censors. "Frances" meant France and "Agnes" referred to England. "Uncle Samuel will come soon, by boat, to help you." Even a child knew who Uncle Samuel was. So did the censor, who, being tired of the simplicity of all this, added his own comments to one of the letters: "It may be true," he scribbled, "that Aunt Frances and Aunt Agnes and even Uncle Samuel will visit you one day, but until that happens, you'll all be buried in the Siberian permafrost."

'Maybe the censor was right,' Jan thought, his lips tight, 'but until you bury me, I will give you lots of trouble.'

Jan, like most of the prisoners, didn't really believe that they would be rescued by their allies; but still, who knew? Anyway, it was somehow easier, after hearing these messages, to fight against the monotony and hardships of everyday camp life, to stomach the dreary sight of the nearby cemetery and endure the bitter cold and everlasting hunger.

One night, toward the end of April, Jan and his family sat on their bunks, weak, hungry and cold. Jan was trying to read Stalin's book on "Comintern". He was not interested in the International Communist Movement, but it was the only book available in the Red Corner of the community hall. 'Red Corner,' he thought scornfully, 'a bloody shrine to Lenin and Stalin!' Helena occupied herself by counting bed-bugs; the rest of the family had their own thoughts.

They were interrupted by Frank Wojek, who had been the postman in Zamosze. He was a widower, with seven children, all girls. One glance at Mr. Wojek's face was enough for Jan to guess the reason for the man's visit. He had come to ask Jan to help him to bury his youngest daughter, who had just died of scurvy.

Jan followed him to his room, where the remaining six little girls were gathered around the little coffin. Mr. Wojek tied a long piece of string around his waist and told the children to hang on to it.

'Hen's blindness,' Jan thought. 'He doesn't want them to be lost in the darkness.'

The pathetic little procession went out into the cold night to bury the dead child. In the next few weeks, Jan helped to bury child after child in the snowy cemetery. Jan never saw Mr. Wojek shed a tear, but after each burial, the man seemed older and greyer.

One day a man passing the cemetery found Mr. Wojek lying on the ground in the cemetery. To his left stood the seven crude crosses that marked his family's graves. He was dead too.

May 18th was also Maria's eighteenth birthday and, in spite of the sorrow around them, Jan not only remembered the date but was determined to make this a special day for her.

Maria worked seven days a week loading, unloading and delivering logs, which, combined with poor nutrition and constant exposure to the cold, had reduced her to a skeleton. Her enormous brown eyes were the only signs of her former beauty. In the evenings she dragged herself to her miserable, cold bed without bothering to remove her clothes or eat the half-rotten soup.

Eleven year-old Helena took it upon herself to look after Maria as well as her dying grandparents. "Eat, Maria, please," she pleaded, kneeling beside her sister. "Have a sip of soup, for God's sake."

Helena, like all of them, was badly infested with lice. They were everywhere, in their hair, their clothes and even under their skin. Her skin was also covered with bites and scabs from bed bugs. There was no soap in the camp. They could not even wash themselves with warm water, since they had no basins or water tubs. Unwashed clothes, unwashed bodies and lack of any kind of disinfectant, made the barracks stink.

On May 18th, Jan lingered in the stable until the other teamsters had gone home. He wanted to talk to Olga Stepanovna, who knew Maria and liked her. When Jan told her about Maria's birthday, she leaned on the stall partition and fell into deep thought. Finally she spoke.

"Malcheek, this is misery. This is hell on earth! There is nothing we can do. You have nothing, I have nothing, everyone has nothing in this goddamned, fuckin' hellish camp and all of fuckin' hellish Russia!"

"Sh, sh," Jan pleaded. "Somebody might hear you."

"Fuck them! Jan, fuck them! I don't care anymore. All my goddamned life I've been nothing but a slave." Her tirade went on and on. Jan did not interrupt. Suddenly she yelled, "I've got it!"

"You've got what?" asked Jan, surprised by the change in her mood.

"Of course, yes, how stupid I am! Come here, malcheek, come closer," she whispered. "I told you I had nothing to offer your sister, didn't I?"

"Yes, you did," Jan answered.

"Well, I don't have anything, but the fuckin' stable has something!" she said, smiling.

"What does the stable have?"

"Oats, you dolt! Oats! The horses won't mind if I take some of them for your poor sister. Oats are nutritious," she continued, "and you can make oat porridge... I'll find you a can to cook it in."

Jan was unsure how to turn the oats into flour and so he asked Olga Stepanovna about it.

"You don't need flour! Just cook the goddamned oats, flavour them with lard, and you have a good meal."

"But where can I get lard?" he asked. "Nobody has lard here."

"I know somebody who has," she said grimly. "The Commissar."

"The Commissar? He won't give it to you."

"Give? That bastard wouldn't give a drop of water to his dying mother."

"So?"

"So," she smiled mischievously, "we will requisition it from him."

Jan was both excited and terrified. Steal from the Commissar? That meant a firing squad, or at best, 30 years in the lager. They whispered for a long time, Olga having to lower her head by a half metre so that Jan could hear her whisper.

The K.G.B. occupied a whole barrack that included the Commandant's and the Commissar's offices, interrogation rooms, armoury room, and common room. The Commissar and Commandant had their living quarters in another barrack.

Olga Stepanovna had been inside the Commissar's living quarters twice, so, as she told Jan, "I know the layout of that bastard's lair. During my first visit, the devil tried scare tactics on me, telling me that I was not doing a good job in the stable and that I was too friendly with the Polish teamsters. 'You, Comrade Konushnaya (teamsteress), are not alert enough socialistically,' he said. Hell only knows what he meant by that, but anyway, he told me to come again the day before yesterday, after work. The loathsome bastard was waiting for me. His table was loaded with all kinds of food. Jan, I tell you, there was everything you could wish for. Kielbasa, ham, butter, sugar, tea, and plenty of vodka."

"And so?" Jan prompted impatiently.

"So, nothing. I ate like a pig, drank a lot and then tried to go home."

"What did he do?"

"Oh, the usual. He had been saying that he loved me and that he would be good to me. Then at the door, he changed completely. Threatened to send me to the lager, swore he would kill me with his own hands." She was pensive for a moment, then said, "Jan, I am not a virgin, I've been with a lot of men here, but to go to bed with that bloody swine, one of those who beat me years ago - No! Oh, no, not me."

That night, at about ten o'clock, Olga Stepanovna, followed by Jan, crept toward the Commissar's quarters. "Watch for the police patrol!" she warned him, "They should be on the opposite side of the camp, but you never know."

The skies were cloudy and the night was pitch black and they hoped that the darkness would be to their advantage. In any event, they planned to move too quickly to give the Commissar a chance to recognize either of them. Jan hid around the corner of the barrack, his heart pounding crazily and sweat streaming down his face. Olga threw some gravel at the door. The Commissar, dressed in heavy underwear, opened the door slowly and saw no one. He then made the mistake of stepping outside. The sledge hammer fist of Olga Stepanovna descended on his head, knocking him flat.

Jan raced to join his friend and they stepped over the Commissar. She led him to a pantry next to the kitchen where she lit a match and Jan saw the riches they had come to steal. There were piles of lard, two large loaves of bread, and a dozen or so bottles of Moskovskaya vodka.

Olga Stepanovna grabbed a loaf of bread and gave it to Jan, another disappeared under her shirt. She did the same with the lard. On her way out, she grabbed a bottle of vodka and hid it in her pocket. As they stepped over the Commissar, he groaned and tried to get up.

"Run," Olga Stepanovna whispered urgently. "Run home, but take a 'round about way. Go!"

He ran faster than ever before in his life and, by the time he heard shouting, he was a safe distance away.

He woke his family and they prepared the feast - the only feast they would ever have in the Soviet Union. Jan settled himself close to the stove and started to devour his booty ravenously. Grandfather ate slowly, as though he was doing it against his better judgment, and Jan felt the reproach in his eyes.

He seemed about to say something, but was silenced by a look from Grandmother. Maria and Helena showed no sign of remorse; they were eating as eagerly as Jan, smiling at each other with stuffed cheeks.

In the meantime, the Commissar had regained consciousness and, shivering in the cold night air, rushed into his barrack. He tripped over a chair and fell, hitting his head on a chest of drawers. Stunned temporarily, he lay on the floor until he regained his wits enough to crawl to his desk and press the alarm button.

In a few minutes, the room was swarming with K.G.B. men. Some of them, seeing their boss in his underwear, had difficulty holding back their laughter. The Commissar, apparently sensing this, stood up and delivered a barrage of obscenities which surprised even the K.G.B. men.

Seldom had Nukhto-Ozyero witnessed such an uproar. The K.G.B. men checked every room in every barrack occupied by the prisoners, searching for the Commissar's bread and vodka. At four o'clock in the morning, they came to Jan's room, overturned every bundle and bag, but found nothing.

****

On May 27th, Aram Visaryanovich, the K.G.B. Commandant of Nukhto-Ozyero, read and re-read the letter he had just received by special courier. The more he read, the less he liked it. The letter was from the Commissar of the Central Committee of the K.G.B. in Moscow. From the corner of his eye, he looked at his second-in-command, Ivan Vasilevich, the Political Commissar, who held a similar letter in his hand.

"Aha!" he thought, with a certain amount of satisfaction, "so that bastard got one too." He hated Ivan Vasilevich; he knew that the Commissar spied on him. He, of course, was spying on the Commissar as well, but that was different.

The letter was brief, requesting an appearance at K.G.B. headquarters in the left wing of the Lubyanka prison in Moscow. The thought of the prison made him shudder. He had been around long enough to know that such a summons foretold nothing good. He remembered all his colleagues who had been summoned to headquarters and had never been seen again. "Shot in the neck or rotting to death in Lubyanka," he concluded sadly.

He glanced again at the Commissar, who was fidgeting in his wooden chair. "That bastard is shitting in his pants," the Commandant thought.

****

The meeting was held two weeks later in a large hall in the GULAG head-quarters. Looking around, Aram Visaryanovich calculated that the large hall could seat at least two thousand people. "Huge, like Mother Russia," he said to himself with a mixture of admiration and fear. He noticed that almost every chair was occupied. He had come earlier than scheduled in order to manoeuver himself toward the centre of the hall. He knew from experience that the centre was usually the safest place during meetings.

Those in front ran the risk of being observed from the podium. If they stopped applauding too soon, during the frequent and long periods of applause, their names would be written down and later they would be asked to explain why they hadn't liked the speech. They would often end up in Lubyanka. On the other hand, if they applauded too long, they could be accused of fawning and insincerity. Those sitting in the back were either cowardly or disloyal; they were afraid that by sitting close to the dais they might inadvertently betray themselves.

Aram Visaryanovich surreptitiously looked around the hall at the hun-dreds of men in their mud-green uniforms. Most of them were chain smok-ing. On the dais, behind a long desk, sat four uniformed men. The chair in the centre was empty.

After half an hour of silence, interrupted only by an occasional cough, the men on the dais sprang to attention and the audience followed their example. From a hidden side door, a short man dressed in civilian clothes stepped onto the dais. He was unpretentious and remarkably self-assured, but nothing in his appearance would distinguish him in a crowd, thought Aram Visaryanovich, except for his eyes, which were dark, penetrating. He had the uncomfortable feeling that the man's eyes were on him, reading his thoughts. Aram Visaryanovich felt colour rise in his face.

Lawrenty Beria, the Supreme Commissar of the mighty K.G.B., took the central seat. He was, as every child in the U.S.S.R. knew, the Number 2 man in the Kremlin. He was the only man in the Kremlin whom Stalin trusted completely. Only Beria could enter Stalin's personal apartment or office at will. Afraid for his life, suspicious and half insane, Stalin formulated his atrocities - and millions lived in terror. Beria proved his unquestioning loy-alty to Stalin by following all orders to the letter, regardless of their brutali-ty.

It was a long meeting, interrupted by numerous bursts of applause. They listened to a long lecture given by an expert on the economy. The gist of his message was that, in spite of a 10% increase in prisoners brought from recently occupied lands, the actual production of lumber and minerals had risen by a mere 2%. In the agricultural sector, there was no increase whatsoever. The only good result, as far as the expert was concerned, was the remarkable mileage increase in railway track construction.

Lawrenty Beria, following the expert's presentation, laid the blame on the audience. "You have failed to properly utilize the potential given to you. You have not shown the determination and will necessary to make these enemies of the Soviet Union work harder. The statistics show, beyond any doubt, that most of you are too soft," he accused. There was strong applause in response to this.

"You have redirected only a small percentage of the prisoners from the labour camps to lagers. Are you trying to tell me, comrades, that these parasites are so good?" he continued. "In the lagers, they work harder! They cost us less. I specifically direct my criticism to you, Political Commissars. You are my eyes, and ears, and you have failed me. Some of you will regret it."

Beria left no doubt that this was no idle threat. His message was clear; they were expected to increase terror in their camps, which in turn would increase production. Aram Visaryanovich abhorred the idea; he wished again that he had followed his mother's advice to become a shoemaker. He shifted uncomfortably in his seat until the meeting was finally over, and he and his deputy were free to board the first train north.

He was not surprised when the door to his train compartment slid open and his deputy entered. In his hand, the Commissar had a piece of paper with several names scribbled on it.

"Well, comrade," the Commissar said, "following comrade Beria's advice, I took the liberty of preparing this list of names." When his announcement met with silence, he added, "You will approve it, of course."

The Commandant wanted to say what he really thought of the list and his deputy, but instead he reached for his pen and signed. He noted that 48 men and women in Nukhto-Ozyero would be arrested and sent to various lagers (heavily guarded labour camps, reminiscent of German concentration camps). As much as he despised his deputy, he knew that the list of people to be arrested had to be made and acted upon, because comrade Beria wanted workers for the Vorkuta salt mines, Krasnoyarsk stone pits, Karaganda iron ore mines, Krivoy Rog coal mines, Trans-Caspian Railway construction, or worst of all, the Kolyma salt mines. He also knew that the lives of those listed wouldn't be worth a kopeck. 'You can write them off for good,' he thought. He found this train of thought somewhat disturbing. 'Well, it's them or us. There is no choice, is there?' he concluded. He closed his eyes and listened to the rhythmic beat of the train wheels as they continued toward

Pleysetsk.

Chapter Four

On June 20, 1940, before dawn, four uniformed men, carrying rifles with bayonets rushed into Jan's room. One of the men grabbed Jan by the hair and pinned him to the wall. Another produced a piece of paper, raised his lantern and read its contents. "You, Jan Tabor, are under arrest under Statute 58. You are to dress immediately and come with us." His voice was matter-of-fact.

The swiftness and brutality of the assault was so overwhelming that the whole family was speechless. Jan put on his tattered clothes and was shoved roughly through the door without a chance to say goodbye.

It was dark outside. He saw a police wagon drawn by two horses in front of the barrack. He wasn't the only one to be arrested. Seven other men from his barrack were being led to the wagon.

"Chorny Voron (Black Crow)," somebody whispered, pointing at the police wagon. Jan recalled reading somewhere about the Chorny Voron. The Czars had used them; the Soviets had merely made them more efficient. The arrested men were pushed inside. Those who hesitated or struggled were given the assistance of a sharp jab with a rifle butt. Inside the Chorny Voron it was pitch dark. The prisoners sat on the floor wherever they could.

Nobody talked. Some, like Jan, were too shocked and frightened. Others knew that in the Soviet Union, the less you talked, the longer you lived.

Jan desperately tried to think, but the suddenness and brutality of his arrest had made thinking difficult. However, after an hour or so of riding, he quieted down enough to realize the horror of the situation he found himself in. By then he had heard enough stories from the prisoners who had experienced similar situations.

"Some prisoners taken from the labour camps are executed - shot in the back of the head," the stories went.

"Those whose lives are spared will end up in the salt mines, coal mines and quarries, where conditions are so bad that the Nukhto-Ozyero labour camp is like Heaven."

"Prisoners like these are murdered inch by inch... their bones are broken, their teeth are knocked out. They will rot in jails..."

Jan didn't want to be shot, nor to be murdered inch by inch. He wanted to live. He must. He had a family, whose life depended on him. He must fight - fight to the very end. He felt, to his relief, that the terror in his heart had somehow subsided.

After about five hours, the wagon stopped. "Pleysetsk," somebody whispered. The door was opened and they were ordered to get out.

They were surrounded by uniformed men and led to a nearby train which looked like the one which had brought them to the Soviet Union. Inside, however, it was different. There were no sleeping decks and no wood stove. The only similarity was the square hole in the floor of the car which served as a toilet. The reason for the lack of decks and a stove soon became obvious. There was only standing room available. They heard the clang of heavy iron as the door was locked from the outside. Those closer to the walls reported later that the door was also secured with barbed wire, precluding any possibility of escape.

For three days and two nights, they stood there, sleeping by leaning on one another, cursing the Soviets and each other in turn. "Don't lean on me, you bastard!" "Fuck you and the whole world!" "Holy Mother pray for us..."

A few fainted and were trampled where they fell. For the duration of the trip, they were given neither food nor drink. Thirst caused the greatest suffering. Jan tried to ignore the pushing, cursing and groaning, and to improve his position by shifting and adjusting his body. The swearing decreased as the stench of human waste increased.

Jan prayed silently, but the calm he usually found in prayer eluded him. His thoughts were in a turmoil, his mind filled with fear of the unknown.

'Where are they taking us?' he asked himself. 'What will happen to me... to my family?' The thought of his family brought tears to his eyes. 'Why do they have to suffer so much? What have they ever done to the Soviets?'

"Soviet bastards!" he cried out, shaking with anger. "You will pay for this - I swear it!"

The train kept on, moving, stopping, jerking and moving ahead again. On the third day, it stopped and didn't move for a long time. This had happened before, so the prisoners didn't think much of it until they heard someone remove the barbed wire and unlock the door. The sun flashed through the opening, blinding those closest to the door.

"Vygroohzay (disembark)," they were told.

Jan took a few tentative steps toward the door and collapsed. The other inmates helped to drag him out of the wagon. Lying on the ground, he saw that there were many others lying beside the train in a long, irregular line. Along this line, with rifles in hand, stood the impassive K.G.B. men. "Half hour's rest," rang a grim voice from somewhere.

Jan lost consciousness and was aroused by an inmate who was lying close to him. "Wake up! Wake up!" he whispered, shaking Jan urgently. Jan tried to get up but his legs were weak, and it took several attempts before he managed to get up.

They were formed in two long lines and ordered to move. Jan heard the familiar warning known to countless thousands of Soviet prisoners: "One step to the left or one step to the right, and I will shoot."

The fresh air and movement revived Jan enough to read the sign on the station. "Vologda," it said. 'So we are still up north,' he thought, 'but out of the Arctic.'

They were marched through a huge gate, flanked by turrets. On each of the turrets, a soldier with a machine gun was posted. There were similar turrets placed irregularly around the large enclosure. In the middle, there were several bleak buildings with barred windows. The column halted. From one of the buildings, a group of soldiers appeared and approached the column. One of the soldiers counted the ten men who were at the head of the column and marched them into one of the buildings. This procedure was repeated until Jan's turn came. He and nine other prisoners were marched into the largest building in the complex. They entered a long, narrow corridor, with heavy iron doors on both sides. They stopped in front of one of the doors and all ten of them were told to enter. A small, high window with bars allowed a little light into the cell.

The cell was very small, it stank, and it was already inhabited by ten other people. The feelings of the old inhabitants were mixed. There was a gladness at having newcomers who could perhaps give them word about the outside world, but there was also annoyance because they now had to share their small space with others.

Jan was interrogated frequently, mostly at night. His interrogators, Political Commissars, accused him of counter-revolutionary activities, actively practiced in the labour camp of Nukhto-Ozyero. "You have violated article 58 of the Soviet Constitution," the Commissars told him, "and you must sign a confession." The confession was a one-page document, which stated that he was 'actively sowing hatred against the Soviet Union and sabotaging the efforts of the workers in the forest of the Pleysetsk region, Arkhangelsk Province of the U.S.S.R.' Jan didn't understand any of these accusations and so he told them that he was not guilty and refused to sign.

"Sign or die!" they yelled during the beatings. After two weeks of such interrogations, Jan wanted to sign the paper just to avoid further beatings, but he was afraid and confused because he didn't know what article 58 meant.

One night when he was returned, bleeding, to his cell, he was elbowed by one of his cell-mates, who, unlike most of the others, was friendly and often spoke to Jan. "They beat you again, *malcheek*."

"Yeah."

"Asked you to sign the goddamned confession?"

"Yes."

"Did you sign?"

"No!"

"Why not?"

"They say I am counter-revolutionary and violated article 58 of Criminal Code."

"Hmm, bad news."

"Listen, Wasily," Jan turned in spite of the pain in his neck, to his fellow prisoner, "what the hell is article 58?"

"Hey, guys," Wasily roared, "this little Polack doesn't know what Statute 58 is!"

All the prisoners, it seemed to Jan, woke up to tell him how stupid he was for not knowing what article 58 was. "You are kidding!" "What do you expect from a Polack, anyway?" "They don't teach them much in Poland, do they?" "They taught them how to eat chocolate and cakes but not real life."

"Fuck beautiful women and ride *troykas* (three-horse sleighs)." "Suck blood from the poor... these Polish *pans* (lords)."

Bleeding, his muscles aching, he resigned himself quietly to the bombardment of curses and verbal abuse. He thanked God that it was night so his tormentors couldn't see his tears, mixed with blood.

"Shut up! All of you shut up. Enough is enough," Wasily thundered. In a milder voice, he asked, "You have been told by the fuckin' Commissar that you are a counter-revolutionary who is sowing hatred against the Soviet Union, no?"

"Yes!" Jan exclaimed, surprised. "Plus sabotage," he added.

"Of course, sabotage, sure," Wasily said. "Except for two of us, we all are counter-revolutionaries in this cell."

"What do they mean by counter-revolutionary?"

Again the cell came alive with voices. "Everything from swearing at the Commissar to spying." "They pin you with 58 for no reason." "Or when they need you in the coal mines." "Or the quarries." The voices were both sad and angry.

"They accused me of sabotage," said another speaker, "You see, I couldn't fix the goddamned tractor in time. I was in Lubyanka prison, before they shifted me here."

"You think that's bad," another voice reached Jan's ears, "I spent almost five years building the Trans-Siberian Railway, burying my weaker friends by the wayside and for what? I swore at the Supervisor."

"My own son, my own blood, denounced me. He told his teacher that I didn't like to work on the collective farm and wanted my own farm."

"I was careless enough to call Stalin a tyrant. My twelve-year-old daughter repeated it to her teacher."

The stories continued until morning. "Vorkuta Coal Mines", "Karaganda Iron mines", "Arkhangelsk lumber lagers", "Pechora River Mouth Lager Camp", "Lena and Yenissey Rivers Barges", "Trans-Siberian Railway construction". The names rang ominously in Jan's ears, places where torture and death were taken for granted. Hardened as these men were, the name "Kolyma" seemed to hold the darkest memories.

Conversation was stopped by a noise at the door. It was time for breakfast. The guards entered the cell and distributed bread and hot water. Jan ate his breakfast slowly, thinking about his experiences of the previous night. Gradually, the misery of all of Russia was unfolding before his eyes. It caused him greater suffering than the beating and kicking he had received from the Commissars. He had not known that such cruelty and injustice existed. He had been raised to believe that one's punishment should fit one's crime, but here, in the Vologda prison, he was learning that there could be punishment without crime. The men around him were being punished, not only for what they had said or done, but even for what they had thought.

****

In his first days in the stinking cell he had looked upon his fellow prisoners with disgust. Their coarse language, brutality to each other and constant anger had kept him apart from them. He had felt that he was somehow better than they were. Now he was forced to re-examine his attitude toward his companions. Listening to their suffering, their tragedy, their degradation, he felt compassion for them. He moved himself as close to the wall as possible to leave a bit more room for the others. He tried to be more tolerant and forgiving, to think of ways to make their lives less miserable. But there was one thing he couldn't do, and that was share his bread. That 400 grams of black, poorly baked bread was more valuable than all the gold and diamonds in the world. It was a gift from heaven for him and only him. His neighbour, a young man, only a few years older than himself, had become skin and bones. Every time Jan ate, the skinny man's eyes followed Jan's hand toward his mouth. When Jan put his last bread crumb in his mouth, there was a deep sadness in the man's eyes. Feeling guilty, Jan would swear to himself that next time he would share at least the last few crumbs with the man, but he lost the struggle every time. He started to eat with his back turned to the man, but he could still feel those agonized eyes following his hand up and down, up and down, to the last crumb.

One day, exhausted and sick, Jan signed the confession and almost immediately was put on a train, destination unknown.

****

After Jan's arrest, the terror of the K.G.B. increased at Nukhto-Ozyero. The rage of Ivan Vasilyevich, the Political Commissar, had reached the point of frenzy, making prison life even more difficult. The Commissar seemed to be everywhere at once: making unexpected visits to the work brigades, observing the long lines for bread or soup, giving long talks during the Thursday indoctrination meetings, breaking into rooms at night. Several men and women were arrested. Some of them, after a severe beating, were sent back to the barracks. Others, like Jan, disappeared.

Maria, like the other workers, had to attend the indoctrination meetings, where she heard repeatedly that they must work harder, produce more, or die of starvation. They were dying. The camp was already decimated by starvation, disease, and overwork. Hope kept her alive. She believed that something would happen to change their lives for the better. She prayed and hoped that Jan was alive and that all of them would somehow survive and be together again. However, these meetings were eroding her hope, bit by bit. After hours of listening to the Commissar's shrieks - "Work or die!" "You will never see your home again!" - she felt so empty inside that in spite of her tiredness she often couldn't sleep on Thursday nights. 'No wonder,' she thought, 'that the prisoners have nicknamed indoctrination night "Black Thursday".'

The health of their grandparents was getting worse. They were too weak to leave their wooden beds. Being almost nineteen, she felt that it was her duty to take care of them. Helena was not quite twelve years old, and there was little she could do to help.

One dreary March evening in 1941, Maria returned from work to find Helena sobbing hysterically beside her grandmother's corpse. A week later, Grandfather died. Helena now found herself alone from early morning until night. Dirty, hungry and tormented by bed-bugs, she lay motionless on the bunk, too weak to cry. A few times she managed to get up from the bunk and leave the room. In the long and narrow corridor, she saw other children, some of whom were her own age. Some of these children, she noticed, stood leaning against the wall, others just sat on the cold, wooden floor, or lay down in silence. She decided not to go out of her room unless she had to.

By the end of May, the snow had finally disappeared and hundreds of coffins, buried too close to the surface during the winter, were exposed. The nauseating stench reached the camp, further demoralizing those who had survived the winter.

One day, Maria was stopped by Olga Stepanovna, who led her to the stable storeroom and handed her a small bag filled with oats. "Hide it, little sister! It is not luxury food, I know, but it is something. Maybe it will help your poor sister." Maria was so amazed that she forgot to thank her.

Maria boiled the oats until they were soft enough to eat. "I never though that I would become a horse one day," laughed Helena, eating the oats with relish. Her laughter brought a warmth to Maria's heart that she hadn't experienced for some time.

A few days later, she got more oats from Olga Stepanovna, who warned her to "take it easy with the oats, or you will soon start to kick like a horse!" Winking, she put an extra handful of oats into Maria's pocket. This gesture restored Maria's sinking hope. Helena, she noticed, was a tall girl for her age and, with her large blue eyes and well-formed nose, she was quite pretty in spite of her hollow cheeks. As for herself, she knew she was pretty too, but in a different way. She had brown hair, which, in spite of her poor diet, was still surprisingly thick and healthy. Her deeply set brown eyes were her most beautiful feature, she had been told. There were many men in the camp who, though hungry and miserable, had noticed and admired Maria's eyes. She liked their compliments and smiled her thanks.

There was one man in the camp who was not satisfied with just a smile. Ivan Vasilyevich, the Political Commissar of Nukhto-Ozyero, had been watching her for a long time. He thought of her often, especially when he was drunk and lying on his bed.

"I must have that girl," he told himself. He started arriving at the stable when Maria returned from the forest. "Good evening, my beauty," he would greet her.

"Good evening, Commissar," she would answer with a smile. It was that smile that Ivan was unable to forget. Nobody, except his late mother, had ever smiled at him.

His frequent visits to the stable did not go unnoticed by Olga. "Watch that dirty police pig, Maria," she warned her.

"Oh, Olga, he is just an old man," Maria laughed. She did not understand the meaning of Olga's warning, so when she was told to appear in the Kommendantura (K.G.B. Headquarters) on June 18, 1941, she went without suspicion.

Soon after her arrival, the few people lingering outside the barrack were alerted by Maria's terrified screams and they ran to help her. As their eyes took in the scratches and blood on Ivan Vasilyevich's face, they realized that Maria had been winning the battle. They helped her back to her barrack, shaken, but otherwise unharmed.

The incident depressed her so much, however, that Helena had to take charge. She brought soup, boiled oats and tried to lift Maria's spirits by regaling her with camp gossip.

"Maria," she told her, "you're a celebrity in the camp! Everyone is talking about you and laughing at the Commissar. They are saying that it's lucky for him that your rescuers arrived when they did - otherwise you might have killed him!" Helena chuckled.

Maria smiled wryly, but made no comment.

"Would you?" Helena asked.

"Kill him? Oh, no, but I certainly would have plucked his eyes out as a favour to all the women in the camp!" She and Helena both laughed at that.

Olga Stepanovna, however, saw no humour in the Commissar's interest in Maria. "Let him come here again and I will kill the bastard with my own hands," she roared when she saw Maria. "Even if I have to rot in the lager for it!"

Ivan Vasilyevich was unable to go to the stable again, however. A few days after the incident with Maria, he was found in the woods with a bullet hole in the back of his head. The gossip was that Aram Visaryanovich had found a denunciation about himself in the Commissar's handwriting. It was said that the Commandant had shot Ivan Vasilyevich to ensure that the higher authorities would never receive it.

Someone swore that he had seen Olga Stepanovna walking toward the woods with the Commissar, shortly before his death. Maria was never to know if Olga Stepanovna had made good her promise, because a few days later the Germans launched an attack on the Soviet Union and the Commissar was forgotten.

It was not clear how this new development would benefit the prisoners, but there was new hope in the camp. "Nice to see our enemies at each other's throats," someone remarked. "Maybe they will kill each other and we will be free!"

Work went on as usual, with no sign of any change. Within a week, though, most of the young Russians - both men and women - were conscripted. Some Polish prisoners were chosen to supervise the work teams. Those who were promoted had a difficult time; the prisoners refused to obey them and the supervisors would not betray their countrymen.

August 20, 1941 was a day that Helena and Maria would never forget. It was sunny and warm, with a cool breeze blowing in from Lake Nukhto. The prisoners were marching to their respective work places when they were halted by the police and herded to the camp square. They were met by the Camp Manager and Police Commandant.

"Comrades," the Manager began. The sisters heard the man behind them mutter, "It must be a trap - he's up to something, he's calling us comrades."

"Comrades! Poles!" the Manager cried. "Today you are free people."

"I think that man must be right; it must be some sort of trap," Maria whispered to Helena.

"We are allies," the Manager continued, "Poland and the Soviet Union are allies. We are friends - friends fighting a common enemy, Germany!"

"We are free! Free at last!" people shouted, embraced, kissed.

"Comrades, line up at the office to get your I.D.'s!"

When the sisters' turn came to appear in the office, the Manager looked the two girls up and down and said, "You have the choice of taking either Polish I.D.'s or Soviet citizenship papers. You will, no doubt, make the right choice. As Soviet citizens, you will be very happy and secure."

They left the office with Polish I.D.'s.

A week later, the Polish survivors were told to board a special train which would take them to the Caspian Sea area, where the Polish army was to be formed. This army, the Soviet authorities told them, "will fight, arm in arm with the Soviet forces, against our common enemies, the Germans."

"Maria, where is the Caspian sea?" asked Helena.

"I don't know, but I heard it is very far - 5,000 kilometres away. To the south, I think."

"Oh, good!" Helena exclaimed. "It will be warmer."

"And maybe Jan will be waiting for us there."

On August 3, 1941, 432 Polish ex-prisoners found themselves in the all-too-familiar train cars. There was one difference; there were no guards in mud-coloured uniforms.

While the passengers waited for the order to embark, they looked at the place where they had spent almost two years of their lives. They did not regret leaving behind the filth, the hunger, the parasites, the hard work, or the Russian guards. Maria and Helena, among many others, let their eyes rest for a long moment on the cemetery where so many friends and relatives were buried. "Almost one thousand crosses," someone said quietly. "Almost one thousand people we must leave behind." The silence of the crowd was broken only by subdued sobs, sighs, and prayers.

The quiet was shattered abruptly by Olga Stepanovna's booming voice. "Maria! Helena! Where are you?" she called, elbowing her way through the crowd. "Well!" she roared, finding them, "Why do you look like you've seen a ghost?" She embraced the sisters with her tremendous strength, leaving them breathless. "Here is something for both of you," she said, handing Maria two huge loaves of black bread. They smiled their thanks to their friend, who beamed at them. "I arranged to have them specially baked," she said proudly. "They are still warm, you see?" Helena rushed to embrace the huge woman. Before she had a chance, her feet were swept off the ground as Olga Stepanovna grabbed her under the arms and lifted her like a baby, hugging her tightly. "I'm glad you're leaving this hellhole, but for my sake, I'm sorry, too. I will miss you." She turned abruptly and strode away without a backward glance. "I'll be damned if I'll blubber like a goddamned baby," she muttered to herself.

Chapter Five

While Maria and Helena were leaving the Nukhto-Ozyero labour camp, Walter Plater, a mining pick in his hands, was striking a large grey salt rock which was resisting his efforts to break it into smaller pieces. His shirt was soaked with sweat and salt, stinging his wounds. He had come to tolerate the constant pain.

His fellow miners were often unable to communicate with one another, being, as they were, of so many nationalities. The prisoners were Russian, Ukrainian, Polish, Turkish, Uzbek, Lithuanian... Plater gave up on the list; there were just too many to remember. The ringing of picks on salt rock was frequently accompanied by the most hideous and blasphemous swearing Plater had ever heard. He remembered someone telling him that the first words one learns of a foreign language are the curses; that was certainly the case in the Kolyma salt mine.

Occasionally, along with the curses, Plater heard the choked mutter of the word "God" in a multitude of languages. 'Some bastard is breathing his last,' he would think, spitting in disgust, 'praying at the last moment, the idiot.'

When the whistle blew, signalling the half-hour break, he set his pick aside and sat on the same rock he had been trying to split. He closed his salt-irritated eyes, trying to rest them. He thought about his escape from Nukhto-Ozyero - about a year ago, he guessed - and how it had ended with him spitting blood, moaning in agony in Gorki prison. Oh, he had prayed then. He had prayed to God, Jesus Christ and the Holy Mother as tears mixed with blood on his battered face. He had prayed for endless hours, oblivious to the mocking words of his cell-mates.

"Pray to Stalin," they would say. "Stupid Polack, praying to God." "Stalin will hear you sooner!" "Where is your God now?" "In Heaven - or in Moscow!"

"Our Father who..." Plater whispered, but could not recall the words that should follow. "Hail Mary..." His mother had taught him those prayers when he was a boy. After her death, his father, an atheist, had discouraged prayer. Later, as a young communist, he stopped praying as a matter of principle. In Gorki prison, he needed prayer more than at any time in his life, but no matter how desperately he struggled to remember even one, the words eluded him. He had invented a prayer of his own, born of his pain, his fear, his isolation.

But his prayer had not stopped the interrogations, tortures, and beatings. They had tried to force him to confess that he was a Polish spy. They had submerged his hand in boiling water, rammed toothpicks under his fingernails, kicked at his stomach and kidneys repeatedly and beaten him until he had lost all but two of his teeth. Finally, his spirit broken and his body weakened, he was unable to bear the thought of any more pain. He had signed the confession and been sentenced to 25 years in the salt mine. He, along with many other prisoners, had been put on a train bound for the infamous Kolyma.

Kolyma! He had heard more than enough about this infamous place. Desolate, rich in minerals, with an extremely harsh climate, Kolyma was known as a place from which no prisoner ever returned - alive or dead. Thousands of miles away from Gorki, it could be reached by train, boat, train again, and then by walking often fifty or more miles to the numerous concentration camps.

Plater's journey started just after Christmas, 1941, when they transported him by truck to a little railway station outside the city and loaded him into an unlit freight car. In the darkness he stood sandwiched among the other prisoners as the train rattled onward for endless days and weeks until he finally collapsed. At last, in the black of night, he was taken off the train and dumped on the frozen ground. It was likely due to the cold but nevertheless fresh air that he awoke from his unconsciousness. It took him a while to realize that he was lying a stone's throw from a huge body of water. Huge, black waves, like mountains, were hitting the shore only to retreat and advance again and again. Prisoners, dragging their feet and cursing one another, were led to a large - two hundred or so meters long - army boat. There they were herded to the lowest deck, close, Plater noticed, to the ship's machinery. The air stank of rotten fish and dead rats. It was dark. A few kerosene lanterns gave only dim light, so the prisoners, pushed by the guards from behind, were stumbling, falling... and cursing, cursing everything and everyone, but mainly cursing their own pitiful lives.

Plater could not say how many days they rotted in that accursed boat, but the overcrowded deck, the stench of rotten fish, the dead rats, and human excreta, and the rising and dipping of the temperature from extremely hot to impossibly cold began to take their toll. Plater had no way of knowing whether it was day or night... or in fact, whether he was alive or dead! Their captors fed the prisoners some kind of fish soup, which even for these hungry men was not edible. Plater became indifferent, oblivious to his environment. Dead prisoners were being carried away more and more frequently, but to Plater, it was... well, normal. There were moments when he thought that he had died and was damned to some sort of purgatory to atone for his unspecified sins.

How long had this journey by boat lasted? Plater couldn't tell. All he remembered was that as the journey progressed, there was more and more room in the lower deck. He later tried to speculate just how many of his cohabitants had died, and he came to the conclusion that only about half of the prisoners had survived the arduous journey.

Those who did survive were driven like cattle from the boat onto another train at a forsaken little port; and a new land journey began.

It was pitch black inside the freight car. It was also dark outside; at least that is what they were told by those prisoners who managed to peek out through little holes in the wooden planks of the freight car. 'This means only one thing,' Plater thought, 'we have not only reached the far East, but also the far North.'

The journey went on for a number of days. When they were ordered to disembark, those who had survived were met with the bleak sight of an abandoned railway station and a few huts. Plater counted eleven dead bodies left behind in the freight car.

Plater, because of some inner strength he hadn't known he possessed, survived the horrible journey. He swore that he would, from now on, survive - no matter what! He would survive regardless of the odds against him. There would be no prayers for him! There was no God or man who could help him; he was on his own. He would take what he needed and would kill if he had to; but he would let no one stop him in his fight for survival!

Now, here they were, stopped in the middle of nowhere, and ordered to disembark. In spite of the darkness, Plater noticed a desolate landscape - treeless, covered by short Arctic grass - a gently rolling landscape, with slightly steeper hills scattered here and there. It was bitterly cold. The winds, whipping off a nearby large body of water, cut through the prisoners' scanty clothes like a sharp knife.

The prisoners were ordered to walk. 'At least it will feel a little warmer if we're moving,' thought Plater. Fortunately, their hike lasted only several hours. Soon Plater noticed the dark outline of barracks. They entered a guarded gate, turned to the right, and were then forced into a long, dark warehouse close to the gate.

The prisoners stood close to one another, shivering uncontrollably. "It's probably twenty degrees Celsius below zero," Plater heard someone say.

"More like thirty below, to me," someone answered through chattering teeth.

"Take off all your clothes," a harsh voice ordered.

At first they thought that the guard was joking. It wasn't the first time they had heard 'Russian jokes', so they stood, astonished, ignoring the order. It was only when the guards used their rifle butts that they realized the horror of the situation. They reluctantly took off their ragged clothes until they all stood naked. Plater felt pain all over his body as though someone was sticking needles into him, followed by numbness in every part of his body. Then, to their disbelief, the guards turned on several water hoses. Streams of ice cold water hit them from all sides. "Welcome to Kolyma!" they heard the guards yelling.

After making sure that they had 'washed' everyone, the guards slammed the big door, but not before they had wished the prisoners: "A pleasant night, comrades."

Since their clothes had not been returned to them, the prisoners lay naked on the floor, some exhausted, but most felled by the shock of the powerful streams of icy water.

Plater knew that if he wanted to survive, he must keep moving at all costs. Summoning all his strength, he got up and started to walk and then run. In the dim moonlight filtering through the cracks in the walls, he saw prostrate bodies. Some were jerking convulsively. Others were still, lying in grotesque formations, their arms and legs intertwined. He started to jump over the bodies, clearing some, landing on others. His mind became confused and his eyes blurred. He thought that he had been sent to Hell to atone for his sins. He could have sworn that he saw demons lurking in every corner; "Have a pleasant night, comrade Plater," they were hissing.

Still he continued, jumping, crawling, falling, getting up again, and running, running. Then, exhausted, he fell on top of some stiff bodies.

The door of the warehouse was eventually opened, and a group of guards entered. Plater slowly turned toward the door and saw that it was somewhat brighter outside. 'It must be morning,' he thought, trying to get up.

The guards began to load the dead bodies onto horse-drawn sleighs which were lined up outside. The corpses were piled five high with the head of each frozen man overhanging the sleigh. One of the guards was smashing the heads with an axe, just to make sure... or was he just following orders?

Plater, and the few others who survived, were led, still naked, to their respective wooden barracks nearby. Plater was lucky because Barrack Number 14 was heated by a woodstove. He was given a pair of felt boots, thick cotton pants and a heavy coat.

Some of his companions, he learned later, were not so lucky. They were sent to new barracks made of poorly nailed boards, which the howling northerly wind easily penetrated. There were no woodstoves. "You will get them soon," they were told by the guards.

To protect themselves from the vicious winds, the prisoners had positioned the bodies of their frozen companions against the cracks in the walls. When the stoves eventually arrived, only a few of the prisoners were still alive.

Plater knew that he had been brought here to die. The camp commander himself had told them so on the very first day. "You will all die here," he had shouted. "It is only a matter of time. You will start work tomorrow, and the harder you work, the longer you will live."

"I will survive," Plater again vowed, "even if I have to lie, cheat, steal or kill!"

****

In June 1941, the Soviet Union was attacked by the Germans and the Red Army was in retreat. The prisoners were unaware of these events. The guards may have known about them, but they told the prisoners nothing about what happened outside. Their orders were to ensure that those still alive would work as hard as possible, and the death rate was high. Almost half of the inmates in Barrack 14 were buried under the permafrost of Kolyma. Normally, old timers were saying, they should have had several batches of prisoners to replenish their ranks, yet no newcomers arrived. There was some speculation, but no one bothered to wonder about it for long.

In September 1941, Plater was called to the camp office, where he was told he was a free man. He was sure it was a trick, so he just stood there, silent. It was only when he reached the Trans-Siberian Railroad, far away from Kolyma, that he started to believe he was free. He headed west, then south toward the Caspian Sea. It took him one month longer than necessary to reach his destination because he stopped in several towns along the way to steal. He was probably the only Polish ex-prisoner in the Soviet Union who was rich when he joined the army.

Chapter Six

After signing his confession, Jan, with other prisoners, was taken to the Vologda Railway Station, where he was put on a train. Caged in the over-crowded freight car, hungry and thirsty, Jan lost all sense of time and direction. Sometimes the train would stop for days. No one knew where they were going, or seemed to care. At first Jan had cared, but after a while, his senses dulled, and he became indifferent like the others.

The corpses, the violent interrogations, and the stench of infected sores had become part of his daily life since he had been taken from Zamosze. He couldn't think of anything worse that could happen to him. His main concern was for the family he had left in the Taiga Forests. How would they survive without him? He tried to convince himself that Maria could take care of them, but his fear for them stayed with him. Worry drained his strength. He managed to creep toward the wall, where, after some manoeuvering, he squeezed himself between two prisoners and leaned against the wall. His thoughts became progressively less coherent. Snatches of conversation with his interrogators in the Vologda prison, recollections from his childhood appeared and disappeared in his mind. He sat there, his parched lips moving. "God, Comrade! Comrade! I am guilty. Guilty because... No more! No more!... Grandfather, help me! The cow is in Marta's garden..."

"The boy must be delirious," observed one of the prisoners, pointing at Jan.

"Yeah, it looks like," answered another, looking at the slumped figure by the wall. "If this goddamned train doesn't stop soon, we'll all go insane."

"Where are they taking us, Kola?"

"Russia is big. Don't worry, they'll find a place for us. They always do," Kola answered. "I think we're heading south."

"Why do you think that?"

"It's getting warmer. Didn't you notice?"

Jan didn't hear this conversation. Neither did he hear the train stopping at its destination. When he came to his senses, he was lying in a tent on some sort of pallet.

Half rising, he peered through the dimness to find out where he was. He saw four other men, two of whom were snoring noisily. Getting to his feet shakily, careful not to wake up his companions, he went outside. He was almost blinded by the sunlight, but after a while his eyes became accustomed to it and he could see high mountains surrounding a wide, U-shaped valley. The mountain peaks were snow-covered and the lower slopes were green with coniferous forests. The valley itself was filled with tents and there were several wooden buildings. The valley's only opening was protected by a high barbed-wire fence, beyond which was a construction site and a pile of metal rails.

The valley was surrounded on three sides by mountains, hundreds of metres high. Jagged and steep, they seemed impossible to climb. At the entrance to the valley were two turrets manned by soldiers with machine guns. 'Clever,' he thought. 'No one can possibly escape from this trap.'

Feeling dizzy, probably because of the cool, mountain breezes, he dragged himself back to the tent and lay on his pallet. Some of his companions had awakened and were busy talking among themselves.

"Where are we?" Jan heard an old man asking no one in particular.

"Hell knows," said a man lying close to Jan.

"It's much warmer here, so we must be somewhere in the southern parts."

"Transcaucasia, maybe?"

"No, it is not," they heard a loud voice. They all turned their eyes toward the speaker. Jan noticed that he was short with yellow skin, slanting eyes, and high cheekbones. 'Tatar, probably,' thought Jan.

"How do you know, Tatar?" somebody asked in an insolent tone.

"I know!"

"He knows! He knows!" jeered the man. "If you know, then tell us."

"We are close to the Afghanistan border."

"Afghanistan?!" someone exclaimed. "You sure?"

"Sure! I have been here before."

"Why have they brought us here?"

"To build a railway," said Tatar.

"Where to?"

"Don't ask me! Ask the Russkys," the Tatar barked.

Jan didn't like the man's tone of voice. He seemed angry and contemptuous of the rest of them. The man's narrow eyes darted like a snake's.

"Maybe the railway will go toward Afghanistan," suggested Jan's neighbour to the left, a huge bony fellow with a pensive face.

They were interrupted by a loud, shrill whistle, followed by shouts in Russian, "Davay! Davay! (Get going!)." The Tatar was outside first, followed by the rest of them. The valley, Jan saw, was packed with prisoners. A number of uniformed men with long rifles were running to and fro, trying to form the throng into a line. The smell of food was everywhere and each man was given a bowl of cabbage soup and a large piece of black bread. Unlike Nukhto-Ozyero, the soup was thick and the portion generous.

"Well, at least the food is better," Jan sighed, eating greedily. After supper, still in the full sunlight, the new prisoners were formed into another line. This time, to their delight, they received new boots, felt trousers and jackets. After that, they were herded to the opening of the valley and informed by a tall uniformed man that from tomorrow on they were going to work, building a railway. "It is hard work," he told them, "but you will be better fed than in any other prison. Do not try to escape," he warned, pointing at the barbed-wired barrier and the turrets above. "A few have tried before, and they are now there," he indicated the ground.

'Only a crazy person would attempt it,' thought Jan, looking around the compound.

They went back to their tents and lay down again. "I hope they don't give us a sixth prisoner," observed the Tatar to Jan.

"They may, there are six pallets," answered Jan.

"Five or six, who cares?!" exclaimed the Tatar irritably. "I will kill any fucker who dares to come in here."

However, the tent flap was suddenly opened and another prisoner forced himself in. The newcomer, Jan observed, was short and wide. He had a huge head, bushy hair, a prominent hooked nose, and a long, red beard. 'He must be a Jew,' Jan thought. 'He looks like old Moyshe in Zamosze.'

The newcomer stood uncertainly at the door. His large dark eyes travelled around the tent, searching for a place to squeeze in. He was totally ignored. "Please," he pleaded. "I was sent here, I must have a place." The man's Russian had a heavy accent.

"Hey, Moses," a harsh voice called from the corner of the tent, "shut up! Can't you see I'm tired?"

"But, I must..." stammered the man called Moses.

"Look, you fuckin' Jewish bastard, get out of here! Go to Palestine! You hear me?"

'Palestine? Oh, God, I wish I could be in Palestine, instead of in this stinking tent,' Jan thought. Seeing the desperation in the man's eyes, he sprang to his feet and approached him. The man interpreted the movement as hostile and started to back up. Jan grabbed him firmly by the arm and said, "Come, come with me."

The man followed Jan reluctantly, as though embarrassed. There was a problem, because Jan's space between the Tatar and the big, bony man, was not big enough to accommodate both Jan and the newcomer. The Tatar, knowing Jan's intention, refused to move further to the left. Instead, he made himself more comfortable by moving the opposite way. The other showed no inclination to move either way. "Move," Jan ordered impatiently.

There was no reaction from the two men.

"You sons-of-bitches! Move!" Jan roared. The bony fellow moved a little to one side, but Tatar turned his back on the intruders exposing his naked rump and lay still.

Jan was enraged. He aimed a kick at Tatar's ass. Fortunately for Tatar, Jan's soft felt boot did not do any great harm. If Jan had known more about the Tatars, he would have thought twice before attacking one of them. Centuries of warfare, conquests, pillages and their struggle for survival had made these people extremely proud and unyielding.

The slant-eyed, short and stocky Tatar was on his feet before Jan had time to think and was at his throat, choking him. Freeing himself, Jan ran outside the tent, hoping that he wouldn't be pursued. The Tatar, however, was on his back before he could go far. They fought savagely, Tatar screaming "Allah, kill!" The fight attracted a crowd of spectators who formed a circle around the combatants, encouraging and jeering.

Tatar would probably have killed Jan if two police guards hadn't arrived in time. Soon Jan and Tatar found themselves unceremoniously dumped on the floor of a damp and dark cave, securely locked in by a heavy wooden fence covered in barbed wire. They lay there side by side for a long time, bleeding and groaning.

"Malcheek," Tatar said in a surprisingly soft voice.

"Yeah?" Jan answered grudgingly.

"What's your name?" asked Tatar.

'Of all the...' Jan thought with annoyance.

"What's your name?" Tatar repeated.

"Jan," he said, hoping that was all the bloody Tatar wanted to know.

"Polack?"

Jan wanted to tell him that it was none of his damned business, but he was too tired. Instead, he said curtly,

"Yeah, so what?"

"Brave people, you Polacks!" Tatar continued. Jan said nothing. Tatar, it seemed, was not ready to sleep. "You are a good fighter, Jan! I like good fighters."

Jan couldn't believe his ears. 'This brute actually likes me,' he thought. He wanted to laugh, but the pain in his jaw stopped him.

"You and I will be good friends," Tatar persisted. "I thought that you were a *gadzeena*."
Jan's Russian was, by now, quite good, and he realized that *gadzeena* was a derivative of "gad" which meant reptile in Russian. Puzzled, he asked Tatar, "Who are *gadzeenas*?"

"Russians, who else?" was the brisk answer. "When you came into the tent, I was sure you were a *gadzeena*. If I had known that you were a Polack, there wouldn't have been a fight."

They talked long into the night; the Tatar's story would have been familiar to many Soviet citizens. His home had been in the Crimean peninsula, where he had worked on the state farm, tending horses. Most of the workers there were Tatars, while the administration was mostly Russian. Tatars, until recently, a nomadic people roaming over the steppes of southeastern Europe, were Moslems. They were akin to Turks, and spoke a Turkish dialect.

Subjugated by the Russians and forced to stay in one place, they were, in effect, condemned to die. Their nature and their lifestyle did not fit into the collective scheme of the socialistic Soviet Union. The slightest sign of disobedience was enough to send a Tatar to the worst labour camp. When Jan asked his companion why he had been arrested, the Tatar was silent for a while. Finally, he said, "I swore at Stalin! They told us to stop praying, so I told them fuck you and fuck Stalin. I am a Moslem, and I will continue to pray whether they like it or not. So here I am."

"Statute 58?" Jan asked.

"Yes, how did you know?" asked the Tatar, surprised.

Jan just smiled sadly. That night he dreamed about the cell in Vologda. On its door was carved a huge number 58.

Next morning he glanced out of the corner of his eye at his Tatar companion. The Tatar was lying on his back, hands behind his head, also awake. His eyes, directed at the roof of the cave, were sad and cloudy.

Suliman, the Tatar, had been awake for hours, remembering his wife and son, whom he hadn't seen for four years. He looked at the boy sleeping next to him. 'He is about the same age,' he thought bitterly.

That afternoon, to Jan's surprise, they were released from the cave and sent to work. "The bastards want to see us working instead of sitting in the cave," Suliman said. They were escorted to one of the gangs working along a narrow pass which had been blasted out of the mountain for the railroad tracks.

Their job was to lift the dynamite blasted rocks and load them onto huge iron wagons. Another gang pushed the wagons away. Since some of the rocks were too large, they had to be smashed with picks before they could be loaded.

Jan knew by now what hard work really was, but even in his boldest thoughts couldn't possibly have imagined that it could be so hard. Lifting big rocks and loading them on the wagons was a back-breaking task in itself, requiring every ounce of his strength. His hands were cut to ribbons by the sharp rocks. The fine dust which seemed to be suspended over the entire valley was irritating his eyes, nose, mouth and lungs.

Preoccupied with his work, he didn't notice at first the noise emanating from every corner of the valley. After a while, he started to distinguish frequent explosions, voices shouting curses in every imaginable language, groans, the clattering of the iron wagons and above all - the coughing. Some dry and short, others seeming to continue forever. In spite of the cool mountain winds, Jan was sweating.

His nearest work-mate was Rettinger, who had been the cause of his fight with the Tatar. David Rettinger was a Polish Jew from Krakow. In the course of the next few months, David told his life story to Jan. He had been a professor of Geography at the Jagiellonian University of Krakow. It was much later that Jan learned that Rettinger was not only a professor, but an internationally recognized academic.

During their conversations, Rettinger subtly assumed the role of teacher and Jan became his only pupil. Jan's mind was receptive and open to Rettinger's knowledge. They discussed geology, geography and environmental science. Their environment was a perfect class situation because the split stones were excellent examples of a geological time table. Jan was intrigued by the time and length of the Pre-Cambrian, Paleozoic, Mesozoic and Cenozoic eras, but environmental science fascinated Jan the most.

"Don't do it!" Rettinger would say when Jan was about to kill an insect which had come too close while they were resting in the shade. "Each of these bugs," he would explain, "has a niche in the ecosystem." There was a deep sense of the interdependence of all living creatures in Rettinger's lectures.

The friendship between the wise, red-bearded scholar and the young man grew stronger daily. Suliman, who at first had looked at Rettinger with suspicion and mistrust, soon began to listen to their discussions. He didn't seem to understand most of the talk between Rettinger and Jan, and they were surprised one evening when Suliman started to ask questions. Rettinger was pleased by the Tatar's interest and answered his questions with the utmost patience.

One afternoon when the three of them were trying to split a particularly large rock, they heard a voice behind them. "L...let me try!" Turning their heads, they saw a huge man with a pick in his hand, regarding them with pity.

They had seen him before, working with another gang. He was in his late twenties with flat Slavic features, and he towered over all of them. He quickly accomplished what they had been labouring over for so long.

His name was Andrey Nikoloyevich. He was a Russian collective farm worker from the Orel area. He spoke slowly and stuttered badly, constantly struggling for the proper words to express his thoughts.

He had been in the camp for six years of a twenty-year sentence. While working on the collective farm, Andrey had been tormented by the Political Commissar who, being short and thin, was jealous of him. "He c...alled me a big st...stupid ox," Andrey told them. One day, when he had had enough, he had whacked the Commissar on the head, "Just to t...teach him a l...lesson." The Commissar had been killed instantly.

Andrey was a simple, good-hearted peasant who was liked by all of the inmates. His innocent smile and readiness to help the weak endeared him to everyone. He became the fourth member of their group.

****

Christmas was approaching, and it was growing colder. They were issued warmer coats called *koofaykas* and felt boots popularly known as *walonkis*.

The prisoners worked from seven in the morning until seven, sometimes eight, in the evening, seven days a week. When they complained about it, citing the Soviet Constitution which supposedly guaranteed prisoners one day a week off, they were told that "Yes, indeed you are right; but there is nothing in the Constitution that would forbid 'volunteering' - and haven't you volunteered?"

Although camp discipline was very strict, there was a certain amount of self-government. The work quotas, for example, were controlled by the inmates themselves. If one of them showed any sign of slacking, the rest of the inmates, afraid of getting less bread, imposed their own justice. Beating up the slacker was the usual punishment. Stealing bread was the greatest crime of all. Quite often, the thief was punished with death. The authorities pretended to have no knowledge of such things.

One evening, when they were lying, exhausted, in their tents, they heard horrible cries so full of agony and fear, it was difficult to determine whether they were human or animal. The prisoners ran out of the tent to see what was happening. They were joined by other groups of inmates. Jan spotted the tall figure of Andrey running at the head of one group.

Following a treacherous path, they descended into a crevice, hidden from the rest of the camp by overhanging rocks. A group of men stood in a circle around a small man whose weasel-like face was covered with blood. Two tall men were thrashing him mercilessly with sticks. "I won't steal any more!" the man screamed. "Let me go! Let me go, for God's sake!"

"Kill him! Kill the bread thief," people snarled from the crowd.

The screams ended as the thief fell, but the attackers continued to swing their sticks and fists. Jan and his group just stood there, gaping. Andrey stepped forward. The men, surprised by the sudden appearance of the mountain-like man, stopped beating their victim. Andrey approached the bleeding man and, lifting him as though he were a child, walked away along the path. There were rumours of protest from the crowd, but no one dared to stop him.

"He is a human being, after all," Andrey said to himself. Jan ran after Andrey and told him to take the man to his tent, where he would be safe. "Thank you," Andrey said simply. He deposited the unconscious man between Rettinger and Suliman, who had not taken part in the drama and were sleeping soundly. Jan woke Rettinger and, after a brief description of events, asked him what should be done.

Rettinger ordered water to be brought in and, wetting some rags, put a compress on the man's forehead. With the remaining water, he wet the victim's lips and eyes. This done, they all sat on their beds and waited. After a while, the man groaned and moved.

When he had recovered enough, he told them about himself, despite his pain. He was a Romanian from the area which had been annexed by the Soviet Union in 1939. During the Soviet invasion, he had been in a Romanian prison.

"I have been stealing since I was five years old," he said proudly. He was a true professional thief, living and prospering from his activities. He and the other inmates of the Romanian prison had been transferred from one Soviet prison to another until he had wound up in this camp.

Grateful for being rescued, he began following them everywhere, like a dog. Amazingly cunning, he always had more food than anyone else, and insisted that they share some of it. Among his paraphernalia, which he once displayed for Jan, was a long sharp knife, a small elaborate axe, a gold ring, needles and thread. Jan couldn't believe his eyes but had enough sense not to ask Gregory where he got it all. Eventually, he became one of their group.

****

By March of 1941, the railway line they were constructing was approaching the Soviet-Afghani border. According to Rettinger, they would be there by August, or, at the latest, mid-September.

Rettinger usually seemed to be composed and at peace with himself, and so the few times he became emotional were surprising. Once, he had reached under his shirt and pulled out a photograph. It was discoloured by sweat and time but was still clear enough to show a beautiful young woman, holding a small child in her arms. "My wife and child," Rettinger said, almost in a whisper. "The last time I saw them was in Lvov." Rettinger turned his head away. When he faced Jan again, Jan could see tears in his friend's eyes.

Another subject which evoked emotion, was Palestine. From their conversations, Jan learned more about Palestine than any school could have taught him. "Imagine walking over the narrow streets of Jerusalem, drinking water from a well my ancestors drank from, or crying at the Wailing Wall for Jerusalem's lost glory, or thanking God for His mercy and help in our survival." These conversations made Jan dream of seeing Palestine.

One day, Rettinger put his pick aside with unusual determination and said matter-of-factly, "Let's escape, Jan."

Jan was stunned. Caged effectively in the valley, guarded day and night by armed men, escape seemed impossible.

"Escape?" Jan echoed in disbelief. "You mean the two of us?"

"No, five of us. I have given this a lot of thought, and I have a plan I would like to share with you."

Jan was silent. He was too excited and terrified to speak.

"Success will depend on many factors," Rettinger continued. "The first of these is the participants. To survive under any circumstances, the group should be well balanced. The men should complement each other in skills." Seeing Jan's perplexed look, he added, "We need a combination of brains, physical force, and cunning."

"How about the guards, the valley, the mountains?" asked Jan doubtfully.

"Aha! The terrain is factor number two." Rettinger was silent for a while, then resumed thinking out loud. "As a geographer, I have given a lot of thought to that important factor." He looked around and made sure that the guards were not watching, then took a stick and drew a map in the sand.

"Assuming that we are 40 - 50 miles north of the Soviet-Afghani border, it shouldn't be terribly difficult to reach there in three days. Crossing the border, it will be imperative to proceed another 50 miles or so south, before turning west to Iran."

"Yes," Jan interrupted, "But the Soviets have control over northern Afghanistan and Iran. At least, that's what I was told by the prisoner from Afghanistan, that short fellow who works in the 'Dynamite gang'. He also told me that the Soviets arrested quite a few people in northern Afghanistan."

"You are right about that. I know that neither the Afghanis nor the Iranians particularly like the Russians. Once we are in Iran, we will head westward as far as we can and with luck we will reach the British, who, by my calculations, should be there by now."

The next day, they resumed their conversation and decided that Andrey, Suliman and Gregory should be informed of the plan immediately. "If, for some reason, they decide not to join us," said Rettinger, "they are discreet enough to keep their mouths shut."

Cautiously, they informed each member of the group. As Jan had expected, they all agreed to participate. Suliman, on hearing the proposal, leapt around screaming "Allah is One," until Rettinger told him to shut up.

"He is a good fighter, especially with a knife," Jan told Rettinger.

Gregory was delighted when he was informed, realizing that this was his only opportunity to escape a life of slavery. The choice of the Romanian was a bit puzzling to Jan. In spite of his apparent devotion, Jan didn't trust him completely. His sly smile, the uncontrollable twitching of his right eye and his continuous stealing disgusted Jan. One day he expressed this opinion to Rettinger and was surprised at his response.

"Gregory is a product of blatant social injustice. There are thousands like him in every corner of the world who have had to survive on the streets, alone. Most of them perish before they reach their teens. Some, like Gregory, develop a facility for survival that keeps them alive. There may be more good in him than meets the eye. Remember that. Besides," he added with a wink, "we need somebody as cunning as he, don't you think?"

Jan had mixed feelings about the whole affair. First of all, he was scared. He knew that if they were caught, they would be executed. They were not the first to try to escape. He also couldn't understand why Rettinger had confided his thoughts to him with no reservation.

"What will be my part in your plan, David?" he asked point blank.

"I thought you would never ask," was Rettinger's answer. Jan noticed mischief in his friend's eyes. "To begin with, you are a bright and good-hearted young man, Jan. Secondly, you, being the youngest of all of us, should survive to tell the world everything you know about this inhuman land." Jan blushed. "You are also the best runner," David added, and laughed aloud.

"As long as I have good boots," said Jan, to cover his embarrassment.

They decided that each of them should save as much food as possible. Gregory, in addition, would try to get some tools. "Let me see, Gregory," Rettinger was saying, "you've told me that you have requisitioned a knife. Now we will need as long a rope as you can find, a pick and a water bag, the kind used by herders, made from leather. I believe that all the guards possess a one-litre bag."

"Leave it to me, Rettinger," the Romanian answered, pleased at his new-found importance.

After many more discussions, they agreed that their escape would take place around the end of April because, as Rettinger concluded, "It will be warmer then, and easier to travel." Rettinger was to inform them later about the exact details of the plan. In the meantime, each man was to accumulate enough food for at least one week.

Spring arrived in southern Turkestan. By mid-April, all the snow had melted, except for the highest peaks of the surrounding mountains. Rivulets of water cascaded from the steep mountains into the valleys and the numerous rivers. The mountain slopes, almost overnight, were covered with short alpine grass and multitudes of flowers. The valleys were covered with shrubs and small conifers. Daily, the mountain breeze grew warmer.

Jan scanned the mountain slopes more and more often, wondering what awaited them on the other side.

An escape at night was ruled out on the grounds that security was stronger then and also because all previous unsuccessful escapes had been tried at night. They would try one hour before the end of work.

"How, for the love of God?" Jan exclaimed when they heard the daytime plan. Looking around, he could see numerous security detachments strategically placed among the work gangs and on the nearby hills. They were armed with rifles and automatic machine guns, and as an extra precaution, machine gun nests were mounted on the overhanging cliffs. Rettinger's eyes followed Jan's and he knew at once what worried him.

"We will create a diversion!"

"How?" they all asked at once.

Rettinger was silent for a long time. He looked at Gregory for what seemed an eternity. The Romanian writhed on the boulder he was sitting on, uncomfortably averting his eyes. Rettinger, pretending not to notice his discomfort, continued, "Gregory! Can you get some dynamite?"

"Dynamite? Oh, God!" Gregory cried. Then, as the importance of the task struck him, he added, "I'll do my best."

"There will be an explosion in the southeast corner of the valley where the K.G.B. headquarters are located. This will attract the attention of the guards. "Suliman!" Rettinger pointed his bony finger at the short man, "You will tell your Moslem friends to create confusion by running toward the explosion. Pass the word 10 minutes before, not a single moment earlier." They all sat for a long while in silence, overwhelmed by the boldness of the plan.

"Then what?" asked Andrey Nikoloyevich.

"We will run," Rettinger replied.

"Run where?" asked Jan meekly.

"That is another point that I would like to discuss with you," said Rettinger.

'Discuss?!' Jan thought. 'The old s.o.b. has thought out the whole plan without consulting anyone!'

"The pursuit, I think, and there will be one hell of a pursuit," continued Rettinger, "will be heading southeast toward the Soviet-Afghanistan border and a detachment will be sent in that direction. In addition, border security at Kushka to the south will be told to be on the lookout. It would therefore be suicidal to proceed in a southerly direction. So, we will head north."

"But that's crazy!" exclaimed Suliman. "Don't you know that north of here is the Kara-Kum desert? We should be trying to get out of the fuckin' Soviet Union, not going deeper into it!"

"Yes, I know that the cursed Black Desert is there, but we are not going there to be fried by the heat. What we will do is take a roundabout way. We will swing southwest from the desert toward the Koppeh Dagh Mountains, west of the railway we built." Seeing the bewilderment of his listeners, he added, "Consider our journey through the Kara-Kum as a brief three-day visit before swinging southwest."

"And then?" Jan asked, increasingly doubtful.

"Once we reach the foothills of the Koppeh Dagh, we will swing eastwards and squeeze between our railway and the mountains, then turn south towards the border. Close to the border, instead of going directly to Kushka, where we wouldn't be welcome, we must proceed along the eastern edge of the Koppeh Dagh until we get to Afghanistan. We will then turn eastward and head for the Iranian border. Once in Iran, I hope that we will meet the British, that is if the sons-of-bitches have had enough sense to get there by now."

The plan was too complicated for them to challenge, so after some deliberation, they all agreed to follow it.

Chapter Seven

An explosion rocked the valley, sending sparks and flames high into the cloudy skies. This was followed by the shouts of men and the crisp orders of the K.G.B. Men ran crazily in all directions, confused and frightened.

Ten yards away, partly illuminated by the fire, a man crawled rapidly toward the gate. It took him only a few minutes to join his fellow conspirators. The others, lying low on the rocky terrain near the gate, were startled by the sudden rustling sounds, but calmed down when they realized it was Gregory. They all started to crawl as if by command and pushed toward the gate. As anticipated, the guards at the gate were too busy observing the confusion and didn't notice a darkly clad figure examining the gate, nor did they hear the metallic cling, cling of shears cutting the heavy chains. Andrey, using his enormous physical strength, cut them in a minute as though they were mere threads. Rettinger, once outside the gate, led his party northwards. He glanced back and, satisfied that all were present, increased the pace and plunged into the darkness.

The path they followed was full of potholes, rocks and dry roots, and was made more treacherous by the approaching night. Their feet frequently became entangled in the roots and brush, causing them to fall, especially the big Russian, who carried the largest bundle.

'At last,' Jan told himself, 'we're moving.' Although still trembling and drenched with sweat, he felt better. Walking over the uneven ground required all his attention and forced his mind away from his fear.

His only desire was to put as great a distance as possible between their group and pursuit. Rettinger was obviously thinking the same thing, but he wanted to confuse the enemy by circling back, not once but several times.

Jan, exhausted, tumbled over a rock and fell heavily, but immediately sprang to his feet and followed his companions. They continued their breakneck march for what seemed to Jan an eternity. Every part of his body was aching, and he was short of breath. He needed to rest, at least for a few seconds, to quieten his fast, beating heart. Oh, how nice it would be to rest right there, close to that big boulder - to lean his aching back against its cool side. Just for one second! For one second. "Oh, my God, I'm falling behind," he cried, realizing suddenly that his preoccupation had increased the distance between him and his companions. 'Rettinger selected me mainly because he believed that I can run fast, that I am reliable and that I am smart enough to know what is expected in a given situation. But look at me now,' he thought, 'I am dragging behind them all, slowing their progress and endangering their lives. What kind of a man am I? Am I weaker than the rest of them? What, therefore, is your problem, Jan?' he asked himself. 'Well, show them what you are made of, Jan!'

He darted ahead, jumping over any boulders and protruding roots that dared to block his path. To his great relief, he caught up with his companions and with a few additional strides, found himself ahead of the group. In spite of the pain in his chest and his extreme exhaustion, he felt happy. He heard Rettinger's laboured breathing and the groans of his other companions.

"Stop, Jan! Stop! We must rest," Rettinger's voice was harsh and halting.

Jan slowed down and stopped and the others soon joined him. "Over there under that overhanging boulder - to the right, see?" Jan pointed.

"One hour - rest, friends," Rettinger told them. "So far we have made good progress, thanks to fast walking." Rettinger glanced at Jan, and Jan thought that he winked at him, although in the dim moonlight he wasn't sure. "After our rest, we'll turn sharply to the east - right here," he pointed to the right. Jan looked in that direction and saw that the terrain was rugged and formidable. In the moonlight, he was able to make out the contours of jagged rocks, buttresses, and overhanging cliffs. At first he was apprehensive, but the realization that they had been able to break out of the camp and travel so far gave him courage and hope. He raised his eyes toward the moon and breathed deeply. They were free - free! - and there was no obstacle in the world that free men could not overcome. He looked at his companions and knew that in their own ways they all had the same feelings.

"Where is the rope?" Rettinger asked loudly, startling Jan.

"I have it," answered Andrey Nikoloyevich.

"We will hold onto the rope so that no one will be lost in the darkness. You!" he turned to Jan. "I want you to be at the end of the line."

As it turned out, he was glad that he was at the end of the line, since he was often actually pulled by the four older men. For hours and hours, they climbed the mountain sides and cliffs. If one of them slipped, hanging suspended over a crevice, the others held him until he managed to regain his balance. When the clouds were finally scattered by increasing winds, visibility improved.

While they were sliding down yet another steep slope, they saw what appeared to be a flat expanse of land in front of them.

"What a relief to see flat land again!" Suliman exclaimed.

"Don't be too happy," said Rettinger, scouting the land.

"But, surely now we can walk faster," observed Gregory.

"And be spotted by the enemy faster," Jan countered.

"Not if we cross the flats in the next three hours or so. See that dark line? Looks to me like a string of low hills. If we could..." he became thoughtful.

After a short rest, they resumed their journey. The plain was covered with small pebbles and walking was difficult, but better than the hellish terrain they had left behind. At sunrise, they reached the foothills, which were covered by stunted and widely spaced coniferous trees.

They found a narrow crevice among the trees where they could rest. The crevice offered an ideal cover for the fugitives, and an unexpected bonus - a small pond fed by the numerous tiny streams that tumbled down the mountain. The cool water quenched their thirst and soothed their scrapes and scratches.

"This feels wonderful!" Jan cried. He splashed water at his companions, and jumped around like an exuberant child.

Rettinger smiled back briefly, then became serious. "Now we must discuss strategy, and clear thinking is required," he announced. The others moved closer to him, then, leaning against the rocky wall, he continued. "I suspect that, by now, the K.G.B. knows about our escape. If I read them well, even now they have detachments combing the area south of the camp and perhaps southwest. They are not stupid so they've sent their men north also. Failing to locate us by noon, they will ask for airplanes from Ashkabat."

"Oh, my God," said the Russian.

"The airplanes cannot possibly see us now," Rettinger reassured him.

"But that means we can't walk in the daytime, doesn't it?" Jan asked.

"Yes, and we can't sit here for too long, either. They will send their men in all directions."

"Today?" the Tatar asked.

"I think they will start tomorrow morning. By that time, I hope we will be far from here."

There was a long silence; they were too tired to speak.

Jan didn't have to be told; he fell immediately into a deep sleep.

His sleep was broken by a thunderous blast that made him jump. The sound echoed through the crevice, bounding off its rocky walls and cliffs.

The crevice appeared to be darker than it had been before, but there was sufficient light to see a man, in uniform, lying face down on the rock. Jan noticed a widening circle of blood on the man's back.

A few feet to his left, Jan saw another uniformed man lying on his back. Gregory stood over him, pointing a still-smoking gun at the man's head. Jan was still too sleepy to understand the full meaning of the drama in front of him, but he understood one thing for sure: Gregory was about to shoot the man on the ground.

Jan jumped on Gregory, knocking him to the ground. The gun discharged into the air causing yet another echo in the crevice. Getting to his feet, Jan saw his other companions looking at him, perplexed.

The K.G.B. guard was still lying silently on the ground. He was a young man, only slightly older than Jan. Their eyes met; the guard's glazed with fear, and Jan's surprised and curious.

"What's the idea, Jan?" Gregory demanded angrily. "Why'd you stop me from killing the Soviet bastard?"

"Because this man is a human being, that's why," Jan retorted.

"Gregory!" Rettinger, who had not been participating in the drama so far, spoke up. "Jan is right, leave him alone."

The others nodded in agreement.

"Where did you get the gun?" asked Rettinger.

"That's my business, Jew!" was the angry reply. "If I didn't have it, we would be marching back to the execution squad!"

They all knew that he was right, and yet they were somehow disturbed by Gregory's previous silence about the gun.

"I wanted to tell you about the gun," Gregory said, as though reading their thoughts, "but running like crazy over these fuckin' mountains, I didn't think about it."

They all sat quietly for a long while, then Rettinger broke the silence.

"It seems, my friends, that the situation has become more complicated. Before making any decision, let us ask our 'guest' some questions." He gestured to the young guard who was sitting quietly on the rock, staring at his dead companion. Rettinger sat down beside the soldier.

"I am sorry about your friend," Rettinger said. "You took us by surprise."

The guard remained silent.

"How many of you were sent here?" Rettinger wanted to know.

"Just two."

"How did you get here?"

"We were parachuted in."

"When?"

"Two hours ago."

"Were there other planes in on the action?"

"I don't know - don't think so."

The man, small in stature, had short, blonde hair and a small, flat nose. His soft-spoken manner and grammar suggested a man of some education.

"What are we going to do with him?" asked Gregory, stating what was on all their minds.

"Let Rettinger decide," said Andrey Nikoloyevich, silent until then.

"Me?" Rettinger cried. "Who do you think I am, King Solomon?"

"Take him with us," volunteered Jan.

"Are you crazy, or what?" Gregory exploded. "First you stop me from killing him, then you want to burden us with a prisoner!"

"Well, there are three possible solutions," said Rettinger. "The first is to agree with Gregory; the second, to leave him here; and the third, to take him with us."

"Killing him would be the least complicated," interjected Gregory.

The Russian tried to say something but was interrupted by the Tatar.

"Tie the little bastard up and leave him for the vultures," Gregory went on.

Rettinger knew that he must decide, so after thinking for a while, he said, "We will take him with us." Then added quickly, "Maybe he knows a few things about the area."

Gregory spat with disgust, picked up his gun, then spat again for emphasis. On Rettinger's insistence, they buried the dead K.G.B. man and started to walk, even though the day was still bright.

Rettinger immediately changed direction, heading northeast. "I've learned from Sciopa, our K.G.B. friend, that the search is concentrated in the area of Ashkabat and along the railway."

They were walking fast. Sciopa, following Rettinger, was well guarded by the other men. They kept close to the forested foothills which offered them some protection from the K.G.B. searchers.

Walking at night and sleeping by day, they were pushing ahead. Unfortunately, their food supply was disappearing quickly and it was becoming increasingly difficult to replenish their water. The terrain became drier with scanty grass and shrubs. There was less protection from the blazing sun and the Soviet pursuit.

On the fifth night of their journey, they entered an area covered by elongated ridges, topped by shifting sand.

"There is no question in my mind," Rettinger told them, while they rested along an indented sand ridge, "that we are still in the area of the Kara-Kum Desert, somewhere south, or southeast of the city of Merv. It would be logical to take a northwest direction from here, bypass the city and then turn southwest of it. That way, we will eventually reach the Koppeh Dagh Mountains, without being detected."

"You mean, walking through the desert all the time?" asked Jan.

Their prisoner startled them by saying, "You shouldn't venture into the desert too much. We will all die from lack of water. Take my word for it, the Kara-Kum is deadly." He paused, then continued. "South of here there are some settlements, collective farms, mostly."

"Aha! He wants us to be closer to the K.G.B.!" Gregory cried.

"As you wish," said Sciopa, offended, turning his back on them.

It was hard for them to know what Sciopa really thought, but his willingness to help carry the bundles, sometimes even insisting on burdening himself with a heavier load, had dispelled their initial hostility toward him. They had almost forgotten that he was a member of the hated K.G.B.; he was, after all, one of them now, sharing their misery. On the third night of his captivity, in spite of Gregory's objection, Rettinger didn't tie him up.

After some deliberation, they swung southeast and, after a night of walking, reached the first settlement. It was a small farming collective, with no more than 25 huts. From their cover, they saw a flock of sheep grazing on the slope of the hill, a mile or so away from the buildings.

The sun was rising from behind the hills, illuminating the flat roofs of the huts. After some discussion, it was agreed that Suliman, who resembled a Turkman, would scout the village, looking for food and water. The rest of the men, hidden from the village, rested all day.

Evening arrived, but there was no sign of the Tatar.

"We must arm ourselves with patience," Rettinger said, trying to minimize his companions' anxiety. However, when midnight arrived and Suliman still had not returned, even he could not hide his concern.

"Where is that bloody Tatar?" Gregory demanded.

"Maybe he got drunk," volunteered Andrey Nikoloyevich.

"Or maybe the K.G.B. got him," said Sciopa. They didn't know if this possibility pleased or worried him.

"We will all go to the village," announced Rettinger.

"All?" asked Gregory. "What about this K.G.B. dog?" When there was no answer, he continued. "I told you we should get rid of him, didn't I? We still can!" he stroked the gun holster with his hand.

Sciopa trembled and averted his eyes.

"No," said Rettinger, firmly. "We can't do that."

"So now what will we do?" Gregory persisted.

"We'll tie him up and leave him here. The villagers will find him in a day or two. By then we will be gone."

This seemed to Jan to be the only solution. He was sorry to leave Sciopa like that, because he had developed a liking for him.

"Where is the rope?" asked Rettinger.

"No!" Sciopa screamed. "Don't tie me up!"

"And why not?" asked Gregory, his voice rising.

"Because... I don't want to go back."

"What?" yelled Gregory.

"Well, you see, if I go back, they will shoot me," he said, misery in his voice.

"Who are 'they'?" Jan asked.

"The K.G.B. They won't believe me when I tell them that my companion was shot and I was spared. They will say that you spared my life because I collaborated with you."

"So, tell them that you escaped, and were wandering in the desert and hills until now," said Jan.

"Are you kidding? They will ask me why I ran away, instead of fighting! You don't know the K.G.B.!"

"So what the hell are we going to do?" cried Gregory.

"Take him with us," said Jan.

"Crazy! Crazy!" Gregory yelled.

"I want to be with you as a friend," Sciopa said. "Not only because I have no alternative, but also because... I want to escape with you."

Rettinger, who had been thinking in silence, suddenly said, "Your uniform, Sciopa, may help us." They didn't know what he meant by this but, trusting his common sense, they said nothing. So Sciopa went along with them.

It was close to daybreak when the five of them went down into the valley and approached the village. Except for the occasional braying of a donkey or mule, the village was quiet, its inhabitants asleep. All the huts were dark except for the longest one in the centre of the village, where there was a dim light. As the group of fugitives came closer to this building, they realized that it was, in fact, a large barrack. They cautiously crept to the longer wing of the building, where the light burned. They hid themselves in the bushes near the building. Jan was sent to look in the window.

He approached silently, peered through the window and froze. In the dim light, he distinctly saw a uniformed man sitting on a chair with his feet on the desk, sleeping. His snoring was so loud that Jan could hear it from where he stood. The door was shut. Gregory, in the meantime, was exploring another wing of the building, which turned out to be a jail.

They huddled together and, in soft whispers, decided on a plan of action.

"First, we must make sure that the Tatar is indeed here," whispered Rettinger. "Gregory! Crawl to that window and call his name, but quietly, please."

Gregory moved at once. On reaching the barred window, he called out, softly, "Suliman, are you there?"

At first there was no answer, but when Gregory repeated the name, there was a faint, but distinct, reply.

"Gregory? Yes, I'm here!"

"We're here to help you; just be still."

"I wonder," whispered Rettinger, "how many policemen there are?"

"Shouldn't be more than three," said Sciopa. "One is supposed to be on duty, the other two are sleeping in the next room. It's typical," he added.

"Sciopa!" Rettinger replied. "Here is your chance to prove whose side you're on. I want you to knock at the door and tell that man that you are K.G.B. on an urgent errand. Once inside, you can tell him that you've come to pick up the prisoner. Oh, yes, and take your gun with you."

Sciopa straightened his uniform and moved at once to the door. Gregory, gun in hand, positioned himself in the shadows not far from the door. Sciopa knocked, but there was no answer. The man was obviously sound asleep. He knocked again, louder this time.

"Yes, who's there?" a sleepy voice said.

"A K.G.B. courier from Ashkabat."

"Who?" The man jumped up from his chair.

"K.G.B., you mother fucker! You heard me!"

Pulling up his trousers and adjusting his shirt, the policeman hurried to the door and opened it. Sciopa entered the room, glanced around, and sat on the vacated chair, placing his dust covered feet on the desk.

"What can I do for you, comrade?" said the policeman, barely controlling his trembling voice.

"I came to pick up an enemy of the people, one calling himself Suliman Bey."

"Oh, yes, comrade, we caught him stealing food from the store."

"We want him for much more serious crimes. Where is he?"

"In the cell," the policeman said, pointing.

"So don't waste my time, comrade."

The policeman had now regained his composure, enough to ask a routine question: "Your papers, comrade, a release order?"

"What papers, you son-of-a-bitch? I have no papers," cried Sciopa.

"Then I must ask my superior."

Before Sciopa had a chance to react, the policeman rushed to another door and opened it. "Comrade, Matvyj! Come here."

Two bulky men, dressed in long underwear, emerged from the bedroom.

"This man wants the Tatar prisoner, but he has no papers. He - what's your name, comrade?"

Sciopa, realizing that the man was following procedure, didn't like the situation at all. "Never mind my name. This is not a social call," he snapped. "Now, bring me the prisoner!"

"Calm down, calm down, Nikolay!" one of the men in long underwear said, turning to his colleague. "If he," he nodded at Sciopa, "hasn't got papers, there must be a reason for it. All we have to do is make a phone call." As he reached for the phone a shot from Sciopa's gun killed him. He fell heavily on the desk.

The door burst open and Gregory, squatting down on the threshold was firing at the other policemen. The rest of the group rushed into the smoky room. Rettinger ordered the big Russian to break down the door leading to the cell. They found Tatar, shaking with fear, but alert. They went through the kitchen cupboards, taking everything edible, and added several flasks of water.

Disturbed by the shooting, some of the villagers opened the doors of their huts. But, seeing that the shots were coming from the police building, decided that it would be more prudent to pretend that nothing was happening, and went back inside. The fugitives ran.

When they had left the town far behind them, the group, keeping away from inhabited areas, headed in a northeast direction. They had enough food for five or six days and hoped to find water along the way. They desperately needed to distance themselves from the killings.

To protect themselves from pursuers, they kept to the hilly terrain which was now more treacherous than ever. They moved on, day after day.

When their food ran out, Gregory's sheep stealing experience was most valuable. Slithering like a snake, he was able to outsmart the most watchful dogs and herders. He always managed to bring back a lamb, or sometimes even two. Water, however, was becoming a problem. There were fewer and fewer creeks in the mountains.

****

It was in the third week after the shooting incident that Jan, climbing a barren slope, lost his grip and fell into a crevice.

Regaining consciousness, he tried to open his eyes, but it hurt too much. He tried to move his legs, but excruciating pain brought tears to his eyes. With bleeding hands, he groped around and discovered that there were rocks all around him except to his right, where there were some sort of bushes. "Help! Help!" he called again and again. He opened his eyes, but pain forced him to close them again. He lay still moaning softly.

'Why am I lying on these rocks?' he thought desperately. 'What happened to me? I must try to remember. I must think chronologically. I must -' but there was a strange buzzing in his head and pain, sharp and piercing.

'There was a barren mountain,' he started again, but the mountain some-how disappeared and its place was taken by huge stretches of marshes. 'There was a mountain,' he repeated. 'The man in front - Rettinger and the others - Suliman, Andrey...' They had been climbing up the steep slope of the mountain. He was holding the rope. There was moonlight and to his right there had been a dark crevice. "Help! The rope is breaking!" he remembered a piercing voice yelling.

He had been lying against the slippery face of the mountain, holding on with every centimetre of his body, his fingernails trying to dig into the rock. He felt blood oozing from his fingers. He shifted position slowly, very slow-ly, to secure a better foothold.

Suddenly dark silhouettes were rolling down the mountain, straight at him. He moved instinctively to the left and lost his grip. He was slipping down, trying to grab rocks, roots, or anything that would slow him down.

Then he was falling faster, bumping against rocks. He felt an agonizing pain in his head that seemed to be spreading through his body. Then there was nothing. He must have lost consciousness. The next thing he remem-bered was seeing the huge ball of the sun over him. Its rays were warm and pleasant, even though they hurt his eyes.

He was thirsty. 'Where is my water bag?' It should be fastened to my vest.' But there was no water bag. 'I must have lost it when I fell,' he thought, beginning to panic.

He lay still for a long time, trying to calm himself and think what to do next. "I guess this is the end for me," he whispered. "I will never see my family again, or Zamosze." He looked up and thought he saw two dark dots almost directly over him. Puzzled, he fixed his eyes on the objects and as they became larger, he realized that they were some sort of birds. He noticed that their vertical descent was very fast - 'like stones thrown from an airplane,' he thought. He heard guttural noises as though the birds were fighting among themselves. Then, to his dismay, he noticed that there were more of the same birds circling above him.

One of them, in fact, was just a few metres from where Jan was lying. The bird had an enormous hooked beak and long, sharp talons.

"Vultures! Vultures!" Jan cried, terrified. The bird, his eyes fixed on Jan, sat on a rock, motionless. Jan felt that the bird was trying to analyze him and assess his strength. Terrified, Jan grabbed a stone and threw it at the bird, but missed. The bird didn't even blink. Jan threw another and another stone, with the same result. "You bastard!" he yelled in frustration. Looking around for more missiles, he noticed something brown under a bush. When he looked more closely, he saw that it was his water bag and so he crawled closer to retrieve it. After satisfying his thirst, he lay still, trying to ignore the bird which, like a guardian angel, continued to watch him.

"So, you are waiting for me," Jan hissed. "You are waiting for me to die, you bloodthirsty bastard. Well, you will wait forever if I can help it!"

He began to examine his injuries and it didn't take long to find out that he had bumps on his head, cuts and scratches all over his body, and worst of all, his right ankle was broken. 'I have to get away from here, before this bird tries to be smart with me,' he thought. Then he remembered, from Boy Scout training, that he needed splints for his ankle. Fortunately, there was plenty of dry wood around, and he had some string in his pocket. He concentrated on securing splints to his injured ankle in the fading light. "Tomorrow I will leave!" he yelled, turning to the rock where the bird had been sitting; but the rock was empty. 'A good omen,' he thought, feeling a little better.

The night was cold and he shivered all night, unable to sleep. 'Where are my companions? What happened to them?' He remembered seeing bodies rolling down the mountain slope. 'Who... who?...' He didn't want to think about it. 'Maybe they are alive, sitting somewhere and waiting for me. Surely they must... oh, God!'

"Rettinger! Suliman! Andrey!" he called again and again, but there was no reply. Tiredness overcame him and he fell asleep.

Next morning, armed with an improvised walking staff, he started his descent, hoping to find a way to flat land. Looking ahead for the gentlest slope, slipping and falling over and over again, he was crawling at an agonizingly slow pace. The sweat from his forehead flooded into his eyes in a profuse cascade, forcing him to blink hard and keep his eyes closed. An ever-increasing pain in his ankle, back, arms and head weakened his strength and his spirit.

"What's the use? It is hopeless! Give up," he moaned.

By then he reached some sort of a barrier, some sort of a wall which barred his progress. With the rest of his will, he opened his eyes, but the piercing pain forced him to close them again. He lay there motionless, with an empty feeling of defeat and with a profound feeling of abandonment and helplessness. He didn't know how long he had been lying there like that, a minute, an hour?

Slowly, his ears started to register sounds, the sounds he missed before - the sounds of tumbling stones, which in the stillness of the mountains, sounded like a squadron of galloping horses. This woke him up from inertia. The curiosity, sense of danger or simple instinct of self-preservation forced him to open his eyes and keep them that way.

To his left was a steep knoll, to his right was a blistering wall of a mountain; so tall that Jan, as much as he tried, couldn't see its peak. 'Probably it extends to Hell itself,' Jan thought. His eyes fell on the barrier, which he felt before, but which he could see in front of him. 'There was a barrier there, alright,' he thought. In fact, it was a ridge, extending from the knoll on his left and connected to the steep mountain to his right. The ridge, Jan thought, was about 5 metres high, covered by small bushes and coarse grass.

"I am trapped," he moaned. "...trapped!"
His upsurging energy gone, overcome by despair, he lay there on his back, his eyes looking into a blue, cool, indifferent sky.

'I guess I am done for. There is no way I can come out of this tomb,' he reflected sadly.

His thoughts were in Zamosze. The faces of his dead mother, his father, sisters... were smiling at him... In his imagination, he heard his father's voice... warm and loving... "Decision, Jan, always make a decision and... look Jan... stick to it... right or wrong... stick to it."

'Ha, decision! What can I decide now? How can I get out of this god-damned enclosure? How?'

His eyes were scouring the ridge before him, inch by inch. They rested on a narrow, shallow depression. It was probably made some time ago by a rivulet of water falling down the ridge. 'Hm...' he reflected. 'Perhaps... I must try! I must!'

He turned himself on his stomach, and overcoming an excruciating pain, raised himself slightly and crawled close to the depression in the ridge. It didn't take him long to find out that in order to get into the depression, he would have to climb an overhang of steep rock, about three metres high. Once in the depression, he concluded there would be a chance to overcome the ridge. "At least that is what I think," Jan whispered.

His first attempt to climb the rock was disastrous. His broken ankle prevented him from hooking onto a rough rock, and he tumbled down, moaning from the incredible pain. He tried again and again, but unfortunately with the same results. His hands were bleeding, head was pounding... and he was losing his strength again. After every fall, he gave himself a short rest, and tried again and again. It took him a long time to realize that his progress was being prevented by his slipping shoes. He removed them and tried again. He felt the sharp rocks were piercing his feet, causing them to bleed, but his determination to overcome the obstacle was by now above the pain. "I will climb this rock, or die..." he muttered through his dry throat.

It was then that Jan had heard two voices within himself. 'Come on, Jan, you will make it, Jan! Remember the horse?'

"What horse?" Jan moaned in his delirium.

'The Priest's horse, stupid! You saved the horse, didn't you?' was the voice's reply to Jan.

'Oh, God, let me die. Let me die here... I cannot make it' said the other voice.

"Oh, God help me!" cried Jan.

'God will help you, Jan, if you help yourself. Remember.'

"But I can't."

'Oh, yes you can!!!'

Jan was grabbing the twigs of small bushes, coarse grasses... rocks... anything to hold him. This time he made it... he was lying in the depression, half dead for a long, long time.

Then, lying on his stomach, he started a slow ascent along the depression.

In the fading light, he reached the peak of the ridge. In front of him was a flatland, stretching as far as he could see. Mobilizing the rest of his strength, he started his descent towards the flatland. He knew that his endurance was reaching the end. "I must keep going - I must," he whispered. "I must reach the plain! I must!"

Then he was there, he felt more than he could see, the flatland under his feet. He tried to stand up, but felt an overpowering weakness, so he started to crawl, trying to leave the mountains behind as much as he could. 'Goddamned mountains, goddamned...' Suddenly, he saw that he was on a country road. Unmistakably a road, since there were two distinctive depressions parallel to each other, thus a horse-cart road. Suddenly, he heard the rattling noise of a cart and human voices. He made an enormous effort to stand up, yelling "Help! Help!" but only a hoarse voice came out of his throat. He moved haltingly forward, then his vision blurred and he lost consciousness.

****

Jan tried to open his eyes. He could hear a quiet bustling somewhere nearby, and the murmur of voices. There was an unfamiliar smell, sharp and unpleasant. Jan forced his eyes open and, for a moment, blinked and squinted in the brightness. He was in a bed. His leg was in an enormous cast and hoisted by a strange apparatus.

'I'm in a hospital. How did I get here?' he wondered. He lay for a long time staring at the ceiling as he tried to remember. His thoughts were interrupted by a nurse who approached him smiling. She was young, with blonde hair, a small up-turned nose and full lips.
"Good, you are awake," she said kindly. "I thought that you would sleep forever." She adjusted the pillow and left, smiling.

Some time later, he was awakened by a hand on his shoulder. "You must eat," the same young nurse told him. Lifting his head with her left arm, she began to feed him some sort of soup. He began to eat hungrily.

"What's your name?" he asked her.

"Vera. I am one of the nurses here."

After swallowing some of the food, he asked Vera if she knew what had happened to him and who had brought him there.

"You were brought here in a farm wagon by two collective farm workers. They found you a kilometre or so from their collective farm, bleeding and badly smashed up."

The next day, he was awakened by a terrible pain in his left leg. Opening his eyes, he saw an older woman with a stethoscope around her neck, moving his left leg.

Hearing Jan's moans, the woman looked at him. Her eyes were pale blue, warm and friendly.

"How do you feel, young man?" she greeted him, smiling.

"Fine, but my leg..."

"My name is Larrysa Ivanow. I am a doctor here," she interrupted him.

"But my leg, Doctor," Jan insisted.

"You will live, *malcheek*! You will live!" she said. "These bones of yours," she pointed at his leg, "will mend like a puppy's." Then she added, "In time, *malcheek*, in time."

"How long will it take?" Jan asked anxiously.

"At least four weeks."

"Oh, no!"

"Well, maybe sooner," she said gently.

"How is your head?" the doctor asked.

"It hurts."

Her long, shapely fingers traveled over his head, as if she was looking for something. "Hmm," was all she said and, promising to be back, she left him.

A few weeks later, when Jan was stronger, he was visited by a young man dressed in a grey, rumpled suit. He was whistling as he sat on the chair in front of Jan's bed, looking at him intently. Jan didn't like the man's eyes or the way he was looking at him. His eyes were small and cunning and he seemed cold and suspicious.

"Your name, young man?" he finally asked.

In the last few days, Jan had given more and more thought to the Soviet police. He knew that sooner or later he would be asked questions about who he was and what he was doing in the Soviet Republic, Turkestan.

"Ivan!" Jan exclaimed.

"Look, *malcheek*! Stop playing stupid and give me your full name."

"Don't remember," Jan said, grasping his head in his hands and pretending to be in great pain.

"Where are you from?" The man's voice was becoming more and more unfriendly.

"From the collective farm," Jan said.

"Which collective farm?"

"I don't know."

"You little mother fucker! Stop this nonsense or I will..."

"Or you will what?" Jan heard an angry voice behind them.

"Comrade Doctor!" exclaimed the man in confusion. "I was merely doing my job. We need evidence."
"Yes, yes, Comrade Commissar, I am aware of your duties, but the patient is too sick to be interrogated."

"Well, yes, doctor, I... I... just want some information... his name, etc... I am responsible."

"Give him some time, wait 'til he is better," she replied as she proceeded with her daily examination of Jan's injuries.

"I will see you later, Ivan," the Commissar said angrily.

"I heard the Commissar's questions, Ivan," said the doctor quietly. "You truly don't remember?"

"No, doctor."

The doctor checked the chart, examined Jan's head and, with a frown, left him. Jan signed with relief. The Commissar's visit had terrified him and he knew that faking amnesia wouldn't work forever. He tried to move his left leg, but couldn't manage to budge it.

Outside, the spring of 1941 was coming to an end. People in the hospital yard were wearing lighter clothes, and the nearby mountains were still covered with flowers.

Jan's strength was returning. Soon, he could walk on crutches, with Vera's help. The nurse, he thought, was unselfish and gentle, always finding time for him, despite the constant demands made on her.

"Ivan," she once asked him, "are you really Russian?"

Jan was deeply disturbed by her question and so he quickly asked her why she doubted his Russian origin.

"In some ways your accent is strange, but that's not surprising in the Soviet Union. But... but..." she was lost for words, then added, "Your manners and... the way you think."

"I think the same way as you, Vera."

"Well... yes and no," she paused, then added, "I heard you praying several times in some strange language."

'I hope the Commissar is not wondering about me too,' Jan thought, but said nothing.

Weeks passed and the Commissar paid Jan several visits, and, to further increase Jan's misery, promised to try to come more often. During these visits, Jan pretended to be in great pain, holding his head and moaning, although he suspected that the young Commissar didn't entirely believe him. Jan knew with certainty that the Commissar was searching all the nearby collective farms and labour camps, inquiring about a missing person of Jan's description.

****

One particularly beautiful, warm day, Jan asked Vera if she would take him outside.

Slowly they reached the vestibule and went out through a wide door. The cool breeze blowing from the mountain was invigorating and he immediately felt better. He headed toward a small bench under a tree and sat down heavily.

The grassy slopes of the hospital grounds were filled with bright, fragrant flower beds. From the nearby village of Merv, they heard the sound of voices and traffic. He reached for Vera's hand and she did not object. Her hand was soft and warm. They didn't talk, just sat there, satisfied with being close to each other.

Jan was now able to walk without his crutches, although he quickly became very tired and weak. Then, on June 22, 1941, terrifying news reached the hospital.

"Ivan!" Vera cried. "Ivan! We are at war! Ivan!" She rushed into Jan's room.

Jan sat up quickly and started to ask questions. "War? Where? With whom?"

Vera told them they had heard, on the hospital radio, that Germany had attacked the Soviet Union that morning. Jan's feelings were mixed. His memory of the German attack on Poland in 1939 made him sad, but it was also good to know that his enemies were at war with one another.

Vera was frightened. "My father and my two brothers will be conscripted. They could be killed, Ivan."

"You mustn't think about that, Vera. Have hope." He tried to comfort her as much as he could. They sat there quietly for a moment.

Weeks passed, and Jan's health improved. Except for his left leg, all the bandages were gone.

The hospital was swarming with new patients that it couldn't properly accommodate. Many of the new patients had to be put on the floors between the beds, or in the corridors. The stench of infected wounds and the moans of the injured forced Jan to spend most of his daylight hours outside.

"The Germans are pushing eastward," Jan heard a man say to his companions who were lying on the floor. "Spreading like a plague."

"Moscow will be their tomb."

"Those Germans are brutes."

"The Red Army will beat them."

"The German dogs burn our villages and rape our women."

"Many refugees are heading eastward."

Jan, who read 'Pravda' every day and occasionally 'Izvestia', was surprised to hear the men talking like this. In 'Pravda' and 'Izvestia', there had been no hint of defeats. In fact, one report after another read: 'Our glorious Red Army has achieved a great victory, beating the enemy back...'

'What is the truth?' Jan wondered, looking at the wounded, fear-stricken and sick men close to him.

Jan, feeling stronger now and bored with his long idleness, decided to help around the hospital. He worked with the orderlies, bringing patients into the hospital, and he carried supplies to the doctors and nurses. At first, the sight of mangled bodies and injured limbs made him sick. He was amazed at the calm efficiency of the doctors. They worked long hours and showed neither shock nor surprise at the dreadful condition of their patients. The surgeons Jan admired most seemed to have mastered their emotions completely. Amputations were performed swiftly and carefully, but mechanically.

Vera was at first shocked to see Ivan plunging into such hard work. She tried to persuade him that he was not well enough to work, but later she was proud of him.

"And how is Doctor Ivan today?" she teased, drying the sweat from his face.
"Fine, fine, Doctor Vera," he countered, laughing. 'We seem to be the only people who laugh in this dreary place,' thought Jan sadly.

One morning, Jan, reading 'Pravda', almost shouted with joy. 'The Soviet Union and Polish Government,' he read, 'have signed an Agreement to renew diplomatic relationship with Poland. Following the reestablishment of diplomatic relationship, the Soviet Union will grant an amnesty to all Polish citizens on Soviet territory, imprisoned as war prisoners or others.' He read it again and again.

The article further mentioned that the government of the Soviet Union agreed to allow the Polish army to be formed on its territory. It didn't say exactly where, but Jan heard a conversation among two Polish speaking patients in the hospital who mentioned the Soviet Republic of Uzbekistan again and again as the area where the Polish army would be organized.

'Since the Soviet Union unselfishly has given sanctuary to many Polish citizens since the beginning of the war...' Jan almost laughed aloud. "Oh, yes," he muttered, as he thought of Nukhto-Ozyero and the Lager in Turkestan 'To those Polish citizens who were hostile to the Soviet Union and found themselves in labour camps, the Soviet Union now grants an amnesty.'

'So, first they lock you up without trial and then they grant you amnesty,' he thought bitterly. He continued to read.

'It has been agreed that the Polish authorities will be allowed to form a Polish Army in the Soviet Union to fight arm in arm with the Red Army, against our common enemy - Germany.' Jan couldn't believe it. He read on with tears of happiness in his eyes.

'The initial concentration of the Polish Army will be in the area of the Caspian Sea around Tashkent and Bukhara. All Soviet citizens are asked to give full assistance to as many Polish Allies as possible, in their efforts to reach this area.'

Jan felt free for the first time in two years. Stretching out on his bed, he felt like singing, shouting, thanking God. After he had calmed down, he started to think more rationally, analyzing this new development.

He wondered whether this so-called amnesty included men who blew up half of a Labour Camp and killed K.G.B. men. But an amnesty is an amnesty, he reasoned.

'Tashkent? Bukhara? Where are these cities?' He tried to recall his long geographical conversations with Rettinger. 'Amy Darya River' came to his mind. 'Aha,' he recalled, 'Tashkent should be east of the Amy Darya.' He almost heard Rettinger's voice.

"Vera," he asked matter-of-factly, "how far is Tashkent from here?"

"I don't really know. Maybe 400 or 500 kilometres." Jan was disappointed that it was so far.

His volunteer work at the hospital had made him popular with the staff. Seeing this young man, still not completely recovered, working 10 to 12 hours a day, they had grown to like and respect him. Even the Commissar, when he was still here, had stopped questioning him.

Jan laughed to himself, thinking about the Commissar. Two weeks ago, he had been conscripted into the Red Army, and his substitute, an old man, didn't even bother to talk to Jan.

At the end of August, Jan told Vera that his memory was coming back and that he thought he was from Uzbekistan, more precisely from Bukhara, where he had attended school. His father, a school teacher in Bukhara, had been sent there in the 30's from Byelorussia to be 're-educated', he explained. He was deeply ashamed of lying to his girl, but he felt that it was prudent not to reveal his identity, even to her.

"How can I thank you?" he asked her before his departure. They were sitting on their bench outside the hospital. Vera turned her head away. How often her work days had been brightened by Jan.. She thought that she even loved him a little. How different he was from the other boys his age. She had grown to rely on him, and now he was leaving.

She handed him a small package, telling him to open it later.

They kissed, first tentatively, then passionately. Reluctantly, Jan left with the package under his arm and disappeared into the noisy city, heading straight for the Merv Railway Station. The package contained a loaf of bread and a can of sardines, the first he had seen in the Soviet Union.

The station was swarming with people, occupying not only the station yard, but spilling beyond it in all directions: the Turkman women with veils covering their faces, the Uzbek farmers with bundles, the Russian soldiers in their tattered Red Army uniforms, the Thadzik herders carrying long staffs with bundles tied to each end, the Kazakhs, tall and unsmiling with their shaved heads, except for one long braid, falling down their backs to their waists...

'I wonder if they are all waiting for the train,' thought Jan. He couldn't imagine a train long enough to accommodate all of them. Meanwhile, he found a boulder, sat as comfortably as he could, and waited. Hours went by, and evening was approaching, but there was no train in sight.

Suddenly, there was an incredible noise and a mad stampede. People were yelling and pushing toward the rails. First, there was the familiar whistle, then the long light beam of the approaching train. Finally, it stopped, panting and hissing. Pandemonium erupted. The people pushed, kicked, shouted and pulled at each other, rushing forward, all trying to get inside at once. Some, failing to get to the doors, used the windows, squeezing themselves through the narrow openings only to be pulled down by others, who took their place.

Jan, stunned by this madness, watched with his mouth open. This could continue for hours because more and more people were coming from everywhere. He decided that if he wanted to get to Bukhara, he had to act quickly, do something. The train was by now packed to capacity. So he, with a few others, scrambled to the couplings and held onto an iron bar. Thus, with legs dangling into the air, he started his journey to Bukhara. 'At least I didn't have to pay for a ticket,' he thought wryly.

By noon the next day, the train had reached the terminal at the Amu Darya River. Anyone who wanted to travel to Bukhara would have to take a ferry boat.

Jan had never seen such a huge river. Straining his eyes, he saw the faint outline of the opposite shore, dotted with white buildings. Beyond, the gently rolling land extended as far as the horizon. The ferry made the crossing twice a day, once in the early morning, and again in the evening.

Having a few hours to wait, Jan walked to the river, and found a narrow, rocky beach. Removing his badly worn boots, he put his feet into the water. It felt pleasantly cool, in spite of the hot day. His eyes followed the river upstream and stopped at the far mountains, the source of the Amu Darya.

'The Pamir Mountains,' he remembered from Rettinger's lectures.

On the other side of the river was his destination, the ancient city of Bukhara. His eyes shifted to the left, downstream of the river. In that direction, thousands of miles to the north was Siberia and his family. 'Are they still alive?' he wondered. 'Did the amnesty reach them too? Did it reach them in time?'

Crossing the Amu Darya River took much longer than Jan had anticipated. The large barge, loaded with people and goods, moved so slowly that Jan thought that it would never get to the other side. It was some time after midnight when the barge finally anchored. Jan decided to spend the rest of the night close to the river.

Next morning, he headed for the nearby railway station. By noon that day, he had reached Bukhara. As the train approached, he saw the distant roofs of the Mosques. The city was flooded with Polish ex-prisoners, men, women and children, all having one thing in common - tattered clothes.

Chapter Eight

While Jan was arriving at the ancient city of Bukhara, where he joined the Polish Army, the survivors of Nukhto-Ozyero were also on their way to Bukhara for the same reason. Maria and Helena, packed like sardines into the freight car, tried desperately to help each other. Everyone had been happy to leave the camp and feel free again. People were talking and occasionally even singing to the rhythm of the moving train. The train moved through forested land, dotted by numerous lakes and cut by fast flowing rivers. They looked at this landscape differently somehow, seeing for the first time in two years its beauty and its splendor. By the end of the third week, the train left behind the flat expanses of the Taiga forest, and entered into the hilly terrain of the Ural Mountains. There, it followed a wide valley with gentle slopes, proceeding directly south.

Their elation over their newly-proclaimed freedom was soon consumed by that all-too-familiar condition they found themselves constantly fighting since they came to the Soviet Union - hunger. The Soviet authorities did not feel obliged to feed them. Only occasionally, stopping in small towns, had they been given boiled water and some bread. The survivors, tired out and often sick, were dying. Day and night, people died in their freight car. At night, the dead were thrown out of the door by other passengers, and landed in the ditches, fields, groves or, sometimes, on the station platforms. It became an everyday event, surprising no one. There was more and more room in their freight car and soon Maria and Helena were able to find enough room on the deck to lie down. Maria saw that Helena was losing her strength. She knew that unless they found some food, they would die too. She noticed that some of the men, women and children were leaving their freight car at almost every train stop and returning with bread, sometimes milk or potatoes, but mostly bread.

Once their train stopped in the town of Sverdlovsk. It was a cool late August morning. They were told that the train would leave no earlier than afternoon. Taking Helena with her, she followed two men from their freight car who, from Maria's observation, were the most successful at finding food.

They followed them to a large square where they saw numerous stalls with bread, vegetables, milk, fish, and some meat.

"Oh, Maria! I'm so hungry!" moaned Helena, tears rolling down her cheeks. Maria was close to tears herself, but she pulled her sister to another stall where the two men were standing quietly, looking at the bread. The merchant was busy with a customer, paying no attention to them. Suddenly, one of the men grabbed two loaves of bread and ran. The merchant, taken by surprise, stood still for a second, then yelled and cursed as he started to chase the thief. His companion, who had been waiting, raked off several loaves of bread and speedily disappeared into the throng of people.

"So that's how they got their food!" exclaimed Maria.

"But that's stealing, Maria. We can't do that... can we?"

"Of course we can't... what would our father say if he could see us doing such things? Or our grandparents? Anyway, we'd be caught if we tried it." They walked back through the market, talking quietly and trying to think of ways to get food without money. When they were passing the last stall, Helena stopped suddenly.

"Maria, I can't stand it anymore," she said. "My stomach is aching... and I'm so weak." She stood still, staring at the bread.

"Come on, Helena! Come on!" Maria urged.

But Helena just stood there, staring at the bread, oblivious to the people around her. The merchant, an old bearded man, noticed and shouted at Helena to "go away, get lost" or else he would call a militia man, or, if necessary, would take care of them himself. But Helena, as though in a trance, continued to stare.

"Helena, come on," Maria pleaded, embarrassed. She grabbed her younger sister and, using all her strength, started to pull her away. Helena reluctantly went with her.

"Just a moment, girls," they heard the merchant say. They stopped and turned back to see him offering a loaf of bread to Helena. "Take it, child," he said softly. Seeing Helena's confusion, he repeated, "Please, little girl. Take it."

They were astonished. "Now, go away! Go away, girls!" he said quietly.

"Helena," said her older sister later when they were sitting on their bunk in the freight car. "I think I know how to get food now."

"How?" asked Helena, her mouth full of bread.

"We'll have to beg." Helena just looked at her in surprise. "Well, it's either begging or stealing, and we can't steal."

"No, of course not."

From then on, they begged wherever they could. They would leave the train, sometimes for hours, and head for a nearby town or village where they could beg for food.

They weren't the only ones who were begging. There were numerous trains passing through this area. Some carried Polish survivors south. Others brought Soviet refugees from as far away as Leningrad, or other Soviet cities threatened by Germans. They were all hungry, and swarmed over the countryside in search of food.

"We don't have food for ourselves!" people yelled at the girls. "Go away! We are starving too!"

Once the train stopped close to the city of Chelyabinsk and didn't move for the next three days. "A collision ahead," they were told.

The sisters, hungry as usual, climbed down from the freight car. To their left was a wide green valley. The green grass was woven with small yellow flowers. After walking for an hour or so, they reached a narrow brook. Its cool water soothed their aching feet and washed away the dirt.

"Look, Maria!" Helena cried. "A butterfly!" And for a moment, they chased it, then they slowed down, paying more attention to the distant village they were approaching.

This village was smaller than Zamosze, about sixty straw-thatched huts, Helena counted. The huts were arranged along the gentle slope of the low, round mountain, reminding Maria of her grandmother's rosary. There was no breeze. Grey smoke rose from the chimneys in vertical columns. The peaceful scene was interrupted only by an occasional dog barking or the cackle of the geese.

"It sounds like Zamosze!" cried Helena joyfully.

"Hmm, maybe it sounds like Zamosze," said Maria, "but it doesn't look like Zamosze." She pointed at the mountains surrounding the valley.

"And no thick forest, like ours," added Helena. "Still it's nice here."

They reached the village and knocked on the door of the first hut. An old man answered, listened patiently to the girls, his hand on the door knob, then muttered "*Nyethu* (we have nothing to give)" and closed the door.

The girls continued their knocking, but the result was always the same. Most people were polite, but some were irritable or hostile.

"*Neechevo nyethu* (absolutely nothing)."

"Get lost, or I'll set my dog on you!"

"Food? You want food? Do you know that hundreds like you have been here already?! What food? We don't have any!"

The hunger, the walking and perhaps so much fresh air all at once, tired them, but they didn't want to give up and return to the train without at least a piece of bread.

"I can't walk any more, Maria," groaned Helena, collapsing on a nearby log. They had reached the last hut, which was one of the smallest, and by the look of it, the poorest in the village.

Helena, totally exhausted, sat down with her head in her lap. Maria slumped beside her sister. A sudden advance of clouds from behind the mountains covered the sun and soon they felt droplets of rain falling on their unwashed hair. Maria lifted her head and looked around, as an eerie feeling crept over her. The village was grey and uninviting, an ominous place with strange people in it. Her head sank into her lap as she sobbed. The rain increased; the little droplets became a downpour; rivulets of water ran off the girls' hair to the ground. They were startled by an old woman. She had a large black kerchief thrown over her head and shoulders and she, like them, was barefoot. There was sadness in the woman's brown eyes.

'She has Grandmother's eyes,' thought Maria.

"Come with me, *rebyata* (children)," she said in a hoarse, friendly voice. They staggered to their feet and followed her to the hut. The woman opened the door and led them inside.

When their eyes had become accustomed to the darkness, they saw that the hut had only one room and a shed. In the corner, occupying one third of the space, was a traditional Russian lime-kiln stove. Another corner of the hut was occupied by a goat which was eating straw. The only other furniture in the room was a wooden table, two chairs and straw-covered bed.

"*Oy, moy Bohze, moy Bohze* (Oh, my God, my God)," the old woman lamented as she removed the girls' wet clothes. Her large, bony hands were gentle and comforting.

The naked girls were told to climb up to the brick shelf built above the stove and lie down. The old lady brought some old, but clean, linen sheets, and gently covered the girls. They fell asleep instantly.

They were awakened by a burst of thunder and a jagged flash of lightning tearing the darkness of the hut. The noise and darkness frightened them.

"Hush children, hush!" They recognized the hoarse voice of the woman, who was sitting on the edge of the shelf, trying to reassure them. "It's only a storm, children. You are safe here." Calming down, they heard the rustling sound of rain outside.

The old woman told them to put on their dry clothes and come down off the stove-shelf. While dressing, they heard shuffling and banging noises as their hostess opened and closed the oven below them. They saw two steaming dishes and a piece of bread on the table.

"Sit down, daughters, and eat these gifts from God. It is not much, but it is at least warm."

The bowls contained some sort of soup, with morsels of bread floating on the surface. The girls set upon the food, cleaning off their plates in no time. Maria felt a bit ashamed, realizing that the old woman had replenished their dishes three times. As was customary in Zamosze, she rose to her feet, clasped the woman's rough hand, and kissed it lightly.

"Thank you, *Babushka*! God bless you."

"*Nichevo, nichevo, detyno*! (oh, it's nothing, nothing, child!)" said the woman, pulling her hand back, embarrassed.

After they had again thanked their hostess and bade her goodbye, she opened the oven and, using a long staff, pulled out two baked potatoes, which she put in their pockets. "This is for the road," the woman told them.

The girls walked back to the train, feeling happy. Their long train journey resumed.

By the middle of September, the train left behind the Ural Mountains and, picking up speed, proceeded over the flat Kazakh plains. On both sides of the railway, extending as far as they could see, were short and patchy steppe-grasslands. They saw many herds of cattle, and occasionally sheep, herded by the tall, head-shaven Kazakhs. They wondered at the women carrying baskets and bundles on their heads.

They arrived at Bukhara in Uzbekistan at the end of September. The train stopped one or two kilometres outside the town and they were told by the trainmen to disembark. Fortunately, the evening was warm with warm breezes blowing from a nearby plain that looked to them like a desert.

The sisters sat on the dry ground, watching numerous donkeys, harnessed to two-wheeled carts. The girls had never seen donkeys and were astonished to see them harnessed to such large vehicles. After resting for an hour, they were told by an official in civilian clothes to follow him.

Staggering on their weak legs, they were led to a donkey cart. The owner of the cart, a fat and tall Uzbek, mumbling something incomprehensible, indicated with a whip where they should sit. The sisters were amazed to see how strong the little donkey was. It moved the cart, with its three riders, with extraordinary ease. Turning left from the railway, they followed a narrow dirt road. Behind and ahead of them were other carts. The Uzbek was quiet, except for some words of encouragement addressed to the donkey. The little animal responded, obviously understanding his master. The springless cart bounced crazily, making them feel nauseated. It obviously didn't bother the Uzbek, who, singing some sort of monotonous song, appeared not to see his passengers at all. They were passing clumps of dry grass, stony outcrops, but mainly sandy patches, barkhans, and dunes.

"It's some kind of desert, Maria," said Helena, looking around her.

"Sort of."

"No trees... not much of anything."

They were wrong, because after another two hours of slow riding, they spotted a large clump of trees, which, in the moonlight, resembled a black island in the middle of the shining sand. As they came closer, they saw several small buildings.

Some of the carts detached themselves from the caravan and headed toward the settlement. They passed several similar 'islands' until, around midnight, they, too, turned to one of them.

It was a village unlike any they had ever seen. In the bright moonlight, they saw small square buildings. They were not made of wood like Zamosze of Bostyn, but from clay. The strangest thing to both of them was that all of the buildings had flat roofs.

The cart, swaying and jerking, moved slowly along a narrow, dust-covered street. They rode in silence, interrupted only by the noise of their cart and the Uzbek's singing. He stopped and, mumbling something to the donkey, directed him into a small compound. Passing a gate, the donkey stopped in front of a hut. The Uzbek, pointing at the hut, delivered a barrage of words which they guessed meant: "This is your home, girls. Get inside."

They got down from the cart and stumbled toward their new home. The Uzbek smiled with approval and left. They went through an opening in the wall serving as a doorway and managed, despite the darkness, to find two bunks. By touch, they discovered that the bunks were covered with coarse grass or something similar. Hungry and thirsty, but above all exhausted, they went to sleep almost instantly.

Suddenly, a horrible noise unlike anything they had ever heard, loud and persistent, made them leap from their bunks. Terrified, they stared at the doorway, but, because of the darkness, they saw only a huge moving shadow.

"Oyee! Oyee!" the noise echoed, almost deafening them. Then there was silence and the shadow disappeared. Trembling, they huddled on a bunk for a long time, too scared to talk.

"What in the world was that?" the younger sister finally managed to ask.

"I don't know, Helena."

"It was so... so... horrible."

"Yes, loud, too."

"Some animal?"

"Probably."

They tried to stay awake, but their tiredness was stronger than their fear, so they slept until sunlight, warm and strong, woke them up. They looked curiously around, wondering what their new house was like. The hut, except for two large bunks, was empty. The dirt floor was littered with dry-looking straw, animal excreta and dry wood chips. The air in the hut reeked of urine, dung, and some other indistinguishable odours that they had been too tired to notice when they arrived.

Their observations were interrupted by a loud bray. "Yeaa! Yeaa!" This time the noise was coming from outside. They jumped to their feet and ran outside. There, a few paces away in the bright sunlight, stood a donkey. His large eyes gazed sadly at the sisters, as though he was trying to tell them what was bothering him.

"He is swaying, Maria!" Helena exclaimed, looking at the animal with compassion mingled with fear.

"Look, he is nothing but skin and bones."

"He is probably hungry and thirsty."

"Just like us."

The donkey plodded toward them and sniffed, trying to be friendly. They noticed that his skin was dirty and covered with sores. He was coated with flies, fragments of grass and other coarse vegetation.

Helena, looking around frantically, found a small stick and tried to chase the flies from the animal's skin. The donkey brayed again, this time, they thought, more gently.

Their acquaintance with the donkey was interrupted by the entrance of a burly, brown-faced man, with bushy black hair. Mumbling something that sounded like a curse, he chased the donkey away, kicking him in the stomach several times. The donkey was too weak to run, so the man kept beating him until he was out of reach.

"I am Yefreem," the man addressed them in Russian, "the collective farm manager." His Russian was poor, even worse than their own.

"You been, here sent by Russkys. This collective farm has a name... Stalin Collective."

"We're supposed to go to the Polish Army," Maria interrupted.

"Polish Army? Oh, yes... The Army! Not yet... Maybe tomorrow, one month... or later. Army not ready yet."

"So why are we here?"

"Ditches... dig! Dig!"

"What ditches?"

"For water."

"We are hungry."

"And thirsty."

"Come me! Come me!" the man gestured. Following him, they walked through the village. On both sides of the street were huts, each surrounded by a clay wall. They all were small and square. A few of the huts, however, were surrounded by tall cactus hedges, instead of clay walls.

They were led to a larger building which, they soon discovered, was used for grain storage. They noticed that the storage space was divided into two sections. In one, the girls recognized wheat, but in the other one was a grain that they had never seen before.

"*Joogara* (millet)," said the manager, handing Maria a small bag of millet. "Tomorrow evening you get... this..." he pointed at the wheat.

"What should we do with this?" Maria asked, pointing at the "joogara".

"Come! Come!" was his answer. He led them to another building, empty except for a small grinding device made of stone. Taking the bag from Maria, he poured its contents onto the stone. He grabbed a handle which moved the stone around.

"Aha," observed Helena, "we are in the flour mill."

"What should we do with this now?" Maria asked the man, holding the bag of millet flour.

"Wait," he said, and led them back to their hut. As they passed the village well, he pointed and barked, "Water!" In the yard outside their hut, he showed them a small fireplace with an iron pot.

"Where is the wood for the fire?" asked Helena.

"Wood?" the man laughed. "What wood?"

"Wood! Wood for the fire!" exclaimed Maria, pointing at the fireplace.

He led them to the side of the hut where they found a neat stack of pie-shaped objects.

"What is this?" they both asked.

"Fire!" the man replied.

"Yes, but what is it?"

The man stared at the sisters as though they were half-wits, then marched up to the donkey. He lifted up the donkey's tail and graphically described the origin of fuel. To Yefreem's bewilderment, the sisters laughed and laughed.

"I wish our grandfather could see this," said Maria, choking with laughter.

"He'd probably be impressed! It's much simpler than chopping wood," Helena retorted.

That evening, Helena asked, "Maria, why have they sent us here?"

"To dig ditches. Didn't you hear that Uzbeck?"

"Yes, but the Army... Where is the Polish Army?"

"I don't know. The Uzbek said it is not ready yet."

The collective farm, they soon learned, grew millet, some wheat, figs, cotton, and vegetables for market. They both started work the next day. They learned that besides them, eight other families from the Nukhto-Ozyero camp had been sent to this collective farm. They, together with the Uzbeks, had to dig irrigation ditches with shovels from 8 a.m. to 6 p.m. Even though it was now October, the sun was hot. It was back-breaking work, especially for thirteen-year-old Helena. Even nineteen-year-old Maria had difficulty straightening up after hours and hours of digging.

Their food consisted of wheat bread which they baked for themselves in the common bakery and porridge made from millet flour cooked outside their hut. Their common well, located in the centre of the village, provided water. There was nothing else to eat or drink. The Uzbeks, except for the manager, didn't speak Russian at all. Any time Maria or Helena tried to speak to them in Russian, they, without exception, spat and turned their backs on them.

"Why are they acting like that?" Maria asked Isaak Shapiro, a Polish Jew from Warsaw. Isaak, like them, was from Nukhto-Ozyero. In spite of his sixty years, he had managed to survive the labour camp.

"Why? Why?" said Shapiro irritably. "Don't you know what the Soviets did to these Uzbeks in 1917?"

"No, I don't know."

"They slaughtered thousands of them, that's what!"

"But, why?"

"Oy, Maria, Maria, you know so little," was all she could get out of him.

Isaak Shapiro almost drove the sisters crazy with the stories he told them. "Oy, girls," he usually started, "what a good life I had in Warsaw! Oy, what a life! I was working in the Wedel Chocolate Factory, you know, the best in Poland, girls; imagine, girls, after a day's work, walking home, I used to eat a big bar of chocolate, bitter-sweet, oy!"

"Stop, Isaak!" the girls would cry, salivating. "Don't torture us!"

But nothing could stop Isaak from reminiscing about the good old days in Warsaw. "And then I would stop at a restaurant and order an ice cream... vanilla... strawberry, sometimes chocolate..."

"Stop it!"

"And an orangeade, girls, such cool, sweet orangeade.."

The girls, plugging their ears, ran from his hut.

By wintertime the girls' health had deteriorated so much they could hardly drag themselves to work. The winter had been preceded by a rainy season lasting for about two months. The ditch-digging became progressively more difficult. Muddy and exhausted, they could barely reach their hut. The winter, although not as cold as in Siberia, was nevertheless too cold for poorly dressed girls. In an effort to warm up their hut, they burned straw and tree branches, but this produced clouds of choking smoke and there was little change in the temperature.

By February, only 25 of the 36 Poles remained alive.

One day in February, about two years after they had been taken from Zamosze, they were told by the manager that there was no millet or wheat left. When Maria asked how they were supposed to live, he shrugged his shoulders and said, "Complain to the Russkies."

Sometime in March, the village was hit by typhoid fever. The first to die were the Maciazek family. The Maciazek widow had lost her husband about two months before the war broke out. She was left with six children, all daughters. The oldest, Danuta, was sixteen and the youngest, Grazyna, was just reaching her seventh year. The Maciazeks were one of the families who had survived the Nukhto camp. The widow and her oldest daughter some-how managed to support them all.

At the time of their arrival at the collective farm, they, like the others, had reached the point of total exhaustion. However, their will for survival, strengthened in the Nukhto camp, had been shown again in the collective farm. Those who were not digging ditches had been sent not only all over the Stalin Collective farm, but into a score of other nearby collectives. They begged, and stole everything they could put their hands upon. They were chased by the Uzbeks and their dogs, cursed, yelled at, and often beaten. It is probable they would have survived if typhoid fever had not struck the fam-ily. They died one by one and within two weeks only the youngest, Grazyna, and her mother were still alive. The Uzbek villagers, awakened in the night by moaning and wailing sounds coming from the Maciazek hut, knew that another hateful "Russian" had departed to Hades. Some of the villagers were annoyed by the interruption of their sleep; others prayed to Allah, asking him to be merciful to all of them. Maria, Helena and the other Poles wept.

One hot and windy day an Uzbek saw the disheveled Maciazek widow, raving as she dragged her youngest child to the sand dune cemetery. She was never seen again.

By the end of March, Stalin Collective farm lost another five Polish refugees and many of the Uzbeks. All were buried in the nearby sand dunes.

In the meantime, the donkey brayed day and night. Nobody, as far as Maria and Helena could see, cared about the poor beast, but chased him away from the huts with sticks. The two sisters, taking pity on the animal, tried to help him, but aside from giving him water and scrubbing his rough skin, there was nothing they could do for him. The donkey, however, was glad that there was somebody who was at least friendly, and therefore considered him-self a part of their family. He continued to wake them up at night, braying as loudly as his weakened body allowed. Thus awakened, they saw his big bony head at their door and somehow felt more secure, although guilty too for being unable to help their friend.

In the meantime, work at the collective farm came to a halt. There was nothing to feed the workers, so the authorities followed the communist motto, "no work, no food" only this time in reverse.

Then they had a visit from Isaak Shapiro. They only had to glance at him to know he was very sick. Walking slowly, as though half-paralyzed, he reached their bunk and sunk onto it, his strength gone. After a while, he opened his fever-bright eyes and said, softly, "Let's kill him!"

"Kill whom? Why?" the sisters exclaimed in confusion.

"The donkey!"

"The donkey? Our donkey?"

"What do you mean, your donkey? He's nobody's donkey!"

"But, why?" the sisters exclaimed.

"For the meat, that's why!"

They were horrified. They told him that he was a heartless man to even think about such things, and anyway, didn't he know the donkey was their friend?

Isaak, with closed eyes, appeared not to hear the sisters' protests and indignation. With great difficulty, he dragged himself to his feet and left their hut. As he passed the donkey, he muttered: "My friend, you are lucky that I am so weak, otherwise..."

A few days later, Maria noticed with dread that her sister was sick. Helena was lying on the bunk, writhing and groaning in pain. Her distorted face, covered by red blotches, made her look much older. Only her eyes, large and blue, revealed a spark of life. Blonde locks of hair, greasy and sweaty, were spread in disarray over the straw under her.

Maria tried to comfort her with a cool drink of water and a cool compress on her forehead. Noticing the vermin in Helena's hair, she decided that she would be more comfortable if she cut her hair short. Bending over her, with sheep shears borrowed from the farm manager, she selected and cut one clump after another, each dirty and full of vermin. Her own brown hair, she knew, was in the same condition.

The work exhausted her, forcing her to lie down on the bunk beside her sister's feverish body. She started to cry. She knew that Helena was dying of typhoid fever and she could do nothing to help her. Yet she knew she had to try to do something. She lifted herself with great difficulty and, using the wall of the hut for support, went outside.

After the wet fall, the winter was dry without a trace of snow on the ground and the air felt warm. Sage and dried up bush were blowing over the nearby fields. Far away on the horizon, a caravan of camels following an ancient path was heading somewhere, probably toward Tashkent or Bukhara.

She must do something for her sister, she must, she decided. She staggered toward the village. Women in black robes and veils passed without noticing her. She turned into a compound and knocked at the door. After a long time the door was opened by a veiled woman.

"Food! Please! I want food... no, no, not for me, for my dying sister," Maria spoke as fast as she could.

The woman scrutinized her, then, before the girl could say another word, slammed the door. Maria tried another, then another, with the same result. At one hut, while knocking persistently, she was confronted by an old bearded Uzbek, who, with an axe in his hand, chased her as far as the next compound.

After several more attempts, she realized sorrowfully that there was no help here. She didn't want to go back to her sister empty-handed. She had to get something, somewhere - she had to. So, instead of going to the hut, she dragged herself toward the fields. The fields, green with vegetables for the market only a few months ago, were now grey and lifeless.

She wanted to be away from the village and her misery. She walked until her legs gave out and she fell heavily to the ground. She was so miserable that she thought she might die, but she didn't want to die in that wretched field. She couldn't die, because her sister needed her. How could she even think of death? She tried to get up on her feet, and when her efforts failed, she began to crawl. Then, darkness enveloped her, peaceful and painless.

She didn't know how long she lay there unconscious, but when she woke up, the sun was almost gone. As her gaze shifted to the ground she was lying on, she spotted short green sprouts hardly visible, growing all around her. She instinctively pulled one of them and put it into her mouth. It was an onion sprout.

She tried another and another and yes, without a doubt, they were onions. Probably, she thought, left by careless farm workers during last year's harvest. Now, because of the warm spell, they had sprouted. She dug deeply into the soil, and pulled out the onions one by one; large ones, small ones, plenty of them! Sweating from exertion, she started to eat them. Carrying as many as she could, she made her way toward their hut, as fast as her weakened legs would allow.

She boiled the onions and brought them into their hut. She forced Helena to drink the onion soup, again and again. For the next few days she ran between the fields, fireplace, and Helena. Helena's groaning subsided, but not her fever. However, on the eighth or ninth day, she noticed with relief that Helena's forehead had become cooler and that some of the red blotches on her face had disappeared. She continued to make onion soup for another few days, until Helena told her that that was all she could take. She decided then to roast and even bake them.

Soon Helena was strong enough to go outside. While Helena recovered, others had not been so fortunate; a number of Uzbeks had died in the last few weeks. And, according to Maria, only seven Poles remained alive, including them.

One day, Maria burst into the hut panting, and in a strangled voice announced that Shapiro was dying. "It is typhoid fever," Maria stated on their way to Shapiro's hut.

Shapiro, dried up like an autumn leaf, was lying motionless on his cot. The stench in the air almost drove them back, but overcoming their revulsion, they began to nurse the sick man. They fed Shapiro onion soup with Maria holding his head and Helena pouring the food into his mouth. The spoon was rusty and bent, but it was the only utensil they had.

They then applied compresses and fixed Shapiro's bed as much as they could, telling the semi-conscious man that they would be back. Sixty year-old Shapiro, knowing that only young and hardy bodies could survive the disease, realized that he was dying. He was a city man, having lived most of his life in relative comfort, with little exposure to the harshness of peasant life.

But, as if by a miracle, the care and attention he got from the two sisters, helped him to regain, at least temporarily, some of his lost energy.

"My two dear nurses," he whispered faintly, seeing them shuffling around in his hut. There was a perturbed look in his eyes that day, as though something very important was bothering him.

"Maria," he whispered, beckoning the older sister to his bedside. "Maria," he repeated, "could you bring me that board, there, in the corner?"

Following his instructions, she brought the board which was nailed to a three-foot long pole. On the board was a large, elaborately carved star. She recognized it at once, having seen it before in Moyshe's house in Zamosze.

"It is the Star of David," whispered Shapiro weakly. "Put it on my grave,

Maria, please."

The sisters were too upset to speak. They just nodded their consent, sobbing quietly.

"Girls,", continued Shapiro, his voice even weaker. "Leave this place! Go to Bukhara! Walk there, even if you have to, crawl. Go there!"

"Why? What's in Bukhara?" asked Maria.

"The Polish Army may be there. That's what they told us, that the Polish Army would be there. Go! Go there!"

When they returned to Shapiro's hut that same evening, they found him dead. They left the hut and wandered toward the outskirts of the village just to be away from death and misery.

Outside the village, they sat on a high, rocky knoll overlooking the vast Kyzyk-Kum Desert, which spread as far as the horizon. A caravan of camels was heading toward the desert. A man sitting on the lead camel, was singing a desert song, a hymn to Allah. Its monotonous melody floated into the darkness of the desert, soaring unhindered over the stony flats and sand dunes as far as the Koppak Dagh. From behind them, they heard human cries and calls, intermingled with the braying and bleating of animals.

The girls begged the manager of the collective farm to arrange Shapiro's burial. He conceded reluctantly. Placing the Star of David on the grave, they cried for a long time.

"Poor Shapiro," Helena sighed.

"He told us before... before he died, to go to Bukhara," Maria said.

"Maybe we should, Maria."
"Then, let's go! Let's go tomorrow!"

But it wasn't to be. The next morning Helena was awakened by Maria's moans and groans. It didn't take Helena long to realize that her older sister's flushed cheeks, red spots and parched lips indicated that she too had typhoid fever.

Helena sank to the clay floor, disheartened. She couldn't even cry. There seemed to be no more tears left in her eye sockets. Only a short time ago, Maria had been bending over her prostrate body, trying to keep her alive. Now she, Helena, was sitting on that straw-littered clay floor, helpless, waiting, waiting for what? She should do something more, much more than just sit motionless.

'Jan would do something more for his dying sister, wouldn't he?' she thought. 'He always came up with a solution, something.' The memory of Jan and her feeling of aloneness brought tears to her eyes, at first only a few droplets, soon changing to a trickle. Feeling a great weakness overcoming her, she lay down, her forehead touching the floor, and cried until she became exhausted. Crying calmed her, and seemed to clear her head.

"I must do something for Maria!" she whispered, getting up slowly. She stumbled out of the hut and without knowing where she was going, started to walk. She passed the clay-fenced huts one after another. The hot winds blowing from the desert filled her eyes with powdery, stinging sand, almost blinding her. Rubbing her eyes with her soiled hand, she made her way to the house located on the outskirts of the village.

The house, she knew, belonged to the Chairman of the collective farm. She had seen the chairman many times and didn't like the huge Uzbek. She feared his loud voice and even more, she feared his small yellowish eyes resembling a snake which had once scared her in Zamosze. And yet she was determined to confront him and talk to him. She wanted to tell him that she needed help, not for herself but for her dying sister.

"If necessary, I will kneel in front of him day and night," she whispered through her parched lips as she stumbled toward the big hut.

It was afternoon and the house appeared to be peaceful. 'They may be in the fields at this hour,' she thought. Unlike the other huts, this one had no customary wall around it and to a small degree, she thought, it resembled the houses in Zamosze. Swaying from weakness, she directed her steps toward the huge wooden door. She was just about to knock when suddenly from behind the house, she saw a huge hairy dog rushing at her with what seemed to be terrific speed.

She stood there motionless, as though hypnotized by the dog's glowing eyes, fixed on her. She wanted to yell, but instead, only a gasp managed to escape her fear-constricted throat. The dog's mere weight was enough to tumble her down into the sand. The dog, growling madly, jumped on her, searching for her throat. Instinctively, she protected herself by trying to push the beast away.

She felt its teeth penetrate the skin of her right hand. She screamed. Rolling over the sand amid a thick cloud of dust, Helena fought desperately for her life. Suddenly, she felt the weight being lifted. She heard voices. She opened her eyes and saw a figure bending over her. A veiled face was almost touching her own. The woman was saying something; however, her shrill words uttered in Uzbek were wasted on Helena. She just lay there bleeding, too weak to get up.

The woman took her by the arms and pulled her into the house. The cool clay floor brought instant relief and she felt better. The woman, talking ceaselessly, more to herself than to Helena, was bustling around the small house as though looking for something. She soon found some clean rags which she used for bandages. Removing her veil, she started to dress Helena's wounds, throwing occasional glances at her, murmuring, it sounded to Helena, her disapproval. Having dressed her wounds, she helped Helena to a sitting position, placing herself opposite. They stared at each other. Helena thought the woman's eyes were sad. Then the woman, with surprising agility, rose to her feet and went to another room. Helena, left alone, was too tired to think or to look around. She just sat there. After a while, a minute? hour?... Helena didn't care to think about the time, the woman appeared through the other door and approached her.

In her hands, Helena saw a bottle of milk, millet cake, and a dish of dried fruits. She gestured to Helena and urged her by signs, to eat. Helena felt saliva coming to her mouth, but instead of eating, she made a denying sign. The woman raised her dark eyebrow, surprised. Helena rose to her feet swaying and using her bandaged hands, tried to explain to the woman that the food in front of her was for her sister, not for her. Poking at herself then at the woman, using the Russian word "sistra" (sister), she desperately tried to be understood. Sweat flooded her forehead and she sat on the floor again, weakly. The woman looked at her again and then, saying "oohhh", disappeared into the other room again.

This time she was there for a long time. When she reappeared, Helena's eyes fell upon a loaf of *lyepyoshkas* (barley flatbread), dried fruit and what Helena thought the most important, two bottles of goat milk. The woman put the food in an old rag, tied it up and led Helena slowly outside. There, she yelled at the dog, which, with his tail down, disappeared from sight. Helena, in spite of the pain, especially bothersome in her right hand, hurried back, happy. Dragging her feet in the deep sand, she felt like singing and dancing. Suddenly, the winds weren't as stinging as they were before, and even the heat from the sun was not as oppressive. The smell of donkeys' dung reaching her nostrils wasn't as pungent; she was too happy to notice it anyway - she had food for Maria, plenty of it.

Thanks to the Uzbek woman whom Helena frequently visited, they were not hungry. By March, the Uzbek's food and Helena's care put Maria back on her feet. Swaying on her legs and sweating, she nevertheless was able to walk. Determination to find salvation for Helena and herself generated energy and strength beyond belief.

It was a rainy April morning when the sisters left the village. Nobody noticed their departure, nor did anyone care. The Uzbeks on their donkey-driven carts couldn't help but wonder what two strange girls, half naked and in rags, were doing walking down the muddy road. Their light complexion and unveiled faces, indicated that they were not Uzbek girls, therefore Russians. Some were pointing with their whips at the naked part of the girls' bodies, laughing heartily. Others pretended to pick them up by slowing down their carts. When the girls tried to climb into the cart, the owner would whip his donkey to a gallop to leave them behind.

"Why, Maria? Why are they so cruel?"

"I don't know. Maybe they think we are Russians."

"But..."

"Yes, yes, little sister. It's a cruel world."

Weak from walking and hunger, they stopped frequently to rest at the side of the road.

"On your feet, Helena!" "On your feet, Maria!" they encouraged each other, after their rest.

They reached Bukhara at sundown and were filled with awe, forgetting the difficult journey and the weakness of their bodies.

"Oh, look, Maria!" cried Helena, seeing minarets for the first time. "Look at those great buildings. They look as though they are made of gold."

"Those are their churches," Maria pronounced with an air of authority.

"And Maria, there are so many smells here. Some are bad, though," Helena continued.

"Yes, but you don't smell so good yourself, sister!" Maria laughed.

People, hundreds and hundreds of them were walking, running, yelling. The streets and little squares were filled with people, mostly pedestrians, but some were riding carts, pulled by either donkeys or mules. Others were riding donkeys or horses. The booths and stalls, with their meager goods, were spread out along the streets and squares. The merchants seemed to be constantly agitated; yelling, gesticulating, pulling customers' clothes, quarreling with one another.

The girls felt lost, moving aimlessly from one corner of the square to another.

"Oh, God!" cried Maria. "I can't walk anymore. Where are we going?"

"Yes, where are you going, girls?" they heard somebody say in Polish.

At the sound of their native tongue, they quickly turned their heads to face the speaker. There were two men; one older, while the other was around Maria's age.

"We're lost! We don't know where to go! We're going to join the Polish Army."

"Look at them, son," the older man said to his companion, winking humorously. "Look at the new recruits."

Both of the men were dressed in tattered clothes, their faces pale and bony. It was obvious that they also had been prisoners.

"You should go to the Polish Consulate instead of the Army," the older man told them. "Just a few blocks over there."

They set off again, dragging their feet, and soon found the building. It wasn't difficult, because it had a huge sign, in Polish and in Russian, "The Polish Consulate". It was besieged by ragged people of all ages. The line was at least three blocks long. The girls were stunned.

"It will take two whole days and nights to get there," said Helena.

Maria was silent. They stood there, not knowing which way to turn or what to do. Maria started to cry. At the same time her legs gave way and she collapsed on the street. Helena tried to lift her. She was desperate, knowing that her sister had reached the end of her endurance.
"Look who's here," she heard a familiar voice say. Looking around, she saw the two men they had met a little while before.

"She's our new recruit, isn't she?" Seeing Maria's crumpled body, the man's tone became serious. "Is your sister sick?"

"No! Yes! Well, I don't know. She just collapsed, sir," Helena said. "She is very, very tired, sir," she added.

"Aren't we all? I'll get some help," said the older man, pushing himself back into the crowd. The youth followed him like a puppy. Soon they were engulfed in the mass of people.

Helena felt her lips tremble as she sat close to her sister. She didn't know how long she sat there. All of a sudden, the people were pushed aside and two men appeared. Without speaking, they lifted Maria onto the stretcher and, nodding to Helena to follow them, proceeded toward the Consulate.

Passing through the corridor of the consulate, Helena was surprised to see the men they had met before. The older man led them to the Infirmary, where he told the doctor to take care of Maria.

"Yes, General, sir!" The grey-haired doctor snapped back, rushing toward Maria.

Leaving Maria with the doctor, the man led Helena to a large office, where he exchanged a few quiet words with an older woman sitting behind a desk.

Stroking Helena's hair, he bade her goodbye and left the office. "Poor orphans," he murmured, more to himself than to his young companion, stepping into the corridor.

Washed, dressed in clean clothes and fed, the sisters slept well that night. After a week of rest, Maria, being an adult, was assigned to work in the Consulate's kitchen and Helena was sent to the Polish orphanage next door.

Chapter Nine

On the evening of March 17, 1942, Jan's regiment boarded the train for Kermine, a town about 75 kilometres west of Bukhara. Kermine, Jan soon learned, was the base for the Polish Seventh Division, which included, among others, Jan's Artillery Regiment. If he had stayed a month longer in Bukhara, the chances were he would have found his sisters. He asked anyone who would listen to him about his family, but the answers were always „I don't know", "never met", "never seen them"...

He had asked his commanding officer, Captain Szober for permission to go to Bukhara, which was the main recruiting centre for Polish soldiers and the transit base for civilians. However, he was told that there was a strict order not to allow soldiers to leave Kermine Base because they were being trained for combat.

In the meantime, long marches, parades and so on occupied his days, although evenings were free. It was during these free evenings that thoughts of his family invaded his mind. He also thought about the army. He remembered the moment when, trembling from excitement and weakness, he had stood before the Recruiting Commission.

Assisted by the two mustachioed sergeants, a doctor had poked at his ribs, ordering him to lift one leg then another, open his mouth, etc. He recalled his visit to Pinsk with his father, where he had seen horses treated the same way. If he hadn't felt so miserable, he probably would have laughed, but as it was, he just stood there, submitting passively to their examination.

Jan had been assigned to the Artillery Regiment, and to his great consternation, found himself to be the shortest man in the battery.

'I am probably the smallest artillery man since Napoleon,' he thought, observing others, who even though gaunt, were nevertheless much taller and older. He calmed himself, however, with the thought that even though he was the smallest, he was also the fastest.

Still, he didn't like the way these men looked at him. There was obvious irony in those smiles. "Well," he said to himself, "I'll show you... you big oxen... I'll show you!"

Now, sitting under a large tent, Jan couldn't help but notice that each of his army colleagues was either scratching his body or killing lice. He was doing it himself. He wondered how widespread the infestation really was. The lice were in his shorts, pants, hair and even under his skin.

Showers twice a day and clean clothes didn't seem to help at all. The army and thousands of Polish civilians camped close by were at war with the lice. The lice were not only in their clothes, but in train cushions, in soft-covered restaurant chairs, on toilet seats, in public baths - in short, wherever there were Soviet inhabitants, there were lice.

"No soap!" Jan was told by a soldier from the Sanitary Company, when he asked for an explanation regarding the infestation. It was true. So far, he hadn't seen a single piece of soap in the Soviet Union.

A grim, daily procession of soldiers carrying the coffins of dead comrades and civilians who had died of typhoid fever, convinced Jan that the lice were definitely on their enemy's side.

Jan helped with hundreds of such burials, almost twenty per cent of the regiment. Some of the soldiers who were ordered to bury civilians confessed to Jan that their task was easy. "Their coffins are mostly small and very light."

In spite of hunger and general weakness, Jan had to participate in an intensive training program. Marching in formation, running, jumping over obstacles under the command of corporals and sergeants exhausted him. But in spite of this rigour, he was happy to be free, preparing to fight the Germans.

But his happiness was marred by his longing for his family. Again, he asked virtually everybody about his grandparents and sisters. He wrote to the Polish Command Headquarters, but the answer was always the same: "We don't know." 'Holy Mary, Our Merciful Mother, take care of my family...' Jan often prayed.

His happiness was also marred by the thought of his companions from the prison camp. Sometimes at night, he would dream of them; the sadly smiling and wise face of Rettinger, the child-like face of the Russian, of Tatar, Gregory and the hopelessly sad face of Sciopa. Who had rolled down the mountain slope into the abyss? Who had survived? Where were they now?

In Afghanistan, Iran? Did they all die on that mountain?

On the night of April 2, 1942, the Battery was told to be ready to move out in one hour. They were marched to the Kermine Railway Station in silence and ordered onto the train. Following the Trans-Caspian Railway southwest, the train arrived at the Caspian seaport of Krasnovodsk. Jan was glad to leave the Kermine Base, which had become a large, sandy cemetery for his countrymen. The cool breeze from the sea was soothing his shattered nerves.

Subsequent events happened so fast that there was little time for reflection. At the end of the day, the soldiers were fed a good meal and then loaded onto an old ship. It was only when they were far from the shore of Turkestan, that they were told over a loudspeaker that they were among the lucky few to leave the Soviet Union. They were told they were heading to Iran to join their British Allies.

Jan wasn't surprised that these soldiers and civilians (mostly women and children) heading toward freedom did not cheer the news. They were silent and sad, with tears rolling down their wasted cheeks. Their eyes were not turned toward Iran and freedom, but instead they looked back toward the Soviet Union, where their fathers, mothers, sisters, brothers, sons, and daughters lay; some buried in the Siberian permafrost, some in the sand dunes of Uzbekistan and some not buried at all, their bodies thrown from trains into ditches, rivers, and lakes. There was no joy in Jan's heart either. Leaning over the railing to hide his tears from the others, he cried.

Half of the world's armies had passed through the town of Pahlavi at some time or another; some were friendly, most hostile. Pirates, vagabonds, fortune hunters, adventurers, the town had seen them all. The Pahlavians were astounded to see thousands of wasted men, women, and children, in tattered clothes, weak and sick. It looked as though Allah had ordered the Devil to open the gate of hell, allowing only the poorest and the most destitute to get out.

It became a common sight in that memorable April of 1942 to see hundreds and hundreds of coffins carried by soldiers, day after day, toward a newly established Christian cemetery. Mainly the children and older people died. Their exhausted and starved bodies, ridden by infectious diseases, couldn't absorb the abundance of food and collapsed almost instantly.

The Pahlavians were surprised that many Polish soldiers and civilians, upon touching land, knelt and kissed the ground. They knew nothing about the old Polish tradition wherein kneeling and kissing foreign soil upon arrival displayed the friendship and good will of the visitors.

The soldiers were issued new British uniforms, boots, shorts, and khaki shirts. More important, they were issued soap; for the first time since Jan had left Zamosze, he was free of lice.

Jan was haunted by the thought of his family. As days passed and his health improved, he felt that he must go back, find his family and bring them to freedom. He went to see his chief commanding officer. The colonel listened to Jan's story and signed deeply.

"Look," he said to Jan, "there are things in this life that neither you nor I can help." Then, seeing Jan's miserable face, he added, "You should never lose hope."

Jan left the officer's tent and stood motionless for a long time. Soldiers were singing nearby. "Sure," he said to himself, "I should never lose hope, but hope alone is not enough. I must act." He walked away from the camp, toward the Caspian Sea. Gulls soared above, their shrieking noise making him irritable and jittery. What if he went back to the Soviet Union and tried to find his family? He would look in the Caspian area first, mainly in Uzbekistan, because sure, he reasoned, they must be somewhere in that area. He had heard from other soldiers that all the Polish prisoners had been moved there. So, he concluded, they must still be there, providing they had been released. He was walking along the beach to the wharf where a Soviet freighter was moored. Several sailors were hastily loading it.

"Hey, *Polachok*! (little Pole)," one of them yelled at Jan. "Do you have a cigarette?"

"Sure," Jan responded, handing him a pack of British V's.

"British cigarettes, eh?" commented the sailor, inhaling deeply.

"Sure, English," Jan answered, "and I have plenty of them." It occurred to him that perhaps he could try to return to the Soviet Union with the help of this talkative sailor. "Look, sailor," he said quickly, "I have not only cigarettes, but a watch too. Look, do you like it?" He pointed at the wrist watch he had bought recently in Pahlavi. "Would you like to have it?"

"Hmm, not bad. Swiss?"

"Swiss, of course. Twenty-one karats."

"It looks good, but..." the sailor hesitated.

"But what?"

"I have no money."

"It won't cost you anything."

"Ha, ha, don't play stupid with me, Polak. I may not be too smart, but I know that there is no such thing as nothing for a good watch."

"Well, there is something I want from you."

"Aha... I thought so. What is it?"

"Smuggle me back to the Soviet Union."

"What?" the sailor yelled in disbelief. "The Soviet Union! You crazy or what? You must be crazy. I thought that you Poles had enough of the Soviet Union."

"Not this Polak. I've had enough of the Polish Army and want to return to the Soviet Union."

"Now!" the sailor exploded with mirth, "that is the biggest pile of horse shit I ever heard!"

"No, but..." seeing a sentry approaching them, he suddenly was silent. Making sure that the sentry was at a safe distance, he put two fingers over his lips. They stood there in silence.

The sailor then waved Jan into the freight shed. "It will cost you fifty tumans and the watch," he whispered and then, as though an afterthought, he added, "and three packs of cigarettes."

Jan returned to camp, borrowed ten cherventsy from his friends and went back to the freighter. Adding his recent soldier's pay, he had altogether twenty-five cherventsy or an equivalent of two hundred and fifty rubles.

Darkness was approaching and the men were preparing for the night. Stretched in a long file, the soldiers were ready for the evening parade. Three times they were counted by the mustachioed sergeant and three times there was one short.

"Which one of you idiots is missing?" he roared like a lion. "One, two, three... the whore's sons!" the sergeant swore. "One, two, three..."

"The kid is gone," said Moritz, a toothless Jew, while chewing his bread.

"Stop the fuckin' chewing," yelled the exasperated sergeant.

"Nu, you vont me to choke?"

"I'll choke you with my own hands, one of these days!"

"Nu, so who will fight Hitler, if you will choke me?"

The soldiers roared with laughter, liking these exchanges between the bullying sergeant and little Moritz.

"The kid, what kid?" the sergeant wanted desperately to stick to the subject matter.

"Looks like Tabor, the little one," somebody said.

"I will break his tailbone!" the sergeant yelled.

"He ain't got none," somebody intervened in the singsong of Eastern Poland. They all laughed, including the old mustachio.

****

At that moment, Jan was approaching the freighter with apprehension and misgivings.

'Was he doing the right thing?' he wondered. He was deserting the Army, wasn't he? He knew the consequences. Yet, he had to make a choice. To hell with the army. A man must do what a man must. Will he find them? Dressed in civilian clothes, with a Soviet navy hat which he had acquired from an Iranian clothing shop, he could pass for a Soviet sailor, at least in the dark.

At the freighter, the Russian sailor was waiting for him. He talked to Jan loudly as they passed the guards, who, to his relief, paid no attention to them.

The sailor led the way to Jan's hiding place, collected half of the Iranian tumans and disappeared. Jan was supposed to give him the other half and the watch on the other side of the Caspian Sea.

When Jan became accustomed to the smelly darkness, his eyes fastened on numerous barrels, boxes and crates. One of the huge grain barrels was half full of rice. Jan decided that it would be more comfortable for him to sleep in that barrel. Sweating from the heat, he tried to stretch, but the barrel was a bit too small. Crouching as much as he could, he burrowed into the rice, trying to hide. Then he began to feel sorry for himself. No matter how hard he tried to think of other things, his cramped position made his army bed look more and more desirable. Finally, he dozed off until voices nearby awakened him. By the sound of their voices, there had to be two of them. They were no further, he guessed, than three metres away from the barrel. They were talking in low voices, but loud enough for Jan to hear.

"Hey, Styepan," he heard one of the men saying. "Do you have it?"

"Sure, Andrey, what else do you expect?"

"How much?"

"375 cherventsy." (10 rubles per chervenets).

"Is that all, you mother fucker? The gold was worth at least 500!"

"Cross my heart, Andrey, he gave me only 375."

"Lousy *Yevrey* (Jew)."

"Where will we stash it?"

"There, in that little box, Andrey."

"Safe?"

"Like in a Swiss bank."

"Jewish bank."

Jan, one eye at a crack in the barrel, saw them jamming some papers into a small box. "Where should we put this box?" he heard one of them ask.

"Good question. Oh, wait a minute. I think there, behind this big barrel, will be the safest." Jan frantically covered himself with the rice, leaving only his nose sticking out.

"Did you hear something?"

"I'm not sure."

"Let's check it..."

Jan stopped breathing, his sweating increased. But the sailors decided to stop searching and soon left the storage room. He climbed out of the barrel and found the little box. The box still smelled of herring, but inside he discovered what he was looking for, the money. He put it under his shirt, and returned to his barrel. "375 cherventsy!" he whistled. "That's a lot of money. Ten rubles for one chervenets makes, let me see..." he calculated in his mind and came out with a staggering sum of 3,750 rubles. "But that's close to five years' wages for a hard working Soviet labourer," he whistled again. He reflected, 'Maybe I shouldn't take this money after all. These poor suckers will miss it. Oh, to hell with them. I'll need this money, won't I? How am I going to find my family with no money? But still... you know the bloody life in the Soviet Union... maybe this money was needed to support a mother?... a wife?... Or a whore,' he added, trying desperately to justify his act.

'Don't steal. Never steal,' he heard his father's voice in his mind.

He and a few of his friends had been stealing apples from a villager's orchard. They didn't have to since they had as many of their own apples as they could eat. But the thrill of stealing...

Then one day they were caught. His father, red faced, gave him a severe belting, which hurt him of course, but it was his words which hurt the most: "You shamed me, son! You of all people. Rolling in your own apples..."

"But if I were hungry?" he managed to break through his father's tirade.

"Hungry?" his father seemed to be a bit perplexed. "Even if you were hungry," he finally said.

"But is it a sin to steal food if you are hungry?" Jan asked. He knew that what he had done was wrong, but it seemed to him that if he had had a good reason, it would have been justified.

"Yes, it is a sin."

"But why, father, why?"

"Because the person from whom you have stolen could be poorer than you... it... it is just like the neighbour from whom you stole these apples. He is poorer than us."

"But if you know that he is richer?"

"Oh, shut up," his father became angry again. "Richer or poorer, it is not for you to judge."

"It is not for me to judge," Jan sighed as he climbed from his barrel and put all the stolen money back in the box. He returned again to his barrel and lay there for what seemed to him an eternity. It was dark in his hideout, so he didn't know if it was night or day. All he knew was that he was hungry, and very, very thirsty. The sounds of the engine seemed to be slowing down, or was it just his imagination? Yes, it certainly was throbbing more and more slowly, then it stopped. The freighter had arrived at its destination, wherever that was. Finally, he heard footsteps, then he saw in the dim light penetrating from outside, a face peering into the barrel. At first, he was frightened, and then he recognized the voice of "his" sailor.

"Krasnovodsk," the man said in a whisper. "Go now, quickly! It is dark outside, but not before I collect my due." Jan gave him the rest of his tumans and his watch, and jumped out of the barrel.

"Thank you, sailor."

"Good luck, Polak."

Jan followed the sailor who, when he reached the deck, suddenly disappeared, as though he had evaporated. Jan left the ship, mingling with other sailors and walked away as speedily as he could. Only when he reached the street filled with people did he feel safe. He passed many men of his age, some in Polish or Russian uniforms. There were many civilians on the street as well. He stopped a Polish soldier and asked him for directions to the railway station. The station was swarming with Polish and Russian soldiers and civilians. He sat on an empty bench in front of the station and waited for the Bukhara train, because he had decided to check the Bukhara region first, since it was there that most of the Polish troops and civilians were concentrated. If he failed to find his family in or around Bukhara, then maybe he could find someone he knew. If he didn't find them, then he was ready to go to Nukhto-Ozyero, but find them he must. There was the usual commotion and rush to get aboard when the train arrived.

By noon the next day the train reached Bukhara. He felt weak from thirst and hunger. Dragging his feet, he approached a stand and bought a rucksack, then stopped at another stand to buy bread, cheese, and milk. First he drank all the milk. After the meal, he felt stronger and began his search. Twenty-five cherventsy became handy.

Again and again, he stopped people in tattered clothes, asking for the Tabors and the Dabrowskis.

The answer was always the same. "Don't know, don't know. Never heard of them." One old woman suggested he try Stalin's Collective Farm,

Lenin's Sovkhoz (government farm), or Tashkent City.

He decided to try the Polish Consulate first, but found it besieged by soldiers and civilians. He tried to push his way through but was cursed and threatened with violence. There was a feverish rush among the Polish soldiers and civilians. True, he thought, they all want to leave the Soviet Union as soon as possible, but what a rush! He overheard some conversation that worried him.

"The Soviets are changing their minds, I believe," a Polish soldier in British uniform said.

"In what regard?" asked the other soldier.

"They don't want us to go to Iran."

"Why?"

"Political! They probably want us to stay here."

"To do what?"

"To fight the Germans with them."

"But... I understood," the other soldier didn't like what he was hearing, neither did Jan so he came closer to the two speakers, "that the Soviets cannot supply us with the weapons and food."

"It's political, I'm sure."

"We have to get out as soon as we can."

"It looks like it, Stefek."
"But first," the man called Stefek said, "I must find my sister."

It was obvious to him that unless he found his family soon, none of them would ever get out of the Soviet Union.

"Jan!" He heard a thunderous voice from the crowd. Pushing people left and right was a tall soldier whose clothes hung on him loosely and shapelessly. They looked at each other.

"Plater!" Jan exclaimed, embracing his old friend. "Plater! Where did you come from?" As soon as he said it, Jan realized how silly his question was. He looked at Plater apologetically and wasn't surprised to see his friend's face, distorted in a grimace, but then he noticed that there was something evil in his face - extreme cynicism, or extreme irony?

"From the Garden of Eden, where else, hm? And you?" he asked.

When Jan told him that he had returned to the Soviet Union to look for his family, Plater was silent for a while, then said, "I think I have seen your sisters."

"You did," Jan jumped with excitement. "Where? When? Tell me!"

"I think I've seen them here."

"Bukhara! Here!"

"I saw them in the crowd, at least I think so."

"But Plater, for heaven's sake, why didn't you talk to them?"

"Why should I?"

"Because..." Jan stopped. This wasn't Plater, at least not the Plater he used to know.

"Maybe they've crossed the Caspian Sea already," grumbled Plater. "A convoy of ships left Krasnovodsk, about a week ago."

"Did you see my grandparents?"

"No."

"Or maybe they are still on one of those goddamned collective farms," said Plater. Then he added, "Most Poles who were released from the labour camps and prisons spent some time on the collective farms."

'Maybe! Maybe' Jan thought, feeling unhappy and at the same time angry at Plater. 'What in hell is wrong with him?' he asked himself.

Plater talked and talked while they waited to get into the office. Jan was becoming completely frustrated by the delay. "Do you have a place to sleep?" he heard Plater ask.

"No, but that's all right." It was not all right, but he didn't want to feel helpless in front of this cynic.

"You can get a hotel room."

"Hotel? But that costs money."

"Money? Look!" Plater reached into his pocket and removed a huge bundle of cherventsy. Jan was astonished. Plater's bundle was by far fatter than the one the Soviet sailors were hiding in the barrel.

When the Polish Consulate closed its doors at 6 p.m., hundreds of frustrated people, including Jan and Plater, had to leave. Jan, having no place to stay, hesitantly accepted Plater's invitation.

They registered in the "Moskva" hotel, the plushest hotel in Bukhara. However, when Jan lifted the soiled sheet, he saw the mattress was full of holes. Plater's wasn't any better.

They went down to the tea shop and ordered the only food that was available, cabbage soup. Plater excused himself for a few minutes and returned with a little parcel under his arm. It turned out to be a bottle of vodka, which he promptly opened. It was only when Plater had emptied his third or fourth glass that he started to talk. He talked continuously until dawn arrived. Jan had thought his experience in the Soviet Union had been bad, but in comparison to Plater's, it had been child's play.

The panorama of Kolyma, as unveiled to him by Plater, was a horror of horrors. He sat there stunned, doubt and disbelief in his eyes. Now he understood the reason for his friend's transformation and was sorry.

"The strangest thing, though," Plater resumed his monologue over their breakfast of tea, the only thing available for breakfast. "The strangest thing," he repeated, "was when the administrators of the Kolyma camp were told to release us Poles. They went mad. They beat us day and night, stalling our release. No doubt hoping that we would all die, you see. The dead do not talk, do they? And indeed many of us died. I would have died too - they did their best in my case - if I hadn't had my little scheme to support my failing body. By then, you see, my best friend in Kolyma was the camp's cook. I told him in plain Russian (even though the s.o.b. was Latvian) that either he would give me some extra food regularly, or he would have an accident. He had an accident that very same day. My partners, two husky Mongols who happened to be the kitchen helpers, broke the cook's left leg. Accidentally, of course. Then... what was I saying? Oh, yes, then the Polish emissaries became more and more persistent. They intervened in Moscow on our behalf, so eventually they had to release us. A few of us, mind you, but they had to..."

"When did you arrive here?" asked Jan.

"Oh, about a month ago, but I joined the army only last week."

"Why only last week?"

"Because I was busy."

"Busy?"

"Yes, busy."

"Oh!"

"Tomorrow, however, I must join my squad. Plater should become a soldier. It has been decided," he smiled crookedly.

"Where is your... um... squad?"

"I don't know but I shall find it. And you, Jan, what are your plans?"

'Good question,' Jan thought. The truth was he didn't know what he should do now. Plater thought he had seen his sisters but then again maybe he hadn't. He couldn't possibly leave the Soviet Union with such uncertainty. He must exhaust every means to find them or find somebody who knew for sure what had happened to them. No, he could not leave yet, even if he wanted to.

They talked for a long time. This time it was Jan who related his experiences to Plater. Plater listened, Jan had to admit, but he wondered about his friend's ironic smile. The story of stealing the commissar's bread and lard resulted in Plater's ironic look, as though, Jan thought, he wanted to say "big deal" or "come on man, this is kid's stuff." Jan's tales about Rettinger and Jan's admiration for this wise man were dismissed by Plater by "another smartass Jew, eh?" That remark angered Jan.

"Rettinger saved my life, Plater. As for being a Jew..."

"Okay, okay," interrupted Plater, "so he was a good Jew." Jan gave up.

"Good luck, Plater," he said sadly as they parted that day. He didn't really know why he was so sad; after all, his friend had made him angry more than once. Yet he was sad. Following the slightly stooped silhouette with his eyes, he almost cried with compassion. "Good luck, you poor fool," he whispered after his departing friend.

After a cup of tea in another nearby tea shop, he decided to visit the near-by farm called "The Lenin Collective". His choice of farm was simple; it was the closest to Bukhara, only 10 kilometres. He made it in less than two hours, walking briskly in the afternoon sun.

It turned out to be a useless effort. He was told by the chairman of the farm, speaking in broken Russian, that yes, they had had some Poles, but none of them fitted the description of Jan's family. Jan asked the Uzbek whether he still had a list of the names of these Poles.

"No, why? They came and went, except for those..." he pointed with his brown finger toward the nearby field.

"What's there?" Jan asked.

"Cemetery."

"May I see it?"

"Sure."

He walked to a little sand dune where he noticed a row of crosses mark-ing graves. There were eighteen graves, some marked by crosses, others marked only by boulders, and who knows, maybe some didn't have markers at all.

Dry sage brush blown by the winds raced ahead of Jan as he walked back to the village. A caravan was entering the village. The Uzbek on the front camel, only his eyes visible through the cloth that swathed his face, was singing a familiar desert song. The sad melody floated over the cemetery, the village and beyond.

Jan returned to Bukhara. The uncertainty was awful; was his family alive or... After spending a sleepless night on a park bench, he was on his way to "The Stalin Collective" before the sun rose. He walked through the quiet countryside but, in his state of mind, noticed nothing. By noon he reached the farm. He was exhausted and incredibly thirsty. "Are some Poles left in your collective?"

"No. They've all gone."

"Do you have a list of their names?"

"No, we haven't."

"Two girls and old grandparents?"

"No."

"Cemetery?"

"Yes, there."

Again the rows of unmarked graves...only far more of them. Under closer scrutiny, he noticed that one of the graves had some faded markings that might have been a star, but he wasn't really sure of it. "Typhoid fever," he was told by the farm manager, the only person with whom he could communicate.

On his way back, he passed a small hut which he probably wouldn't have noticed but for a skinny donkey which, with his head in the doorway, was braying continually.

For six days, he walked from one collective to another, but learned nothing. Fortunately, in his haste to return to the Soviet Union, he hadn't changed his boots. His British boots, comfortable, and above all, strong, withstood all his walking.

'Blessed be the British shoemakers,' he thought with a smile. He quenched his thirst at the farm wells and occasionally was able to buy a *lyeposhka* (flat bread made from either millet or barley) or when he was lucky, a *shashlik* (a sort of Uzbekistanian shishkebob).

After visiting virtually all the nearby farms, he decided to take the train to Tashkent, the capital city of Uzbekistan, and a caravan town, Kagan. He asked everyone he could - civilians, Polish and Russian soldiers - about his family, but the answer was always the same.

"*Nye znayou.*" (Russian: I don't know). "*Nye vyem.*" (Polish: I don't know).

Jan received silent and often hostile treatment from the Uzbeks, wandering Turkmen and Kazakhs. He returned to Bukhara, penniless, thirsty and hungry, but what was worse, dejected and broken in spirit.

Maybe he should take the train going up north. Maybe his family had never left Nukhto-Ozyero. Perhaps he should go back to the Polish Consulate again. Throngs of people or not, he must try again. After standing in a long line from early morning he was, to his relief, admitted by late afternoon. Little did Jan know then that Maria was working in the kitchen at this very Consulate and that Helena was in the orphanage right next door to where he stood. A woman in her late 50's received him. Her tired face was filled with pity.

"Son," she addressed Jan, smiling sadly. "You are asking an impossible question."

"But..."

"You have seen outside, haven't you... We have thousands of people to deal with. How can we remember?"

"But... do you have a list of those who were evacuated?"

"No, it would take a ton of paper to make such a list."

"So, what do you do with these... here," Jan waved his hand around.

"We send them to Krasnovodsk, and hope that the Russians will supply us with boats."

Jan was silent. Behind him, the line of people was impatient.

"Get going, man!"

"You don't have all day, you know."

"Go to Krasnovodsk! Go now. Get out of here as fast as you can, please!"

'Why such urgency?' Jan thought when he was on the street again.

"The last boat! The last boat!" some people shouted. He moved closer, listening to every word. It didn't take him long to understand that the Russians would allow only one more ship to cross the Caspian Sea. It became clear to him that unless he wanted to stay in the Soviet Union, he must go to Krasnovodsk as soon as possible. He would have to make a decision, stay in the Soviet Union and search for his family, or leave for Krasnovodsk and freedom.

He decided to go to Krasnovodsk, hoping to God that Plater had been right when he told him that he had seen his sisters.

Jan rode all night on an incredibly overcrowded train. Krasnovodsk was swarming with Polish soldiers and civilians. There was an air of urgency in the city. People were pushing in a great throng toward the harbour. Most walked, but Jan noticed that some were carried. In the distance he could see a large boat, whistling intermittently.

Every girl and every old man and woman in the throng reminded Jan of his family. Eventually, exhausted, he sat on a boulder with his face buried in his hands, trying to shut out the sights and sounds.

"Cigarette?"

Opening his eyes, Jan saw a Polish soldier standing in front of him. The man was short, in his forties, Jan thought, and, like everyone else, pitifully thin. The hand in which he held a package of cigarettes was trembling.

"Going on that ship?" he pointed toward the harbour.

"Ship?" Jan asked.

"Yes, ship!" The man sat down beside Jan and exhaled smoke with a sigh.

"This is the last one."

"So I understand," responded Jan with difficulty.

"We are leaving this hell-hole, after all." Without waiting for Jan's reply, he continued. "It is a happy moment, yet a sad one too, to... to leave this... inhuman land." Jan was silent. "I should be happy, but I'm not," the man persisted.

"Why not?" Jan asked, just to be polite.

"If only I didn't have to leave my family behind." He pointed his bony finger toward the desert stretching beyond Krasnovodsk.

"You left your family behind?"

"Seven. Six children and my wife. They are all there, buried."

"Oh!" exclaimed Jan. "I am sorry."

"And you?" the soldier asked. "Did you leave your family there?"

"Yes, two sisters and my grandparents."

"Dead?"

"I don't know."

"You are lucky," he replied, rising to his feet and walking toward the ship. People were struggling and pushing to get on board. Jan moved with the throng. On board, he found a little space near the bow, sat and closed his tear-filled eyes.

Chapter Ten

Rettinger, grasping his head in both hands, sat on a boulder as though paralyzed. A few paces away, between two slight lips of rock, lay Tatar and Andrey, breathing heavily. A cold wind was whistling, making them shiver. Rettinger tried to think, but his thoughts were confused.

He remembered that they had been moving up, climbing one at a time, searching for any foothold to protect the vulnerable climber below. They had perched in order on the rope, Rettinger and Andrey occupying the higher ledge, Tatar and Gregory the middle, Sciopa and Jan the lower. Climbing without pitons to secure themselves and their meager belongings was extremely difficult and often treacherous. Nevertheless, Rettinger recalled he had managed to reach his stance and secure his end of the rope around a protruding rock. Tired, he was about to sit down when he heard shouting, tumbling rocks... then an ominous silence.

He tried to shout, but could only whisper. He stood there in the moonlight, petrified. It took him a long time to notice that he wasn't alone. Andrey and Tatar were standing in front of him like two monuments, staring at him in silence.

"We lost them," Tatar said softly.

"All three of them fell into the crevice," Andrey said in a monotone.

The two joined Rettinger and they all sat on the huge rock.

Rettinger couldn't sleep that night so he sat until morning. Guilt was exploding inside his heart. 'What right,' he thought, 'had I to lure others to escape with me, especially that young boy, Jan. He wasn't quite eighteen yet. Poor Jan! Why him? Oh, God.'

At dawn, he awakened the big Russian and Tatar and asked them to follow him. He must see what had happened to his friends.

First, they found poor Sciopa, his head smashed to a pulp. Then, only about ten feet away was Gregory's shattered body. "Where is Jan?" asked the big Russian, trembling. They checked every depression, every rock and bush, but couldn't find Jan's body. They descended, step by step, until they reached the edge of the rocky precipice, but there was still no sign of him.

Below them, there was an abyss, dark and endless. The stone thrown by Tatar fell forever and ever before it hit the bottom. They didn't speak. Their eyes told all.

They buried Sciopa and Gregory in a small depression, covering their bodies with rocks and grass. It was only then that they noticed several vultures hovering overhead, as though waiting for their departure.

They drew on all their reserves and resumed their climb. By sundown, they had reached a plateau or mesa, which soon merged with a wide, gently rolling valley. They mobilized all their strength and walked as fast as they could. Soon they spotted a cluster of buildings overlooking a small mountain brook.

"Looks like a sheep collective," observed Tatar.

"Who cares whether it is a sheep collective or not? There are people there," said Andrey.

"Yeah, sure, people and the K.G.B.!" cried Tatar, spitting. "And it is the K.G.B. we should avoid."

"K.G.B. or not, we need food," observed Rettinger, "and we must get it somehow."

They decided to wait and try to reach the farm at night. Finding a sandy spot, they fell to the ground and tried to rest for at least a few hours.

It was dark when they crept toward the farm buildings. The absence of light in most of the buildings suggested that it was late and, except for the barking of dogs, the farm was quiet. After circling for a while, they found a building which had a large wooden door with a padlock.

"It must be the food storage building," whispered Tatar.

"How do you know it's food?" asked Andrey. "Maybe tractors, or maybe..."

"Maybe, maybe," jibed Tatar. "There are no maybes here. I smell sauerkraut... I can smell anything, but especially cabbage."

"Let's break the padlock," decided Rettinger, but soon realized that they had no equipment to do it.

"Wait a minute," said Andrey quietly, "I think I saw a pile of lumber nearby. Let me..." he turned around and found three rifle muzzles pointed at him.

They were forced to walk until they reached a large building, where they were separated and put into cells. It was a lonely December night for the captives. Rettinger immediately fell upon the straw-covered floor and tried to sleep.

Memories, like an avalanche, invaded his tired head, most of them uneasy and some even tragic. The memory of his childhood in Krakow. His wise father and gentle mother, who, poor as they were, had somehow found money to educate him. The memory of becoming a university teacher, too late for his father and mother to see his achievements and to be proud of them. Then his marriage and son. His son must now be seventeen, like Jan, smart for his age. The memory of Isaak, his son, brought tears to his eyes.

1939, the war, and the German occupation. The family had run eastward as far from the Germans as possible. They had escaped from the Germans, but had fallen into the hands of Russians. One February morning, the K.G.B. arrested all three of them.

"Don't separate us, please," he had pleaded, "we are a family! Let us stay together..." The memory brought more tears to his eyes. But they scattered them over the vast Soviet land.

The Soviet judges sentenced him to 25 years of hard labour. "For what?" he had asked them naively.

"Anti-state activity," they had told him.

His train of thought was interrupted by the sudden entrance of two uniformed men. They handcuffed him and put him on a freight train. He was surprised to have the whole freight car to himself and wondered what had happened to his companions. After a day and night, the train stopped. The door to his freight car was opened, and he was escorted to the station by two heavily armed men. The inscription on the station building told him he was in Tashkent.

'So I am in Uzbekistan,' he thought. He was pushed into a 'Black Raven', and after half an hour, he was told to get out. He found himself in front of a huge grey building, surrounded by a wall. Once inside, he was taken to a steam bath, his hair was cut and he received a clean, roughly pressed jail uniform. The cell he was placed in was also clean with a comfortable bunkbed fixed to the wall. At first, he was pleased at the cleanliness of the cell and his clothes, but after a while, he became perturbed.

'Why such civilized treatment?' he wondered. His surprise increased even more when the guard brought him a meal: soup, almost half a loaf of bread and meat, with mashed potatoes and vegetables. It was the meat that bothered him most. During his stay in the Soviet Union, he had forgotten what meat looked like, but here was a big chunk of beef.

After three days, this royal treatment abruptly ended. He heard the door and two huge guards entered his cell. He was curtly told to follow them. They passed numerous cells located on both sides of the corridor. At the end of the corridor they turned left, then left again until they reached a large iron door over which there was a brass plate with the inscription: "Colonel Ivan Ivanovich Fedorov, The K.G.B."

They entered a large, well-lit office. It was sparsely furnished; a desk, a small sofa, four chairs and a bookshelf with a dozen or so books. Behind the desk sat a middle-aged man in a well-tailored and well-pressed uniform. His sharp facial features and Semitic nose suggested that the man was not a Slav. 'A Jew?' Rettinger asked himself with a ray of hope in his heart. The man was smiling at Rettinger, scrutinizing him closely, as though trying to assess what kind of species he was.

"Cigarette?"

"No. Thank you."

"Coffee?"

'Coffee?' thought Rettinger. He would sure like to have some, but instead he heard himself saying, "No, thanks."

"Please have some, really. It is good British coffee." The Colonel's voice was pleasant and well-accented.

"No, thank you," Rettinger repeated. "Even if it is British," he added.

"You don't miss British coffee, Rettinger?"

'The bastard knows my name... but why this emphasis on British coffee?' thought Rettinger.

"When did you leave Britain?"

"Britain?"

"Yes, Britain. You are British, Rettinger, we know it."

"I am not British, Colonel."

"What are you then?" The Colonel leered.

"A Polish citizen."

"You are a British Jew, Rettinger!" The Colonel's voice rose a few octaves.

"No, I am a Polish Jew."

"What was your mission, Rettinger?"

"Mission? What mission?"

"Don't play stupid. You are a British spy."

"A spy? I am not a spy and never have been."

"Come on, Rettinger! We know all about you, so don't lie to me."

"If you know everything about me, then you know that I have nothing to do with the British - or any other - government."

"You are lying! Admit it, goddammit!"

"I can't admit something I didn't do."

"Admit it, Rettinger. This is just a formality. Then after you sign this paper, we will send you back to England as an exchange."

"No!"

"Rettinger, are you a Jew?"

"Yes."

"I am a Jew also. We are treated well here." Receiving no response from Rettinger, he gestured toward the guards and ordered them to take the prisoner back to his cell.

Rettinger was interrogated every day, and often at night. The accusation was so ridiculous that Rettinger was sure even Colonel Fedorov didn't believe it. In fact, the colonel occasionally displayed a certain amount of sympathy and seemed to welcome the encounters with Rettinger. It occurred to Rettinger that perhaps the colonel was glad to have an opportunity to exercise his intellect. This was borne out when he was brought to the colonel's office one night. The colonel ordered the removal of Rettinger's handcuffs, and offered him a pot of tea.

"Look, Rettinger," he started. "Let's speak freely and off the record."

"Sure."

"What do you think about the Soviet Union?"

'What is he after?' Rettinger wondered, surprised, but decided to tell him the truth. "Not much," he said.

"I thought so. Why?"

"Because this country's government is not serving its people, but the reverse is true."

"Really?"

"Yes. And furthermore, from what I've seen, life here is based on fear: parents are afraid of being denounced by their children; neighbours are afraid of each other; you, Colonel, are afraid of your superiors and probably your friends... maybe even your own wife..."

"Shut up!"

"I thought I could speak freely."

"Well, go on, go on."

"Suspicion is your national motto, it seems. Take me, Colonel. I am accused of being a spy... You and I both know I'm not."

"When we say you are a spy, then you are a spy!"

"There you are, Colonel. I must prove that I am not a spy, whereas in the civilized world..."

"The so-called civilized world wants to destroy us."

"One day you will realize, Colonel, that the greatest enemy of your people is the system itself."

One night, Rettinger was told "the holiday is over" and he must sign his confession one way or another. Another way was, of course, beatings.

"Sign! Sign, you dirty swine! I, David Rettinger, a member of the British..." Then the brutal beatings started, but he refused to sign.

Many times, he was carried from the interrogation office on a stretcher, and lay unconscious for hours.

Then suddenly, there was a two-day lull. 'Maybe it is all over,' he thought. 'Maybe they will leave me in peace or, more likely, they will shoot me.' He felt very weak. The beatings and lack of food were telling on him. What was worse, he reflected, his spirit was weakening. He felt terribly alone, abandoned and dehumanized. The treatment he had received made him feel like a cornered animal.

Despite the pain, he raised himself on the bunk and, nodding rhythmically, started to pray. His prayer was interrupted by a guard who entered the cell and barked an order to follow him. Entering the interrogation room, Rettinger was taken aback when he saw his two friends standing there. Both were handcuffed.

Rettinger's eyes first fell upon the big Russian. The skin on his face had been torn by some sharp instrument and was now hanging in strips in several places. Suliman's face resembled a rotten beet, and one of his eyes was bandaged. There was an ominous silence in the room. The interrogating Commissar's eyes darted from prisoner to prisoner, curious about the reaction this confrontation would bring. The three bulldog-like guards were standing waiting for their master's order to jump on their victims.

"Now, Rettinger," the Commissar began smoothly, "you can't deny your spying activities."

"You! Big ox!" he addressed the big Russian. "Tell us who you are."

"I am a British spy!" the big Russian said with a choking voice, averting his eyes from Rettinger.

"And you?" he turned to Tatar.

"I am a British spy, too."

Rettinger was too surprised to react. He just stood there. 'Oh, my God,' he thought. 'This is incredible.'

The Commissar read a prepared statement by the two prisoners, a detailed document about the spying expedition led by David Rettinger. At the end of the statement there was a paragraph in which these two men begged the people of the Soviet Union to forgive them for their crimes. The two men, still averting their eyes from Rettinger, were taken away and Rettinger was asked to take a seat.

The Commissar was very polite. "And now, comrade Rettinger," he said softly, offering a cigarette which Rettinger refused. "And now," he continued, "all we have to do is sign here! This little scrap of paper. It is just a formality."

"No!" yelled Rettinger with strength that surprised him.

"No? But that is stupid! Stupid!" cried the enraged Commissar.

Rettinger was taken back to his cell, this time without being tortured. He was surprised and then again he wasn't because by now he knew that anything was possible in this land.

He recalled the big Russian and Suliman giving their testimony. 'So,' he thought, 'they were told they must confess that they were spies or die. Now, because they have confessed that they are spies, they will die anyway.'

As if in response to his thoughts, he heard a noise in the corridor. For some reason, his cell door had been left ajar. So, curious about the noise, he went to the door and saw, to his horror, his two friends being dragged along the floor by the two guards. They were pulling the victims by their feet, their heads bumping along the floor like bags of potatoes.

Passing Rettinger's cell, they slowed down, giving him a chance to recognize his friends, or what was left of them. Both men were bleeding copiously, leaving a trail of blood behind them on the stone floor.

"*Oh, Bohze* (Oh, God)," the big Russian moaned. Suliman's body was limp. This horrible parade turned down the corridor which led to the basement. He remembered now that during his interrogation, one of the Commissars had threatened him with a visit to the basement. He had not paid too much attention at that time to the full meaning of the 'basement', but now the thought sickened him.

He was startled from his numbness by two dry, cracking sounds as though someone wearing heavy boots had stepped on hazel nuts. Then there was silence.

Rettinger's interrogation continued and the beatings intensified in frequency. Driving toothpicks under his finger nails, kicking and twisting his testicles, and employing high-frequency sounds in his cell were only a few of the tortures.

Still, he would not sign.

Rettinger understood that in the minds of his torturers, the execution of his friends was supposed to soften him, causing him to confess. They had spared his life precisely because he hadn't confessed. Thus, in spite of his pain and suffering, he was determined not to sign the confession.

In constant darkness in his cell, he lost all sense of time. 'It must be the end of spring, or maybe it is already summer,' he thought, looking at the barred and boarded-up window.

His health was failing. Diarrhea, chest pains and a diseased bladder had weakened his already emaciated body to a point where he had to be carried to the interrogation room. During one such interrogation, after being kicked in the groin and kidneys several times, he lost consciousness. Usually a bucket of water poured on his head revived him, but this time it wasn't enough. The interrogating Commissar ordered that he be taken to the prison hospital. There, the doctors, also prisoners, saved his life. Not so much because of their medical care which, being short of drugs and equipment, wasn't much, but because they persuaded the authorities to allow their patient to stay in the hospital.

It was during his third week in hospital that he heard from one of the doctors, who was also a Jew, that Germany had attacked the Soviet Union. Doctor Rosen was a Polish Jew from Warsaw who, like Rettinger, had escaped the Germans only to fall into Soviet hands. "Whoever wins this war," the doctor whispered to Rettinger, "what is there for us Jews?"

It was the doctor who brought the news about the amnesty for Polish prisoners. "We are free, free at last!" he cried.

"An English spy doesn't receive amnesty," Rettinger remarked, smiling.

"Oh, come on, all you have to do is prove you are a Polish citizen."

"How? I have no papers to prove it."

"Yes, that is a problem," the doctor agreed, but then he went to work. Dr. Rosen found two professors from Lvov who personally recognized that "Professor Rettinger was from Poland." It didn't work. Dr. Rosen then involved the Polish authorities, who, in turn, exercised pressure on the Soviets to free the prisoner. He even alerted the Polish politicians in London, but that didn't work either.

Then, one day Rettinger was brought in front of Colonel Ivan Ivanovich and told point blank that he would be released providing he would do "a small service for us."

"What service?"

"Well, we don't trust these little Poles, so you will keep an eye open on our behalf."

"Informant, eh? No!"

The Commissar, looking venomously at Rettinger, told him that he was free and could go to the devil. Next day, Rettinger was on his way to Bukhara in search of the Polish Army.

Chapter Eleven

By the end of the summer of 1942, when Rettinger was crossing the Caspian Sea with the last contingent of Polish troops, Jan was heading toward Iraq. A convoy of twenty military trucks, fifteen soldiers in each, followed the meandering dust-covered roads and crossed several stretches of salty deserts. They passed some scantily-vegetated oases, stopping only in two of them.

The English thermometers showed 130 degrees Fahrenheit in the shade, which, for the Polish soldiers accustomed to Celsius measurement was, at first, incomprehensible. However, the infernal heat spoke for itself, thermometer or not. Linen bags, filled with water, hung on both sides of the trucks in the hope that the wind, hot and dry though it was, would have some cooling effect upon the water. Jan's khaki shirt was covered with a thick layer of salt which chafed the skin on his back and shoulders. Fortunately, the nights were cool and Jan could have a good sleep, lying on the ground.

After returning from his unsuccessful trip to the Soviet Union in search of his family, he had rejoined his regiment.

His desertion from the army had fortunately been covered up by the regimental commanding officer, who, in an official statement, thanked Jan for "a well-accomplished mission", lauding his "courage and determination". There was not a word in the statement about Jan's search for his lost family. Now, sitting in the truck, swallowing dust and sweating, he thought about the last hectic three months. He recalled his few hungry days on the ship which had brought him back to Iran. He remembered the agony of leaving the Soviet Union without his family. His sense of loss would always remain with him.

"How can I ever return to Zamosze without them? What will I say to my father if I ever see him again?"

Jan was transferred to a special unit which consisted mainly of young, physically fit men who were, according to gossip, being trained for a special task. What kind of task, nobody really knew, except perhaps the senior officers. For the past three months, the unit had been subjected to a strenuous training of drills, marches, parades, target and bayonet practice, running, alarms - all under the blazing middle eastern sun.

At the beginning of fall, they had established their camp on the stony desert about 20 kilometres from the great petroleum centre, Mosul. The unit was comprised of two combat companies, 120 men in each company. The remaining 60 men or so had administrative functions - all in all, 300 men.

"You will be trained for special tasks," the commanding officer, a major, told them. "You are not infantry, artillery or cavalry men! You are a special commando unit which will be all of these!" He was silent for a while, to let the words sink in, and then he continued. "You will be trained to kill. To kill quickly, efficiently and without mercy." His pale blue eyes swept from one face to another. They were cool and hard. "Every soldier, of course, is trained to kill," he continued, "but this unit is different. You will trap the enemy or descend upon him when he least expects it. You will be parachuted in front of your enemies, behind them, and amidst them."

There were no questions. The soldiers were staring hard at their commander without moving a muscle. "For a start," he continued, "we will deal with the German paratroopers who, dressed as Arabs, are blowing up oil pipes and refineries even while I'm talking to you. It will be excellent training for you. The German paratroopers you will encounter are a well-trained and merciless lot. You must be tougher than they are and have no mercy for them."

Jan didn't like it at all. He knew, of course, that as a soldier he would have to kill, but this unit sounded like a bunch of assassins, cold-blooded murderers. He was very disturbed.

For the next few days, their training consisted of nothing more than marching, running, jumping over obstacles, and swimming in polluted creeks.

Then on one hot day, late in the afternoon, three military trucks unloaded a strange looking group of men. Some of these men, short, with yellowish skin and high cheek bones were Asiatics. "Ghurkas," somebody said, pointing at the little yellow men. A smaller number were young, blonde men, tall and husky, who turned out to be Englishmen. They were the new instructors, assigned to teach them the art of killing.

Training began the next day. Jan was fascinated by the strength and agility of the little Ghurkas. It was quite a surprise to see the young, strong Polish boys flying through the air and falling heavily on the sand. In make-believe combat, they were taught how to remove eyes, smash groins, tear out tongues. Slowly and painfully, Jan learned the art of hand-to-hand combat.

In the next phase of training, they were taught how to effectively use a knife and machete on make-believe enemies. Jan was terrified to see that one Ghurka with a knife in his mouth and a machete in his right hand, could, if necessary, overpower and even kill three of his "opponents". Even though he was apprehensive, Jan was learning quickly. Occasionally, the Ghurkas slapped him on the back, or shook his hand, saying "Good! Good!" as confirmation of his progress.

The English and Polish instructors taught them parachute jumping, machine gun and rifle shooting, map reading, explosives and the Arabic and German languages. Jan liked the Arabic language and learned quickly, enjoying the throaty sound.

After three months of training, they were sent to hunt for German paratroopers and spies. Jan felt strange and uncomfortable in the Arab turban that he wore to conceal his blonde hair. The intelligence sources had sent warning reports regarding increased activities by German saboteurs, who had already inflicted serious damage to several oil pipelines and had blown up one refinery in the area of Kirkuk and Mosuh.

These saboteurs, highly trained German paratroopers, were aided by dissident Arabs hostile to Britain and their own governments, or by unscrupulous mercenaries.

The Iraqi oil fields were the main German targets because they were important suppliers of crude oil. The Polish troops were to protect this vital source of power.

The group, during Jan's first 'hunting' expedition, was led by the very professional Sergeant Majewski. Jan liked the sergeant. He was thirty-five years old and 6'4" tall. He impressed Jan with his quiet behaviour and extraordinary physical strength.

The second-in-command was a short, wiry fellow, called Corporal Oprzedek, who, though he would never admit it openly, had been a member of the French Foreign Legion. The rumour was that, after murdering his wife, he had to run from his native town of Lvov, finding sanctuary in the French Legion. The presence of this quiet, hard-eyed man increased Jan's courage, since Oprzedek's knowledge of the desert was legendary. Oprzedek was also fluent in German and French. Jan was chosen because of his knowledge of Arabic.

Surprisingly, short, fat Kozak was the fourth choice. He was twenty-eight years old and totally bald. His bulb-like eyes in his round face showed fear, mockery and dog-like humility, all at the same time. A perpetual talker about his great deeds, full of humour, he was both liked and despised. Kozak had another unusual quality. He could imitate everything that moved or made sounds: men, beasts, birds.

Even now, riding his donkey behind Jan, he was singing a monotonous Arab song. It wasn't really a song, since Kozak didn't know Arabic, but the melody was authentic and it was sung in a beautiful tenor. The melody perfectly fit the surroundings of the desert they passed, reflecting its desolate monotony.

The song was suddenly interrupted by Kozak's imitation of a donkey braying. Jan could have sworn that it was genuine donkey's braying. Jan's donkey responded, confirming that Kozak's braying was indeed authentic.

The night was bright and cool. Listening to the rhythmic clopping of donkey hoofs and Kozak's wailing melody, Jan felt a part of this vast desert. They were passing a stretch of badlands, sculptured into bizarre forms by the winds. There were arches, cupolas, and long corridors. Gigantic heads stared at them as if displeased by the intrusion. The winds, trying to find an outlet, whistled eerily through the openings. 'How different from the marshes of my childhood,' he thought. And the people? While wandering through the desert in the past few months, he was stopped several times by Bedouins on horseback. Squatting on the sand or stone-covered surface of the desert, they had gladly shared their food with him: dates, dry mutton and goat's milk. The same, he reflected, as the Byelorussian hay mowers offering him water, black bread and milk when he and his sisters wandered in the marshes.

Jan was lost in thought when their little caravan stumbled onto an oasis. It wasn't much of an oasis. The ground water supported a few palm trees and five or six clay huts.

Sergeant Majewski led his cavalcade toward the largest of the huts at the edge of the oasis. The sergeant halted them and gestured that they move closer. In a whisper, he gave several rapid orders. Instantly, they dispersed. Kozak led his donkey to a palm tree about 30 metres away from the hut and, after tying it to a tree, squatted on the ground. Almost at once he started to sing, lauding Allah and thanking Him for the successful journey. It was a meaningless song, but Kozak managed to put in the word 'Allah' here and there. Then Jan realized that Kozak was interweaving Arabic words with obscene Polish and Russian sayings, and he had to make an effort not to laugh.

Majewski ordered Jan to follow him. Jan noticed Oprzedek leaning on the hut's wall, nonchalantly eating a date.

Jan and Majewski entered the hut, which served as a restaurant, hotel and social club to wandering herders. The herders, traveling with their flocks of sheep from wadi to wadi, used this kind of oasis to replenish their food supply, meet other herders and sometimes sleep overnight.

Upon entering the hut, they were met by the loud, guttural voices of Arab singing, coming from a huge, old radio in the corner. There were six turbaned men seated close to the radio, all holding small cups of steaming coffee and talking animatedly.

To their left, on a long bench, sat another three Arabs, tall and muscular. These three, unlike the others, were sitting quietly, their eyes scanning the smoky, semi-darkened room. Behind the bar was a short, fat Arab wearing an apron, serving coffee, dates, pomegranates, and dry mutton. Jan ordered coffee for each of them and they sat in the darkest corner of the hut.

"Those three there," whispered Majewski, "they're our birds." Jan glanced in the direction of the three Arabs. They did look different from the rest. In the dim light, their eyes seemed to be blue.

"Muhammed is great," they heard Kozak wailing above the noise in the hut. "I hope the bastard doesn't use Polish," whispered Majewski.

"We should capture the three fellows along the wall," Majewski said quietly. Then he added, "The more I look at them, the more I think that they're Germans."

"Probably, but... Well, we're not sure, are we?" They continued to sip their coffee.

"Let's go and take these three, Jan."

But Jan didn't think that this was a good idea. 'What will happen if the others are Germans and those three are not?' he thought.

"We'll take them all, sergeant," Jan said as he jumped toward the bar, the muzzle of his tommygun pointed toward the greatest concentration of Arabs. "Hands up!" he roared. He heard Majewski's whistle and, from the corner of his eye, he saw Oprzedek rush into the room with his tommygun in his hand.

One by one, the Arabs raised their hands, too terrified to argue. Taken by surprise, they offered no resistance. There was one man in the room whom they hadn't considered seriously enough. While the three Polish tommyguns were covering the Arabs in the room, the barman pulled out a gun. Jan was saved by the cool Oprzedek who, being positioned at the door, saw the barman's gun aiming at Jan's back.

A long, deafening series of bullets shattered the barman's head. He fell backward, crashing bottles and glasses.

In the confusion, two Arabs tried to reach the window, but were cut down by Majewski before they could move three steps. Jan ordered the remaining five Arabs to lie on the clay floor, face down. Almost at once they began to wail, calling Allah as their witness.

'Excellent Arabic, considering that they're bloody Germans,' Jan thought.

From outside, Kozak's wailing reached their ears, this time the words were nothing but Polish obscenities.

It was morning by the time they escorted the prisoners back to the base and, exhausted, went to sleep. Not for long, though, because they were awakened quite brutally by a sentry and told to report to the major. Something was terribly wrong.

"So you sons-of-bitches accomplished your mission, eh? You did, eh? And went to sleep happy, eh?"

"But sir..." Majewski sputtered.

"Shut up," the major yelled, thunder in his eyes. "You brought five Germans instead of eight..."

"Sir?"

"Yes, five Germans, and you killed a German officer."

"Officer?"

"Yes, sergeant, the fuckin' barman was a German officer."

'So what?' Jan thought.

The major, as though hearing Jan's thoughts, screamed, "Never kill an officer, you hear me? Never! We could have obtained so much information from him."

"But, sir... the barman... pardon me, the German officer was about to sh..."

"No buts, Sergeant. Next time, remember." Then he added, more quietly, "Any fool can shoot, but only a few can think."

"I guess we have to get used to all these shitty things, Jan," Majewski remarked, after they left the major's quarters.

Jan got used to it. He went on many other expeditions, some successful, some less so. In one such encounter, he killed his first man, in turn receiving a knife wound in the left arm and a gash on his face. He couldn't sleep for a week, remembering the last moments of the man he had killed. Sure, he knew how to kill quickly and mercifully, but still... in his heart, he felt sadness and guilt.

During the hot Iraqi evenings, he would walk alone into the desert, sometimes kilometres away from the camp. These solitary excursions had a soothing effect upon his soul, taking him away temporarily from military camp life and his conscience.

One night, he was walking into the desert over the sand dunes, boulders, and sharp stones. It was late, past eleven, but he continued to walk until the camp disappeared from view. Cool breezes brought relief from the earlier sizzling heat. The full moon cast enough light for him to see the arroyo he was approaching. He sat on a large boulder as comfortably as he could. It still retained some warmth from the day's heat.

"Oh, God," he moaned. "What is your will? Why did I have to kill that young German? He was my age... His mother is probably... Why am I here instead of in Zamosze? And that man I killed, maybe he wanted to be in Bavaria or Rhineland or wherever!"

"If you hadn't killed him, he certainly would have killed you," he remembered Sergeant Majewski's stern admonition.

"Kill or be killed, eh?" Somehow he couldn't accept it. He didn't exactly know why, but he couldn't.

Only two weeks ago, reports had come that the German paratroopers were about to blow up an oil refinery, close to the town of Khanakin. Since Jan's patrol consisting of 9 men in jeeps was only 3 kilometres away from the refinery, they were given orders to intercept and destroy the German commandos. The number of Germans was vague, but they were warned that there could be at least 15 men, heavily armed and well trained.

The Poles, led by Sergeant Majewski, their jeeps at full speed, had rushed toward the refinery. Just in time, because the Germans, blowing up the iron gate, were ready for an "anshlous" on the refinery itself.

The Germans met them with a volley of fire. Two Poles in the first jeep were killed instantly; another jeep was set afire. Covered by the machine guns in the two remaining jeeps, five of them, tommyguns in hands, advanced toward the Germans. The German commandos fought well. It took them only a minute or two to realize that their safety was in break-through tactics. With automatic pistols in hand, they moved toward Majewski's men. Judging from the intensity of fire, he estimated at least a dozen men were advancing toward them. The fire from the Polish jeeps at first checked their advance, then those who were still alive sprang to their feet and ran forward.

In the full moonlight, Jan suddenly saw a huge turbaned man, firing a machine gun and advancing toward him. Jan pulled the trigger and by all logical explanation, his bullets should have found their target, but the advancing German made an amazing somersault and rolled down the hill like a ball. Jan sent another, then another series of shots, but the man, like a gymnast, managed to avoid them all. Jan heard the familiar thud of a falling object coming from the direction of the enemy. 'Grenade!' he thought as he leapt to his feet, and then jumped aside. Not fast enough, however, because he felt pain in his left arm. He pointed his tommygun in the direction of the enemy, but, to his dismay, the tommygun didn't respond. In the meantime, the German paratrooper, after firing a few additional shots, also became quiet. By the sound of the bullets, Jan guessed that the enemy was only a few metres from him, but since he didn't know his intention, he lay quietly. He heard shooting, but decided it sounded as if it were far away. 'So,' he thought, 'it is you and me.' He was thinking of ways to outwit his enemy when he saw him rising to his feet.

Jan sprang to his feet as fast as he could and lunged at him. The man raised his automatic with the obvious intention of smashing Jan's head, but somehow lost his balance and fell to the ground. Jan was on him in that instant. Rolling in the desert dust and over the stones, uttering groans and curses, they fought. The German, freeing himself from Jan's grasp, reached for his throat. Then Jan produced his spring knife and pushed it with all his might into the man's stomach. The man screamed, jerked a few times, then lay silent.

Jan rose to his feet and looked at his enemy. The turban slipped from the man's head showing short, blonde hair. His eyes were staring at Jan as though full of reproach and sadness. The memory of those eyes would haunt him for a long, long time.

He shivered, as he always did recalling that night. The desert creatures were looking for their shelters, nestling under the boulders, tufts of vegetation or in the cracks of the earth. They had survived the day. The silence of the desert was profound. Jan rose, took a deep breath of the cool clear air, and started back toward the camp.

"I, too, survived the day," he whispered, lifting his head toward the stars. "Thank you for letting me be free. Free like this desert." His eyes moved over the dark, seemingly lifeless, surface of the desert.

From then on, Jan's life was divided between chasing German paratroopers, training and waiting. He was waiting for news from his family, thinking that maybe, just maybe, he would receive a letter. Others were getting letters; some from parents, wives, sisters, brothers or friends. But Jan had received nothing.

Chapter Twelve

While Jan was chasing the German paratroopers in the Iraqi desert, Rettinger, after two weeks in Habanya, the British Air Force Base in Iraq, was on his way to Palestine. His regiment, a part of the Fifth Division of Infantry, was glad to be leaving Iraq. The summer of 1943 had been particularly oppressive. At Lake Habanya, it was 130 degrees Fahrenheit in the shade, and the water was too hot even for swimming.

He was looking forward to seeing the land of his ancestors, his spiritual fatherland. Sitting in the big military truck, he leaned on his rifle and let his thoughts wander.

"Palestine!" The name itself created a strange feeling in his heart. "Palestine!" How many times he had heard this word spoken with reverence, respect, and warmth. His grandparents, friends, teachers and rabbis had told him, since he was a child, about the significance and glory of Palestine.

They reached the first kibbutz in three days. It was mid-afternoon when their trucks, cannons, carriers and tanks entered a wide street in the Jewish agricultural settlement. They were instantly surrounded by people of all ages. The farm workers had thrown down their implements and run toward the column of Polish soldiers. Rettinger was surprised that virtually all the settlers spoke Polish.

"Warsaw! Who is from Warsaw?" "Brest-Litovsk! Who is from Brest-Litovsk?" "Pinsk?" "Kobryn?" "Krakow?", they were shouting.

Rettinger jumped from the truck. He found himself in the arms of an old bearded man who embraced him, tears rolling down his cheeks. He was saying something to Rettinger half in Polish and half in Yiddish, but all Rettinger could understand was, "My little grandchildren, my poor little grandchildren. They are in Warsaw, my good sir, they are in Warsaw."

Rettinger understood what the old man was trying to tell him. He had already heard of what was going on in German-occupied Poland. He freed himself from the old man's embrace and walked along the street of the kibbutz. On both sides of the street were orange groves. "Do you know Sruel from Krosno? Did you meet Seliek from Lodz? Seliek the barber, everyone knew Seliek. You didn't see Yankiel? Yes, yes, Yankiel, the tailor. Oh, you know him, Oh God! Listen! Listen, he knew Yankiel."

Rettinger heard the cries, but his eyes were sweeping the green hills, the colourful houses of the kibbutz, the endless groves of citrus fruits, and then he saw the temple. It wasn't much of a temple, certainly not as magnificent as the one in Krakow, but it appeared to be warm and inviting. He went inside. When he finally left the temple, he had to run to catch his truck, which had joined the convoy and was gradually gaining speed.

The soldiers were happily chatting about the welcome and hospitality of the Jewish kibbutsim. Each of them had bags full of oranges and grapefruit. Rettinger didn't participate in the talk because his thoughts were still in the temple where he had thanked God for sparing his life and getting him out of the Soviet Union, and he had asked Him to have mercy on his wife and child.

They passed valleys covered by lush orchards and vegetable gardens, interrupted by small fields of barley. Wherever he turned his eyes, he saw sprinklers, shooting life-giving water high into the air in lazy arcs. Often their convoy was slowed down by a horse-drawn lorry or an occasional farm truck. The serenity of these farmers was apparent to Rettinger. They were doing their daily chores as though there were no concentration camps in Europe, or labour camps in the Soviet Union - just them and their land. Rettinger was both surprised and pleased. The children were dressed in light clothing. They were playing in the streets, yelling at each other. Laughing mothers walked with baby strollers, storekeepers stood behind their counters, barbers with razors in hand; they all peered curiously at the passing column. All these things seemed strange to Rettinger, and pleasing at the same time. 'Damn it! It is normal life again,' he thought. He wasn't alone in these sentiments. His buddies, who hadn't smiled for months, were now grinning, waving and blowing kisses to clusters of giggling girls.

"It's like a homecoming," he heard a big corporal telling his closest companions.

'Six hundred years of Poles and Jews living together have done something,' thought Rettinger.

They made camp close to Rekhovot, right in the heart of the fruit belt. The orchards stretched along the Mediterranean Sea like a flowing ribbon, producing the best citrus fruit in the region. Rettinger spent every free moment walking through these orchards, vegetable fields, and beaches. He never got tired or bored. In fact, every pebble he picked up on the beaches, every leaf he touched, filled him with joy. He felt an integral part of this land, which he had never seen until now. The land of great history, the land of suffering, the land of his ancestors - and the land of hope.

The winter of 1943 was approaching, but Rekhovot enjoyed warm and sunny weather. Rettinger had no problem obtaining two weeks' leave to visit Tel Aviv and Jerusalem; in fact, he had been encouraged by his superior officer. Rettinger had been promoted to military correspondent with the rank of captain two months earlier. The appointment gave him a lot of freedom of movement.

It was early afternoon in December when he parked his jeep and approached the Wailing Wall. Until he arrived in Palestine, he had thought little of the Wall and its traditions. Now, however, it had taken on significance. At the Wall, there were several older men and women swaying to and fro, praying in Hebrew, a language Rettinger didn't know.

Besides Jerusalem, Rettinger visited Tel Aviv, Jaffa, Haifa, and in each of them, he found a part of himself. To the surprise of the pedestrians, he touched the stones of temples and other old buildings, as though caressing them. He visited every major library and learning institution, perusing for hours the old books and documents. He talked to and learned to respect the Jewish farming settlers, who were slowly, but visibly, transforming yesterday's desert into blossoming orchards and endless green vegetable gardens.

Driving back from these excursions to his military quarters, he thought about the significance of this land and its people to him. "Maybe, when the war is over, I will settle in this land," he sighed.

Chapter Thirteen

"Dear Brother," Helena wrote the two words again and again. Impatiently, she left her small desk and walked over to the window. This April day in 1943 was sunny and warm in Santa Rosa, Mexico. In fact, it had been sunny and warm and the roses close to her window had been blossoming since her arrival two months ago.

"Dear Brother," she tried once again, when she returned to her desk. This time she had to write the letter.

"I don't know how to start this letter. I really don't know. You see, I don't know if you are alive. I was advised by my teacher, Mrs. Rosinski, to write a letter to you anyway. She thinks that maybe you are in the Polish Army. Everybody who is with me writes their letters to their father, brother or to somebody. I am attending school. They put me into grade six, it is too easy for me. Maybe they will put me in grade seven soon, but I don't know. I like it here in Santa Rosa. Mexicans are nice people and take good care of us. There are many of us here - six hundred or maybe more. We are all Polish orphans except for a few teachers who are teaching us the same subjects as in Poland before the war, except that we are taking English too. We arrived here from India about two months ago. We spent four months in India. Maria is in Africa. She lives in a place called Nairobi. She told me in one of her letters that it is close to a large lake. She is happy there. It is a camp run by the British, but she told me she likes the African people too. They are nice people and they are black.

I wish you could be here in Santa Rosa; it is so nice here. I am sad, because I am alone. I often cry remembering my grandparents who died in Nukhto.

Maybe the good Lord will help us and soon you and Maria will be able to come here and stay with me.

Dear Brother, I love you.

Your sister, Helena."

She sat quietly for a long time. She wasn't in a hurry today. It was Saturday, and so she could do anything she liked with her time. She started to read a book, Gulliver's Travels, which she had read twice already. However, at that moment, she had no interest in the book. She felt restless. She thought about the time in 1942 when she and the other Polish orphans from the Consulate orphanage in Bukhara had been loaded onto a large ship which took them across the Caspian Sea, away from the Soviet Union. They had been the lucky few to leave the Soviet Union. They heard from their teachers that many children had not been allowed to leave that terrible country.

She would never forget the moment when they had been told that they were leaving. She had been very sick at the time and had been worried about what had happened to Jan and Maria. She had felt so alone. Many other children were sick too. Everybody had been crying, she remembered, and the noise, she was sure, could have been heard a long distance. She didn't know how long it had taken them to cross the sea because she had been too weak to think about it. She didn't remember when they had arrived in Iran. Well, that was not exactly true. She remembered that someone had carried her in his arms, some big man dressed in a green uniform. She remembered feeling secure in his strong arms. For a moment, she had thought that he was her father.

"Hush child, hush... don't cry! Please don't." The man's voice was trembling. She was brought to a hospital. She remembered clearly. It was so white there. The men and women who helped were all dressed in white. They were nice to her. They had even dried her eyes when she cried and she had cried often, almost all the time she was awake. Then one day when she was well, a man took her to a large ship and she found herself once again looking over endless water.

They were on that ship for almost two months. The ship made frequent stops. The children cried less this time, although some were still sick. They finally arrived at their destination, Calcutta, India. It took a long time for the trucks to cross the city. They then traveled for a full day until they arrived at a camp. There were hundreds of tents in that camp, waiting for them.

It was nice there, except for the heat. Many children became sick again, probably because of that terrible heat. Those who weren't sick attended a Polish school which had been organized for them. Helena noticed that all the teachers were very old. She asked her older friend Rosie, why there were no younger teachers here. Rosie told her that all the younger ones were in the Army.

After four months in India, they were loaded onto a ship again. This time, their voyage was so long that when the time came to disembark, some of the children didn't want to leave. The ship had become their home. Helena had been reluctant to leave. Now they were in Santa Rosa and happy. They were getting pretty good food. Almost every can of meat, biscuits, chocolate, Helena noticed, had the inscription 'Made in U.S.A.'. All their fruits and vegetables were Mexican, fresh, tasty and plentiful.

"Good Jesus Christ and Holy Mother," she prayed every night, "thank you for saving me and Maria. Please save my father and Jan, too. Please!"

She always felt better after these prayers and slept peacefully in her clean bed. At the end of April, she was called to the camp office where she was given a letter. With trembling hands, she opened it and saw that the letter was from Maria.

The letter was short. It began

"Dear Helena,

By the time you read this letter, I will probably be out of Africa. On my 21st birthday, I joined the WAF and soon will be on my way to fight the Germans. I will write more to you later. Did you hear from Jan or Father?"

It was signed

"Your loving sister, Maria."

"What is the WAF?" Helena asked her teacher later.

"Women's Auxiliary Force," answered Mrs. Rosinski.

"What is 'auxiliary'?"

"Sort of helping those who fight at the front."

Helena didn't really understand, but it sounded exciting, so she asked her teacher: "Do they accept 15-year-olds?"

"Fortunately, no" answered Mrs. Rosinski, smiling. "They want 15 year-olds to stay in school to make up their three lost years."

****

In the summer of 1943, a contingent of about 700 Polish women, all volunteers, left Nairobi for an unknown destination. Maria was glad to leave Nairobi, although she knew she would miss the peaceful life she had experienced in the last few months.

Leaning on a rail of the large Polish freighter, Batory, she looked with sadness at the disappearing East African Coast. She would miss the oval African hut which she and three other Polish girls had shared. The clay hut had had a straw-thatched roof with a small garden surrounding it. In spite of the high temperatures, the hut had been pleasantly cool. It had been spacious enough to accommodate four of them comfortably.

They had decorated its walls with flowers, pictures cut out of British and Polish newspapers and a variety of African handicrafts which they had placed on the wooden table. In the daytime, the girls had attended a school with Polish and British teachers. In the evenings, the camp was full of life.

The camp had had a theatre where British and American movies were shown. For those who preferred dancing, there had been several dances every week. Often, though, the girls had preferred to stay in their hut and sing together. There had been one serious problem, however, in the otherwise ideal camp; there had been a severe shortage of men. The only men were either very old or very sick.

She turned her eyes from the great expanses of greenish water to the deck and the machine guns pointing to the cloudy sky. The soldiers manning these machine guns were constantly searching the sky, as if expecting something.

That evening, Maria was frightened by the sirens and the frantic, pecking sounds of the machine guns. Several airplanes with black crosses approached their ship. She heard a muffled explosion as though something heavy had been dropped on the deck. Their ship had been hit by a bomb, but the damage was minimal.

After that, Maria was so scared that she refused to leave her cabin until they reached their destination. They disembarked in Plymouth, England and they were almost immediately loaded onto large military lorries and driven off. Even though the summer was almost over, Maria was amazed by the green of the English countryside. Among the groves, she saw small clean houses, often surrounded by carefully clipped hedges. It's so peaceful here, she thought. It was hard to believe that there was war and killing in the world. They passed small, well-fenced meadows, with many cows and horses. The people they met when they stopped were friendly, offering them cakes, apples and tea. Maria's English was poor, consisting of a few hundred words she had picked up in school in Nairobi. However, the people showed a lot of patience, smiled at her a lot, and tried hard to guess what she was saying. What impressed her the most was the appearance of normal life. She saw the newspaper vendors, postmen, shoppers, all going on with their business as though the war did not exist.

They were brought to Nottingham Air Base where they were quartered in barracks. Next day, they were issued dark blue uniforms. Maria couldn't wait to see herself in the long mirror which hung in the recreation room. After putting on her uniform and fixing her hair, she regarded herself in the mirror. The uniform suited her tall, slim figure and her short, dark hair looked attractive with her hat. She smiled and winked at herself, then she marched into her quarters.

"Dear Brother," she wrote to Jan, a week later.

"I don't know what's happened to you. I know one thing, however, that if you are alive, you must be a soldier. I am a soldier too, but that's all I am allowed to say. Helena is in Mexico. She is attending school there and she is all right. Our dear grandparents are not with us. They died in that horrible Siberia. Did you hear about Father? Please respond.

I cry often thinking of our father, you and Helena.

Praying for you, I remain your loving sister, Maria."

She sent it through the military mail service, hoping that the letter would reach her brother. She had often heard her friends complaining about lost letters and parcels.

Chapter Fourteen

Meanwhile, Jan's unit in Iraq was ordered to be ready to leave. There had been many such orders given before, but the unit had stayed in the same place for almost a year. The German paratroopers' attacks had virtually stopped, mainly due to the troubles which the German Armies were having on all fronts.

However, this time they were given only two hours to be ready, or, as Sergeant-in-Arms Zebrowski told them, "you will join the jackals forever."

During their hot, dusty journey, the news somehow spread that they were going to Palestine. They travelled only at night. During the day, they camped in one of the numerous depressions called *wadis*. They arrived at their destination at night, so Jan couldn't see much of the landscape.

They were quartered in wooden barracks, close to the village of Barbara. The barracks had real beds and showers. The pleasure of standing under a cool stream of water delighted Jan. He probably would have spent the rest of the night under the shower if it hadn't been for Sergeant Majewski, who physically kicked him out of the shower, yelling, "You've already used enough water for five men. Water is scarce in Palestine."

Jan was learning fast. After a week of rest, the companies started training again. Parachute jumping, use of dynamite, hand-to-hand combat, day after day and often at night as well. It became obvious that they were training for some special assignment.

Leaves were seldom given. Jan asked three times, and each time he was refused. After two months, however, he was summoned by the commanding officer and told that he had seven days that he could spend as he liked. The absolute joy of having some free time at last was beyond description. He thought it would be a good idea to hitchhike to Tel Aviv the next day. He had heard so many interesting tales about this city, which had been built by Jews fairly recently.

So, on Saturday, dressed in a clean and well-pressed uniform, he was about to leave camp, when he heard Sergeant Majewski yelling excitedly at him, holding what looked like an envelope in his hand.

"Yes sir, what's the trouble?"

"Letters, Jan! You have letters, two of them."

Jan felt his legs go weak. "Letters? Oh my God! What letters? From whom?"

Both letters were in small, thin envelopes, with no sender's name on either of them. With trembling hands, he tore open one envelope. His eyes fell upon the last line of the letter, "Your loving sister, Helena."

"Helena, Oh my God, she's alive!" he shouted excitedly.

After reading it, he sat on a nearby boulder and cried. He cried out of happiness and despair. His sister was alive, but his grandparents?

He opened the other letter. A faint smile appeared on his face. "Maria is a soldier too," he whispered, more to himself than to Majewski, who was observing Jan curiously. "My grandparents are dead, in Siberia." They stood there in silence.

"Jan," he finally heard the sergeant say in a trembling voice. "Jan, I... I never told you but maybe I should tell you now." Tears ran down his cheeks, falling on the parched Palestinian ground. "I never told you," the sergeant repeated, "that I had a wife and three children, yes, a wife, two boys and a girl... between three and eleven. They... they are all there, buried in the sands of Uzbekistan. Typhoid fever. They all died." The tears continued to roll down his cheeks. Jan jumped to his feet and embraced his friend as tightly as he could. They stood there, crying.

"Go, Jan! Go!" said the sergeant, freeing himself.

On his way to the highway, Jan changed his mind. "No, I want to go to Jerusalem instead of Tel Aviv!" Oh, how many times Jan had heard that name in Zamosze.

"Jerusalem! Jerusalem!" Moyshe's voice would become soft when he spoke that word in his blacksmith shop in Zamosze. Even the expression in Moyshe's eyes would change. They became somehow dreamy, with a spark of hope, Jan thought.

Now, seeing the magnificent Jewish temples, the great gold-roofed mosques rising over the buildings like watchtowers, the narrow streets, upon which generation after generation of Jewish and Arab people had trod, the ancient houses which had witnessed some of the greatest events in the history of mankind, he felt that he understood Moyshe's longing.

"Jerusalem!" He heard his grandmother's voice pronouncing the word with solemnity and devotion. "Jerusalem!" the thought of the boy Jesus teaching in the Temple, Palm Sunday and the Crucifixion. Jan walked softly along the Via Dolorosa as though wishing to diminish his presence, asking forgiveness for the temerity of treading on the ground upon which He had walked toward His final Passion.

That night, Jan arranged for accommodation in a building requisitioned for Polish soldiers. After walking for miles in the streets of Jerusalem, he approached his quarters after dark. He heard Polish singing coming from the building. Strong male voices reverberated over the narrow streets, echoing in the lanes and alleys. "We shall return to the land of our fathers. To the land for which our hearts are longing. We shall return all, young and old..." Jan walked down the hallway to his room.

Jan spent four days visiting the many shrines, or just strolling in the narrow streets of the old city. The remaining three days he decided to spend in Rekhovot, 'the city of orchards'.

Rekhovot, with its orange groves and charming little houses hidden in the lush green vegetation, relaxed him, and he felt happier than he had been for months. He admired the Jewish settlers who, by hard work and determination, had managed to convert this semi-desert into an eye-pleasing and economically important agricultural belt. As he walked along the shore, the cool breeze from the Mediterranean cooled his face and soothed his nerves. He found a bench overlooking the sea and sat down.

A young girl was sitting at the other end of the bench. Their eyes met. The girl's eyes were large and intensely blue, accentuated by high cheekbones. Her smooth, clear complexion and shining hair radiated health and vitality.

"Good afternoon," he greeted her in English.

"Good day," she answered him in Polish.

She shifted on the bench, trying to settle more comfortably. Seeing Jan's eyes following her movements, she quickly pulled her skirt around her knees.

"From Russia?" Jan asked.

"Yes, of course."

"Sorry, how stupid of me. Of course you are from Russia. Aren't we all?... Siberia?"

"Yes, Siberia."

"Are you with your family here?"

"No, my family is there," she pointed eastwards, "buried in Siberia."

"Oh, I am sorry." Then, after an awkward pause, Jan added, "I just learned that my sisters are safely out of the Soviet Union. My grandparents are..." there was no need to finish the sentence.

"Parents?"

"Mother died before the war. Father... I don't know, he went to fight the Germans."

For a while, there was silence. The girl was looking pensively at the sea. He, observing her unobtrusively, waited for her to speak again. She had, he noticed, thick, dark hair, falling in soft waves to her shoulders. In the approaching twilight, it gleamed softly. Jan guessed she was about eighteen. They talked about their experiences in the Soviet Union, their childhood in Poland, enjoying each other's company.

"Ah!" she exclaimed suddenly. "I must go. I am late for my shift."

"Shift?"

"I work as a nurse in the Polish Military Hospital."

"I must go, too. My furlow is almost over."

"Then we will walk together. The bus stop is on my way."

As they walked, Jan became conscious of her firm, rounded breasts and curving hips. He felt his face flush.

The girl suddenly stopped and started to laugh; a girlish, carefree laugh. "My God!" she cried. "We have been talking for almost an hour and I don't even know your name."

Jan, also laughing, introduced himself.

"Olenka," she responded, curtsying, and then added, "Alexandra in full, but don't you ever call me that. It is too dignified for me."

"Does that mean that I will see you again?" asked Jan, his voice trembling.

"Maybe... well, actually, it will be rather difficult, because..."

"Please, Olenka, I really would like to see you again. It was such a pleasure..."

"Okay, then. You know where to find me - Hospital 2, Section 6."

His eyes followed her until she disappeared around the corner. "Hey, soldier, are you getting in?" he was startled by the bus driver. "Hurry, will you?"

'She is so beautiful,' he thought, settling himself in a corner of the bus. 'She has such a melodious voice... I must see her again. I hope she'll remember me.' He felt like opening the window and yelling out that he had just met a beautiful, wonderful girl.

When he returned to his unit, Jan was told by the commander that he was being transferred back to his original artillery regiment.

"But why, Major?" Jan asked, sorry to learn that the "elite" unit, which he was beginning to like, was about to be disbanded.

"All of you are going to be sent to your original regiments," said his superior officer. Jan, noticing the sadness in the major's voice, didn't pursue his questioning any further. "I guess they need you there," the major added.

The artillery regiment to which Jan was re-assigned was stationed close to Tel Aviv, the largest city in Palestine. Because of his previous training, he was promoted to the rank of sergeant. Not quite nineteen, he was the youngest sergeant in the Regiment.

A month later, he was appointed instructor of the regimental scout detachment. In spite of the speed of events and many duties, he found time to think about Olenka. "I must see her again," he told himself often, but his instructor's job and the pressure that went with it prevented him from returning to Rekhovot.

It was only about two months later that he was allowed to go on a three-day leave. Dressed in a well-pressed uniform, with sergeant's stripes on his shoulders, he looked at himself in the shop mirror in Rekhovot. He saw a lean, but wiry young man with thick, blonde hair. His slightly aquiline nose and cool, blue eyes gave him a stubborn look. A slight scar on his right cheek, a souvenir from the German paratrooper he had killed gave him an air of mystery, he thought.

Normally, he didn't really care how he looked. Of course, he had to comply with regulations which demanded neatness and cleanliness, but beyond that, he, unlike some other soldiers, didn't spend too much of his energy or time on his appearance. He couldn't understand some of his companions, who, before they went on leave, spent hours and hours "beautifying" themselves. He considered it unmanly and unworthy of a soldier like him.

This time, however, was an exception. He was about to meet a girl, a beautiful girl, who stirred in him an emotion never experienced before. He walked briskly and energetically toward the outskirts of town, where the Polish Military Hospital was located.

It was Sunday, the 3rd of December, 1943, when, after a half hour's walk, he reached his destination. The guard at the gate didn't like the idea of letting Jan go through. Too many uniformed men tried to get inside the compound to meet nurses. The old guard had been fooled many times by these smart alecks who would say anything to see a woman. They would either invent sad stories to soften the corporal's heart, or try to intimidate him with rank. But they couldn't fool an old soldier like Corporal Stash. He had been an experienced corporal when most of these young officers were still in school.

"Yes?" he barked at Jan.

"I must go to the compound, corporal!"

"No!"

"But, but..." Jan stammered, "I have an important message to deliver..."

"Don't say it... I know, a message for a nurse."

"Yes!" Jan exclaimed, surprised.

"Everybody has a message for a nurse, especially on Sunday."

"Corporal, please. It is important."

But the corporal turned his back on Jan and pretended to be deaf. After several more tries, Jan gave up and walked away, fuming with anger. After walking for a few minutes, he suddenly stopped. "I can't walk away. I must see her," he muttered under his breath. "I must find a way to get into that compound."

The compound, he observed, was surrounded by barbed wire. However, it was spaced widely enough to squeeze through. The side of the compound was guarded by an armed soldier walking along the fence. Choosing a moment when the old soldier's back was to him, Jan, forgoing the indignity of squeezing between the wires, jumped over the fence with the agility of a mountain goat.

"The fence wasn't planned for commando-trained fellows like me," he smiled sardonically.

Once inside, nobody asked any questions. He was just another sergeant, who had good reason to be here. Otherwise, he would have been stopped by the good Corporal Stash, wouldn't he? Marching energetically toward the hospital office, he whistled softly.

A plump, young nurse behind the desk smiled at him. "Sure, Sergeant... Olenka? Hmm...a nurse, you say? No." Jan was crestfallen. "Wait a minute," she was checking the list. "Oh, yes... tropical diseases... there she is, Section 2, Unit 6... you can't miss it."

From that time on, they saw each other whenever their duties permitted. Long walks in the citrus orchards, sipping cool soda-drinks in restaurants, drinking coffee in small coffee shops, or just simply sitting on the beach and gazing at the waves of the Mediterranean Sea.

Jan felt greater and greater attachment for this girl. He felt her presence even when she wasn't with him. While training, marching, or teaching his subordinates, he thought of her, even if it was just for a moment. It was good to know that there was somebody, not far away, somebody close to his heart with whom he could share his thoughts, hopes, and dreams.

"Jan!" she cried one day, "Jan! Where have you been for so long?"

"Olenka!" he said excitedly. "Wasn't I here the day before yesterday?"

"Ah, yes, Jan... too long ago," she teased him, laughing like a child.

But during one of those peaceful evenings when they were sitting on the beach, Olenka became suddenly sad and restless. She wasn't her usual self,

Jan noticed. He felt a tension about her.

"What troubles you, Olenka?" he asked, hugging her and caressing her long dark hair.

She didn't answer at first. She had been thinking of Jan, and of herself quite often the last few weeks. She had decided to tell him... everything about herself. 'He deserves to know. He's such a sweet young man...good at heart and... so dear.' She had never felt so happy in all her life as she had since she'd met him. 'There is nothing false about him, and he is strong... Strength emanates from him and is somehow transferred to me, making me stronger, too. Do I love him?' she wondered. She honestly didn't know. She didn't even know whether she could really love anyone. One thing she knew, however; she didn't want to lose him. Losing him now would mean returning to an empty life, with no commitment and no hope, the life of her painful past. Sure, there were many men who were interested in her - a doctor, two officers... But for some reason they reminded her of her past. With Jan, she was looking into the future.

"Jan," she said, her voice trembling, "I must tell you something about my past."

"Hush, Olenka, hush. You don't have to tell me anything," he told her quietly.

"No, Jan. I must!" Then, amid the sound of the waves, she told him about her past. "I, and my sister Natalia were sent to a labour camp in Siberia. It was cold in the barrack and cold in the forest. There were the cold eyes of the guards and the suffering eyes of the prisoners. Up to our waists in snow, my sister and I loaded heavy logs, day after day... falling deep into the snow, getting up... I can still see my sister - she was sixteen, then - with her hands bleeding, scratched by tree branches, tears in her eyes from the pain and cold. 'Olenka! Help me!' she cried. 'Olenka, I'm dying!' I knew she was dying, Jan. She was so gentle and fragile."

"Please, stop, Olenka!" Jan exclaimed. "Don't torture yourself, please!"

"She had long hair," Olenka continued as though Jan hadn't spoken. "Longer than mine, and it was blonde. She was beautiful... I did everything to save her, Jan, I truly did. Please believe me."

"Olenka..." Jan tried to reassure her.

"No! Listen, please! I must tell you the rest, I must!" she interrupted. "I shared Volkov's bed, thinking that I could get more food for Natalia."

"Volkov?"

"He was the camp commander, a really evil man. At first, Natalia and I had more food. Then one day he told me that he didn't want me anymore. I felt filthy and defiled. Some time later I discovered that I was pregnant."

"Olenka, please stop! I don't want to hear anymore!" cried Jan urgently.

"It was a boy," she continued, tears rolling down her cheeks. "Born prematurely, dead... I buried him in the snow..."

Jan hugged her closer, trying desperately to comfort her, his heart pounding madly.

"Then Natalia died, too." She grasped Jan's hand tightly, as though afraid of losing him.

They were silent. Jan didn't know what to say, how to give voice to the compassion and understanding he felt for her. All he knew was that he held in his arms a girl who had made a great sacrifice for another... a girl who had become a victim of the evil times.

Jan wanted somehow to assure her that he understood her tragedy and respected her feelings. He felt that he must protect this girl, with his life if necessary. If poor Olenka thought that her confession would put an end to their relationship, she was heading for a great surprise.

Jan gently took her hands in his. Looking into her eyes, he said: "Listen, Olenka. Only those of us who have tasted the bitterness of life truly understand it. I love you, and I always will."

They clung to each other in a fierce embrace, trying to forget the horrors of their past.

****

One fall day, without warning, Jan's unit was ordered to move. A few hot and dusty days later he found himself in Egypt.

"This is not farewell, dearest Olenka... it's just goodbye," he wrote to her hastily. He knew these words were clumsy and inadequate and did not convey his feeling of loss and desperation.

Jan's regiment was stationed close to the town of Ismailia on the western edge of the Sinai Peninsula. The town almost touched the Suez Canal, which cuts through the desert, separating Asia from Africa. The regiment's sixteen medium calibre cannons, pointing toward the canal, protected this important transportation artery. Ismailia itself was a busy market place, but there wasn't much else to see or do.

"I hear you're complaining about being bored here," said the Battery commanding officer, Captain Kalas. He had just been appointed, and the soldiers couldn't make up their minds about him. He was a thin bow-legged man with an ascetic face and a high-pitched voice. He had been decorated for his participation in the battle of Tobruk in Libya.

"He is one of those Tobruk rats," a soldier whispered.

"He looks like a rat," somebody added.

"Well," continued Kalas, pretending not to notice the insolent glances of the soldiers. "Training will start this afternoon... and it will be thorough."

It was. From six o'clock in the morning until five in the afternoon, the Battery practiced the art of war. Fortunately, the Egyptian winter was relatively cool.

Two weeks after their arrival, they were given two days' leave. It was a great relief from the effort and tedium of training. Jan left immediately, and luckily he got a ride in a British Army truck going straight to the city.

A noisy, busy place, Cairo was rightly called the capital of Africa and the Middle East. Cars and pedestrians crowded the squares, restaurants, theatres, and brothels. Jan went straight to a crowded bar and ordered a drink. Normally, he didn't drink at all, but his longing for Olenka made him want to. He was soon joined by three Polish infantrymen who had also decided to start their exploration of Cairo in a bar.

After an hour of continuous drinking, one of the soldiers at Jan's table became sentimental. He was a tall, wiry fellow in his early 30's.

"Look at those soldiers," he said sighing. "Poor wretches far from their homes and families. They are lost like us in a foreign land." He raised his glass. "Their health." Everyone downed his drink. But after a few more rounds, the same soldier's mood changed to hostility.

"Look at those bastards, there," he jerked his thumb at the group of British soldiers sitting at the next table. "Bloody, cool limeys. Mustachioed gentlemen's gentlemen. Didn't do a damned thing for us in 1939. Now they want us to fight for them." He took another long drink. "Fight for them?

The bastards!" the soldier continued.

"You can always quit, soldier."

"Quit? Quit and do what? Manicure camels? Look at them," he cried. "Pompous bastards."

"Be quiet, Steve, quiet," pleaded the big corporal, putting his hand on the soldier's arm.

"Quiet! Quiet yourself," the soldier cried, turning his chair toward the British soldiers. To Jan's relief, the Britons were absorbed in their own conversation and drinks and were not paying the slightest attention to the shouting Pole.

Jan left the bar soon after and wandered in the Cairo streets for a while before deciding to book into one of the hotels.

The Capri Hotel was small, but clean. Night was approaching, and he was hungry and thirsty. After taking a shower he decided to go to the hotel's restaurant he had noticed earlier. It was a small, cozy restaurant, almost full at that time of day with civilians and allied soldiers. Drinking coffee and absorbed with his own thoughts, he failed to notice a group of soldiers who had just arrived, taking a table close to his. It was only when he heard Polish that he turned his head toward them.

There were four of them, all captains. One of them, a stocky powerfully built man, had green shoulder stripes, worn by war correspondents. He looked at the man again and had the feeling that he knew him.

"Rettinger!" Jan roared with such force that people around him jumped. Rettinger recognized him, too. They lunged at each other and embraced.

"It really is you, Jan!" cried Rettinger.

"And you, Rettinger? Where is your red beard?"

"I left it in the Soviet Union!" he chuckled, pointing east.

"With the vermin, I suppose."

They laughed, embracing again. Rettinger excused himself to his companions and they went to another restaurant, which, as Rettinger said, "is smaller than this one, but has better coffee." It turned out to be a good idea, Jan thought; they needed a lot of coffee, because they talked until morning.

It was nine o'clock when they finished their breakfast and said goodbye to each other.

'Oh, God, I'm so glad Jan didn't die in that crevasse,' Rettinger thought, relieved.

Jan, heading toward the auto shop, was equally happy. 'It is thanks to Rettinger that I am alive today. Who knows what would have happened to me - to us - in that Turkestan labour camp?'

From then on, events moved too fast for Jan's liking. Returning to the base in Cairo, Jan found his unit ready to depart. That March night in 1944, they traveled to Alexandria, an Egyptian port on the Mediterranean Sea. There, as a warm rain fell, they boarded the Polish freighter, "Sobieski".

By the rising sun, "Sobieski", escorted by two destroyers, took a northerly direction toward Europe.

The coast of Africa and the port of Alexandria receded as the "Sobieski" gained speed. In the setting sun, the distant mosques gleamed brilliant gold and red. It seemed as if Alexandria was all glowing colour. Then gradually the glow died and only the dark green of the Mediterranean remained.

Jan's feelings were mixed. He was glad he had survived the horrors of Siberia and the heat and hardships of the Middle East. And yet he was sad. The memory of his grandparents, friends, and acquaintances, whose graves he left behind, filled his heart with sadness and pain.

He had survived, when stronger and wiser people had perished. What was the meaning of it? What did destiny have in store for him? What was expected from him at this stage of his life?

His homeland, like most of Europe, was under the boots of Germanic Teutons. The news, though incomplete, was nevertheless sufficient to visualize the enormous suffering inflicted upon people by Germans. Maybe he, and others like him, had been spared so they could repay their enemies. He had been trained to kill, even though every fibre of his soul was against killing, even his enemies. He abhorred killing, but he would kill!

He joined a group of men who, leaning on the rail, were talking among themselves.

"Where are we going?" a soldier asked no one in particular.

"Italy," answered another. Then added: "It is no secret anymore. I heard it straight from my commanding officer, just a while ago."

"It looks like the Americans have already exterminated the Germans, like cockroaches, in Sicily," somebody else said. "Apparently, the allies have occupied the southern part of Italy."

"Oh, so it looks like we'll fight in Italy?"

Jan shifted to a more comfortable place, listening to the soldiers.

"I remember," one said, "when I was on a similar voyage a year ago. We had just left the Port of Aden, going to Basra, standing at the rails, as we are now. Suddenly the Messerschmidts attacked our convoy. Holy Mother! They sank three of our ships, one with a hospital crew on board. The bastards! They did it in spite of the huge cross painted on the deck!"

"A similar thing happened to us," said another soldier. "When we left Tobruk, there were three ships, but only one arrived at Alexandria Port."

The ship was now swinging wildly, climbing the huge incoming waves, only to dive into the abyss of the dark sea. Holding the rail tightly, he wished he was in Zamosze now, strolling over the marshes, instead of looking into the bottomless chasm beneath his feet. Still he knew that Zamosze was far away and the road leading there wouldn't be easy. He suspected that the road would most likely be over dead bodies - perhaps his own.

He went below, reached for his knapsack and removed an English-Italian dictionary he had bought in Alexandria. "I might as well study Italian," he said to himself. "I may need it. It looks like a beautiful language to me... I'll learn it in no time."

Chapter Fifteen

Next morning, many soldiers remained in their hammocks or lined the railings. Seasickness had destroyed their dignity and there was much deck-swabbing. Jan, too, was nauseous. Fortunately, by next evening, they had reached the port of Taranto, right at the heel of Italy. The destroyers vanished, leaving "Sobieski", which they had been protecting, along with several other freighters. Behind them, huge, black and distant, lay Sicily, which had been freed from the Germans. Ahead of them lay the city of Taranto, or what was left of it.

In Taranto, wherever he looked, Jan saw the shells of burned buildings, overturned vehicles, bomb craters, stumps of shelled trees, and the ruins of schools and offices. The stench was sickening. The streets swarmed with hundreds of young ragamuffins with pale faces and feverish eyes.

"*Il pane! Prego! Il pane.* (Bread, please, bread.)"

Clusters of grownups were standing aimlessly nearby. They, like the children, were in rags, unwashed and pale. 'So this is what the end result of war looks like,' Jan thought. He stood there petrified, until he noticed that his unit had marched out and disappeared into an oak grove on the periphery of the city. With his head down, he followed.

Seasickness forgotten, the soldiers began to set up camp on the wet clay, cursing as they waded through ankle deep mud. Bobko, one of the soldiers from Jan's battery, was struggling with his tent and swearing.

"For two bloody years my ass froze in Siberia, and for another two, it was frying in the desert. Now it looks like it will be rotting in this goddamned mud."

It was already dark as Jan splashed through the puddles to the two storey farmhouse that served as battery headquarters. He climbed the stairs and entered a brightly lit room. At the dining table sat Captain Kalas, Sergeant-

Major Kirpa and two cadet officers. Before them on the table was a large carafe of wine; 'Vino Roso' read the inscription. Bent over the table was a farmer, who had thick, shaggy hair and small, eager eyes.

"Come in! Come in!" Captain Kalas exclaimed when Jan entered. "First, we must have something to eat, then we shall fight the war. So grab a fork and sit down."

"Yes," echoed Sergeant-Major Kirpa, "it is a matter of priorities."

It didn't take long for Jan to realize that his colleagues had gathered together to sample the homemade Italian wine. 'Why not?' he thought. 'Let's try this Italian "vino".'

He sat down on the nearest chair and looked around him. He was sitting in a European house for the first time in almost four years. How many times, in Siberia and the desert, had he dreamed of being back in Europe? But he hadn't dreamed that Europe would be smoldering ruins, stench, and hunger.

A woman was sitting on a small bench by the far wall. The deep furrows on her face and her pain-filled eyes, told of her hard life. She was dressed in black: black dress, black stockings, and black run-down shoes. Sitting quietly, she looked at the strangers with her large, sad eyes, trying to assess them. In the corner, at the opposite wall, stood two frightened little girls, dressed in rags. Fascinated by the strangers, they watched every movement. Their black eyes particularly followed the movement of corned beef from plate to mouth. Jan suddenly wasn't hungry. The Nukhto-Ozyero camp came in to his mind. The other soldiers also became uneasy.

The commanding officer leaned toward the sergeant-major and spoke to him quietly. The sergeant-major rose from the table and left the room. The remaining soldiers stared at their plates, full of steaming corned beef, but no one could eat. The silence was so heavy that Jan began to feel uncomfortable.

Minutes later, the sergeant-major returned with a half dozen cans of corned beef and a few bars of bitter-sweet chocolate. He handed them to the woman, who quickly went to the fireplace and began banging pots and pans around. The man, who had been silent until now, finally spoke in a sudden, nearly incomprehensible rush of words. The gist of what he said was that the Germans had taken everything, that is everything except some wine. There was nothing to eat.

The wine carafe was quickly emptied. The farmer went to get another bottle - 'Vino Bianco' this time. There was another rush of words as the farmer brought the wine. Captain Kalas, who had studied Latin in school, translated that there was some kind of connection between Mussolini, Germans, and the lack of bread.

The mixture of the vino roso and vino bianco loosened their tongues. "It tastes like horse piss, but it's wine," observed the sergeant-major.

"As they say in Russia," the commanding officer added, "in a foreign land, even an old babushka is a gift of the gods, so don't complain, but drink."

"When in Rome, burn Roman candles," added one of the cadet-officers, who hadn't said much until now.

"Rome," said Captain Kalas pensively, "Rome is a long way ahead of us my friends. I'm afraid it will cost us a lot of blood."

They celebrated their return to Europe until the Italian farmer explained to them, mostly by gestures, that he regretted that there wasn't a single bottle left. They left the farmhouse and went to their tents.

Their regiment was stationed in the Taranto area for about a week. In the middle of April, they decamped and traveled northward. Just before reaching a larger city called Bari, the column turned to Capurno, passing Palo, Bitento and Andria. They passed war-devastated towns and villages. The townspeople, standing by the roadside, waved and occasionally threw flowers at the passing column. On walls in these towns they read newly-painted greetings: "*Viva Polachi* (Long live Poles)". Some of these signs were side by side with others that read "*Viva Tedeschi* (Long live Germans)". There had been attempts to remove the signs welcoming the Germans, but some remained.

"It seems the Italians aren't fussy about who they welcome," grumbled Ted, the cadet-officer sitting beside Jan in the cab of the truck.

"Perhaps," said Jan, "they figure this is not their war."

"Well, maybe not theirs, but Mussolini's for sure," Ted retorted.

They passed Foggia, more than half of which was in ruins. The wrecks of several Allied aircraft told what had happened here. Their column camped in a desolate, hilly area that night.

The next day was sunny and warm. Cool breezes from the hills were pleasant and refreshing. They decamped immediately after breakfast and continued their journey. The footprints of war were progressively more visible as they traveled northward. The towns they were passing were more and more devastated, and the number of graves was increasing. The graves, marked with crude wooden crosses, were often only a few feet away from the roads. The top of each cross was decorated with a helmet: German, American or British.

By the second night, they had reached the town of Campobasso, which had also been wrecked by bombs and artillery shells. The town, located in a large valley, was surrounded by rounded hills, richly covered by grass and poppies, like a crimson carpet from a fairy tale, interrupted only by fast-flowing streams and vineyards. May of 1944 had arrived in Campobasso.

****

Jan and his commanding officer, Kalas, were sitting in a little summer house which served as battery headquarters. The evening was warm and peaceful, except for the ominous thunder of heavy cannons, which occasionally reverberated from the north. The house was surrounded on three sides by a cherry orchard. Through the window, they could see the dark hills. They were soon joined by Ted and Kirpa. Sergeant-Major Kirpa appeared to be more stooped that evening. They all sat in silence around the table with an open bottle of scotch. Captain Kalas poured a very large shot for each of them. Clearing his throat, he raised his glass in a toast.

"To next year in free Poland, gentlemen."

"In free Poland," they all responded except for Ted.

"Free Poland?" he said after a moment's silence. "There will be no free Poland after the war." A long, uneasy silence settled on the room.

"What do you mean, Ted, no free Poland?" Jan burst out, offended.

Ted slowly raised his eyes, which had been staring into his glass. They were full of grief. "The Russians are at the Polish border already, pushing the bloody Germans westwards."

"And at the same time, they have broken their treaty with the Polish government in exile," added Kirpa.

"Yes, so they won't have to account to our government for any future occupation of Poland," added Ted.

"Do you mean that the Russians could occupy Poland and disregard the

212

Polish government, their ally?" cried Jan.

"Oh, no," joined Captain Kalas, who hadn't said anything until now. "There will be talk between the Polish government and the Russians, but it will be the Polish Communist government."

"I don't understand," said Jan.

"Simple," continued Captain Kalas. "They will create a communist government the moment they reach Polish soil."

"So what's the point of fighting?" cried Jan, unable to contain himself.

"The Second Polish Corps here in Italy, our Navy and Air Force, and the First Polish Corps in Britain will fight nevertheless," stated Captain Kalas flatly.

"Fight for what?" yelled Ted.

"For Britain?" Kirpa demanded.

"Or for America?" Jan added, feeling hopeless.

"We want to fight the Germans, don't we?" demanded Captain Kalas.

"Sure, but..."

"Well, it seems to me," said Captain Kalas, "that if we fight the Germans, and we sure seem to want to fight them, then maybe, just maybe, our comrades in arms, the British and Americans, won't allow the Russians to take over our fatherland."

"So fight we must," stated Ted.

"And die! Maybe for nothing," said Kirpa.

"Oh, come on!" Jan, emboldened by the wine, yelled. "I'm ashamed of you. You should have more faith in Great Britain and the United States. I refuse to believe that they would give in to the Russians and give them a free hand in Poland."

"And why not, my boy?" asked Ted ironically.

"For our loyalty to them, if for nothing else," cried Jan. "We were the first to say no to this bloody bastard Hitler, weren't we? And we have fought well. We reorganized our Army in France a few months after the fall of Poland, and our airmen were dying in the Battle of Britain." Kalas tried to restrain Jan, but to no avail. Jan continued, "And now, now we are ready to meet the Germans head on! To show them..."

"That's all true, Jan," said Ted quietly. "Nobody's arguing that. And I hope you are right, I hope you are right about the honour of our allies."

"Yes, we will do our duty, gentlemen," said Captain Kalas.

"Or die," added Kirpa.

"Or die," they echoed, somewhere between patriotic fervor and fatalism. Through the window, they heard another volley of artillery fire.

****

The next day in the afternoon, they left Campobasso. Their long column moved into the mountains to the accompaniment of the distant artillery fire. "Look!" said the driver of Jan's truck. Jan turned and saw a man with a yoke on his shoulders, climbing the hillside, a short distance from the road. It was dusk.

"What's he up to?" Jan asked.

"He is carrying water to a garden... up there on the mountainside," said the driver. "Did you know, Sergeant," he turned to Jan, "that some of those gardens are no bigger than the floor of a small barn? They have a great thirst for land here."

'Who doesn't?' Jan thought, remembering his own small farm in Zamosze. He wondered whether there was at least one country in the world where the farmers were not "thirsty for land". "If there is one," he sighed, "I would like to see it."

They continued to drive along the mountain road, passing many anti-aircraft guns, ammunition dumps, stores of gasoline and food, all camouflaged by green nets. Several times they passed long mule trains, carrying supplies of ammunition, water, and food.

In the morning, they reached a crossroads. A military policeman signaled them to stop and warned each driver to keep at least 100 metres between his vehicle and the vehicle ahead. All were told to proceed with all possible speed. There was a sign at the crossroads with an ominous message: 'This Road is under Fire'. Under this large sign there was a smaller one which read: 'Don't be stupid. Don't let yourself be killed'.

"What do you make of..." Jan started to ask his driver. He was interrupted by the whine of shells and then a series of explosions all around them. He heard several smacking sounds on the truck's tarpaulin. The driver pressed the gas pedal and the truck, with a heavy cannon hitched behind, leaped forward, jumping crazily over the deep craters and holes. They heard shells passing over their heads, whining and whistling and then exploding somewhere away from the road. Some others, however, swishing and hissing satanically, burst in front and behind the fast moving truck, sprinkling it with a shower of shell fragments. The crimson light of the exploding shells lit up the sky repeatedly; each flash barely long enough for Jan to catch glimpses of overturned tanks, wrecked trucks, and dead mules all along the road.

****

The road suddenly turned left and entered a small dale with a narrow ditch cutting it in two almost equal parts. The regiment's cannons, pointing their barrels at a high mountain called Monte Cassino, were installed along the ditch.

Early in the morning, amid heavy smoke which protected the small valley from the German observers, the regiment was preparing itself for the battle of Monte Cassino. While drinking his tea in the battery kitchen, Jan was summoned by his commanding officer. He found Captain Kalas and a young cadet-officer, leaning over the topographic map.

"Good! Good!" he responded to Jan's greeting. "Come here, sergeant! Come close." The captain's pointer danced on the map, showing Jan the Polish Second Corps' position. The captain stopped at one point. Bending closer to the map, Jan read: "Phantom Ridge".

It seemed as if Captain Kalas was giving Jan extra time to memorize the name of the ridge. In the dim light in the tent, their eyes met.

"This is the first bloody ridge that our 5th Infantry Division must capture from the bloody Huns," Captain Kalas stated. "After that... look!" he moved his pointer behind Phantom Ridge. The pointer moved from one hill to another. Jan moved closer to the map and noticed that some of the hills had sharp peaks, others had steep slopes and virtually all were separated by wide rifts and deep, narrow cracks. Beyond these treacherous hills, overlooking the Liri River Valley, was the high mountain called Monte Cassino. The Captain halted his pointer at the mountain, and stood there, musing.

"Monte Cassino," said Jan, just to break the silence.

"Yes, Monte Cassino," repeated Captain Kalas. "Our main objective," he added.

"Yes, but these...these hills, Captain, they must be taken first."

"I'm afraid you're right."

"But that is an enormous task."

"Very, Sergeant, very much so."

"What will our artillery's function be, Captain?"

"We are going to help our infantry by softening up the enemy positions with our cannon shells, Sergeant. You and I will be there with the infantry, right in the front line. You and I will be the eyes and ears of our artillery."

So far this softening had been deliberately limited. Most of the big cannons were silent. Only one or two were belching their deadly shells upon the waiting enemy.

"The moment to settle accounts with the Germans is approaching," observed Captain Kalas. "In these hills," he continued, pointing at Monte Cassino, "sit our enemies. We must win this battle!"

"It will be a piece of cake," exclaimed a young corporal, known for his prattling and smart-alecky manner. "We will get the sons-of-bitches..." However, meeting the captain's stern, cold eyes, he stopped abruptly.

"The German paratroopers and elite S.S. divisions are in a strong position in these hills." The captain swept his blood-shot eyes around the tent. Staring at the talkative corporal, he added, "And they are not a piece of cake, my friend. They are probably the best trained and experienced soldiers on earth. Remember that." There was silence in the tent, broken by the occasional sound of whistling cannon shells over their heads.

"These seasoned German troops were especially chosen by Hitler to block the road - the only road leading to Rome. Therefore, we must take these mountains if we're going to clear that road."

That evening, May 5, 1944, Captain Kalas with his second-in-command Sergeant Jan Tabor, a radio-man and four signalmen left the battery's position and headed toward their artillery observation post. The post was located close to Phantom Ridge. The Ridge itself was still occupied by the German troops. They saw that their observation post was a deep hollow cleverly dug out from the mountainside. They were told that the Americans, the previous inhabitants of the dugout, had attempted to storm Monte Cassino several times and failed. Similar attempts were made by the British and with the same results. Bleeding and decimated, they had retreated to another position. Now the task of taking Monte Cassino had been given to the Poles. Jan, crawling, explored the area around the dugout and found that it was littered with supplies left by the American troops. The cans of Carnation milk, boxes of biscuits, cans of corned beef, blankets, army boots, helmets, and empty water canisters were bent and twisted, or full of bullet holes. The carcasses of several mules in various stages of decomposition, and human excreta were scattered around, filling the air with a sickening stench. Among the rocks and cans lay American magazines, newspapers, and fragments of letters.

"Either our American friends are exceedingly rich," said Captain Kalas reflectively, after he heard Jan's report on his findings, "or they had to leave this position very quickly."

"Probably sloppy," added one of the signalmen.

"Whichever it is, we have some extra supplies," noted Jan, then added, "No water, though."

They were all thirsty and hungry. Conversation, through their parched lips and dry throats, became a considerable effort. Several brave attempts to deliver food and water to them resulted in disaster. Two vehicles were hit and four men in them were burnt alive. In desperation, the men started to drink the condensed milk; soon, however, they got diarrhea. Captain Kalas, it seemed, was affected most by it.

Under continuous artillery, mortar and machine-gun fire, they tried to identify the enemy's defence positions. For five days and nights, they were observing, calculating, occasionally shelling the enemy, and waiting - waiting for D-Day.

Then at 11 o'clock on the evening of May 11, all hell broke loose. 1,800 cannons and countless machine guns, and mortars opened fire. The dark night was illuminated by continuous firing. From the Adriatic to the Mediterranean, half-naked gunners, bodies glistening with sweat, fired deadly charges at the enemy. The shelling lasted forty minutes; then the infantry moved forward. Some of them were armed with tommyguns; others carried bazookas, or lugged deadly flame-throwers. Battalion after battalion, like giant ants, climbed the slopes of the mountains, or descended into the depths of the crevices, searching for the enemy.

Jan saw Captain Kalas giving orders over the field radio. The artillery almost at once extended its range and kept up their barrage ahead of the advancing infantry. Jan's duty as an observer was to detect and pinpoint the enemy positions and destroy them with artillery shells. He, and the observers from other artillery regiments, had to move forward with the infantry; therefore they would be in the first line of an attack. At first, it was a steady march.

An intensive artillery barrage managed to daze and suppress the enemy temporarily. The Polish troops moved smartly, one after another, heading toward their objectives. After such incredible artillery fire, they thought there could be only few enemies left to deal with.

Then the Germans opened fire. Shells and mortars fell among the marching troops. Jan heard the whine of the shells, explosions, then the cries of wounded men. He suddenly felt scared, and fought an impulse to turn and run.

"In case of calamity," Grandmother's words flashed through his mind, "the best thing to do is to pray; it will calm you down." 'Our Father, who art...' His prayer was interrupted by an explosion very close to him. He wasn't, strictly speaking, afraid - at least not scared enough to run or panic. What really bothered him was the invisibility of the enemy. "The sons-of-bitches," he swore harshly, "are hiding somewhere in the mountains. Come on, you Teutonic bastards, show your ugly faces!"

"Come on!" echoed several men around him. "Come on, you German bastards!"

The ominous ridge was not too far away now. A barrage of fire burst forth. A fearful explosion deafened him. There was sand in his mouth, his nostrils and his eyes. He wiped his eyes and looked back, expecting to see Dashevski, the corporal from Jan's battery, with his radio gear. Instead, he saw a severed arm, legs, and feet thrusting upward from a huge hole. Shocked and nauseated, he had to get away from this gruesome scene.

As he started to run on, he glanced at a shrub beside the path. Fragments of Dashevski's guts and parts of his battle-dress clung to the swaying branches.

He paused for a second or two, just enough time to realize the horror of Dashevski's death. First, he felt disbelief. It couldn't be one of his men there on those bushes. It must be some sick joke. Within seconds, however, incredulity was replaced by outrage, untamed and ferocious. He took a firmer grip on his tommygun and, jumping over boulders, short bushes, and his fallen comrades, he ran on.

"Forward!" he heard somebody order repeatedly. The clamour of machine guns, the rumbling of exploding artillery shells and the air-tearing howling of mortar shells spread their deadly harvest around Jan.

"Jesus, Mary!" Jan heard a cry and from the corner of his eye, saw a tall soldier, falling like an oak.

A few paces further, Jan almost collided with a soldier who, in a crouching position, was trying to stop his guts from pouring out. Normally he would vomit from seeing such a thing, but now he just by-passed the man and continued to run forward. Oblivious to the explosions, the rattling noises of machine guns and the screams of wounded men, he was only concerned about getting to the ridge to kill his enemies.

They encountered accurately-aimed machine gun fire from several points. A bullet struck his helmet, slapping it against his head. He felt a trickle of blood from his left temple, but ignored it. Gasping for breath, they climbed the slope as fast as their lungs permitted.

Suddenly, just before they reached Phantom Ridge, Jan saw the ridge ahead of him come alive. The Germans were descending like an avalanche.

"Forward!" a voice commanded somewhere to his right.

Jan increased his speed, running toward the Germans. The Germans came in force, their automatics pumping a hail of bullets. Their extended line moved toward the Poles with admirable efficiency.

In the bright moonlight, Jan saw them rising and falling, almost like on manoeuvers. By-passing a clump of thick bushes, Jan nearly crashed into a German paratrooper standing on a flat rock. In the moonlight, the German seemed enormous. The sudden encounter surprised them both.

Jan saw the barrel of the German's automatic move in a half-circle, but before his enemy could pull the trigger, Jan shot him in one short, but deadly, burst. He swiftly moved to the right and joined another score or so of Polish soldiers moving forward. Ahead of them, a group of Germans tried to escape; but, caught on a barren stretch of the ridge, they fell one after another; some tumbled forward on their faces, others spun around as though performing a last crazy dance, and still others, lifted by the force of the lead, hit the ground and rolled down the slope.

Then, when Jan thought that victory was in their hands, they were pinned down by a barrage of machine gun fire. Those who were too late to find cover, died before they could blink their eyes. Jan was hit twice, but luckily one bullet only grazed his left arm and the other one bounced off his helmet. He lay gasping for breath behind a large boulder. He tried to assess the situation calmly. The intensive fire of machine guns seemed to be coming from the area which, in the moonlight, looked like long overhanging cliffs. He could just see the bunkers, cleverly built along the face of the cliffs. He knew that the Poles had three choices: to retreat, move forward and take the bunkers, or stay where they were and be killed by the German artillery which should, in his judgment, start to fire soon.

'What's going on?' he thought angrily. 'Who's leading us anyway?' During the early stages of their assault, he had seen several officers, one of them a colonel. It was only when he heard the nearby explosions of enemy artillery that it occurred to him there might not be a single officer left. He knew then that he must act, and act fast.

Glancing around, he saw a soldier with a bazooka. He crawled toward him, attracting a series of machine gun bursts from one of the bunkers. Securing himself in his new position, he scanned the area around him, trying to assess how many of them were left, but he soon realized that even though the night was bright, it was impossible to count heads.

"We must take these bunkers, or we'll all die," he murmured to himself. He sent a message along the line that on his order, they were to open up with everything they had. Returning to the soldier with the bazooka, he pointed at the biggest bunker.

"Fire!" he roared as loudly as possible. The gun coughed and one of the bunkers was hit. To his right, he heard the rhythmic coughing of the Bren and the bursts of the automatics.

"Forward!" he roared. "Faster! Faster!" The soldiers, glad that someone was leading them, ran after him. However, some were cut down before they could take ten paces.

Jan saw flames coming from a nearby bunker. He fell to the ground and rolled toward it, wishing he was much faster. He saw the barrel of a machine gun blazing from an opening. Crawling to the side of the bunker, he pointed his tommygun into the opening, and emptied its magazine. He fumbled around his belt and grabbed a grenade. Removing the pin, he slowly and carefully threw it into the opening.

He heard an explosion, and then silence. He got up on his feet swaying, and ran toward another bunker. Before he got there, he saw it falling apart. He passed a German soldier rolling in agony, his uniform ablaze.

One by one, they knocked out the bunkers, nine in all, and when they thought that victory was finally theirs, the horrible thunder of German artillery struck them again. To Jan, it sounded as if a thousand devils had broken through the gates of hell. The ridge shook under the tremendous explosions. An instant later, he was rolling down the slope. He heard voices. A bearded man with a Red Cross band on his arm was injecting a needle into his arm. Then he saw a man's back in front of him. He was stumbling as though he was carrying some burden. Who or what was he carrying? Then he passed out.

Chapter Sixteen

Jan opened his eyes, and promptly closed them, bringing his hands up to protect them from the sunlight. When he could finally focus, he saw row after row of beds, few were empty, all were covered with white sheets.

He tried to get up but something was holding him down, something invisible but heavy. He pushed the blanket aside and saw that a wide belt held him firmly to the bed. Why was it so difficult to move a blanket? 'Am I tied up, a prisoner?' he wondered.

He tried to move his fingers - then saw that his hands were in casts. He made an effort to move his legs and immediately knew that they were also in casts. Sweat broke out on his face. "I'm wounded. God, my legs!"

"Nothing wrong with your legs, soldier. It will just take a little time for the bones to knit."

Jan turned to the man who had spoken. He saw a bandaged head and sharp black eyes looking at him. "You were in poor shape," said Jan's neighbour. "We thought you were a candidate for heaven - or hell."

Jan felt no pain. He felt very tired, wanting only to sleep, but then memories began to return, a series of clear images. "How long have I been here?" he asked.

"Three or four days."

Jan closed his eyes. Memories of the mountain and the artillery duelling filled his mind. He remembered the howl of artillery shells, the explosion of mortars, and the angry barking of machine guns. He did not want to think about it, but the images were too vivid to dispel. He slept again, the dreamless sleep of utter exhaustion.

****

He felt a cool hand on his forehead. He opened his eyes, then promptly closed them. The strong light was painful. Someone was beside him, but he was too tired to bother, and went back to sleep.

Jan didn't know how long he slept. When he woke up, the daylight didn't hurt so much.

"Hello! Feel better?" asked his neighbour.

"Yes, a bit, thank you," Jan answered.

"You sure were raving. I heard about the whole battle from you."

"What happened? Where are we?"

"Easy, easy. One question at a time. What happened? Well, in simple words, it was like this: we stormed the bloody Monte Cassino hills once and failed; we stormed them the second time, failed again. Whole regiments were wiped out. It seemed that every lousy bunker had to be burned and every German killed. Then every camp straggler, cook, batman, anyone who could still walk, was thrown onto those damned hills. Finally, we won. Only a few of us are left, but we won."

"Hmm..." was all Jan could say.

"But what a price! The newspaper said that more than 1,000 were killed, 3,500 wounded. That means one out of every ten is either dead or hurt. Well, I've told you, now it's your turn to tell me something - who's the girl that's so anxious about you?"

"What girl? Who do you mean?" Jan asked.

"Come on! You can't have a luscious brunette girlfriend like that and forget her! Or is she your sister? Don't worry, I won't compete. She's only interested in you."

Jan was puzzled. A girl - what girl? What woman was he talking about? It couldn't be his sister Maria. She was in the Air Force. The soldier said a brunette. 'Olenka? No, it would be too good to be true. Still, Olenka is a nurse. Couldn't she...' he closed his eyes and dozed. He heard voices and opened his eyes. A doctor looked down at him. The nurse he was talking to was partly obscured from Jan's vision.

The doctor grinned at Jan. "Awake at last. Good! We got you through all right."

Before Jan could say anything, the nurse came up beside his bed and smiled at him. It was Olenka! Her face was alive, her eyes full of warmth. Jan smiled. Her face seemed to brighten even more.

"You recognize me. That's so good, that means you'll be fine," she said.

"But, what are you doing here?" Jan asked. "It doesn't matter why you're here," he added quickly, "I'm just happy that you are."

"You know one another?" said the doctor. "In that case I shall leave you to talk. Nurse, see me when you can."

As soon as the doctor left, Olenka was bending over Jan's bed kissing his forehead. She was crying. Jan was too overcome and too weak to say anything, he just stared at her. He was close to tears.

"Oh, how silly of me!" cried Olenka softly. "Here I am crying instead of laughing! I'm so happy, Jan. Thank God you're alive... and we can be together again."

San Basilio, in southern Italy, is an ancient town overlooking the blue waters of the Adriatic Sea. High cliffs on the rugged coast defend the town from intrusion by sea. The heat of summer is moderated by cool sea breezes, and the nights are balmy - a perfect spot for convalescing soldiers.

Gradually, Jan's strength returned. After a month, he could walk about the hospital with the assistance of a nurse. After exercise and physiotherapy, he often sat in the garden, watching the bees circling busily about the bright flowers and listening to the crickets signaling in the shrubs. As his health improved, his spirits rose. For the first time in years, he knew contentment.

Olenka had a lot to do with Jan's peace of mind. Smiling and cheerful, she helped him in many ways - taking him in a wheel chair to the physiotherapist, then following the physiotherapist's direction to exercise his slowly mending muscles. Often they wandered through the sunlit garden, talking and laughing. Sometimes they talked about the war, or the good times they had had in Palestine, but never about the Soviet Union and their experiences there. They enjoyed the present and dreamed of the future. The past was merely a painful memory, far removed from San Basilio's healing serenity.

On a rainy afternoon in June, Jan sat on his bed, reading. Water streamed down the window, thunder rumbled in the distance. Tired of his book, Jan set it down. He looked about the familiar ward. The fresh-smelling sheets no longer seemed luxurious. Olenka was tending to an infantryman who had suffered severe chest wounds. She talked softly to the man, too low for Jan to hear, as she changed the dressing on his chest.

Jan had seen Olenka perform such tasks a hundred times. Today he watched with a particular intensity. 'She's kind and gentle,' Jan thought, 'there is tenderness and grace in her work.' Jan was thankful to God for allowing him to meet a wonderful person like Olenka. He felt a need to cherish her, to protect her, and to do everything possible to help her forget about her past.

Olenka left her patient, who smiled his thanks. As she walked to the next patient, she sensed Jan's intensity and stopped. Why was Jan staring so? She hurried to him.

"Olenka! Please sit down," Jan said, pretending to be severe. He took her hand and drew her down beside him on the bed.

"What is it? What's wrong?"

"Oh, nothing. I just want to tell you for the nth time that I love you, that's all," he said, smiling.

"I love you too, you dear... dear, crazy boy! But I must do my duty." Placing a kiss on his lips, she left the ward.

They spent hours together when Olenka was off duty. Sometimes they went into town, more often they wandered around the countryside, comfortable in the peace and warmth of summer. Jan's love for Olenka deepened, even though he never spoke of it. Usually, she was happy with him. But sometimes she was serious and withdrawn, and Jan could guess why.

The day finally came when Jan was to be discharged from the hospital. The Polish Second Corps, strengthened by reinforcements, was moving northward along the Adriatic, pushing the Germans back with its advance. It was time to rejoin his artillery unit. Olenka was unusually quiet and sad, but she never spoke of what was going on inside herself.

When Jan was set to leave, he put on his uniform and went in search of Olenka. A nurse informed him that she was in the nurses' residence. Jan hurried to her room. He knocked gently at the door and then pushed it open. Olenka was standing by the window, her face pale and tear-stained. She forced a smile.

"Jan! I hoped you would come."

"Yes, I've come to say goodbye." Jan stood awkwardly by the bed.

There was a long silence. The moment became unbearable until Olenka in a sad and tender voice broke the silence.

"Jan, God guard you! I will pray for you. I love you, and I always will." A tear rolled down her cheek.

Jan rushed to her, took her in his arms and kissed her. "Don't cry Olenka, don't cry. Olenka, I love you, too. I love you with all my heart! I'll come back to you, wherever you are, as soon as the fighting is over."

Olenka could barely speak. In a choked voice, she said, "I will wait for you, Jan." Then she burst into tears. Jan, holding her in his arms, let her cry. He dried her eyes and cheeks with his fingertips, then kissed her again. Calmer now, between sobs, she looked up into his eyes. Jan read in her eyes more love for him than any words could ever express.

He kissed her again, then turned on his heel and left. He never looked back. He knew the sight of her sobbing would break his heart.

****

Jan rode in an army truck traveling north. They drove through one town after another. Some had escaped destruction, and these bustled with life and activity. Cars, trucks, and horse-drawn wagons moved through the streets. The shops were open, but few goods were available. He saw farmers spread their meager produce in marketplaces they were passing.

Some of the towns showed the full brunt of war's ravages. Bombed buildings, craters in the streets, burned-out houses. He turned his attention to the Adriatic, as though expecting to find consolation and peace in its blue water.

Jan's truck came to a halt. A long column of military trucks had stopped by the side of the road. He approached a group of soldiers who were talking excitedly.

"What's going on?" he asked a short soldier.

"An uprising in Warsaw," was the reply.

That was all anyone seemed to know. Jan was stunned. He sat down on a nearby boulder. 'Why?' he thought. 'Why an uprising now?'

"You know what will happen to the people of Warsaw now," one of the soldiers standing in the group commented. Those bloodthirsty Germans will slaughter every one of them. Women and children can't beat German tanks."

"Then what are we doing here?" somebody asked. "We ought to be there with them."

The column moved ahead. Jan sat in his truck, feeling angry and helpless. He finally caught up with his regiment in the town of Ancona. He reported to the regimental commanding officer, Colonel Rydel.

"Congratulations! It is my great pleasure to inform you that you have been promoted to the rank of lieutenant," Colonel Rydel said formally.

Jan thanked the commander politely, but as he left to find his own quarters, he felt no pride. The honour meant little to him in the face of Warsaw's tragedy. His depression deepened.

The Germans were retreating north. Jan's regiment pursued. It was almost fall, with cold rain and cooler weather as they reached the Plain of Lombardy with its muddy fields and roads of clay. Jan's regiment was shifted east to the area of a town called Catolica, where they were assigned to the Canadian Infantry Brigade for two months.

Jan, thanks to his knowledge of English, was assigned to liaison with the Canadians. He became friendly with Major Page, the Commander of the Canadian Infantry Battalion. The major, a short, stocky man of forty, was a farmer from Saskatchewan. Jan learned a great deal about Canada from him. He also learned that Major Page had a bad temper.

"Your bloody English is Chinese to me," he once commented, about Jan's clumsy translation. But seeing that Jan was offended, he apologized: "Forgive me. My English father says that my French mother is responsible for my bad temper."

One day while waiting for the Major at the battalion headquarters, Jan was approached by a tall Canadian sergeant.

"Do you have a match?" the sergeant asked. Jan lit his cigarette. The sergeant inhaled deeply, then sat on the boulder beside Jan. "Where are you from?" he asked.

"From Poland."

"Oh, Polack, Polski. I am from Toronto," he pronounced it 'Tronna'.

"You're a long way from home now."

"Yes, and I hate soldiering."

"Who doesn't? Are you a professional soldier?"

"Me, a professional soldier? In civilian life, I worked in a machine shop."

"Were you drafted?" Jan asked.

"Yes, goddamnit. Two months ago. Were you drafted too?"

"No, I volunteered," Jan answered, then added, "Sort of."

"What do you mean by 'sort of'?" the Canadian was puzzled.

"Well, I had to volunteer, you see. I had to volunteer, otherwise I would still be in the Siberian camp." However, the Canadian's blank expression suggested that he didn't see at all. Jan wasn't anxious to talk about his past, so after a few more polite words, they said goodbye to one another.

Winter brought snow to the rolling hills and wide valleys, concealing some of the ugliness of war. The opposing armies, separated by a river, dug themselves in and waited. Except for patrol skirmishes now and then, the front was quiet. The Polish troops were impatient and restless. They were all aware that their country had been overrun by the Russians. They knew what that meant.

"Once the Russians set foot on a neighbour's land, they stay forever, unless overwhelming force can be brought against them," Captain Kalas said to Jan. "Britain or America will object for a while, then they will accept reality and agree to a Poland controlled by Russia. After the war, a couple of Red Army divisions will remain in Poland. Just to be sure that the people don't throw out the Communist government."

"Very likely," Jan agreed. "But what should we do?"

"There are two courses open to us, the way I see it," said Captain Kalas. "We can go back to Poland on the Communist government's conditions or not return at all."

Through the night, from one of the Polish batteries, came an old Polish song:

"We shall never leave the land of our fathers
The land of struggle and glory
So help us, God, so help us, God."

Jan went for a long walk, trying to decide where he should go, what he should do.

The Polish Second Corps, forming the right wing of the British Eighth Army, was pushing the Germans north, along the Adriatic Sea. The German forces, veterans of many battles, did not retreat willingly. Utilizing every mountain, every hill, river, and creek, they put up an impressive fight. They burned and dynamited every town, village or farm house. They destroyed miles and miles of paved roads and railways, setting all sorts of mines, traps, and snares. They killed anyone suspected of supporting the partisans.

One day, Jan was passing an area which had been particularly devastated by the war. Following his regiment and having no immediate duty to fulfill, he took his time, paying greater attention than usual to the landscape he drove through.

He was passing the smoldering ruins of roadside houses, dead mules, cows, and other domestic animals, some of which were lying in the ditches, others run over by military vehicles. He manoeuvered his jeep in an attempt to pass the huge craters and holes dug by the air and artillery bombardments.

He felt sad. 'Why is it,' he thought for the thousandth time, 'that man destroys things it took so long to build? What evil forces are behind this destruction? And why, above all, inflict such horrible suffering upon the children, women and elderly? How long will it take to rebuild these ruins, so those who have survived will have a roof over their heads? I hope,' he thought sadly, 'that our house in Zamosze has not met the same fate.'

His train of thought was broken by a woman sitting so close to the road-side that he had to swerve sharply to avoid her. He stopped his jeep and walked over to her. Garbed in traditional black, she was sitting on a small bench with her head down. She appeared to be preoccupied and it took her a while to pay attention to his presence. Behind the woman were the smoldering ruins of a house. The stench of burnt flesh, acrid and nauseating, filled the air. A few feet away lay the carcasses of two partially burnt cows. Their stomachs had been ripped open and were covered by swarms of flies.

Jan walked toward the ruins of the house. Even before he reached it, he saw something protruding from the rubble. Coming closer, he realized to his horror that it was a foot of a small child. He resisted the impulse to run from that gruesome scene; how could he leave just like that, he reflected. He found an iron bar and began to dig. It didn't take him long to uncover the body of a little girl, not much younger, he thought, than his sister Helena. Close to the girl were two dolls which he pulled from the ashes. He lifted the girl's body and gently placed it on a nearby stretch of grass. He continued to explore and found, in the ashes, the bodies of a man, a woman, and a child no more than two years old. The bodies were partially burned.

"The whole family," he whispered, "the whole family, except for the old woman."

The house, he concluded, had been bombarded by artillery shells. Those who weren't killed directly by the shells died in the fire started by them. After removing the bodies from the ruins, he lay them, one by one, on the grass. He stood there, looking at them for a long time. He was too moved to cry; he just stood motionless. Then he returned to the woman, who was still sitting quietly on her bench.

"Signora," he said huskily, touching her arm gently. He felt her tremble as she stifled a sob. The woman raised her head with great effort and looked at Jan. Jan saw her face for the first time, full of lines and wrinkles. Her tear-filled eyes showed such deep sorrow that Jan began to cry too.

"*Tuti sono morti,*" she whispered harshly.

By then Jan knew enough Italian to know what she had said. "They all died," he repeated.

He wanted to console this poor creature somehow, to give her something to hang on to, but he couldn't find the words. He took her old hand in his, trying to convey his message by a touch. Her hand was rough and calloused by hard physical work. For a moment he imagined that he was in Zamosze and that the hand belonged to his grandmother. He gently lifted her hand and kissed it warmly, as if she were his grandmother. He rose to his feet and started toward his jeep. He stumbled on something and stooped to the ash-covered ground to discover what it was. He brushed aside the ashes and dust to uncover a simple wooden crucifix with a metal image of Christ, fastened by three common nails. Assuming that it belonged to the old woman's family, he walked back with the intention of returning it to her. She looked at the crucifix for a long while, then raised her eyes to Jan.

"Take it. I want you to have it. Please, young man, take it."

"But signora, it is yours, so..."

"Carry it with you," she interrupted, then added, "Take it to your home, my son, because my home..." she waved her hand toward the ruins.

'My home?' Jan thought. 'I wonder...' He was too tired and too unhappy to finish his train of thought. He walked away towards his jeep, with a slow and fatigued walk of an old man.

Chapter Seventeen

The colonel was dressed in a splendid uniform, adorned with numerous decorations. He spoke matter-of-factly. In front of his desk sat ten officers of various ranks. There were three majors, four captains and three lieutenants. Judging from the insignias on their sleeves, the officers belonged to various divisions and brigades comprising the Second Polish Corps; the Fifth Wilno Division, the Armory Brigade, the Artillery Group, the Carpathian Division, etc.

"Gentlemen, I will be brief," said the colonel. "The aim of this meeting is to choose the courier to Poland. As you know, our country is occupied again, this time by the Soviet Red Army. Thousands of our partisans, mainly in Eastern Poland, are fighting against the new occupants. We don't know how events are going to develop, but in case there is war between the west and the Soviet Union, we want to be ready. Thus, we must help our partisans in every way we can. There is an urgent need to deliver much needed money to our partisans in Poland so they'll be able to acquire arms, food, and clothing. Also some important documents should be sent as soon as possible."

"Who will sell them arms?" one of the captains boldly interrupted.

"Money talks, Captain. Russkies themselves will sell, if no one else. Returning to my theme... besides the money, we are sending a coded list of suspected traitors who have infiltrated the partisan ranks. They must be stopped before it's too late." He sat for a while in silence, then resumed his address. "The courier we send must be, first of all, familiar with eastern Poland. He must be physically fit, tenacious, intelligent, able to speak the Byelorussian language, and, above all, honest and loyal."

"I would love to meet such a man," one major remarked.

"You won't! There's no such animal in the Second..." somebody intoned. He didn't finish the sentence. The colonel's steel-like stare silenced him.
"This is hardly a subject for your wit, gentlemen. Your jocularity is out

of order," he thundered. "I want you to think, now. Surely there must be such a man in one of your units."

There were many who came close to meeting the requirements. Under closer scrutiny, however, none were fully qualified; some did not speak Byelorussian, others were not familiar enough with the area, still others had the necessary qualifications, but could not be trusted fully.

"Jan Tabor," the baritone voice of a tall major from the Artillery Group said triumphantly. "He has all the qualifications," he continued, "and one extra you didn't mention, Colonel."

"And what is that?" the colonel asked.

"He is from the marshlands, where most of our partisans are at present."

"Send him in, Major," the colonel ordered.

Two weeks later, a two-passenger plane with Jan aboard left the Bari Airport in southern Italy and headed toward central Europe. Jan, now known as "The Fox", was dressed in long knee boots, a warm lumberjack shirt, grey linen pants, and a short, heavy woolen jacket. A Russian style fur hat completed his attire. He looked like a young Byelorussian farmer. In his inside coat pocket, he had personal identification documents, a set of Russian and Polish certificates, and affidavits which stated that "Wasyl Kulik, born in Bostyn, was a citizen of the Byelorussian Socialist Republic." The parcel he was delivering was wrapped in grey oil-cloth and cleverly concealed in his heavy coat.

His attempts to communicate with the pilot sitting in front of him had failed. All he got from him was "yes" and "no". Closing his eyes, he thought about the events of the last few weeks. He recalled his summons to the colonel's office, and his initial reluctance to comply with the colonel's request to take the assignment. When this was getting nowhere, the colonel simply changed his request to a direct order. By then, Jan smiled to himself, he had changed his mind and decided to go anyway. An opportunity to see his beloved marshes and maybe find out what had happened to his father was too good to refuse. However, he didn't want to show the colonel his eagerness to go. His thoughts switched to the mission ahead. He had been told to get to Bostyn and wait there in the only restaurant until the partisan's contact led him to "The Wolf", the commanding officer of the partisans.

"If you fail to meet The Wolf, you will deliver the parcel to 'The Birch'. Remember, Jan, The Wolf or The Birch, nobody else. You'll be parachuted into the Carpathian Mountains. That is as far as our plane can go. If you're caught," he was warned, "you're a dead man. Either you'll shoot yourself, or they will torture you... and then shoot you."

Now, remembering these ominous words, he tried hard to be calm. His thoughts wandered from his village, the marshes, the Polish Army, his family, and the Soviet Labour Camp, then back again to his village.

'Soon, I will see Zamosze again,' he thought with a sigh. His fears somehow subsided and he felt happier. They had been flying for six hours. 'Soon I'll be on Polish soil... after five long years.'

"Ready?" he heard the pilot call, followed by: "Jump!"

He jumped into the cloud beneath him, falling into bottomless darkness. Instantly, the cumulus clouds soaked him to the skin. Gasping for air, he pulled the string of his parachute and was relieved to feel the jolt as his parachute opened. Descending slowly, he peered down, hoping to see where he was headed, but saw only darkness beneath him. April rain lashed his feverish face, cooling it. He began to shiver uncontrollably.

His feet touched something soft, something very wet. Almost instantly, he realized, to his horror, that it was the tree line. He kicked furiously to keep his feet from the tree crowns, but felt only the air and an instant later, he hit the ground. He began to roll down a slope, then he hit something hard and passed out.

When he regained consciousness, it was already morning; sunny and pleasantly warm. He lay still with his eyes closed, trying to regain his wits. He recreated the events of last night, up to the moment when he was sliding, terrified over the tree crowns.

"My parachute," he suddenly remembered. He jumped to his feet, but immediately had to sit down again because of the pain in his head and his left arm. "Thank goodness for this heavy Russian fur hat," he whispered, feeling the tender spot on his head. Looking around, he realized that he had landed on the steep slope of a mountain just a few metres from a grove of trees.

He checked his coat and felt relieved. The parcel was still there. He found a small depression where he concealed his parachute with stones and branches. When he had settled his immediate problems, his anxiety returned. "Steady man, steady," he told himself. "Sit on that boulder and think... think..."

He looked around again, more slowly this time. The landscape, as far as he could see, was gently hilly. "Must be in the Carpathian foothills," he concluded. Judging by the lush grasses, it was probably used for cows or sheep, so, he thought, there must be a settlement nearby. At least there should be. He began to follow a path which led to the valley below.

The narrow path unwound like a snake, bypassing rocky outcrops and occasional clumps of trees. The day was becoming brighter and warmer. On both sides of the path, the meadow was covered with wild flowers. Jan was elated, inhaling the fresh mountain air and feasting his eyes on the colourful meadow, almost forgetting his reason for being there.

There was a noise from behind a rock outcrop to his left, like the heavy steps of somebody walking. Jan fell flat and lay motionless. The noise stopped, and as Jan lay, sweating with fear, he heard the neighing of a horse. He peered from behind the rock and laughing, jumped to his feet.

A few paces behind the rock was a short, grey horse with the thick, deformed legs and heavy bones of a working horse. The horse, hearing Jan's steps, raised its head for a second and then, reassured that there was no danger, continued grazing.

Jan petted its mane and back, chasing the flies away. The horse, as if to thank him for his kindness, waved its tail and neighed.

The slope was much gentler now as he resumed his walk, and soon he found himself in a wide U-shaped valley. The valley was cut by a narrow stream, its water hardly reaching Jan's knees. On the other side of the stream, Jan saw a village about half a kilometre away.

The path soon merged with a narrow road leading to the village. The road was unpaved, bumpy and full of potholes. Two narrow furrows had been carved by the wheels of inumerable farm carts. And indeed, there were two such carts, a short distance ahead of Jan.

Jan once again was reminded of Zamosze and bygone springs. He came upon a small wayside shrine next to a linden grove. It was a wooden structure with a triangular roof, only a few metres away from the road and partly hidden by the trees and bushes.

He hesitated, then turned to his right and approached the shrine. It contained a crudely carved statue of the Holy Mother. The body of the carving had been done with an axe and a crude chisel. The Madonna's face, however, had been carved with a knife, with much attention given to the expression. To Jan it was a face of sadness, thoughtfulness, and suffering. He sat on a wooden bench, his eyes on the statue, and he felt the sadness in his own heart. The artist who had carved this statue had reflected, perhaps unwittingly, the suffering of his people, trampled through the centuries by the hooves of the invading Tatars' and Turks' horses and more recently, by the tanks of the Germans and Russians. Jan felt a deep sense of kinship with his people, symbolized by this Madonna, the sad Queen of Poland.

From far off, he could hear the barking of dogs and see smoking chimneys. It was as if the village was welcoming him. Soon he was walking through the only street in the village. Women were working in their little gardens; children were playing on the wooden sidewalks. Men were driving their horse carts or walking on the street. Nobody paid any attention to a youth walking alone. The war was still going on and more than one stranger had passed through this street lately; partisans going home, having left their sanctuaries in the hills; slave workers who had been captured by the Germans then freed by the Red Army, returning to their villages; men, women and children looking for lost members of their families. Nobody paid any attention to Jan, not even a passing Red Army convoy.

He continued walking, hoping to reach some railway station and take a train to Warsaw. From there, he was planning to swing east, also by train, and head toward Pinsk. In the meantime, he was thirsty and hungry. He reached into his tunic and removed some Polish money, given to him in Bari.

In the next village, or what was left of it, there were only a few people. Those few were busy rebuilding their burned out homes. The men and women were so busy with their task that when Jan tried to start a conversation, they did not respond. He continued his walk.

All the villagers he met bore the hardship and suffering of war. They were, almost without exception, shabbily dressed, with undernourished pale faces, looking exhausted. Barefoot, half-naked children, many with rickety legs and bulging stomachs, stared sadly at the unknown passerby. Some children, stronger and perhaps better fed, were playing, splashing each other in the puddles formed by the recent spring rainfall. Their chattering delighted Jan, who had almost forgotten the sound of Polish children at play.

In spite of his ever-increasing hunger, Jan kept pushing on, leaving several villages and hamlets behind him. The road, judging by the position of the sun, led roughly in the desired direction, northwards. His shadow was lengthening and it was getting colder.

His body ached with tiredness and the after-effects of the parachute jump. He walked on for another two hours. Instead of fields on both sides of the road, he was now passing an elm forest, with no sign of buildings or human habitation. The twilight had turned to darkness. The sky had clouded over and Jan had to strain his eyes to follow the barely visible outline of the cart track. As he turned the corner on one of the numerous curves, Jan saw a dim light to his left, through the trees. It was flickering hesitantly, as though somebody was playing with it.

He left the road, and plunged into the forest, heading toward the light. Stumbling over tree roots and stumps, he walked over the soft, damp forest floor, until he felt firmer ground under his feet. It appeared to be some sort of road, narrow and bumpy. Soon he heard a barking dog. He slowed down, watching and listening for any sign of danger. Everything seemed calm. Entering a clearingm he saw a house about 50 metres ahead of him. It was a solitary log building. The absence of barn and stables indicated that it was not a farm but probably a forester's house. A huge dog on a chain guarded the only door leading to the house. Its barking suddenly became a raving howl, terrifying Jan. He stood, stunned in the light cast by the dimly lit window. The door was thrown open and a man came out, pointing a rifle.

"Who are you?" the man demanded.

"A traveler."

"Go away! We don't need travelers here. Go away before I shoot!"

"I... I... just thought that perhaps I could buy some food, sir."

"Food? You crazy, or what? We don't have food! Go!" the man repeated.

Jan returned to the road and continued walking. The main thing, he told himself was to stick to the northbound road. Sooner or later it would take him to a larger town or to a railway station. In the meantime he decided to rest for a few moments beside the road.

Morning was breaking through and soon, he thought, it would be warm. Sitting on the grass, he began thinking about what he should do next. In spite of his extreme tiredness and inability to find lodging, he was happy about the development of events. At least so far. After all, he reflected, he was alive and heading toward his home. Hadn't he been in much worse situations before? Didn't he have a considerable amount of Russian and Polish money?

What he needed was some sort of transportation. That should be first, if he really wanted to get to Zamosze soon. A horse? Maybe he should try to buy a horse. He had seen quite a few people passing him on horseback. However, after further thought, he dismissed the idea. A horse, he thought, reliable animal though it was, was too slow. No, it must be something faster, but what? He rose stiffly to his feet and resumed his walk.

236

The sun rolled up from behind the hills and he noticed a farmhouse. Being afraid of the same reception as before, he circled so that he could enter the barn rather than the house. He met a yapping puppy. He stroked the little animal and it soon became friendly. Jan sneaked into the barn where, as he had expected, plenty of hay was stacked in the loft. Climbing a ladder which he found in the barn, he reached the loft and, burrowing deeply, went to sleep almost at once. The puppy, left alone, sniffed for a while, then left the barn.

Jan didn't know how long he slept, but he was startled by the complete darkness enveloping him. 'Is it night time?' he thought. His ears registered the lowing of cattle coming from outside and human voices muffled by distance.

It had to be evening, around milking time. Perhaps he should wait for a while until it was quiet and then he should move. He closed his eyes and lay quietly. However, he was so tired that he went to sleep again. This time he was awakened by a cock crowing, a sound he had not heard for a long time. The sound was loud and was coming from below. 'Well,' he thought, 'wherever there's a rooster, there must be hens.' He climbed down the ladder, lit a match and started to search the barn. It didn't take him long to find a flock of hens, bunched together in one of the corners. Amid cackling, he chased them away and found what he was looking for - eggs. He was thirsty and hungry, what could be better than raw eggs? After the meal, feeling refreshed, he left the farm as quietly as he could and in the light of dawn, soon reached the main road.

In the dim light he spotted a sign-post: "KATOWICE 25 km."

"Aha!" he exclaimed with satisfaction, "so I am heading in the right direction. Then I should be in Katowice by tonight."

Early morning found him in a little village, a mere 40 households or so. Despite his raw egg feast only a few hours earlier, he still felt hungry. He cursed his superior officers in Italy for not providing him with rations. It would have saved him a lot of trouble and, what's more important, it would have been safer. Then he remembered the young major's last words: "You must live off the land, Jan." Little did the major know, Jan thought, that the land he was referring to had been devastated and its people were hungry.

He stopped at the first house, where an old lady in a black dress carrying a large pail of milk was leaving the barn.

"Good morning, mother," he greeted her with the traditional Zamoszan salutation for elderly women.

"Good morning," she replied without slowing down.

"May I buy some milk from you, mother?"

"It is not for sale."

"I will pay you well."

"I can't drink money, can I?"

"I will pay you twice what it's worth. Three times," he was walking behind her, feeling desperate.

"Three times, you say?"

"Yes! Yes!"

"Wait!" she commanded.

"Some bread too," he yelled after her.

A long time passed before she reappeared, but it was worth the wait because she was holding a bottle of milk and a good-sized loaf of bread. He paid her in Polish currency, throwing in some extra zlotys. He passed the village and, finding a comfortable spot along the road, he sat down and started to eat. The bread had a sour taste and was stale, but the milk? 'Still warm,' he thought, emptying the bottle and throwing it into the nearby ditch.

He reached Katowice at sundown. It was a large town, half devastated. Every street and every square he passed was jammed with Soviet military vehicles and marching infantry. Some of the marching soldiers in ragged, long, mud-coloured coats, rifles hanging carelessly on their arms, were singing their beloved "Katusha". "Katusha" brought back memories of the first Soviet troops he had seen in Zamosze.

It was getting dark quickly, so he started to look for the railway station. He stopped a few people to ask directions and after half an hour reached the large station, crowded to its limits with peasants dressed in heavy, shabby coats even though it was the end of April and the weather was turning warm. Some of them, women mostly, were loaded with bags and sacks of all descriptions. Some were carrying meat wrapped in linen cloth, and two men were carrying sacks of flour. Jan looked at their faces; almost all pale, some wrinkled and all tired, a testimony to starvation and hardship. Here and there, he noticed the green uniforms of the Polish People's (communist) Army. Their lean, pale faces and ragged uniforms also suggested years of hardship. Some wore bandages, while others were on crutches, hopping from one end of the station to the other. Jan became aware of two militia men who, with Soviet built automatic guns, stood at the door of the station. Jan moved as far from them as he could and found a little space to sit down.

He had to devise a plan to fulfill his mission. He was listening to radio music, coming from a loudspeaker placed somewhere outside the station. A monotonous folk song was interrupted by a news announcement. He tried to listen through the noise of the crowd. "The glorious Red Army together with the Polish People's Republic Army, have reached Berlin. Savage fighting over the last remaining few square miles of Nazi soil is going on right now. Hitler's nest is under constant bombardment. The Allied forces are advancing slowly, very slowly from the west. They want the Red Army to bleed."

'Even if the Americans and British advance faster,' Jan thought bitterly, 'it is too late for Poland, already "liberated" by the Soviets.'

The long-awaited train with its broken windows finally arrived. The crowd rushed toward it en masse. After a considerable struggle, with frequent use of his elbows, Jan found a seat on a wooden train bench, squeezed between two peasant women. One of them had a sack of potatoes between her legs, and was holding it with both hands as though there were diamonds inside. Another, thinner and smaller, was holding a big chunk of raw pork wrapped in a huge kerchief. The blood had soaked through the material and was staining Jan's left pantleg.

"Mother," he turned to the woman, "would you..." he never finished his sentence.

"Oh, yes. Thank you, young man," she spoke in a sing-song dialect. "I knew at once that you were a good boy and wanted to help me." So saying, she placed the meat on Jan's lap and sighing heavily, closed her eyes and pretended to sleep. Jan noticed, however, that one end of the string around the meat was firmly wrapped around her left hand.

'She wants me to hold this goddamned meat, but at the same time, she doesn't trust me,' he thought, shaking his head.

The train coach was packed to full capacity. People were standing, crammed into the corridors and compartments, or sitting on the floor. Only a few lucky ones like Jan sat on the benches. There were bundles everywhere: on shelves, under benches, between the benches and in the corridors, piled as high as the broken windows. It was hot and stuffy in spite of broken windows but, to Jan's surprise, quiet. The poor wretches were too tired to talk, he concluded.

The train moved slowly, stopping at every station, large and small. It puffed and jerked along as though it was also tired. Jan calculated that with this kind of speed, he would be lucky to get to Warsaw by noon of the next day. He desperately wanted to see the countryside, but there was no way to get close to the window, and it was still dark, so he closed his eyes and tried to sleep. His soggy trousers made him uncomfortable and miserable. Fortunately, after three hours, the woman with the meat got off, relieving him of his burden. Her place was taken by a little girl of about ten years old, giving him, thankfully, a little more space. Soon, he fell asleep.

He didn't know how long he slept. When he opened his eyes, standing before him was a tall, uniformed man with three stars on his shoulders. He was flanked by two other soldiers.

"Documents," barked the big captain. "Byelorussian?" the captain said, looking at Jan's papers with suspicion.

"Yes," Jan answered meekly.

"And what are you doing here... on this train?"

"Going home, comrade."

"From where?"

"From enforced labour in Germany, captain," he replied, then added hurriedly, "A document explaining this matter is attached. Look for yourself, it is in Russian."

The captain, after glancing once more at Jan's document and after weighing the information for a while, gave the papers back to Jan and left.

"It worked," Jan sighed, drying the sweat from his face. The train, after a torturous series of stops and back and forth manoeuvers, finally arrived in Warsaw in the afternoon. Jan followed the crowd.

He had never been to Warsaw. It had never been necessary for Michal Tabor, Jan's father, to go to Warsaw. In any case, the distance and expense prohibited a Pripet Marshes farmer from visiting the capital, never mind taking his son along. Jan's knowledge of the Polish capital came from the stories of those who had the means to travel and from his reading.

He had visualized the capital as a large and bustling centre. What greeted him was piles of rubble stretching as far as he could see. He had seen bombarded cities in Italy, like Foggia and Rimini, where whole blocks lay in ruins. But here he saw a whole city completely and totally devastated, a city that, before the war, had a population of one million people. He stood there shocked, not knowing what to do next. After a while, he returned to the station, or more correctly, a clearing among the rubble serving as a station. He found a half burned log and sat against it, tired.

Somebody touched his back, gently. He turned his head and saw a man in his late thirties, with shaggy, unkempt hair, standing before him. The man's clothes were also soiled and ragged, like most of the people he had seen so far. Then Jan realized that the man was wearing a priest's garb. His collar, white originally, was now the colour of mud.

"In which direction do you intend to travel?" Jan heard the priest ask in a tired voice.

"East."

"Oh, so am I," then added: "If we are lucky, that is."

"I don't understand."

"The train may or may not go east today. Besides, it is full of Soviet soldiers. Well, I guess we will have to wait and hope." He sat silently for a long time. Then the priest noticed Jan's eyes scanning the ruins over and over again. "Nothing left," the priest said.

"But... it's incredible!" exclaimed Jan, almost crying.

"I can guess you were not here during the uprising." Then without waiting for Jan to respond, the priest continued. "250,000 men, women and children perished. And our allies," his eyes pointed to a group of Soviet soldiers approaching the station, "were camped on the other side of the Vistula River." His voice was full of bitterness and anger.

"How could that happen?" Jan asked.

"The city rose against the Germans. We fought for five weeks, hoping for Soviet help. But all we heard from them was radio propaganda. They, incredibly, were telling the world that the adventure-seeking Poles had started the uprising against the good judgment of the Soviets." He was silent for a while, breathing hard. Then in a quiet voice, he resumed his monologue. "They wanted us dead. The Germans, after evacuating those who survived and taking them to their prison camps, dynamited virtually every house and every building. This is all that is left."

After a long silence, Jan and the priest decided to take a walk. They took a narrow path which had once been a street. Now it led nowhere. People, bundled in heavy, soiled clothes, were clearing heavy cement blocks, moving them from one place to another.

"What are they doing?" Jan asked, turning to his companion.

"Building shelters, caves, actually. Look there," he pointed to his right.

Jan saw several huts. Some were without doors or windows, some had doors made of canvas. Men, women and children, their faces determined and stoic, continued their work without even a glance at Jan and his companion.

"They will survive," said the priest.

"You think so?"

"Sure, every generation of Poles has."

"But look!" Jan cried. "Look around!"

His companion was grim, determined. "For thousands of years we have survived the Tatars, Turks, Germans, and Russians... and we shall survive the Soviets." Jan observed his companion's strong, Polish face as he spoke.

The priest resumed. "You know, for five years, the Germans have tried to destroy us as a people. They have been good at it, very good. Employing their modern technology to its fullest, they have managed to murder six million of us; with bullets, in crematoria, in slave labour camps... and of course like this," he waved his hand over the Warsaw ruins.

He stopped as though short of breath, then added, "And yet they have failed! They failed to kill our spirit and our faith. Oh, they tried that, too. Ninety percent of the Polish priests are dead, thousands of teachers and professors have perished. But they have failed. Look at those poor wretches rebuilding their shelters. There will be a priest here on Sunday to celebrate mass. These surviving slabs of cement will be the altar. I know, I have done it."

"Will the Russians and the Polish Communists allow these masses?" Jan asked.

"Allow? They will try their best to stop us, but like the Germans, they will also fail. Listen to me, young man. Don't be afraid of losing everything, but guard your spirit and stick to your faith." Their conversation was interrupted by a sudden whistle and the noise of an approaching train.

"We'd better hurry back," the priest said. "I'm supposed to meet someone. He's also a priest who is going to work in our diocese. It's only a few weeks since he returned from the west... England, I believe."

"Oh?" Jan exclaimed.

"Nice fellow," the priest prattled on. "He would rather live in England, but as he told me, he is needed here more."

As they approached the "station", Jan saw a tall, burly figure waving at them from the milling throng. "Father Stefan!" the man's powerful voice pierced the noise. "Father Stefan!" he repeated, running toward them. Then noticing the priest's companion, he stopped. "Oh, you have company," he said in a quieter voice.

Jan looked at the man in astonishment. It was Zamosze's parish priest, Father Kowalski. He looked older and stouter, but unmistakably the same priest whose chestnut horse Jan had helped, many years ago.

Father Kowalski looked at Jan, too. Then he addressed Jan. "I know you, young man... but..."

"Zamosze."

"Zamosze!" roared Father Kowalski, causing Father Stefan to jump. "Jan!"

"Father Kowalski!"

They hugged each other, oblivious to the world around them. It took a while for Father Stefan to separate them and lead them to the train.

"It seems," said Father Stefan, chuckling, "that you know each other."
"Know? What a question!" cried Father Kowalski. "You are looking at my best altar boy, Father. Former altar boy," he corrected himself, laughing. "He saved my horse, a chestnut to be exact... he..."

"Prepare yourself for a battle," Father Stefan said with a wink. And indeed it was a battle. It took them half an hour to get places on the train. The clerics' collars, soiled though they were, helped, and they found a space in the corridor to accommodate them all.

They talked about the past for hours. Jan told Father Kowalski almost everything except, of course, his mission. Father Kowalski, it turned out, had spent almost two years in Soviet prisons, "confessing" as he told Jan, "all of those who asked me to do so. The prisoners, the Russian prisoners included, on learning that I was a priest, asked me to be their confessor. Not all of them, however. Some others told me 'If you are the Lord's priest, you should be able to make a miracle and all of us can walk out of this prison'," he said, laughing.

"Why did you return to Poland, Father?" Jan asked.

"I am needed here more than in England. There will be a battle again - a battle for the souls of our people. Because it is against the soul that the new order will strike..."

"The Soviets will try to kill our spirit, mark my words," Father Stefan broke into the conversation.

"And you, Jan? Why did you return?" Father Kowalski asked, staring.

"To... to find my father."

"Oh? I hope you will."

The train arrived at the town of Byalystock. "Good luck! Good luck!" the priests cried, leaving the train.

'I need plenty of good luck,' thought Jan, looking at his fellow passengers, mostly Soviet soldiers. In their filthy and worn coats, they were a tired looking lot. Some, in bandages, stared sadly through the train windows. Their faces showed the years of hard suffering and deprivation. They had fought their enemies step by step, at first kicking them out of their own country and then pushing them as far as Berlin. Now, they were going home, but facing them was the rubble of their towns and cities, and starvation on the collective farms. Some of them could even end up in Siberia. Perhaps he should hate them for what they had done to him, his family, and thousands of other innocent people. But he knew what the Soviet system really was; he had experienced it. He had seen how this system treated not only prisoners, but its own people as well. It was somehow difficult, although there was good reason, to hate these people knowing that they, too, were victims.

In the morning of the next day, the train arrived in Pinsk. Jan left the train and stood on the platform stunned. The district adjacent to the station was all in ruins. He remembered it had been inhabited by Jews and included the town's market, which he and his father had so frequently visited. Now, as far as he could see, only the skeletons of burned houses and impassable streets remained. Fortunately, other districts of the town had survived, and so, after some hesitation, he walked into Pinsk.

The few people he saw were apathetic and lifeless. There was no sign of rebuilding of the destroyed districts. Pinsk, he concluded, resembled a cemetery. Since his destination was Bostyn, he decided to leave at once. After a final glance at Pinsk, he started to walk toward Bostyn, hoping to reach it by the end of the day. He was overtaken by a horse and farm cart driven by an old, bearded peasant.

The peasant, seeing Jan's raised hand, stopped his horse and looked at Jan appraisingly. "Where to?" The man's melodious, Byelorussian voice was pleasant and friendly.

"Home... Bostyn," Jan answered.

"Oh, good thing you have a home. Not like this." The peasant waved his whip toward Pinsk. "So you are from Bostyn?" the peasant asked.

"Well, not exactly Bostyn, a bit further, a place called Zamosze."

"Zamosze?" the man's tone of voice changed. "Zamosze, you said?... I knew the village, I knew the village." Jan was worried about the word "knew", but said nothing.

The country road hadn't changed since Jan had last traveled over it with his father. It was narrow and sandy, with numerous puddles through which the grey horse had to splash, sometimes up to its knees. On both sides were flat, sandy fields, and beyond them, the lonely marshes, stretching as far as Jan could see. Here and there he noticed a peasant ploughing his field. Some farm workers were sowing rye by hand, just the same as before the war. The fresh ridges of ploughed soil were covered by flocks of noisy crows. Further, over the marshes, clouds of birds were descending over the turf islands, seeking shelter for the night. Jan's eyes filled with tears. His lungs were breathing in the sour-sweet smell of the marshes that he had dreamed of so many times. This was a part of him. He had longed for this moment while in the vastness of Siberia and in the deserts.

His eyes were scanning the sandy fields, leafy groves, and marshes. The peasant nudged his arm. He had been asking Jan some question repeatedly, and wanted to bring him back to reality.

"Where were you during the war?"

"In Germany," he answered, drying his eyes.

"You were working there?"

"Yes."

"Many others did the same," the peasant said, "but only a few have returned... so far," he added.

"You have a good horse," Jan said to change the subject.

"Yes, he's not bad," the man agreed. Then, as an afterthought, he added, "I'm lucky to have a horse at all. Very few left, you know."

They drove through a village familiar to Jan. Most of it had been burned.

Small groups of peasants in ragged clothing were rummaging in the cinders, some with shovels, some with their bare hands, hoping to find something that could still be used, Jan supposed. Some others were just standing with their feet buried deeply in the ashes, staring vacantly at what used to be their homes.

Children, unwashed and half-naked, sat quietly on half-burned logs, probably thinking about yet another night they would have to spend without a roof over their heads.

'They, too, have become homeless and uprooted,' Jan thought sadly. 'Who is responsible for the misery of these people... these children?'

"The soldiers and partisans," the peasant said, as though guessing Jan's thoughts. "Always there were soldiers and partisans here; Polish, Soviets, Byelorussian, even Jewish. They descended upon our villages like vultures, always looking for the same thing - food. On their tails, like hunting dogs, came the soldiers of the occupying armies; Germans looking for partisans and taking our bread again; Russians looking for Germans and taking our bread. They were burning and killing each other and us. We Byelorussians were killing Germans, sometimes Poles and Byelorussians." He stopped, out of breath. "Our property was burned and our food stolen. Whose side to take? Who should you support? You couldn't trust anyone, not even your own. And now? Do you think this is the end of it? The bloody Russians are taking away our land - our land, young man! These few furrows... they are taking them away from us. They are telling us it will be better for us. Better? How could it be better? I love my land, meager though it is, I love every bit of it, so do others like me. Now the Soviets are taking it away from us. They are merging our small holdings together into what they call a collective farm. A child, I am telling you young man, a child could tell them that a farmer without his own piece of land is not a farmer anymore. Tfoo!" He spat in contempt.

"Why won't he be a farmer anymore?" Jan asked.

"Because... because," the peasant was obviously looking for the right word.

"His pride..." Jan said, trying to help.

"Yes, exactly, pride!" exclaimed the peasant. "The collective farms will kill the farmers' pride. And killing? Still going on, let me tell you." He bent closer to Jan. "Just two days ago, Polish partisans came to Bostyn and killed the Soviet Commissar. There will be more trouble, young man. There will!"

He swung his whip in the direction of the marshes. "These marshes, young man, these marshes are red with the blood of men, women and children. Yes, red... Tfoo!" He spat again.

Jan hardly recognized Bostyn when they arrived there in the late afternoon. The houses he remembered were gone. The streets had been renamed. The voices he heard were different. He expected to hear Poles speaking Polish, Jews speaking Yiddish. He heard only Russian and Byelorussian. He walked to the place where his school had stood. It was gone. The Catholic Church was still there, but it had been converted into some sort of warehouse. The town centre had undergone the greatest change. The square, which had had numerous Jewish shops, was gone. So was the old city hall.

Jan strolled about. His rendezvous was in a restaurant on the other side of the town. He noticed that there were few people in the streets and to his relief, he saw no familiar faces. Men and women walked around silent and unsmiling. What had made this once lively town so lifeless? Was it the lack of shops, or the noise and activity of the Jewish merchants? Where were they? There had been scores of them before the war. They had been everywhere in their long, black coats, bewhiskered, vigorous, gesticulating, enjoying their trading skirmishes hugely. Others always had worn the latest fashions and it seemed that their conversation had invariably been humorous, as if there was fun in everything they did. It was the Jews who had given the town its vigor and its colourful appearance, Jan saw that now.

He decided to go to the town cemetery. He wanted to pray and reflect at his mother's grave. The cemetery, he was certain, would not have changed like the rest of Bostyn. The cemetery had been on the eastern outskirts of the town. Beyond it was the road leading to Zamosze. Jan, as a school boy, had passed the cemetery twice daily. He reached the place where the cemetery should have been. There was no cemetery. In its place were row after row of Russian tanks. Most of the tanks showed the scars of battles: broken turrets, shattered caterpillars, holes, dents, and scratches. Jan was stunned. The cemetery, before the war, had been divided into two sections - the larger Christian part with crosses, and the smaller Jewish section with stars of David on the stones. Now there were no markers.

"Could I be in the wrong place?" he asked himself. He scanned the street closely, looking for someone he could ask about the cemetery. There was no one in sight. He waited for some minutes until he spotted an old, stooped woman walking slowly along the muddy street, supporting herself with a cane. She was at least eighty. He walked quickly, caught up with her, and greeted her in Byelorussian. She answered him in Polish.

Jan, walking slowly beside her, asked what had become of the cemetery.

She raised her tired, sad eyes to meet Jan's. "The cemetery," she said, "is gone."

"Gone? Gone where?"

"Everything is gone, young man! Everything!" her hand moved in a broad circle.

"Everything," Jan repeated quietly. 'Everything means that our house and maybe the village are gone, too.' He felt a heaviness settling in his heart and a sense of hopelessness. He just wanted to sit on the first log he could find and cry. 'But I have to carry on,' he thought. 'I must fulfill my mission; I must do my duty.'

He left the woman and hurried toward the restaurant. He didn't know how he would be contacted. All he had been told was to go to the only restaurant in Bostyn and wait for the contact. The code words, "the birches are blooming", would be spoken to him by the contact and Jan's answer should be "yes, the birch leaves are green".

He remembered the restaurant well from before the war. He had been there many times. It was a small place consisting of a kitchen and a dining room. Inside the restaurant, several people, mostly peasants, were sitting at the two long tables, noisily eating soup. There were three smaller tables in the corners; two were occupied, so he took the remaining one and sat, discreetly looking around. A young waitress simply brought him a large bowl of cabbage soup, a spoon, and one thick slice of black bread. Not a word was spoken. He tasted the soup. It was spicy and extremely hot. After days of near starvation, Jan attacked the soup. In a few minutes, the bowl was empty and Jan wouldn't have minded another, but not knowing whether it was customary to order another one, he thought better of it so as not to attract attention.

He began to observe the people around him and listen in on their conversations. The farmers were talking in Byelorussian and bits of sentences reached Jan. They were discussing their daily problems such as crops, cows, etc. The young waitress, after serving the soup, stood near the kitchen counter. Jan noticed that her eyes were often directed at him.

She was a tall, slim girl with a shock of blonde hair down to her shoulders. She wore a full, flowered skirt and white linen blouse. In the corner, also at a small table, sat a man. Like the others, he was eating soup. But unlike the farmers, he wore a rumpled old town suit that was a bit too big. He also wore a large gangster-style hat which he hadn't bothered to remove. He was one of those men whose age was difficult to guess. He could be forty-five or sixty. On the other hand, his black, alert eyes, sad though they were, were the eyes of a young man. The man was looking over at Jan far too often, making him uncomfortable. The man finished his meal, but made no move to leave. Was this man his contact, or was he a police officer?

Jan's thoughts were interrupted by the waitress, who came to take away the dishes. She seemed to take an unusually long time to clear his table. As she placed herself between the man in the far corner and Jan, he was startled to hear her whisper, "The birches are blooming."

"Yes, the birch leaves are green," Jan swiftly whispered in a trembling voice.

Jan stretched out his legs and pretended to rest. Out of the corner of his eye, he noticed an old man entering the restaurant. He was carrying a large basket of raw cabbage. Grunting, he passed through the restaurant and disappeared into the kitchen. Probably a further contact, Jan concluded.

The waitress returned after a while and, bending over his table to replace the ashtray, whispered softly, "Come here tomorrow night. Nine o'clock." She left Jan's table and headed toward the kitchen.

Jan rose to his feet and walked away from the restaurant as fast as he could. He passed the tank yard and turned on to the familiar road leading to Zamosze. He walked quickly, jumping over the pools of water, but occasionally sinking into the mud caused by the May rainfall. The marshes, partly submerged, welcomed him with the croaking of frogs and chirping of birds. Drier ground, forming numerous islands, was covered by lush grasses and small bushes. To his left was a narrow ribbon of sandy fields mostly ploughed and seeded, beyond which was a green wall of forest. He reached Zamosze when the sun was still high. But the lengthening shadows of the roadside trees suggested that it was late afternoon.

As he turned the last bend, he stopped. Like Warsaw, Pinsk and Bostyn, there was no Zamosze. Built of logs, it had been burned to the ground. As if in a dream, he started to walk along what used to be Zamosze's only street.

He had to bypass broken glass, heaps of smoke-darkened clothing, and to jump over half-burned logs and twisted pipes. A feeling of loss crept into his heart. He slowed down, as though afraid to go any farther, thinking 'Maybe my house has survived. It was on a hill, away from the street, so...'

However, turning into the land leading to his house, he saw that this had been wishful thinking. There was little left but cinders.

He stood there for a long time, mud and ashes reaching his ankles. His eyes moved from one familiar object to another, recognizing most of them. He saw a half-burned kitchen table, an oak bench, rusted iron burners of the stove and bent and twisted spoons and forks. Close to this pile of rubble, submerged in sluggish fluid lay broken cups, remnants of clothing, and twisted pipes.

Slowly, he approached the bench and sat down. The bench had been a part of Grandmother's orderly kitchen. Looking around, he spotted something red protruding from the rubble. He pulled it out and discovered that he was holding Maria's red shoe. He remembered how, in Siberia, Maria had often cried because, in the rush of packing when they had been arrested, she had managed to take only one shoe with her. They had been her favourite shoes.

He turned his head away, tears rolling down his cheeks. How many times, while in Siberia, Iraqi deserts or Italian battlefields, had he dreamed about his homecoming? In these dreams he had always seen his home as he last saw it: small, sunk deeply in the ground, surrounded by flowers. Now, he scanned the area which used to be an orchard. But all he saw was several uprooted trees lying in disarray, like fallen soldiers after a battle.

It was true that he had suffered in Siberia and in the quarry of Turkestan, but there had always been the hope that, if he survived, he could go back to Zamosze... back home, with his people and his marshes.

He had been lonely in the Iranian and Iraqi deserts, separated from his family and his home; but, in the moments when the heat and blowing sand made his life almost unbearable, he had held onto the hope that one day, somehow, he would see his home again.

But now? Now, that hope was buried under the debris, along with everything he and his family had owned and cherished.

As he sat on the bench, his sadness gave way to a growing anger against those who - by some evil design, or out of sheer hate - had chosen to destroy instead of create. Anger against the forces of evil which engaged themselves in uprooting, starving and scattering innocent people. He had to continue to fight them with every means at his disposal. He would remain with the partisans if they chose to have him. He wanted revenge on those who were responsible for the destruction of his hopes and the murder of his people. He must act! He stood up with restored energy and looked, for the last time, at the ruins which had been his home.

Raising his head toward the sky, he saw a black and white stork flying in low circles above the ruins of the barn. As though it had been waiting for him, the stork circled lower and made its familiar clatter. It was a sad sound, as though the bird wanted to complain.

After making a few more circles, the stork stretched its huge wings and flew westward.

Jan began to walk toward his special place overlooking the marshes where he had sat for hours and hours, contemplating and dreaming. He found his usual boulder and sat down. The evening mists were descending over the marshes, as they had a long time ago. He heard the same croaking of the frogs, and 'yet,' he thought sadly, 'it is not the same.' He would never hear his grandmother's voice calling him for supper. He would never hear Helena's and Maria's laughter from the house or garden. He would never again see his grandfather's stooped figure walking from hive to hive, speaking to his bees as though they were human.

Instead, immediately behind him lay the ashes of his village and his family's home. A thousand kilometres away, in the vast Siberian permafrost, were the graves of his grandparents, their half-buried coffins whipped by cold northerly winds. His sisters, uprooted like thousands of other Poles, were trying to survive in foreign lands.

He wanted to scream and tear apart those who were responsible for their suffering. His anguished cries reverberated over the mist-covered marshes.

When he could cry no more and was just about to get up, he heard steps behind him. Jumping to his feet, he prepared to defend himself. In the twilight he confronted a tall, lean man, slightly stooped. The man, seeing Jan preparing to fight, raised his hand in a friendly way.

"Terribly sorry for startling you... but," the man spoke in halting and accented Russian, "but, you are sitting on my boulder."

"Your boulder?" Jan asked, also in Russian.

The man laughed loudly. "My boulder is only a figure of speech. It is the place where I come often to contemplate." Then he added quickly, "I live there," he waved his hand in the direction of where Shloma's Inn used to be.

"You live in Shloma's Inn?" Jan asked.

The man was visibly startled. "Did you know Shloma?" he cried.

"Yes."

"Who are you?" the man asked in a trembling voice. He moved closer to Jan. Jan noticed that the man was dragging his right leg with difficulty. Moonlight shone on the man's face and Jan thought it seemed familiar.

"Roova!" he yelled.

The man grabbed Jan by his coat and peered into his face. "Jan!" he cried, joy in his voice. "I can't believe it! I can't believe it's you, Jan!" Then, as though remembering something, he said, "Come on! Come on to my place. It's the only place in Zamosze which still has a roof."

They laughed and shook hands heartily. He led Jan to his father's inn. Even from a distance, Jan could see that the inn, like the other houses in the village, had been burned. However, the brick walls had survived. In fact, the western wing of the inn was untouched by fire and now served as a home for Roova. It was a one-room shelter with a small wooden stove, a bunk bed, and one rickety chair.

Roova put a pot on the stove and said that he still had enough tea left to welcome his friend. The hot tea and the warmth of the room made Jan drowsy. Roova was looking at him, curiosity lighting his face.

"You'd like to know what happened to me, Roova?" Jan asked.

"Well, of course, yes."

Jan was in a dilemma. He couldn't possibly tell him the whole truth about himself. On the other hand, he was talking to a friend and he didn't want to lie.

"Roova," he said thoughtfully, "Roova, my friend, forgive me, but I cannot tell you everything about myself, except that my grandparents are dead, my sisters are in foreign lands, my father is lost somewhere and I... am on the verge of leaving this place, our place. Not because I want to, but because I have to. Before I leave, though, I must do a few things. They are important to me, Roova."

Roova sat quietly, staring hard at Jan. "I understand, Jan," he said finally. "In these days, there are many things that should not be said - even between close friends. It may be better for both of us."

"And you, Roova? Tell me something about yourself. Where are your parents, sisters, Moyshe, Wasily, Jossif? What happened to our friends in Bostyn, Roova... that cute looking Rose Wolanski? The little one who used to call me Napoleon, remember? Sruel Rabinovich, David Cohen, all those Jewish boys who defended me against the Byelorussian boys?"

Jan stopped. Roova's face had become as pale as paper and was distorted with pain. The memory was obviously dreadful. Jan said quickly, "Roova! You don't have to tell me anything. Some things perhaps shouldn't..."

Roova's grave voice interrupted him. "It was June 28, 1941." He paused, as if to gain strength, and then went on, "Yes, it was June 28, 1941, a warm and sunny morning. We were awakened by the roar of motors. I ran outdoors, half-dressed. The village street was packed with tanks, trucks, soldiers on foot, all German. I heard machine gun fire. People were running in all directions, screaming. Screaming! My father pulled me back into the house. There we sat, the five of us, until night came, terrified, but praying and hoping. The noise had subsided by nightfall. Mother prepared food but nobody was hungry."

"My little sisters started to cry... then our mother... myself... well, I was scared, looking at my father's eyes - hoping for some kind of hope in them... Instead, there was a pain in his eyes... or sorrow, perhaps. Later that night, we saw a red glow over Bostyn and muffled noises of people wailing and... shots... many shots: cannon, rifles, explosions. We hardly slept that night. Then at noon the next day, the Germans, Gestapo, you know, came to our Inn. They pounded on the door with rifle butts, then burst into the inn. 'Are you Juden?' they yelled at us. Without waiting for an answer, two of them grabbed me. One held me and the other pulled my pants down. 'Juden... no doubt about it.' They laughed with satisfaction. The same thing happened to my father. The other German soldiers were holding my mother and sisters. 'You sure that these women are Juden?' 'I don't know, maybe yes, maybe no... Juden women have different cunts.' They laughed and nudged one another."

"We understood all this talk because Yiddish is similar to German. I wish

I hadn't understood, Jan..." He was silent for a while, sweat rolling down his face. "I don't know how much you remember about my father, but he was a good man who abhorred violence. He pleaded for them not to harm his children. 'Shoot me, if you must, but please spare my children,' he said. But they beat him savagely with their rifle butts and dragged him, unconscious to the truck. Then they loaded the rest of our family and Moyshe's family on trucks. They drove us to Kopya's farm about one kilometre from Bostyn, near the sand dunes."

"Kopya's farm? Wasn't that the smelly place where they buried dead horses and dogs?"

"Yes, the very same one."

"They unloaded us on those sand dunes," Roova continued. "We saw people digging. They were Byelorussians. I recognized some of them. One of them was our friend Wasili, who recognized me too. He looked at me, horror in his eyes. A German hit him with a rifle for that look. I felt certain, Jan, that I was going to die."

"I should have run, all of us should have run. Maybe some would have managed to escape. But I couldn't run. It was as if my legs were paralyzed. I just stood there. After a while, they lined up a group of people in front of the ditch. Everything was done in silence, except for the orders of the German officers; clear, precise, god-like. None of the victims cried, ran or fought. We stood petrified. Then came the staccato sounds of firing. I saw bodies falling, one by one, into that horrible long pit that is the grave of all the Jews of Bostyn, Zamosze, and many villages around. I saw my whole family falling... falling into that common grave. Jan! I... I..." he stopped, sobbing.

"Roova, Roova!" cried Jan.

"They put shovels in our hands, ordering us to cover the bodies," continued Roova. "I was just about to throw a shovelful of earth into the ditch when to my horror... I... noticed that some of them were still alive... I recognized Rose Wolanski - you asked about her...to her left, my little sister - you remember her, the merry one, remember? She had been wounded, but was still alive. She was staring at me, her eyes... accusing... shifting from me to my shovel - as though I was responsible... I wanted to scream at the executioners, 'she is my sister, a child... still alive'. I wanted to call them to... to come to the ditch and shoot... shoot again - this time, to aim better... aim at my sister... aim well this time... but my throat was too dry; nothing but a meaningless croak came out." His voice broke in a sob. "She was just a child, Jan! A child."

Jan wanted to stop his friend's talking, but he only managed to whisper "Roova..."

"Then they lined up our group, facing the other half-filled ditch, the same ditch where my family's bodies were. A woman was praying. I can still hear her voice. I stood at the edge of that ditch and... I wanted to die, to join my family... to be with them," he sobbed. "I stood at that ditch, waiting, welcoming death... believe me, welcoming...Then someone barked an order in German. I heard shots, many shots, then I felt as though my heart and my legs were exploding... and I was falling... falling..."

They sat in silence. Jan knew better than to interrupt his friend now. Roova gazed at the clear, starry sky. Then, as though awakening from a deep sleep, he turned to Jan and continued, "It was Wasili who covered the rest of the ditch I had fallen into. I was wounded but still alive. It happened that our group was the last one to be executed that day. When the Germans left, Wasili dug me out and carried me to his home." Roova stopped and looked away. Then he added, "It was not a great effort to dig me out, Wasili told me - the ditch was filled with bodies almost to the brim."

He turned to Jan. "I wish he had never done it! Look at me now, lame, and look here," he unbuttoned his shirt, showing two bullet scars: one on the right, the other on the left side of his chest. "Alone," his voice faltered. "Alone in this huge, horrible world. I'm not really alive, Jan. Most of me died there with the others. Some of the people here, the Byelorussians and Russians think I'm crazy. 'Crazy little Jew', they call me. Maybe I am, Jan. Maybe I am." Tears rolled down his cheeks.

"What happened to Wasili?"

"He's dead. He joined a partisan unit, Russian partisans, I think. They were caught here in Zamosze. That's when the Germans burned the village and shot your uncle Wladysaw, your aunt, her daughter-in-law and her 2-year-old child. I think that your uncle tried to hide Wasili. They were shot by the German Wermacht. Not the Gestapo, Jan, just ordinary, God-fearing German soldiers. Why children, Jan? Tell me why? Why kill little children?"

"Why children?" Jan repeated in a choking voice, remembering Wojek's children dying one after another in Siberia. "Yes, why children?" he said again.

It was a while before either of them could talk.

"And what now, Roova?" asked Jan, who regained his composure first.

"I don't know. I suppose I will stay here. At least I can walk to the place we met tonight and talk."

"Talk?"

"Yes, talk to my dead family and my dead friends. The marshes don't mind listening to a crazy Jew, Jan."

Jan left Roova's place the next day by sundown and headed back to Bostyn. He allowed himself one final glance at the village and his beloved marshes. It was too early for his rendezvous, so he strolled on the town's streets, trying to find buildings which should have been there, but weren't. He was just approaching the restaurant when, to his surprise, he noticed the same man in the crumpled suit and gangster hat who had been in the restaurant during his first visit. The man, leaning against the wall of the building opposite, was gazing at the sky, observing the formations of geese flying by.

'A policeman,' Jan thought, breaking into a cold sweat. He changed his direction and walked swiftly away from the restaurant. From the corner of his eye, he noticed that the man seemed to be following him. Jan dashed into a narrow street, jumped over a low fence, and hid in a clump of bushes. Soon the man appeared, running and looking around frantically. Jan was scared. There was no doubt that the man was following him, and that was a bad omen. Crawling among the bushes and circling for half an hour, he arrived back at the restaurant. He was surprised to find the door locked. He stood at the door, trying to decide what to do next.

"Hello!" a girl's voice said. Startled, he whirled around, trying to see who was calling him. "Hello," he heard again. This time he was sure that the voice was coming from the nearby garden. Moving closer, he heard, "psst... take that little path - quickly, before that bloody Soviet spy sees you again. Follow that path, it will lead you through the garden into the bushes. Quickly!"

He jumped over the low gate and found himself in the garden where a winding path led him to a small apple orchard, and eventually into a forest grove. It was much darker in the forest and he started to wonder if he could find the girl. Then he saw a figure emerging like a phantom from behind a bush. His military training made him react instantly, so he fell to the ground and rolled behind the bushes.

"It's me!" she exclaimed.

He rose to his feet, embarrassed by his reaction, and glanced at his companion. In front of him stood a tall, slender girl, dressed in long cavalry boots, riding pants, short, heavy jacket, and a heavy, Russian style hat. The hat with its long ear flaps, covered almost all her face, except a pair of large sparkling eyes. He recognized at once that this wasn't the girl from the restaurant. The other had been much shorter and older. Taken by surprise, he stared at her.

"My name is Zoshia," she said. Sensing Jan's perplexity, she added quickly, "I am from the forest... from..."

Jan sighed with relief and, shaking Zoshia's hand, introduced himself.

"I was sent to fetch you and guide you to the commanding post," said Zoshia, starting to walk with surprising speed and confidence. After half an hour of walking in silence, they left the grove and reached a meadow. Asking him to wait, she scrutinized the meadow ahead of them for what Jan thought was a long time. Satisfied, she came closer to Jan and beckoned him to follow her.

They started to walk rapidly. Jan felt that the girl wanted to put the meadow behind them as soon as possible. Jan, keeping his eyes on the tall, agile figure in front of him, had to make a great effort to keep up with her.

The terrain was indeed difficult. They were sinking in the marshy quagmire from time to time, avoiding puddles of water, bypassing huge boulders, so their progress was much slower. The girl's skill was amazing. She seemed to foresee every difficulty just in time, pulling him out of bogs, stopping him at the right moment before he fell into a lagoon or pierced his eye with a sharp, protruding tree branch. They walked for hours. To Jan, who was using all his strength following her, it seemed like an eternity. Mercifully, they left the marshes behind and entered the forest. The forest floor, boggy though it was, was nevertheless much easier to walk on. Zoshia, it seemed, had an endless amount of energy, something he had to admit he didn't have.

He was tempted to ask her to stop for a rest, but his pride wouldn't permit him. 'What will she think of me?' he thought, dragging his numb feet along. However, to his relief, he saw her suddenly sit down on a large log. She was panting from exertion and obviously sweating. She removed her heavy hat, revealing a thick mane of dark hair. In the moonlight, her round face, large sparkling eyes and small mouth made her beautiful.

"We'll rest here," she said, smiling.

"How far now?" Jan asked.

"We'll get there by dawn."

"By dawn."

"It's only three more hours - maybe less."

'Oh my God,' thought Jan, trying to change the position of his numb legs. They were sitting on the log in silence. Jan had many questions for this girl beside him.

"How many of you are there?" he asked, but before he had finished his question, the girl - without a word - sprang to her feet and started to walk again.

"She's a bloody goat!" he swore, soon lagging behind again.

Walking became even more difficult. This time, they had to climb numerous fallen logs, which, Jan thought, had probably been put there by the devil himself. When he had reached the limit of his endurance, he was startled by a voice emanating from the bushes to his left.

"Halt!" its baritone sound echoed over the forest. "The password."

He was too tired to listen to this exchange, leaving it to the girl. Leaning on a large tree, he tried to catch his breath. Suddenly, from nowhere, they were surrounded by four men, armed with light machine guns. To Jan, they looked threatening and dangerous. Jan and Zoshia were searched, presumably for concealed weapons, and then ordered to walk. After 15 minutes of circling to avoid booby traps, Jan surmised, they saw a large clearing ahead.

In the pale light of early morning, except for their escort, he could not see any sign of the partisans. It was only when they passed the clearing and approached a grove of trees that he noticed smoke coming from beneath a large oak tree. Zoshia went up to the tree and raking with her fingers around the roots, revealed to Jan's surprise a large, cleverly concealed wooden door leading to a dug-out.

In the dim light of a lantern, Jan was met by a man armed with an automatic pistol. Following a narrow passage, they entered a room. At first, it was too dark to see anything clearly, but as his eyes adjusted, Jan saw that the room was surprisingly large. It was reinforced by thick wooden beams and furnished with a narrow cot, a table, and a stove. The air was stale and heavy with odours of cabbage and smoke. Jan felt dizzy and sweaty.

Behind the table sat three men. The one in the middle, slender with a long, grey beard, rose to his feet and, extending his hand, said, "My name is The Birch. Welcome!"

"The Fox, reporting," answered Jan, saluting. Then added, "The Fox reporting to The Wolf."

The men at the table were silent. Jan noticed signs of trepidation. Then the man calling himself "The Birch" said quietly, "The Wolf is dead."

"Oh, I am sor-"

"He was a soldier and met a soldier's death," The Birch interrupted, then asked, "Where is the parcel?" Seeing Jan's hesitation, he quickly said, "You may give it to me. You were told, I hope..."

"Yes, sir! Of course, I had orders to give you the parcel in case..." He took his coat off and handed it to The Birch.

Once their mutual identification had been completed and the parcel delivered, the atmosphere in the room changed as though by magic. The men surrounded Jan, questioning him about the Polish troops in Italy, international politics...

Jan, though tired and sweaty, answered each question as well as he could.

Finally, The Birch rescued him from the ordeal. "Gentlemen, gentlemen!" he exclaimed, turning to his companions. "Where is your hospitality? Don't you think our guest is tired and, I'm sure, hungry?" Turning to Jan, he said, "Please excuse our poor manners. Allow me to arrange a few things. Captain!" he turned to one of the men in the hut, "take this young man to the kitchen and then make sure that he has a good sleep." Facing Jan again, he said, "We'll talk later, after you rest."

Jan was led by the captain to yet another dugout which served as a kitchen. He was served eggs and sausages by an old, mustachioed man who spoke in the Byelorussian singsong, so familiar to Jan. "It ain't much," he said in his broad accent, "but this ain't a picnic."

"It ain't much but it's tasty," Jan answered with the same accent.

"Oh my God!" the cook jumped as though burned. "You're local. Where from?"

"Zamosze."

"I'll be damned! Zamosze, you say. I think we have some people from there."

"Who? Tell me, who?" Jan shouted excitedly. As far as he knew, all the Zamoszans had been deported by the Soviets.

"I heard somebody mention Zamosze, but kill me if I remember who," he said, distressed. "But I will find out," he promised.

After he had finished eating, Jan was taken by the man referred to as "captain" to an empty dug-out where there was a cot in the corner with a straw mattress covered by a coarse, soiled blanket. In a few minutes, he was asleep. He was awakened by the sound of a bugle.

'Aha,' he thought, rubbing his eyes, 'it must be a reveille. Just like the real army!' He wanted to go back to sleep, but curiosity was stronger than his fatigue, so he rose to his feet with difficulty and peeped outside through a wide crack in the dugout's door. In the middle of the clearing, straight rows of men and women stood at attention. There were at least 100 of them, Jan calculated. Fifty feet away stood another similar group.

"Holy Mother!" he exclaimed, "there's a lot of them."

The Birch emerged from one of the dugouts flanked by the two men Jan had met earlier.

"Hail, soldiers!" The Birch greeted his troops.

"Hail, Colonel, sir!" they answered in unison.

'Aha,' Jan thought, 'The Birch is a colonel.' The rank didn't matter very much to Jan, but still...
"At ease," rang the command.

"When the early sun is rising," the colonel started to sing a traditional morning prayer.

"The earth and seas are singing praises to Thou, O God Almighty," the partisans joined in.

The song reverberated over the forests and marshes; the song, Jan thought, was as old as Poland's history. They sang it while in Russia and in the Middle Eastern deserts... or wherever there were groups of Polish soldiers or civilians.

He returned to his cot and tried to go back to sleep, but tired as he was, he somehow couldn't. Thousands of thoughts invaded his mind, confusing and deeply disturbing thoughts. Maybe it was the sight of these men who, dressed in shabby clothes, sleeping in these murky and stinking holes, were carrying the torch of freedom. Don't they know it's a lost cause? That they are alone and abandoned by everyone? Or maybe it was the morning song he had just heard that disturbed him. Eventually, he fell into a restless and feverish sleep.

It was dark when he opened his eyes. At first, he couldn't remember where he was. A melody reached his ears, sung by many men.

"Do not weep, my willow tree..."

He recognized the words. This was an old song of the Polish partisans, sung by them after so many battles.

"Because my heart is torn apart.
Do not weep, my beloved one,
The war will soon be over..."

'The war is over?' he thought. 'For whom? Not for these people. Not for me. For us, it may never be over.'

"...Do not sway, the weeping willow,
Do not weep, my beloved one..."

He sensed that he wasn't alone. Someone seemed to be standing over his bed. He told himself that he was imagining things, but he still felt that some-one was in the room with him.

"Jan!" a voice said. "Is it really you?"

Sleepy as he still was, he was astonished that anyone here knew his name. He was sure that even Colonel "Birch" didn't know his name. To the colonel, Jan was "The Fox" and nothing else. Who was this person who knew his name? Had he been betrayed? He didn't respond, trying to think.

"Jan! Jan!" the woman repeated. There was something familiar about that voice, and yet, for the life of him, he couldn't place it.

As though guessing Jan's perplexity, the woman moved toward the dugout's door and opened it. For a moment, the brightness made Jan squint his eyes. Opening them, he saw a powerfully built person, dressed like the other partisans he had seen.

"Aunt Fela!" he roared. "My God, it's Aunt Fela!" he cried, jumping off the cot.

Aunt Fela rushed toward him, her arms open. They embraced each other in silence.

"Jan! Jan!" she cried, tears rolling down her cheeks. They looked at each other for a while and embraced again. "You're alive! You're alive!" she said through her tears.

Like so many others who had been separated for a long time, it was difficult for them to know where to begin.

Jan wanted to know, first of all, whether his aunt had heard anything about his father. Fela, on the other hand, was anxious to know about Jan's grandparents, sisters and his own experiences. It took Jan a long time, patience and pleading to make his aunt tell him the tragic truth about his father.

According to Fela, his father had survived, although he had been wounded in the war against the invading hordes of Germans. With great difficulty, he had avoided German captivity and somehow managed to return to Zamosze.

"Imagine, Jan" his aunt said, "your father's feelings when he found his house empty. After learning what had happened to all of you, he almost had a heart attack. It would take me all night, Jan, to explain his agony and his suffering. Then, on top of all of this, he was arrested by the K.G.B."

"Arrested? Arrested for what, Aunt?"

"For being a Pole, that's what. Don't forget that, on the morning of February 10, 1941, all Poles were supposed to be deported, like you were. However, as it was, some were unwittingly left behind. Take me, for example. At the time of deportation, I happened to be in Pinsk. When I returned, to avoid arrest, I ran into the forest where I joined the Polish resistance fighters, or partisans as we are now called. There were a few others like me, who were away that morning. The K.G.B. arrested your father three days after his return home. He would have ended up in one of the Siberian labour camps... but his fate was worse than that; he was arrested by none other than that Polish traitor, Szymanski."

"Szymanski!" Jan exclaimed. "The commander of the Polish Police Post in Bostyn before the war?"

"The same."

"But, Aunt Fela..." Jan broke off, confused. "He always led the parades on national holidays! He was... such a patriot."

"Patriot, indeed!" spat Aunt Fela with disgust. "The fact is that he was an ardent communist, even before the war. A concealed one, to be sure."

"But I thought the Russians deported all the policemen."

"Exactly. That's why we were so surprised when the K.G.B. didn't deport him," Aunt Fela said indignantly. "Believe it or not, he changed his uniform from the navy blue of the Polish police to the mud-green of the K.G.B., and returned to his position... On the very same day the Red Army occupied our area," she added.

"Bastard!"

"He certainly is, but let me tell you the rest."

"What happened to my father?" Jan asked.

"He was in hiding, but someone denounced him to Szymanski, who, with the Soviet K.B.G., arrested him. He tortured your father."

"But why, Fela? Father never harmed Szymanski!"

"Well, you probably don't know it, but your father was on the jury which sentenced Szymanski to six months in jail and a fine, just before the war. For defrauding the police fund, or something like that. Anyway, that skunk, Szymanski, never went to jail because the war broke out!"

"So Szymanski wanted revenge?"

"Yes. It was a personal vendetta; plus, that bastard knew about your father's strong anti-communist feelings."

"What happened to Father, Fela, please?" Jan asked in a trembling voice.

"As I said, Jan, he was tortured by Szymanski." She sat quietly for a while then said softly, "I'm sorry, Jan, but it's better than I tell you this... this terrible story that somebody else." .

"Go on," Jan urged, a catch in his voice.

"Szymanski's K.G.B. broke your father's legs, and," she paused as tears welled up in her eyes, "and permanently damaged his health. But," she added quickly, "he is alive, he wants to live... until he sees at least one member of his family."

"Where is he, Aunt?" Jan cried.

"He is with a group of partisans, about 20 kilometres from here... but, Jan, he is dying."

"Lead me to him, Aunt Fela!" Jan cried, jumping from his cot. "Right away!" He started toward the door, then turned and asked, "Where is Szymanski now?"

"That traitor retreated east with the Red Army after the German attack on the Soviet Union, but now he has returned with the same army. This time in the rank of K.G.B. colonel. Why are you asking about him?"

"Because I am going to kill him," Jan said forcefully.

He was just about to leave the dugout when the door opened and The Birch entered.

"Oh, so you know each other?" he said, surprised.

"This is my nephew, Colonel," said Aunt Fela.

"Aha, so our courier is a local boy. I thought so."

"How did you know?" she asked him.

"He has a similar accent to yours, Fela." The Birch patted Jan on his back and asked, "Why so gloomy?"

"His father is Sergeant Tabor," said Fela, quietly.

Birch's face twisted with pain. "Oh my God, I am sorry." Turning to Jan he said quietly, "Your father is a brave man, son. You should be proud of him." Before he had even finished speaking, he realized how inadequate his words were. "Goddamn," he swore to himself, "what else can I say, really," and started toward the door.

"Colonel!" said Fela. "Jan, my nephew, that is, should be taken to his father."

The colonel, turning his head, said, "Yes of course, I will attend to it."

Emerging from the dugout half an hour later, Jan was surprised to see six horsemen, automatic pistols across their shoulders, sabres at their sides, waiting for him. The seventh horse, a beautiful chestnut held by a partisan, was obviously for him, saddled and packed.

He stroked the chestnut's mane and patted its slender neck affectionately. The horse responded by snorting and neighing impatiently. "Looks the same as the horse we pulled from the marshes centuries ago, Aunt Fela, doesn't it?"

"It should," smiled Aunt Fela ruefully. "It came from the same stable."

Jan, bidding goodbye to his aunt, joined his escort and rode away. The narrow path they followed was firm and relatively clear of obstructions, so in spite of the darkness, the cavalcade moved quickly. The chestnut trod resolutely and surely, dancing happily under Jan's competent yet gentle lead.

On both sides of the path were continuous walls of dark forests broken by lagoons and patches of swamp. Riding cooled his feverish cheeks and diverted his thoughts from the tragic news about his father. The cavalcade pushed ahead without stopping for a rest or to water the horses. Rounding a bend, they stopped suddenly. Jan heard voices from the front of the cavalcade and then they moved ahead, much more slowly this time. He had a feeling that they must be close to their destination and he felt an increased anxiety.

A few minutes later, they were surrounded by a group of people, who in silence, led them to a large shed, where their horses were taken from them by two silent men. Jan was approached by a youthful partisan who led him to a forester's house built of logs. The youth opened the door and beckoned Jan to enter. The room was full of people, some sat at the table, others were sitting, half reclined on the floor with their backs against the wall, some were lying on the floor, presumably sleeping. All except those who slept came to attention as one, clicking their heels and saluting. One of them, a tall clean-shaven man approached Jan and, shaking his hand, said "We were informed about your coming. Sorry about your father, we are all truly sorry. My name is Wladek, Sergeant."

"Where is he?" Jan's voice was choked with emotion.

"Follow me," said his host. He was led to another room. Two kerosene lanterns lit the room enough for him to see a huge bed and a person lying on it. He rushed toward the bed but was stopped by Wladek, who grabbed Jan's sleeve trying to hold him back.

"Sir, please... don't... He... your father is very, very sick. Let me..." He moved quietly toward the bed and bending over it, removed a thin sheet which was partly covering Tabor's face.

His eyes were closed. Jan was looking intently at the face on the bed; emaciated, hollow-cheeked and covered by a blonde beard. He hoped that there had been a mistake, that this man was not his father after all. Then the patient opened his warm and somewhat humorous eyes that Jan would have recognized among millions of men. Their eyes met, but there was no sign of recognition in Jan's father. Michal Tabor's eyes were immobile and steady. He stared at Jan in silence.

"Father, Father!" exclaimed Jan, stroking his father's sweaty hair. "Father, Oh, my God, Father!" he cried, placing a kiss on his father's forehead. "Father! It's me, Jan!"

He noticed - or was it that he just imagined - a slight frown on his father's forehead and a smile. It wasn't so much his mouth that smiled, but his eyes... the same as before... he used to smile like this when he was pleased with something.

"Oh, Father!" the tears poured from Jan's eyes. His father's eyes were wet, too.

Then Jan heard a quiet, weak whisper. He bent closer, his ear almost touching his father's mouth. "Jan! You're alive."

"Yes, yes, Father, I'm alive!" he cried.

"Maria and Helena?" he asked.

"They are alive! Alive, Father... they love you, Father."

He saw a smile, yes, this time it was an unmistakable, broad smile. "Give them my love, Jan."

"I will."

"Grandparents?" the whisper was so weak that Jan guessed more than heard. Jan didn't answer... he just looked sadly at his father. He noticed that the frown on his forehead reappeared. Jan felt a gentle touch on his shoulder.

"He must rest now, sir, please!"

Jan knelt beside the bed and, covering his head in his hands, remained there for a long time.

"Jan," a gentle voice said. It was Wladek, again. "It's over Jan... it's over... your father, Jan, just passed away." He helped Jan rise to his feet. He felt a great emptiness in his heart and numbness in his body. He saw that Wladek and other men had come from the other room, and were kneeling around his father's bed. He heard a prayer being offered by one of them, loudly. He joined them, but as much as he tried, he couldn't remember the well-known words of the prayer. So he just knelt there in silence.

A bugle sounded at the funeral of Sergeant Tabor. It didn't surprise Jan. He had seen many, far too many, such funerals of soldiers; in Russia, Iran, Iraq, Egypt, Italy, but what surprised him was the behaviour of the partisan soldiers. Many were crying openly like children. Jan felt that these men and women were not just burying a comrade in arms, they were burying a friend, a person close to their hearts. After the last lump of soil had fallen upon the coffin, Jan was accosted by a short, grizzly man of about 50. He introduced himself as "Captain Lynx", the commander of the outpost.

"Look, young man," he said straightforwardly. "I know what you are going through, but life has to go on. There is nothing that you or I can do, you understand."

"Oh, no?" Jan roared. "The hell there isn't! There is that butcher, Szymanski! He's the one who killed my father, isn't he? Isn't he?"

"Yes, it was that fuckin' renegade Szymanski," said the captain, "but there is not much we can do about it. At least not yet," he added.

"We should kill him! He deserves it, doesn't he?"

"Oh, sure he does, a thousand times he does, but we can't just go there with a few men and face three thousand." Then, as an afterthought, he added, "The son-of-a-bitch could have a division of the Red Army if he wanted."

"Isn't there any way we can get him?"

"Maybe there is, or maybe there isn't, young man, but remember, we are soldiers, we act on orders. Don't expect an order to be given to attack Szymanski's troops. It would be suicide, Jan."

"Then let me kill the bastard alone."

"So, help you commit suicide? Hmm?"

They were walking across the seemingly deserted compound, but Jan knew that it was full of well-concealed life. They walked toward the shed, listening to the neighing of horses. The shed was longer than Jan had thought and, according to the captain, sheltered 32 horses. Jan's chestnut was there too.

From the shed, the captain led Jan to a large hut, which he was told was the outpost's headquarters. Inside, he was introduced to another three officers, two lieutenants and one cadet officer. They were all young and seemed to be very anxious to talk to him.

They were served stew with black bread, which Jan didn't touch. There was not much talking until after the meal. The captain dried his mouth with his sleeve, turned to Jan and asked, "Lieutenant, forgive me for bothering you with questions at such a difficult time, but we know you are from the west so we are curious."

At first he didn't want to talk to them, or anybody else. He wanted to be left alone in his grief, but looking at the men's eager eyes, he said, "Go ahead captain, I will try my best to answer you."

"You see," another officer joined the conversation, "we are fighting the Soviets and we would like to know," he looked to Jan for the right words, "whether we can count on any support from the west."

Jan was silent, trying to think what to say.

"The Soviets, as you've probably heard," said the captain, "want to establish the Soviet system in Poland. They have already found some collaborators, like Szymanski, to do what they want. What is the attitude of the western nations, our allies, to that?"

"They don't care about us at all," Jan said finally.

"But, but..." they all started to talk, "our army abroad", "brotherhood in arms with the British and Americans"...

"Don't count on it." There was no use in giving these brave men false hope, he thought. It would be better if he told them the truth, painful though it was.

"So you're saying we are facing the Red Army alone!" the young officer exclaimed.

"Yes."

There was a silence in the room, broken only by voices from outside.

"Then we will fight alone. Maybe, just maybe, our allies will force the Soviets to respect our wish for an independent Poland."

"I don't think so. The British and Americans are preoccupied with their own affairs. Besides," he added, "they trust Stalin. Well, I don't really believe they trust him entirely, but they trust him enough to make a treaty with him."

"They will pay for that trust one day," somebody observed.

"Sure, but it won't help us in the meantime."

"In the meantime," Jan was interrupted by an officer, "we will fight the best we can alone."

"And you? What are you going to do?" one of the officers asked, turning to Jan.

"I must avenge my father. Szymanski must die!" Jan said purposefully. He thought of his father's sad, tired eyes... his whispers for him and his sisters. Jan wanted vengeance, he wanted to kill that fat renegade even if he died in the process.

"What will you do after you kill Szymanski?" asked the captain.

"I don't really know, Captain. I don't really know," he repeated.

The captain looked at Jan pensively. "Join us, Jan."

"Yes, join us. We need young officers, like you," someone else said.

Jan saw their eyes on him, expectant, intense. He realized now that he had known from the beginning what his answer would be. He, like his father, wanted to be one of these patriots. "Yes, I'll join you," he said without a moment of hesitation. "It will be an honour to fight together with you for an independent Poland. But not before I kill Szymanski," he added forcefully.

Saying this, he rose to his feet and left the hut. There was a prolonged silence in the hut after he left.

"We must do something about this bastard, Szymanski," the captain said finally.

"Yes, before he kills that hot-headed young man," somebody added.

"I have a suggestion," said the captain. They moved their chairs closer to his so as not to miss a word. After a brief discussion, one by one, they left their hut in a hurry.

A couple of hours later, Jan was riding at a full gallop. 'It's strange,' he thought, 'that even though the war is over, no one is really happy. Victory over Germany should make us truly happy and, of course, to a certain degree it does. After all, we were the first to tell that bastard Hitler no, and fight against him. But how can we be truly happy when victory over one enemy has resulted in being occupied by another, equally vicious. Why is it that there is no place for us in our own country? Why,' he sighed, 'is this happening to us?'

Leaning over the horse's mane to avoid overhanging branches, he sped toward Bostyn and Szymanski. His eyes cold, he approached the outskirts of Bostyn at dusk. Slowing his horse's pace, he reached for his breast pocket and felt the short, sharp dagger given to him by the captain. Only now he realized that in his hot-headedness, he had no plan of action or the slightest idea as to how he was going to kill Szymanski. Instinctively, he knew that he must develop some extraordinary plan or forget about his vengeance. There was another problem that had to be solved immediately. What was he going to do with the horse, useful for getting here, but a burden now. He could let the horse go free, but he might need it later. He must find a place for the horse within easy access. Zamosze? Surely that would be the best place... Roova! No, the poor man has suffered enough. Why endanger him more? He loosened the reins, letting the horse walk freely at its own speed. Deeply absorbed in thought, he didn't realize that the horse had turned to the left and had taken the road leading to... Zamosze.

"Of all places!" he exclaimed. "The horse is thinking of Zamosze too!"

The horse, flicking its tail to drive away mosquitoes, walked confidently, as though it knew exactly where it was going, and why. Shortly, they reached Zamosze and Jan was full of admiration for the chestnut's ability to bypass the scattered remains of burnt wood, bricks, and stones.

Hatred for his father's killer had invaded his thinking. His only goal was to kill the man responsible for his father's death, regardless of how, when or where. He realized now that without an ally, he could not do it. Well, he had an ally - the chestnut.

The horse increased its pace and soon they left the rubble of Zamosze behind. 'Where is he taking me?' Jan wondered. The path they were following led into the thick deciduous forest, uninhabited as far as Jan could remember, except for a few isolated farms, a flour mill and the forester's lodge. The horse suddenly turned to the right and followed a little-used track.

It was getting dark and Jan started to doubt the horse's wisdom. 'Maybe,' he thought, 'the horse knows some clearing with rich grass.' How was it that he, a soldier of so much experience, was entrusting his fate to an animal, smart as it seemed to be? But since he didn't know the best place to leave the beast, he let the horse's instinct lead him. His thoughts were interrupted by the urgent barking of a dog coming from a deep dale to his left where the horse seemed to be taking him. The dog's barking, deep and hoarse, changed into a continuous howling.

Reaching the hill, Jan's eyes swept the dale and rested on a dim light glowing from below. He tried hard to remember the people who had lived there before the war, but he couldn't recall them.

"Probably some one-horse farmer I never met," he concluded. The path they were following suddenly disappeared, but the horse, circling skillfully, was walking on until they reached some buildings.

The buildings weren't much, a small house or more correctly, a hut, and equally small, almost touching the house, a barn or a stable. It was only when he rode closer that it dawned on him that the place had belonged to the village herder before the war. He had used the common pasture of the dale to raise his few cows and horses.

He had been referred to by the villagers as "Wojtek, the Fool". Now, Jan recalled that he had been here once or twice with his grandfather. According to his grandfather, Wojtek was no fool. The epithet had been bestowed upon him for his manner of laughing frequently and without apparent reason.

Facing the "Fool's" house, Jan was perplexed and confused. Why, for the love of God, was he brought here? In spite of his misery, he couldn't help but see a certain amount of humour in his situation. Chasing a murderer, he had been brought to the "Fool".

"And it is all your fault," he said, patting the chestnut affectionately. The horse circled the house and proceeded straight toward the barn. In the yard, chained to the house was a huge mastiff, which, for some reason, stopped barking, whimpering quietly. The horse halted in front of the barn door and stood there as though waiting for something or somebody. Jan was just about to dismount when he heard a ringing voice coming from one of the house windows.

"Stay where you are or I'll shoot!"

"I am a friend... I just want..." In truth, he didn't know what to say, but even if he did, he wouldn't have been able to finish his sentence.

The horse, which had been standing quietly until now, suddenly lifted its head and neighed repeatedly. "Kashtan! (Chestnut)" Jan heard a woman's voice call from the window. "Is that you, Kashtan?"

The horse stomped his feet impatiently, neighing again. Jan heard the door open with a squeak and saw a slender figure emerging, shot gun ready.

"Whoever you are, stranger, you have my horse."

"Your horse, really?"

"Yes. Where did you get it?"

Jan thought for a moment, then decided to tell her the truth. "Lynx gave it to me. Captain Lynx."

"Lynx or not, put your hands up and be still." The woman came close and ordered him to turn around.

As soon as he saw her face, he cried: "Zoshia!"

She recognized him too. "I thought you were still with The Birch. What are you doing here?" she asked as they led the horse into the barn.

"Ask Kashtan," he said ruefully.

"Oh, Kashtan," she said caressing the horse's mane. "This beast is smarter than many men, you know."

Zoshia took Jan into the house, first ordering the dog to lie down. The beast's glowing eyes were constantly on Jan as though assessing his intentions. The house was in fact a one-room cottage which Jan remembered from his visit there with his grandfather.

"I thought," he said sitting at the table, "that this was Wojtek's house."

"It is, it was; Wojtek is dead."

"Why do you live here now?"

"It's a long story," she said. "One thing at a time."

Sitting in front of the stove, they talked almost all night. Jan told her, among other things, of his determination to kill Szymanski. She, in turn, informed him that she was The Birch's daughter.

"We lived in Pinsk before the war; I was an only child," she told him. "My father was an officer of the Polish army and like your father - I'm sorry about your father, he was a brave and good man - went to fight the Germans. My mother died at the time when Pinsk was occupied by the Soviet troops. I went to live with distant relatives, but when my father arrived one night and told me that he intended to join the partisans, I begged him to take me with him. After all, I was 18 and wanted to do some good for Poland. The partisan command concealed me in this house, because it's remote but fairly safe. I am a go-between for the Polish partisan groups. One of my duties was to take you to The Birch."

"Aren't you afraid to live here alone?" he asked her looking around the small room.

"A little," she said, smiling, but added, "somebody has got to do it. Besides, my father and Hector protect me."

"Who is Hector?"

"The dog, you met him."

"And Kashtan," Jan added.

"And Kashtan," she agreed and they both laughed.

Zoshia wasn't happy about Jan's determination to kill Szymanski. "I know how you feel about that renegade, Jan. I want him dead too, but..."

"Will you help me, Zoshia?"

"Help you?" she said, frowning. "Sure I'll help you. Who else do you have besides me?"

They racked their brains until dawn, considering and rejecting plan after plan. "Let's sleep first," she finally said. "Maybe tomorrow we'll come up with something."

The word 'sleep' prompted Jan to look around the house for a place to sleep. She understood his embarrassment. "You will sleep with Kashtan.

There's enough room for you and Kashtan in the barn," she said, smiling. Indeed, in the corner of the barn, he found plenty of hay and room to sleep comfortably.

A week went, by during which time Zoshia made several trips, the nature of which she didn't explain to him and he, of course, didn't want to appear too inquisitive. Jan himself went to Bostyn several times, observing the police post, the number of soldiers and militiamen around the post, and troop movements. Once he even saw Szymanski, whom he recognized at once. Dressed in the Soviet Colonel's uniform, Szymanski hadn't changed much, except he was fatter than ever. He saw him leaving his headquarters, surrounded by a dozen militiamen, all armed with light machine guns and and pistols.

Zoshia's associates in Bostyn supplied a thorough account of Szymanski's daily routine. It appeared that the bastard was well guarded, careful and cunning. He was never alone. The house he lived in was impregnable. All these accounts suggested that it would be difficult, if not impossible, to kill him.

Jan wanted revenge. He couldn't allow the murderer of his father to go free. He checked and rechecked Szymanski's daily routine.

Little did he know that The Birch, afraid for Jan's safety, had taken it upon himself to "fix" Szymanski. Unlike Jan, though, who wanted to kill Szymanski with his own hands, The Birch decided to use a different method. He was well aware that the Soviet functionaries and other collaborators lived in constant fear. Fear, he knew, permeated the whole Soviet society from Stalin on down. He had had ample opportunity to observe it in the Soviet Union, where he had spent two years in prison and from which he had escaped. This fear, to the point of paranoia, had been brought by the Soviet Army to his hometown. Fear of a supervisor of his subordinates, fear of a worker of his colleagues and friends, fear of a teacher of his pupils... the list was endless and all-embracing.

The whole system was thriving on fear, fear of each other. Writing a short letter denouncing another fellow was enough to send him or her to Siberia, jail, or worse. Knowing this, he decided to denounce Szymanski as an active member of the Polish partisans.

The days came and went and nothing had been decided so far. In the meantime, Jan's friendship with Zoshia was increasing as the days passed. He liked this resolute girl, whose dedication he envied.

"Zoshia," he asked her once, "why don't you leave this shack? It's too dangerous and... uncomfortable for a lady like you."

"And go where?" she shot back. "Anyway," she added, "we have decided to fight to the end."

"You should think of living, not dying."

She didn't say anything, but he noticed that she was frowning. He couldn't tell if it was a frown denoting worry, stubbornness, or a desire to cry.

One evening, Zoshia ran into the house breathing, sweat running down her cheeks. "Jan! Put out the lantern. Quick!" she shouted excitedly. "The Soviet spy followed me. I think I shook him off, but I'm not sure."

"In a crumpled suit and gangster hat?" Jan asked.

"Yes! How do you..."

"Never mind," he said quietly. "I think the bastard knows I'm lodging here. I'm sorry I endangered you, Zoshia."

Jan slept badly that night. He was scared, but at the same time angry. Angry at himself for his inability to find a way to kill Szymanski, and for putting Zoshia's life in jeopardy. "What sort of man am I? Hiding behind a woman's skirt," he reproached himself. "I must kill that renegade tomorrow, or leave this house. There is no other way."

He was wrong. There was another way and the idea came from Zoshia. The next day, while they were eating breakfast, Jan sensed that Zoshia wanted to say something but somehow didn't know how to begin.

"What's on your mind, Zoshia?" he asked finally.

"I have an idea of how we can get rid of Szymanski!" she blurted out.

"Well, for goodness sake, girl, what is it?"

"We could denounce him to the Soviet authorities," she said quietly.

Jan thought about this for a moment. He had heard that a letter which cast suspicion on someone was enough to ensure that person's arrest, particularly if the public prosecutor or K.G.B. received more than one letter of denunciation. "Are you sure it will work, Zoshia?" he asked.

"It will," she said firmly. "I have a feeling ours will not be the only letter sent - the man is hated around here, and if others do the same thing, then Szymanski's life..." It wasn't necessary to finish her sentence. They had both heard about such denunciations before; many people - innocent or otherwise - had been sent to labour camps, or even executed, because of them.

Jan felt that denunciation was not a courageous or honourable method of dealing with his enemy, but he realized it would eliminate Szymanski, and could not help but appreciate the irony of Zoshia's plan.

Time was against him, too. He was sure that he was being watched by the K.G.B.; the only reason they hadn't arrested him was that they wanted to know his reason for being there and to identify his contacts. "I know their methods," he told Zoshia. "They want more than just me; they want to capture and destroy the whole Polish resistance organization." He looked over at his companion. "Including you," he added.

"Then we must act fast," Zoshia said matter-of-factly.

"So be it," he said quietly, accepting pen and paper.

They signed the letter "a loyal citizen of the U.S.S.R." and sent it from Bostyn the same day.

A week later, Zoshia learned that Szymanski had been arrested. Rumour had it that he was sitting in the Bostyn jail, waiting for the "people's court trial". Numerous notices announced that the trial would take place on May 22, and all citizens were invited to attend.

In the meantime, to avoid the possibility of arrest, Jan spent his nights in a little log cottage a quarter kilometre away from Zoshia's house. The tumbledown cottage was empty and partially hidden in the bushes. He was grateful that the nights were warm, since the cottage was unheated.

Kashtan, grazing in the small clearing, was always within reach.

Covering himself with Zoshia's blanket, saddle serving as a pillow, Jan tried to sleep, but fear and uncertainty made it difficult. He would have like to have had Hector with him, but he felt that the dog should be with Zoshia. His conscience bothered him for endangering not only his mission, but Zoshia as well.

****

Szymanski's trial began with all its "kangaroo court" drama. It was a typical Soviet trial.

A throng of people attended; there was standing room only. At first, it was fairly quiet. They stood, Jan among them, staring at the three judges, two in mud-green uniforms and one civilian.

The prosecutor, also in uniform, read a long list of accusations, many of which were taken from Jan and Zoshia's letter. The severity of the crimes was obvious to everyone. The prosecutor requested the death sentence, hoping that Szymanski's fate would serve as an example for other traitors.

The accused, his face showing numerous bruises, sat in a stupor, oblivious to his surroundings. The prosecutor read Szymanski's confession, an inevitable part of Soviet trials. It took him almost half an hour to finish it. Of course, Szymanski had confessed to all the crimes for which he stood accused.

The spectators started shouting: "Shoot the bastard!" "No! Hang him!" "It's too good for him!"

The judges called for silence and pounded on the bench with gavels to regain order.

Szymanski's lawyer stated that his client had confessed, and was repentant. He asked the court's mercy and suggested that justice might be better served if Szymanski were sent to a labour camp to learn the virtues of hard and honest work.

Szymanski was sentenced to twenty-five years of hard labour in the Kolyma salt mines.

Jan pushed through the throng of spectators and left the court room. He felt sick. Turning into the familiar street, he walked swiftly toward Zamosze.

As he was walking, he glanced back, a habit he had acquired recently. At the corner of the street, he almost bumped into the man in the crumpled suit and gangster hat. The man, he noticed, was "busy" talking to a militia man and at the same time, eyeing Jan intently.

Increasing his speed, Jan hurried toward Zamosze. Away from the town, he jumped over a ditch. Choosing the shortest path to Zoshia's house, he ran as fast as his lungs permitted. Sweating and panting, he knocked at the door, but there was no answer. He kept knocking until his knuckles bled, but there was no sign of Zoshia.

Suddenly, Jan heard the thunder of horses' hooves and saw many horsemen galloping along the narrow path leading toward the house. Their pointed, triangular hats were unmistakably Soviet. He knew that they had seen him, so he jumped into the nearby bushes, fell, got up and ran toward the cabin.

'I hope Kashtan is still there,' he thought, increasing his speed. He was relieved to see that the horse was grazing in its usual place. He jumped on the horse, slowing down only slightly. Kashtan, sensing danger, immediately broke into a run.

Jan heard shouts, curses and horses neighing. Glancing back, he saw them - only about a hundred metres away. He heard a harsh Russian voice ordering the cavalry to ride in two directions, in order to encircle the clearing and the cabin.

He swung Kashtan to the left and took the path toward Zamosze. Kashtan was dancing under him impatiently, but the treacherous path did not allow him a full gallop. Still, thanks to Kashtan's extraordinary strength and alertness, Jan was leaving his pursuers behind. He knew that the Soviet horsemen would have anticipated his manoeuver, and that one of the wings of cavalry would try to cut him off from the road. He knew that he was racing for his life and that only Kashtan's speed could save him.

He heard shots and bullets whining around him. "Please, God, let me get to the road first," he prayed. "Get me out of here."

Kashtan seemed to understand the gravity of the situation and, skillfully avoiding obstacles, pressed on. When they reached the road to Zamosze, Jan urged Kashtan forward.

Feeling the solid ground under his hooves, Kashtan leapt forward and raced ahead. The Soviet horsemen, seeing what was happening, shouted excitedly and spurred their horses. For a while, the distance between them remained the same, but Jan soon realized that they were closing in. He heard shots again, dangerously close. Lying low, touching the horse's mane, he continued his flight.

"Try to catch me, you red bastards!" he yelled, feeling elated. The horse, ears flattened to its head, hardly touching the ground, carried him farther and farther from his pursuers. Soon they reached the ruins of Zamosze. Kashtan dodged debris, slowing when necessary, then galloping at full speed.

At the other end of the village, to outwit his pursuers, Jan turned onto a narrow forest path leading to the marshes. Unfortunately for him, his pursuers had done the same thing. Now there was no retreat. Riding at full gallop, he reached the marshlands.

At the edge of the marshes, Kashtan reared and hesitated. Spurred savagely, he leapt into the marshes below. At that moment, Jan heard a volley of shots, and felt a pain in his right shoulder. In the midst of the shooting, yelling and horses' neighing, they hit the shining sheet of cold water below them. The impact knocked Jan from the horse and he felt himself sinking.

Kicking and splashing frantically, he rose to the surface, then almost immediately dived. He swam underwater, trying to gain distance from the shore. Swallowing mud and sour-tasting water, emerging for an occasional breath, he kept swimming toward one of the small islands indigenous to the marshlands. 'About a hundred metres to go - I have to reach it or I'm finished,' he thought desperately.

Finally, exhausted, he reached his destination and concealed himself in the reeds and osiers. Glancing back where he expected to see Kashtan, he saw a wide stretch of water-covered marshes separating him from the shore. Kashtan had disappeared.

'He must have been hit by that volley,' he thought sadly. He scanned the shore and was relieved that there was no sign of his pursuers. 'They must think I drowned,' he decided. Shivering in his wet, muddy clothes, he rose to his feet and examined his surroundings. He was on a small, grassy helm, surrounded by dark water. Most of the helm was soggy and wet, but a small part of it was elevated and relatively dry. He picked up an armful of dry reeds and began to put together a make-shift bed.

Hidden in the grass, he lay on his back, blessing the warm sun. There was no doubt in his mind that his life was in danger. Maybe the Soviets thought that he had drowned. Still, he felt that he wouldn't be safe for long, because it was almost certain that someone among them would want to be sure about it. They would be back to search for him.

'And if that happens, then my life won't be worth a *kopeyek*,' he thought. He must be careful about his next move. One thing he could not allow to happen: he could not be captured by the Soviets. He had not the slightest doubt that, if captured, it would mean certain death for him, and, if tortured, there was the possibility that he could betray his mission. He couldn't possibly jeopardize the lives of these brave men in the forest. The most prudent thing to do, he thought, would be to leave Poland. Now.

Chapter Eighteen

In the Italian town of Ancona, in a little villa overlooking the Adriatic Sea, sat four uniformed men. The oldest of the four, a colonel, was addressing a fifth man standing at attention in the middle of the room.

"Lieutenant Tabor," he started, "it is my pleasure to congratulate you on the excellent completion of your mission. We all congratulate you. It is our pleasure to inform you also that you will receive the Cross of Valour."

"Thank you," said Jan, without enthusiasm. He felt no joy. The image of his burned house in Zamosze, the rubble of the Polish cities, the deaths of his father... the partisans... all that was still fresh to him. And his mission! What was the point of it? His revenge on Szymanski still left an empty feeling when he thought of it.

"Congratulations," they had said. Who would congratulate those brave men and women in Poland who, caught in a confused world, were almost certainly condemned to death or slavery for something they believed? "Tell the world about us," Zoshia had said once. "Get out of Poland as soon as you can. Tell the world about our tragedy, Jan!" 'Tell whom, Zoshia?' Jan thought. 'Who wants to know, anyway?'

"Son-of-a-gun!" the colonel addressed his colleague after Jan left the room. "He actually did it. He crossed the Russian-Polish border, and the Polish-German border by playing refugee all the way through - wounded too," he added.

"So what's next, brothers?" asked the colonel.

"Next? Who knows?" said the major... "All these sacrifices and suffering were for nothing... our homes, if there are still homes left, are sealed by the Iron Curtain. No, friends, there is no returning to our homes for us."

"Don't despair, Major!" said the colonel, "you and I, if we're lucky, may be given a dishwashing job in one of London's hotels, and you, Captain," his eyes went to the captain's armless shirt sleeve; he stopped suddenly, blushing. They sat in silence for a long time.

"Is it true that The Birch and his followers were all captured by the Russians?" asked the captain.

"Yes," answered the colonel, "The Birch was shot and the rest were sent to Siberia."

****

For Jan, the war was over. It was true that he had no home to return to, but at least the war was over. His friend, David Rettinger, also had no home or family to return to. Worse, it appeared that his war was not over.

The end of World War II found David Rettinger in Rome. His duty as the Polish liaison officer in the Italian capital was to gather and record information regarding the families of the members of the Polish Armed Forces. The International and Polish Red Cross had encountered difficulties in obtaining such information. The newly established Polish Communist Government was unwilling to release the information on the basis that it considered members of Polish Armed Forces abroad to be enemies. The Polish High Command in London and Italy was swamped with questions from Polish soldiers and civilians who wanted to know if their families had survived the German deluge.

Rettinger, with his connections and tact, was an excellent choice for the job. Many survivors, mainly Polish Jews, trekked into Italy and from there, some of them tried to get to Palestine, some to the U.S.A. or anywhere... anywhere that would take them. All of them wanted to leave Europe, the graveyard of their families and their dreams.

It was from one of them that Rettinger had learned that his wife and son had been murdered by the Germans. The news was a confirmation of what he had suspected. It had been presumptuous, he thought, to expect that his family would have been luckier than thousands of other Jews. Still, in his heart, there had been a spark of hope that perhaps, perhaps by the grace of God, they had survived. That hope was gone now, like all his other dreams. Now he was alone, truly alone. Americans, Britons and so on were returning home, but he, like many of his Polish companions, could not go home. His old home and the country he was born in were sealed off by the Iron Curtain.

Now what? He was too old and too tired to find a new country and to build a new home. He was like a tree without roots, wilted and dry, waiting for inevitable extinction. Every day, he listened to people from Majdanek, Auschwitz and Tremblinka tell stories of agony, suffering, and degradation. Every day, he was asked by these people for advice as to where to go and what to do, questions he couldn't answer even for himself.

"Why?" they asked him. "Why don't they let us go to Palestine?" "Why do they turn our boats away from the shores of the Promised Land?"

He pondered these questions day and night but couldn't find an answer. Then one day a man was admitted to his office. At first, he didn't recognize him. He was still a young man, around 30 perhaps, but his face, yes, his face, wrinkled and hollow-cheeked, was the face of an old man. His eyes, even though tired, were steady and forceful. It took Rettinger some time to recognize Monachem Mendel, his former student from Krakow. How could he forget this hot-headed youth who dressed in shorts, green jacket and that hat with David's Star on it? He had been a Zionist Youth Leader. Monachem, he recalled, had been both an embarrassment and a source of pride for the Jewish Community in Krakow.

He had caused unrest among the Jewish youth, disrupting the peace with marches and rallies, fighting with fascist lunatics, breaking windows in the buildings of unfriendly newspapers and... at the same time, reading the Talmud, studying Hebrew and lecturing in Yiddish. To Rettinger, the scholar, Monachem was an abomination, and a man with zeal and purpose. The Monachem he remembered was a man Jews were proud of, but with whom they wouldn't like to have a cup of tea. Now this man was sitting at his desk staring with his hard eyes, probably trying to analyze and assess him, resting his eyes several times on the captain's stars with a look of reproof or disapproval.

"You ought to fight for Palestine, Jewish Palestine, not for Poland," he finally said.

"Fighting for Poland was fighting against Hitler," Rettinger retorted.

"Maybe," Monachem replied.

"Fighting for Palestine, you say? But fighting against whom?"

"Against the British and the Arabs."

"And you, Monachem? Why don't you fight them?"

"Oh, I will, I will, as soon as I have the opportunity." Then he added, "I must get to Palestine, Captain, I must! Will you help me?"

Later Rettinger pondered these words. He didn't like Monachem, the arrogant bastard, but he had to agree with him, at least on one point: if the Jews truly wanted their own homeland, they would have to fight for it against the British, the Arabs or the Devil himself. He had no sympathy with the British, whose Appeasement Policy was instrumental in Stalin's occupation of Poland. The fact that they were chasing the Jews away from Palestine was another thing he couldn't understand. The survivors of the concentration camps, like Monachem, wanted to have their own country so that their children would not have to face another Holocaust. But why were they not allowed into the land of their ancestors? Why?

Maybe Monachem was right after all. Take his own situation for example; what future did he have? These thoughts were invading his mind more often than he wanted. Fighting for a Jewish Palestine would give him a purpose in his life. Oh, he was not really thinking about his own life, but rather about the lives of future generations of Jews. Sure the war had anaesthetized these dreams, but now they were awakened again like wadi-grasses after a rainfall.

A Jewish state for the Jewish people should become the watchword and action of every Jew, regardless of where he had come from or where he lived. In the meantime, Monachem and many other Jews, old and young, were disappearing from the streets of Rome. They were boarding ships of all sizes and heading over the Mediterranean Sea. Rettinger's colleagues from the Polish military headquarters, sympathetic to the Jewish cause, had told him again and again about the Jewish men and women who, in order to confuse the British authorities, were taking roundabout ways to get to the Holy Land. Some went there through Egypt, others through Syria and yet others through Lebanon. There were those, he was told, who went straight to Jaffa, trying to elude the British coastal patrols. Some had managed to land, disappearing among their own people, but some had been caught and imprisoned. "Imagine, Rettinger," his colleagues told him angrily, "how those who survived the German concentration camps must be feeling in British prisons?"

'Yes, how must they feel?' he thought, with an aching heart.

"I am resigning from the Army," Rettinger announced to his Commanding Officer who, listening to Rettinger's reasons, was speechless for a few minutes.

"You, at your age, want to fight for Palestine?" he said, regaining his voice.

"I have nothing to lose, Colonel, and anyway, I believe in the cause."

"But you will have to fight the British among others."

"Yes, I'm afraid so."

"You should be, you old fool," said the colonel, smiling warmly. They switched their talk to generalities as though this were the real reason for Rettinger's visit. Then Rettinger rose to his feet and, saluting smartly, marched to the door.

"Rettinger!" he heard the colonel's stern voice. "Just a moment!"

"We need a courier to go to Jerusalem. Major Matoga is sick, I understand, so we need somebody reliable... you don't happen to know someone like that?"

"Thank you, my friend!" exclaimed Rettinger and then they both burst into loud laughter. "So, unlike poor Moses," observed Rettinger on departure. "I shall enter the Promised Land... in style."

****

Almost two months had gone by, reflected Rettinger, since he had joined the Irqun Zvay Leumi, a Jewish underground organization. Even though there were other organizations whose objective was to fight for a Jewish state, he had joined the Irqun.

'I didn't have much choice,' he smiled wryly. 'Monachem conscripted me before I had time to open my mouth,' he thought.

"You will report to Lev Warshavski, the leader of Section II," Monachem had ordered.

Lev Warshavski disliked his new conscript and Rettinger felt that at once.

"That... new fellow, Rettinger, the one you sent to my squad recently, he's too soft," he complained to Monachem.

"What do you mean, Lev, by too soft?"

"He hates blood."

"Really?"

"Yes, he hates killing of any kind."

"So, can't you give him something else to do that doesn't involve bloodshed? Paperwork or something?"

"No! I need fighters, not professors."

Rettinger disliked Lev too. He thought that the big brute was too bloodthirsty, a professional killer, in fact. Lev's squad took credit for several recent attacks on the British garrisons and Arab settlements. In each case, they had left behind corpses. Some of the victims were unarmed soldiers and civilians, and that broke David's heart.

So far, Rettinger had managed to avoid killing personally, only because Lev, considering him a coward, was assigning him only non-violent tasks. But today was different. Their squad of 30 men was to attack an Arab village north of Nazareth as a reprisal. Only three days ago, the Arab fighters had raided a Jewish Kibbutz, killing 14 people, among them four children and three women.

Rettinger's task was to be on the lookout on the narrow road connecting the village with the shrub-covered hills. Armed with an automatic pistol, he was sweating under the blazing sun. A feeling of extreme loneliness overcame him. He felt as though he was tired of life itself.

He saw a score of women and children, yelling and crying, run toward his post. His orders were to shoot anyone who showed up on the road. However, recognizing that they were women and children, he lowered his pistol and stood at the edge of the road, perplexed and immobile. He couldn't bring himself to shoot children and women.

At that moment, he heard volleys of bullets whistling over his head, coming, it appeared to him, from the nearby hill, outside of the village. He knew that he should throw himself to the ground to avoid them, but instead he stood there as though petrified. Then there was a hot and piercing pain, then darkness.

"Son-of-a-bitch got it!" yelled Lev, infuriated, running toward his fallen companion. "I hope the bastard dies," he added angrily.

"Don't be too hard on him, Lev," one of his subordinates remarked.

"Too hard?" Lev screamed. "Half of the terrorists escaped because of him. Look! Look at his pistol. Not a single bullet was used."

"Well, yes, but he is an old fellow and..."
"Too soft."

"He is bleeding, but still alive, I think."

"Let him bleed to death."

"Come on, Lev, don't be such a brute!"

"Well, carry him to the jeep."

Rettinger didn't hear these words, nor did he know that he was carried to the jeep which followed the country roads toward Tel Aviv.

"He is dead," said the doctor. Then, shaking his head, he added: "He lost too much blood."

"He was a good man," whispered Monachem.

"Yeah, he was a good man, but soft, and passive, like... like most of the Jews in Europe. 'Obey the law! Obey!' the rabbis told their flocks. Then came the round-ups, the raids and the journeys to the concentration camps and the crematoria. All nice and orderly... how else," said Lev, bitterly.

They rose to their feet, and glancing at Rettinger's body once more, went out.

"Oh, yes, Monachem, is there someone we should notify about... Rettinger? Family perhaps?" asked the doctor.

"Family?" exclaimed Monachem. "He was a European Jew, wasn't he?"

"Friends, perhaps..."

Chapter Nineteen

Jan heard that there was a Canadian Recruiting Commission in Porto Recanati, not far from Ancona. The Commission had come to select young Polish soldiers for work on Canadian farms.

Jan heard that Canada was a free country with wide open spaces. 'What does it matter where I go?' he thought with resignation. If he could have a choice, he would rather work on his own farm in Zamosze than go to Canada as a hired hand.

"But there is no such choice," he told himself. "I should go and see what these Canadians have to say, anyway."

There was a large bundle of mail waiting for him. He found letters from Maria, Helena and Olenka. There were other letters too. One was from the Divisional Commander informing him that he was promoted to the rank of Captain. He scanned this letter quickly. The other letters he took with him and went to a secluded place where he could read them in peace.

Helena wrote:

"Dear Brother, it is a long time since I received a letter from you. I worry, day and night about you. I hope and pray to the Holy Mother for your safety, dear brother. Oh, how much I would like to see you again. I hope you will recognize me. I am sixteen years old now. Our Polish settlement, Santa Rosa, is near the large city of Leon. I didn't know the name before, so I am telling you now.
Lately, our colony, as we call it, has been extended. We have more comfortable rooms and classrooms. We even have ourown theatre and library. The people in charge often take us on trips to Leon and other beautiful Mexican places. I also want to correct my previous letter in which I gave you wrong information. There are 1500 people all in all in Santa Rosa, out of which 400 are orphans, like me. After the Battle of Monte Cassino, many children got terrible news about their dead brothers and fathers."

"There is a rumour, dear brother, that some of us will have an opportunity to move to the United States. The Polish American Associations are looking for foster parents. I signed my name. Maybe you could come to the United States too, so we could be together.

I pray for you and love you.

Your sister, Helena."

Jan put the letter aside, smiling for the first time since his return from Poland. He took another letter from the pile in front of him. It was Maria's letter.

"Dear brother, I am deeply disturbed by your silence and you can very well imagine what terrible thoughts go through my head. Dear Jan, I have some important news to tell you. I got married two months ago. He is Polish and has your name - Jan. He was one of the Polish pilots taking part in the Battle of Britain. His friends tell me that Jan downed four enemy planes, although he never told me about it himself. He is a wonderful man. He loves to tell stories and he is fun to listen to, believe me. You'll like him. Now since the war is over and we don't want to return to Poland, we are thinking of emigrating to the United States or perhaps Canada. It would be nice if you could go there too, don't you think?

Love, Maria."

"Married!" he cried, shocked. It never occurred to him that such a thing could happen. She was too young! Then he realized that he was thinking of the teenager she had been when he had last seen her. He was almost 22, which meant that Maria was 24 by now.

He hesitated to open Olenka's letter, afraid of what she might have written. He opened it with trembling hands.

"Dearest Jan, This will be a short letter. But even in these few clumsy words of mine, I want to tell you how much I love you. Believe me, there is no waking moment when I don't think about you and cry over you. What happened to you? Why didn't you write to me for such a long time? Every time the postman passes my home, I ask him if there is a letter for me - your letter."

"I am in England, now, working as a nurse in a hospital. However, I am trying to emigrate to Canada. Perhaps you will come to Canada too. I love you very much, Jan, and hope that one day we will be together.

Yours, eternally loving, Olenka."

"I love you too, Olenka, more than ever," he whispered. After thinking for a while, he said aloud, "Let it be Canada, then."

Canada was on his mind often. In fact, he already had perused three books about Canada's geography. Not that he didn't know something about that country already. Even while still in Zamosze, he had met two men who had spent five years in Canada as immigrants, then returned to Poland. He remembered them well. They were sort of celebrities in Zamosze. They were rich and had so many interesting stories to tell the Zamoszans about the beauty and riches of Canada.

'Perhaps it will be wise to make a new home there,' he thought. Canada, he knew, was a haven for many other homeless people - people like him. 'With Olenka... and my sisters...' He tried to picture the mighty Niagara Falls, the endless wheat fields of Saskatchewan and the thick forests of British Columbia. Perhaps there would be a place for him, too, in that vast country.

October of 1946 was hot and dry in Italy. Southerly winds, blowing for the last two weeks, had brought an oppressive heat. The 'Scirocco', as the winds were called, invaded the Peninsula almost every summer, carrying with them sharp particles of sand, inflicting damage on crops and buildings and what was left of the forest. Its hot and dry winds were known to remove paint from buildings, chop grain into chaff and drive people and animals into a frenzy. Jan, like almost everyone else, felt irritable, restless and depressed. The soldiers, cursed 'God's whip', as they had nicknamed the Scirocco, quarrelled and fought among themselves.

One day, Jan requisitioned a jeep and took the road to Monte Cassino. Upon his return from Poland, he had been told that half of his unit had been annihilated. The least he could do, he thought, was to visit their graves. Walking among the thousands of Polish graves, kneeling at each of the graves of his friends, he prayed for their souls, wishing them eternal peace. As he was leaving, he passed the Jewish section of the cemetery. Hundreds of graves marked by granite stars of David, shone in the hot Italian sun.

Leaving the cemetery, Jan scanned the nearby barren hills. The artillery shells had left not a single tree intact. Instead, the hills were crimsoned with poppies the colour of blood.

A plaque at the cemetery gate read:

"They gave their souls to God, their bodies to Italy, and their hearts to Poland."

Epilogue

The "Sea-Snipe", on its way to Halifax, approached the Strait of Gibraltar, slicing through the waves of the Mediterranean. It was a small ship, a freighter in fact, converted in war time to carry soldiers. Elbows on the rail, on his left the blue mass of the Atlas Mountains of North Africa, on his right, the rugged rock of Gibraltar. He was alone in the dawn, enjoying the fresh salt air. He was swaying to the rhythm of the little ship, as it rose and fell with the waves.

The rising sun cast its rays on the Iberian Peninsula as though wishing Jan to see Europe for the last time in brightness. Europe had been the birthplace of his people, his home. The ship was carrying him away from everything he knew. What lay beyond the Atlantic Ocean, he could not guess.

Deeply engrossed in his thoughts, he didn't notice a man coming up to the rail a few feet away. Turning his head, his eyes fell upon a tall, slightly stooped figure. "Plater!" he yelled.

"Oh, no! Not you again!" Plater smiled crookedly, extending his hand. "For the sake of all living and dead gods, I can't shake my past, even if I want to," he added.

"So you're heading for Canada too, Plater?"

"Where else? Poland doesn't want me."

"Or you don't want Poland - Communist Poland."

"Comes to the same thing, doesn't it?"

They went down to the ship's restaurant and ordered coffee. It was only in the full light that Jan noticed his friend's nose. It had been broken in several places and later patched, poorly at that. It was a bumpy and ugly looking nose.

"You were wounded at the front, Plater?" he asked his friend as delicately as possible.

"No! Poles did this to me!"

"Poles?"

"Well, Polish communists," Plater said. "Right after the war, I decided to return to Poland. You see, my - let us say - socialist inclinations clouded my common sense, so, like many others, I went back."

"And?"

"They locked me up, precisely one week after my return," he said angrily. "They told me I was a British spy. I wasn't the only one arrested. Many Polish war veterans who returned are either in jails or... dead."

"So what's new!" exclaimed Jan. "It sounds all too familiar, doesn't it, Plater?"

"It surely was! Kolyma revisited. They were transporting me from Czestochowa prison to, I assumed, Krakow. I had reached the point where I would rather be dead than continue to sit in their stinking prisons... it is a long story, Jan; but briefly, six of us managed to escape. After that, it was sleeping in the forests during the day and marching at night, marching west that is, until I crossed the Polish border to East Germany and finally reached the West German border and freedom."

"Then what happened?"

"From West Germany, I returned to Italy and the Polish Second Corps." He paused for a while as though tired of talking, then added, "Then I heard that Canada needs farmers, so here I am."

They talked until dawn. Plater, Jan noticed with satisfaction, was more amiable, certainly less cynical than he had been the last time he had seen him.

He returned to the deck. It was a sunny day, although the cold winds heralded winter. Wrapping himself in his army coat, he reached into his pocket and pulled out a small tattered envelope...

"Dearest Jan," he had read this letter many times, but each time it was as though for the first time.

"The Queen Elizabeth is leaving the docks in Liverpool on September 10.

We were told that we should reach Canada on September 15. Halifax, I believe. I hesitate to leave England, which, even though separated by the channel, is still Europe to me. I wanted to put these terrible experiences behind me, to be as far as possible from them. And yet, I feel sorry to leave, maybe because I am going into the unknown, away from my homeland, from the graves of my parents and sister. I don't know, I really don't know."

"I was offered and accepted a nursing position in Montreal, The Royal Victoria Hospital to be exact. Who knows, maybe you too will come to Canada, Jan. It will be the happiest day for me if you would. You see, Jan, it was thanks to you, thanks to your unselfish love that I found myself again... that I am able to hope and dream. I do care about you more than I ever cared for anyone else."

"Maybe, my dearest, we will meet again... together, we shall build a little house (how silly I am to let my dream run away....) somewhere on the outskirts of a forest... a coniferous forest, similar to that of eastern Poland... some marshes close enough so we can wade, hand in hand, beside them..."

Jan raised his hand toward the sunny skies, tears in his eyes. The cold westerly winds suddenly didn't feel as cold.

The "Sea Snipe", buffeting from wave to wave, ploughed labouriously closer and closer to the shores of Canada. Down on the lower deck a group of Polish war veterans struck up a song:

"We shall never abandon the land of
our ancestors, nor shall we forget
the Polish language; so help us God,
so help us God."

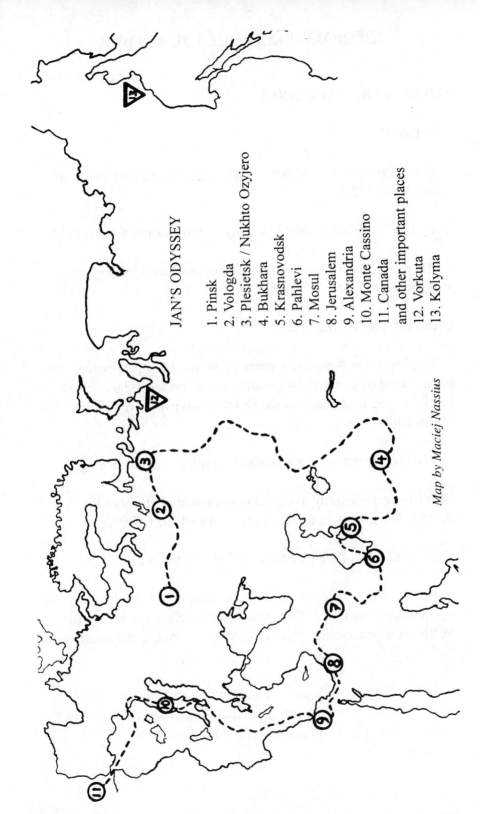

JAN'S ODYSSEY

1. Pinsk
2. Vologda
3. Plesietsk / Nukhto Ozyjero
4. Bukhara
5. Krasnovodsk
6. Pahlevi
7. Mosul
8. Jerusalem
9. Alexandria
10. Monte Cassino
11. Canada
and other important places
12. Vorkuta
13. Kolyma

Map by Maciej Nassius

INFORMATION ABOUT THE AUTHOR

WILLIAM B. MAKOWSKI

EDUCATION:

Completed Masters of Art in Philosophy at the University of Montreal in 1951.

Ph.D. Candidate at the University of Ottawa from 1952-1954.

Attended McGill University in Toronto studying Geography specialization from 1967-1972.

CAREER EXPERIENCE:

Employed for twenty-six years in the teaching profession, serving as Head of Geography Department at the secondary school level. Served four years on the Ontario Advisory Council on Multiculturalism.

Worked for ten years on research, writing and publishing.

Performed specially assigned environmental study of the Eastern Townships in eastern Canada for McGill University.

WRITING AND PUBLISHING ACHIEVEMENT:

History and Integration of Poles in Canada, published in 1967 by the Canadian-Polish Congress. A comprehensive historical treatment of the contribution and cultural heritage of Canadians of Polish origin.

Polish People in Canada; A Visual History, published in 1987 by Tundra Books Inc. A comprehensive historical treatment of the cultural heritage, including a chapter on Multiculturalism in Canada.

The Uprooted, published in Polish under the title "Wyrwani z korzeniami" by Gazeta Inc. Toronto, 2000.

Short Stories, (3) published in the Guidepost and Catholic Readers' Digest between 1962 and 1967.

PERSONAL ACHIEVEMENTS:

Various military awards and decorations (from both the Canadian-Polish Congress and the Polish Armed Forces), including Virtuti Militari.

Fluent in Polish, Russian and English. Working knowledge of French and Italian.

Traveled all of Europe, most of Asia, north Africa, most of Canada (including Resolute Bay) and the United States.

OF PARTICULAR INTEREST:

Intellectual, cultural, social and personal growth drawn from various life experiences. Have good standing in local (and broad) Polish community.

Pictures in this book were made available by the Museum of
Independence, Warsaw, Poland.

The author expresses special thanks to Mrs. Marique Weslawskia
from Warsaw, Poland for the help in obtaining pictures.

Back Cover Photo: Polish deportee with a bowl of soup.

J. Siedlecki: The Fate of Poles in USSR in 1939-1986
London, 1987

Polish children in exile.

J. Siedlecki: The Fate of Poles in USSR in 1939-1986
London, 1987

Polish orphants and half-orphants in Wrewskoje.

J. Siedlecki: The Fate of Poles in USSR in 1939-1986
London, 1987

Polish female deportees beside a well - June (in the 1940's), Village of Lajda, Karaul, Khazachstan.

Floated timber. Siberia, May 1941.

Construction of a chanter in the village of Bultusuk (in the 1940's).

Slawa Brotkiewicz in his homestead. Krasnojarski Kraj, Monski region, Bultusuk village, Russian FSSR (in the 1940's).

Polish deportees with a team of dogs during a trip a geese hunting trip to an island. The village of Lajda, Khazachstan (in the 1940's).

Polish deportee in front of a log shed, to the side dead reindeer to be taken to a purchasing centre. Lajda - Khazachstan.

A view of the Lajda village in Khazachstan.

A herd of reindeers beside a sleigh in the village of Lajda, Karaul, Khazachstan.

Workuta. Home of the deportees. In the background a heap of coal.

A house in a housing estate in Lajda (Khazachstan), inhabited by eigth families. In the front a female Polish deportee dressed in "an elegant summer" dress.

"The outfits" of Polish camp inmates and deportees.

J. Siedlecki: The Fate of Poles in USSR in 1939-1986
London, 1987

Polish deportees in Siberia.

J. Siedlecki: The Fate of Poles in USSR in 1939-86, London, 1987

A line-up in front of the recruiting commission to the newly formed
Polish Army.

J. Siedlecki: The Fate of Poles in USSR in 1939-86, London, 1987